*Totally Bound Publishing books by Sandra Carmel*

**The Cure**
Capture
Discover
Reckoning

# The Cure

# RECKONING

# SANDRA CARMEL

Reckoning
ISBN # 978-1-83943-871-4
©Copyright Sandra Carmel 2020
Cover Art by Erin Dameron-Hill ©Copyright March 2020
Interior text design by Claire Siemaszkiewicz
Totally Bound Publishing

Published in 2020 by Totally Bound Publishing, United Kingdom.

# RECKONING

# Dedication

To those who point to new paths and encourage
exploration of fresh ideas.

# Chapter One

The Secondment

*Hobart, Tasmania, October 2011*

Rick burst into the kitchen. "It's official."

Eden stepped away from the stovetop, trying to school her expression so he wouldn't see the surprise and worry in her face, in her eyes. "So we're actually going."

He reached into his pocket, pulled out four airline tickets and plonked them down on the bench. "Yep. Though I've factored in a bit of a European vacation, a sort of belated honeymoon, before I start the Norway secondment."

She swallowed, then swallowed again. "How long will we be gone?"

"Unsure. As long as it takes. Management has been pretty flexible, surprisingly. They can't have any idea about us or our link to Salvator."

A film of moisture coated her eyes and she blinked in an attempt to stop the tears from falling. "Poor Salvator."

Rick slipped his arms around her waist and kissed her forehead. "I know. I wish we could be at his funeral, but I'm sure he'd understand."

Eden lifted her head and a couple of droplets trickled down her cheeks. "Yes... So when do we leave?"

"In two days."

She stumbled back and stared up at him, swiping the tears from her face. "In two days? You could have given me a bit more notice! We've still got to pack—and how about the kids' passports?"

"Don't worry. I've got everything sorted." And she didn't doubt it. Since their Rick and Eden incarnation, he'd constantly demonstrated that he had everything under control.

She shook her head and smiled. "Of course you do. What was I thinking?"

"Exactly." He pressed a gentle, loving kiss to her lips. "Speaking of the kids, how has Scarlett been?"

"Great, thank goodness. Introducing the animal blood has really made a difference...so far. She not only slept better last night but also went down for a nap this afternoon as well."

"I did notice she seemed to settle a lot easier when I put them to bed."

Eden adjusted his shirt collar. "Now I'm just hoping that she'll start putting on weight and catch up to Blake."

They spent the rest of the night planning for the upcoming trip and playing with the kids. Eden fell into bed, exhausted, and awoke to Rick lapping at her clitoris and an orgasm so intense that she almost shot off the bed. Before she could come down from her high, he crushed his mouth to hers and thrust his magnificent

8

cock inside her, treating her to a bone-melting session of morning sex.

They snuggled afterward until Rick had to get up for work, and Eden drifted back to sleep...with no disturbances. For months, the first few hours of the day she'd spent in a sleep-deprivation-induced zombie state, trying to satiate Scarlett and stop her screaming.

But not anymore. Scarlett seemed to finally be on track, along with Eden and Rick's incredible sex life, which should have been a relief. But how long would it last? They were about to uproot what she'd thought was a stable life that had turned out to be false—a lie— to relocate overseas, to expose themselves to higher, but necessary, risk.

The disruption of their routine to move into the danger zone had to have unsettling side effects, and to think otherwise would be delusional. However, they could no longer guarantee their safety if they stayed in Hobart. They had to go. Her past had taught her the importance of making the most of whatever time she had left with the people she loved.

In life, there were no definites outside of death and an obscene amount of taxes. She could wish all she wanted that things were different, but they weren't, and living in a bubble of ignorance wouldn't protect her and her family.

Dwelling on uncertainty and assumptions was pointless. She had to focus on the pressing here and now—on the facts—and deal with any changes as they arose.

Eden stretched and glanced at Rick's alarm clock. Ten a.m.! She sat up, snatched her mobile off the bedside table and the notification light flashed, indicating she had a message. She couldn't believe she hadn't heard it come through. Those three orgasms

Rick had coaxed from her body must have wiped her out.

She unlocked the sleep screen and found a text from Rick.

*Good morning, darling. Hope you had a good rest. I'm still recovering from our little session...wow. Sensational. Every time I think of you coming on my tongue then on my cock... Fuck. Do you know how difficult it is to concentrate on work with a raging hard-on? Anyway, I miss you, I love you and I can't wait to see you and the kids when I get home.*

She slammed her hand to her thumping heart. Such a thoughtful, sexy man. He was probably busy tying things up at work, but she couldn't resist messaging him back.

*If you're a good boy, I'll show you just how much I love you when you get here.*

She went to get up, not expecting a response, when her mobile buzzed. A reply from Rick. He must have been sitting on his phone.

*Great... Now all I can think about is your heavenly mouth wrapped around my cock.*

She laughed and typed out a reply.

*How did you guess?*

*If you keep up the brazen attitude, as soon as I get in the door I'll bend you over my knee and spank you. Hard.*

*I hope so.*

*Enough. If we continue this, I'm gonna blow in my pants. That's not a good look at work. I'll see you later, sweetheart. Have a great day xox*

She sighed, frustrated and aroused. Now she had to search for something to do to fill in the time until he got home. Maybe a little self-pleasure would tide her over. She lay back against the bed, bent her knees up and spread her legs, reaching her hand down to stroke her sex.

*So wet.* She was always wet for Rick. She trailed her fingers through her folds and thrust two inside her entrance. With her other hand, she reached down and rubbed her clit, slowly at first, while she got into a steady pumping rhythm in her core. She picked up speed, imagining herself riding Rick's face, with two of his thick fingers thrusting into her and two slipping into her back hole.

Her insides clamped down, her climax obliterating all rational thought, all sense of time and reality. She bucked and cried out, giving over to pure physical sensation, her heart racing, her breathing fast and erratic. When she returned to the present, she panicked and sat up. Had the twins heard her? Had she missed one of them calling, sobbing, crying?

Eden listened for any little distressed baby sounds and was greeted by silence. *Thank goodness.* She got dressed and crept downstairs. She could totally get used to beginning the day with four orgasms and no niggly interruptions. Now she just had to find something meaningful to indulge in for her newly acquired spare time.

With no more Scarlett screams of discomfort, Eden suddenly had several hours free, and she felt somewhat at a loss. She still couldn't quite get used to both twins behaving.

Eden tidied up then grabbed a book and reclined on the couch, with Smokey and Thornton curled up by her side, basking in the morning sunshine. But she couldn't concentrate.

She persevered for half an hour then went to check on the kids. Old habits really did die hard. She tiptoed into the twins' room and straight over to Blake's cot. His chubby cherub cheeks were rosy with warmth and he still slept peacefully. She sighed. Such a sweet little thing...

"Mummy, food please?"

Eden spun around. *Scarlett?* It couldn't be, could it? She couldn't be speaking at her present developmental stage. *Am I going insane?* Did she have some odd form of post-traumatic stress or post-natal psychosis?

Scarlett sat up and stared at her with her large, purple-flecked jade eyes. "Mummy?"

Her little rosebud lips formed every letter. It was either that or Eden had descended into the depths of hallucination.

Eden walked over to her crib. "Scarlett, are you hungry?"

Blake opened his eyes and babbled, as though answering her question.

Scarlett smiled at Blake then focused her big, super-alert eyes back on Eden. "Yes, Mummy, both of us are."

So not only did Scarlett exhibit signs of accelerated learning, but also, she could understand her gurgling baby brother? Eden spun her head around like her coffee had been spiked with a triple shot of Scotch. She lifted Scarlett and Blake out of their cribs, carried them downstairs and placed them on the play mat in the living room. "I'll just go fix you both some Oat Brits with milk."

Blake glanced at Eden then at Scarlett and rattled off a sequence of unintelligible words.

When he finished chattering, Scarlett turned to Eden. "Um… Blake wants vegemite toast with butter — and raw mince for me, please."

"O-kay…" Eden hesitated. Had she fallen asleep on the couch and started dreaming? Maybe Rick could confirm her sanity when he got home in a half an hour or so.

"Daddy!" Scarlett squealed.

*Shit!* Could she read minds as well?

Insane or not, Eden was having a conversation with her six-month-old, baby-babble-interpreting daughter. Eden glanced at the clock — three-forty-five p.m. — then at the front door. "No, honey. It's a bit too early for Daddy."

Gravel crunched under tires and Eden raced to the window. Rick had arrived all right, parking his car in the driveway. She pinned Scarlett with a confused stare. "How did you…?"

"I felt him. I can feel you too, Mummy — and Blake."

Eden sat next to her on the play mat. "What do you mean by 'feel'?"

"Um…"

"Do you mean hear? Smell?" Eden prompted, still not quite believing the level of conversation she could have with her baby daughter.

"Both, through the air."

"How about 'see'?"

Scarlett nodded. "Yes, in my head."

"Wow…"

The front door latch clicked and Rick strolled into the living room. "What are my two special ladies talking about?"

*Wait until I tell him.* "Where do I start?"

He bent down and kissed Blake and Scarlett then took Eden by the hand and helped her up. "How about at the beginning?" A mischievous smile tugged at the corners of his lips.

"Ha-ha—"

He pulled her close and kissed her like they'd been separated for weeks instead of hours.

When they broke apart, she felt lightheaded, drunk with an ever-growing desire for her husband. "How come you're home so early? Not that I'm complaining... It's great to have you here but—"

He put his finger to her lips. "Don't worry. Everything's fine. I just wanted to spend as much time as possible with you and the kids, in our family home while we still have the chance. Plus, I've done so much overtime lately, my line manager practically pushed me out of the door."

"'Scuse me, Mummy..."

A mix of surprise and confusion washed over Rick's face and he turned toward his daughter.

"I can talk, Daddy!" Scarlett beamed like she'd discovered a self-replenishing store of fresh, warm animal blood.

"I can see that." He curved his lips up in an awe-filled smile.

"That's not all. She understands Blake and she can 'feel' us, as well," Eden said.

He furrowed, his forehead carving deep frown lines there. "*Feel* us?"

"From what I can understand, her senses are highly attuned...to us, anyway. She's almost hypersensitive,

14

but in a good way. She knew you were nearly home minutes before you arrived. She could hear, smell and see you."

He stared at Scarlett, disbelief clearly warring with fact in his usually composed face. "That's amazing! I'm still trying to get my head around her level of articulation and comprehension."

"Me too. Imagine what she'll be able to do by the time she's one."

Rick's stare turned internal, deep into thinking mode. "I wonder... Are these special abilities linked to her vampire heritage or her mixed-clan origin?"

"Probably a bit of both. I bet Salvator would have known..." Eden's eyes filled with stinging tears.

\* \* \* \*

*Café Destino, the next day, 18:35*

Rick tapped his boutique bottle of beer to his best mate's, and they each had a sip. "Can I ask you a huge favor?"

"Again?" Simon smirked then nodded. "Of course."

*How exactly should I say this?* Rick swallowed the rest of his beer and fiddled with the disposable beer coaster. "The thing is, you're going to want to ask questions, but you need to understand that if you agree to my request, I won't be answering them."

Simon scrunched up his forehead as though fighting his need to question, to ignore the alarm bells blaring in his head. "Okay..."

Rick shifted forward and whispered. "While I'm away, I may need to ask for your assistance and send some stuff to your private email..."

"No worries."

"You can't open anything, though. Your inbox will just be used for safekeeping, at this stage."

The waitress walked past and directed three people into the next booth.

Simon leaned in and mirrored Rick. "Safekeeping? What the hell are you up to?" His voice rumbled low and gruff, edged with concern.

Rick dropped his gaze to the damp coaster in his fidgety hands. "Sorry, mate. I can't go into it."

"Don't you trust me?"

His gaze reconnected with Simon's. "Believe me... It's not that." Rick had already put his family at risk. *Again.* He didn't want to add his best friend to the list.

"Then what?" Simon took a swig of his half-full beer.

"I can't explain any further at the moment. All I'll say is there are two exceptions to reading the emails. One, if I ask you to or, two, if you truly believe my safety is compromised."

Simon reached over and grabbed Rick's wrist, the coaster falling flat onto the table. "What are you planning on doing over there? It's not just you anymore, Rick. You've got a young family."

He didn't need reminding. The whole idea of putting them at risk ate him up inside. He hated that it had come to this, after what had happened in the past. However, he no longer had an option. Either way, they were in danger.

They could only ever be safe if he stopped Sub Rosa. Permanently. And to do that, he needed to somehow free the Violets and the Jades—and collect more incriminating evidence. "I wish I could explain but I can't...yet."

Simon retracted his arm and shook his head.

"Please don't mention anything to Grace."

His frown lines slowly disappeared in the light of realization. "Oh, I get it. The fewer people that know, the less chance of anything getting out and the less danger they're in."

"Precisely."

Simon tapped his fingers in a jumpy, rambling rhythm on the table. "You've got me worried now."

"It'll be fine." Or so Rick hoped. It had to be, this time.

Simon adjusted his position in the booth and had a big gulp of beer. "Grace and I could look after the kids, as well as Smokey and Thornton, if you'd like."

"Thanks, mate. The idea had actually entered my mind, but I think it's best we stay together...for lots of reasons. I wouldn't want to put such a huge responsibility on you, for one, and I want things to look as normal as possible too. And although the kids love you guys, it would be hard on them being away from us for who knows how long." *Plus, I have to keep Scarlett's little party trick hidden.*

Simon's sigh was weighted with resignation. "Well, if there's anything else I can do..."

With his brilliant black-hat-hacker skills and awesome research expertise, he could help heaps, though Rick refused to increase the risk to Simon any more than he already had. "I promise I'll let you know."

# Chapter Two

Norway — The End of the Road?

After spending a week in Paris and one in the Greek Islands, their vacation had officially come to an end. Now they were only minutes away from commencing the 'Norway Adventure', as Rick called it. A coil of worry curled around Eden's spine and speared through her mind.

The plane touched down at Oslo airport, the sky as black as the tarmac. Although it was only four p.m., it looked more like midnight — so much for the afternoon sun guiding them to their final destination. With the speedy planning of their trip, it hadn't even occurred to her that it would be heading into winter there.

Eden stepped into the tunnel connecting the plane to the airport, a shiver running right through her body. She'd envisaged a warm greeting, not all-consuming cold. Was it an omen for their Norway stay? An avalanche of anxiety crashed into her mind and her stomach clenched. *No.* She had to be strong for Rick and the twins.

After a series of deep, steadying breaths, she assisted Rick to load Blake, Scarlett and their bags into the hired car. Then, using the GPS function on Rick's mobile, they made their way to the pre-booked guesthouse, an estimated six-hour drive, assuming they had a straight, uninterrupted run.

Four hours into the trip, Rick's phone lost reception. Eden's gaze shot across to her husband, as though he could pick up the slack for the disconnected map app and rattle off the required directions. "What are we going to do?" Her heart jackhammered in her chest.

He glanced at her, his facial expression calm, reassuring. "Don't worry about it. I studied the paper map before we left and brought it as a backup."

*Of course he did.* The stress leaked out of her shoulders, like a deflating air mattress. Eden should have known he'd have done all the required research. After his impulsive overconfidence that had nearly cost them their lives, Rick had learned the importance of patience and thorough planning.

He'd switched to being supremely organized and not only forward thinking but also thinking ahead, considering all the possible pros and cons, positives and complications. Her husband was her rock, and little Blake already showed signs of having the same temperament as his father, a true chip off the Rick-block.

After traveling for another hour along a dark, deserted freeway, a structure appeared in the distance, lit up by a vibrant, Violet-Jade sparkling star overhead. Were they far enough north to see the Northern Lights? She hadn't had time to investigate the possibility before they'd left. They'd been too rushed, and she'd been too busy to even consider researching what the area offered.

Perched partway up the hill, a house appeared to jut out into the ocean like a magic castle floating above the sea.

"Wow!" Scarlett's sweet little voice sang out from the backseat.

"That looks incredible!" Eden said.

"Big time," Rick replied.

The freeway soon ended, and after driving for forty minutes along a narrow, snow-cleared, curvy road, they arrived at a T intersection.

Eden turned to her husband. "Where to now?"

Rick's glowing green gaze connected with hers. "Right."

"Let me see what the map says." Eden rifled through the glove box for the hard copy Rick had referred to earlier.

He stilled her hand and she stopped to stare at him. "It's all up here." Rick tapped his temple. Then he reached into the pocket of the driver's-side door and handed her the map. "Though I'm happy if you want to double-check."

"No, that's fine. Right it is." *I trust him. I trust him. I trust him* — or so her gut said, pushing her to resist her rational brain's urge to snatch the directions out of his hand, just to make sure.

The car wound around the hill and the road leading to the left continued to the beach. *Good choice. A perfect choice, really.* She needed to stop letting her fear create unwelcome room for doubt. The bright star shone its Violet-Jade light, like a torch along the steep street.

For several kilometers, an eerily beautiful, snow-covered wilderness created a canopy around them, with icicles hanging like Christmas decorations off the pine-tree branches.

Rick rounded a corner and the road opened up, with the 'magic castle' directly ahead of them, bathed in the star's Violet-Jade rays. About one hundred meters away, a gate with an illuminated sign welcomed them to 'Ansfrida', the guest house where they had booked to stay.

"I don't believe it. It's like the universe doesn't trust technology either and sent us a guiding star," Eden said.

Rick's laugh rumbled with a mix of joy and relief.

Once they'd unloaded everything inside, Rick insisted on putting the already-sleepy kids to bed. Eden didn't object. Consumed by fatigue, she collapsed onto the downstairs couch, picked up a brown leather compendium off the coffee table and scanned through its contents.

When Rick returned, he cozied up to her, swept her hair aside and planted a soft kiss on the corner of her jaw. "What are you reading?"

She leaned back against his sturdy chest. "The history of the place. It's really interesting. For instance, did you know that 'Ansfrida' means 'protected by the gods'? Just knowing that makes me feel slightly less anxious about being here."

"Let's hope the name holds up to its meaning." Rick pressed a gentle kiss to her temple. "So, what else can you tell me?"

She angled her head to the side and he brushed his lips along her neck, nipping that special spot at the juncture of her shoulder.

A zing of pleasure zapped her sex and Eden squeezed her legs together. "Well, from what I've read so far, the house was found deserted in the late 1700s, except for some old, decrepit furniture and a wooden chest filled with records written in ancient Nordic."

Her voice sounded breathy, lust-charged. She closed the compendium and forced herself to continue.

"The archeologists at the time couldn't make sense of the writings, and it wasn't until the Rosetta Stone deciphered hieroglyphics in the 1820s that it gave them just enough of a hint to use a similar strategy to decode the documents found in the chest. And it worked."

"Anything else?" Rick persisted with the sensual torture, trailing his lips and tongue along her ear, neck and the exposed skin on her shoulder.

"Mmm-hmm." She breathed out a shaky breath. "Apparently, a missionary lived here alone in the Middle Ages and kept a detailed diary of everything that went on, from mundane, everyday tasks to alchemical formulas and special events. His writings gave the archeologists a really good insight into the general lifestyle during that period.

"The missionary often referred to two tribes also living in the area, but he kept his distance from them. It sounds like they were probably our Violet and Jade ancestors, in which case I can totally understand. It goes on to say that this used to be a two-story log cabin."

Eden reopened the compendium and flipped through the pages with shaky fingers. Among the pictures were a couple of sepia photos of the original cabin with snow covering the roof and forming icicles on the eaves. "Oh, that's gorgeous."

"You're gorgeous." Rick pinched and rolled her nipple through her boatneck top, and she gasped.

She slapped his hand. "Concentrate."

He didn't let go. "I am..." *On seducing you,* his desire-husky tone said.

Her body responded, and she pressed against him and tilted her head some more to give his lips better access to her heated skin.

He chuckled and glanced over her shoulder at the photo. "It looks cold, very cold."

*Always such a tease.*

Rick resumed his distracting ministrations and she tried to ignore him, pointing to the next paragraph and summarizing it as best she could. "In the later part of the missionary's life, he converted his house into a refuge for unsupported couples, to give them a head start as they tried to make a life together. Isn't that lovely?"

"Yeah, he sounded like a top guy," Rick whispered, his sultry breath stroking the shell of her ear.

"I'd say so, because this place turned into a sort of shrine to him. The original building stood in this spot until October 1965, when it got hit by a tidal wave, leaving only a few parts standing. Afterward, the community rallied together and had it rebuilt, incorporating some of the initial structure and features."

"May I?" Rick gestured toward the information folder on her lap.

She handed it to him, her body protesting the loss of his intimate touch, and he flipped back to the photos. "They used to build things to last in those days."

*Damn that compendium and its interesting history.* "Yes... I love what they've done with the place, though. It seems to have retained the old feel—but with the modern conveniences."

Rick slapped the folder shut and put it on the coffee table. "Yeah, it's pretty cool." He snuggled in close to her again, brought her fingers to his lips and kissed and licked the tips. "So what would you like to do now?"

His hot breath skittered across her skin and her libido flared to life.

The suggestive tone of his voice combined with his electrifying touch made her squirm in her seat. "Um...what did you have in mind?" All traces of sleepiness had disappeared, as though they'd never existed.

"Well, we can watch a movie." He licked from her shoulder right up to the top of her neck, leaving a trail of flaming heat.

"Or?"

"I can put on some music and maybe get us a drink..." He ran his hand under her skirt and along her bare thigh.

"I think I might have a better idea." She cupped his angular jaw and pulled his mouth to hers.

\* \* \* \*

Early the next morning Rick woke to the sound of some Nordic pop song blaring from the bedside table alarm clock. He glanced at his sexy, naked wife lying beside him, still sound asleep, wishing he could reprise their earth-shattering sex from the previous night.

However, the Sub Rosa compound awaited him, and he didn't want to be late on his first day. He couldn't afford to draw any unnecessary negative attention to himself.

Rick reached out from under the toasty doona, switched off the alarm and forced himself out of bed. If he wanted to continue to create memories with Eden and the twins, he needed to get moving, to get some results, so they could finally live without fear.

He pulled open the fridge door and stared at the eggs and milk. His stomach churned like he'd swallowed a carton of curdled cream, quashing his appetite. The Norway site staff were supposedly expecting him, but what if they weren't? It could all be an elaborate set up. Then what?

At that point, he doubted he and Eden would get a second chance. Though, being paranoid wouldn't help and neither would an empty stomach. He forced down some scrambled eggs, scrawled an *I love you, sweetheart* message on the back of a business card and left it on the kitchen table for Eden to find, snatched his black leather man bag off the hall stand and drove toward his destiny.

A smattering of cars dotted the parking lot, so he found a space near the exit, in case he needed to make a quick escape. Rick stepped out of the car and patted his jeans pocket, the malleable plastic of his ID badge pressing against his hand. *Phew!* No way he'd get in without it.

Automatic doors welcomed him into a large, modern, minimalist front foyer that smelled like a combination of brand-new car and sickeningly-sweet lily of the valley. Only one receptionist sat behind an expansive maple-wood desk.

"Can I help you?" A wide, flawless smile complimented her refined Norwegian accent. She looked to be in her mid-thirties, which probably meant she was over forty. A lanyard hung around her neck with a photo ID and the name *Rochelle* in block letters.

"I hope so. I'm normally based at the Tasmanian office but took up a temporary secondment here. I've been working on the Norway Experiment."

"Can I see some identification, please?" Her eyes traveled not-so-subtly from his shoes right up to the top of his head and back down to his mouth.

"Sure." He handed over his Tasmanian ID badge.

She reached forward to grab it, emphasizing her ample cleavage. "Thank you, Mr.... Hartman."

He forced a relaxed, friendly smile. "Rick." His hand shook. Hopefully her full-on flirting diverted her from his nervousness. Then again, maybe she used this strategy with everyone to make people feel flustered, distracted, thrown off guard. That was when secrets were revealed.

Rochelle scanned his ID into her computer then gave it back, her impeccably manicured hand lingering against his. "Thank you. It'll just take a minute."

"No worries." He shoved his hands into his pockets to stop the incessant fidgeting — his stressed tell.

Rick surveyed the neutral-toned reception area while he waited. The simple, covert design looked like any corporate foyer — keen to promote its brand while keeping ugly realities concealed.

She cleared her throat and his gaze reconnected with hers. "Thank you...Rick. You've got the all-clear. Do you have a mobile phone with you?"

"Ah...yes." *Shit.* He couldn't let her confiscate his lifeline.

"Excellent. There's an online orientation tutorial that will take you through each section of the building. I'll just give you the WiFi password."

As she read it out, he entered it straight into his phone and instantly got connected to the network. Relief chased away his pent-up anxiety. Sometimes being wrong was a blessing.

"Please make your way to the door on the far left and it will take you into the lab area. Enjoy your stay." Her eyes said, *I know I will.*

"Thanks."

She leaned forward, her gaze unrelenting. "If you're free later, maybe we could get a coffee?"

"Sorry. My schedule is pretty flat out. I'll barely have time to see my wife."

Rochelle slid back into her office chair, her face now a carefully constructed mask of professional fake friendliness, her spine as stiff as a storefront mannequin. Rejection was not a word she knew well, by the looks of things. "Oh, I see... Well, if you change your mind, you know where to find me."

Part of him was impressed with her persistence, a quality he needed to embrace if he had any chance of success.

Once inside the main part of the building, he stopped and scrolled through the orientation package on his mobile. An overview of the campus layout popped onto the screen and he studied the exits then wandered down the wide gray passageway to physically familiarize himself with the escape points.

In contrast to the foyer, this section of the site smelled of Bunsen burners and cooking compounds, like a secondary school lab. A sprinkling of staff sat in an open-plan office space, tapping away at their tablets, and others were spread across a sequence of labs, staring through microscopes, stirring concoctions and rushing around benches.

No one looked up or seemed to notice him. No one seemed to care about anything other than their work. He couldn't fault Sub Rosa for their exceptional recruiting skills and the employees' dedication, except the staff would have been sold a totally skewed picture. And he needed to rectify that...somehow.

At the end of the long corridor, he entered a new building. No, it was more like stepping into his own living version of *Alice in Wonderland*. The unexpected contrast between the areas disoriented him, like he'd gotten sucked through a portal into another world.

Instead of the office and lab environment, it looked residential, open and bathed in soft, golden sunlight.

An eerie quiet filled the sterile hallway, stretching out ahead of him. Open-fronted flats lined both sides of the space with an abundance of light streaming down their entrances, the windows and exit doors, brightening up the whole area without being glary. And yet the place reeked of misery, suppression and depression.

Rick had read about the sunlight bars, envisioning them to look a lot more restrictive. It highlighted that appearances could be totally deceiving. The naturalness of the design gave the area a false sense of freedom.

Back in Tasmania, he had seen architectural drawings of the captives' residential facility, which focused on the use of concentrated sunlight-infused, steel-reinforced concrete, with meter-thick walls to build the outer shell. The information referenced the sunlight bars but provided no details about the intricacies of the system.

At one point, he had asked to see more in-depth visuals of the living quarters and read up on the specifics of the sunlight system to get a feel of the compound — however, his request had been shut down. In other words, classified information was 'for management eyes only'.

With such groundbreaking technology came an associated high risk that someone could leak the sensitive information or even sell it to the highest bidder. On top of that, legalities existed around what constituted ethical restraint. Rick fit into the final risk category — a sympathizer, focused on finding a way to sabotage the technology to release the captives.

"Excuse me."

A woman's gentle, magnetic voice broke him from his reverie.

"Yes?" Rick approached what looked to be a Jade, half-caste woman in her early forties, trapped inside a flat on the right. Her characteristic light golden-brown hair tumbled over her shoulders and her piercing jade-green eyes glowed with a warmth that filled his heart.

"Can you come in, please? I have a maintenance issue I would like to report."

Everything about her seemed so familiar, even her Norwegian-accented speech. Had he met her before? His brain strained, sifting through his moth-eaten memory. *Bloody memory eraser!* "Ah...sure."

He hesitated. Would the sunlight bars affect him? *There's only one way to find out.* He took a deep, steadying breath, psyched himself up and tentatively stepped forward, ready for some resistance. Instead, the sunlight brushed over him as though he'd walked through a multi-colored strip door.

Rick breathed out a huge, relieved sigh and followed behind the woman.

"You're new, are you not?" she asked.

"Yes." His laugh had nervous, jagged edges. He'd thought he'd blended in, looked convincing, inconspicuous. "How could you tell?"

A melodic, tinkling laugh escaped her lips, as though her vocal chords were encased in a piano rather than a person.

She reached the lounge room and turned to face him. "You seem...unsure. I promise I will not hurt you." She studied his face, like she recognized him too.

Rick smiled. "I know." Odd as it seemed, he could sense it, like his gut had prior knowledge, something deeper than a sixth sense. And maybe it did, stemming right back from his 'Richard' days.

Whatever red blood she had in her cheeks drained away, turning her skin an ashen, almost blue-white. "Richard?"

*What the fuck? Can she read my mind?* "Yes, but I go by Rick now. How did you...?" He searched her eyes—the same shape as his—her mouth and teeth, almost a mirror image. A woman from the same clan, yes, and so much more. "Mum?"

She went to hug him...and stopped. "Better not. Not here," she whispered and gestured for him to have a seat. "You can call me Rhoda if you would like."

His mum had a point. They had to be careful. CCTV monitored the corridors, so there shouldn't be any vision inside the cells, though if staff doing their rounds saw them embracing, too physically close, they would start asking questions. And he had to keep his voice down—both of them did—in case of eavesdroppers or recording devices. "Thanks. But I quite like 'Mum'."

She sat next to him on the black leather couch, her smile so bright that he almost needed to shield his eyes from the glare. "You look so much like my Richard in a picture your father sent me when you got married in 1965 that I knew it had to be you. But how can that be? That happened forty-six years ago and you have not aged.

"Vampire genes slow the aging process, but a quarter-vampire like you should appear older, not the same age. Though, you are wearing the cross jewelry I gave to Salvator, a researcher who said he knew you, so it has to be you. I trusted him to pass on the jewelry and my instinct proved right."

"Yes, he helped us a lot. Without him, we wouldn't be here." Rick clenched his jaw and swallowed back the choking bolus of emotion. "Unfortunately, he passed away before we left."

She stared into his eyes. "I am sorry to hear that. Was he unwell?"

"No. That's part of why we're here. So much has happened...but I won't burden you with it all now. I'll explain more another time, okay?"

"Whenever you are ready."

"Thanks, Mum." Just saying the word swelled his heart with joy—and hers too, going by the pure happiness radiating off her face.

"I realize it is a bit superstitious, but I hoped the crosses would protect and watch over you. And so far, it seems they have, and I am forever grateful. Most of our kind don't believe God would look out for us—however, I disagree. If there really is a God or higher power, then I am sure he or she would want all species to thrive. I do not believe God would be selective, do you?"

He wasn't sold on whether to put his faith in God after what he, Eden and Salvator had experienced, but if such a powerful being did exist... "No. I mean, otherwise what would happen with full castes and hybrids like us? Unless there's some higher purpose we're not privy to..."

Rick twisted the cross ring around his finger. He had to get moving soon or else risk drawing too much attention to their little chat. Should he tell her about his dad first? He didn't want to turn their reunion into a downer, yet he couldn't afford to waste the opportunity either. "There is one other thing... Um... Dad passed away about four years ago."

The joyous glow on her face disappeared like snuffing out the flame of a candle. "Oh..." Her eyes filled with bulging tears that wouldn't fall. "Did you see him?"

"No, unfortunately not. Salvator did, though. He found him about ten years after meeting you, and Dad died soon after. Salvator wanted to say something but didn't want to put you or himself in danger. He felt terrible about not being able to let you know..." *Among other things.*

She reached for his hand and stopped a couple of centimeters before making contact. And yet a jolt bridged the gap between their connection, like their auras had touched. "I understand. Thank you for telling me. Do you know how it happened?"

"Apparently he had a heart attack and died peacefully in his sleep."

"He deserved some peace after all the unrest in his life. Abe was such a wonderful man... I wish I could have seen him one last time."

"Me too. I only ever knew him as my uncle—and even then..." Rick's mind raced, trying to crack the chemical code in his brain to allow him to access the locked-away memories. "Everything is so blurry. I wish I could remember..."

She searched his eyes, darts of worry spearing his heart. "Why do you not remember? Are you all right?"

"Sort of... I can't go into it now though, okay?"

Her lips formed a firm line, like she'd forced herself to hold back from demanding an explanation. She took a couple of deep, controlled breaths. "Maybe if you see a photo of Abe from when you got married..." She grabbed a picture frame off the nearby lamp table and handed it to him.

Three photos filled the frame—a portrait of Rick's mum and dad on their wedding day, a candid shot of him and Eden coming out of a small blue-stone church on the day of their nuptials in 1965 and a picture of him and his dad before they left for the church, leaning against the Psyche and Eros fountain.

Rick stared at the picture, willing it to be the correct key to unlock his imprisoned memories. *Come on!* His dad looked familiar, but no other details surfaced. He put the frame down on the coffee table and buried his head in his hands.

Rhoda touched his upper arm. "I am sure it will all come together when the time is right. Just have faith."

He shot his gaze to hers and sat up, his spine steel-rod straight. "After everything that's happened, how can you possibly have faith?" He couldn't conceal the utter disbelief in his tone.

"Richard—I mean Rick—without it, I do not think I would still be here. Though, let me be clear. I am not talking about blind faith. I am talking about a belief that things will work out for the best, even if it seems impossible at the moment. It can be difficult and trying, yes, but I have never given up hope. And look what has happened. You are here, my son."

She clutched his face for a brief moment, her hands exuding a tenderness and loving energy that seeped straight into his skin. "I have always believed that what is right will prevail, even if it takes a while. That is the thing about faith. It is not time restricted." She paused. "Just be patient."

"Trust me. I know all about patience." He twisted his cross ring again. "What you're saying makes sense, but I'm a realist, so I need to focus on the practicalities, on working out how to make things happen rather than hoping and waiting."

A wistful smile tugged at her lips. "You are so like your father. I always had faith in him and he did great things—and I have equal faith in you."

"Thanks, Mum. No pressure or anything."

Rhoda laughed, the sweet sound removing the last traces of tension in the room. "Tell me, are you still married?"

Every cell in his body sung with elation. "Yes. Happily."

Her high-voltage smile matched his. "I am so glad. Is she here with you then?"

"Eden and the kids are staying nearby. We have six-month-old twins, Blake and Scarlett."

"That is so wonderful. I would love to meet them —"

"You will. I'll make sure of it. I'm going to get you out of here."

"No, Richard. It is too dangerous! Abe tried for years..." Her voice took on a total Mother-knows-best tone.

"Rick." He had to ensure that no one else made the connection to his previous self. "I know what I'm doing. I'll be careful..." *This time...* "I promise."

"Rick, please..."

"I don't want to worry you, but the truth is, Eden and I are already in danger and the only way out of it is to take some big risks and try to make things right."

"You sound just like your father." She sighed, lines of worry deepening on her youthful face. She picked up the photo frame off the coffee table with a shaky hand, and a red rose motif on the back drew his attention.

"Your father sent this to me around the time you were married, though unfortunately I did not receive it until several years later. I have cherished it from the moment I saw it."

"Would you mind if I have another look?"

"Please..." She handed it to him, but instead of reviewing the photos, he turned it over and scrutinized the back.

Underneath the rose was a sequence of odd letters. "Intriguing..." Rick pointed to the obscure etching. "Do you know what this is?"

"Probably some romantic sentiment from your father. Abe used to write poetry for me...in code. He worked as a cryptographer and his coded messages became a little game, just between us. I loved it." The look in her eyes turned all bittersweet-nostalgic.

"Anyway, I have tried for years to decipher it and have gotten nowhere. It is so frustrating. I worked out all the others. He always got so thrilled when I finally solved his puzzles.

"I still remember the proud look on his face. I never had the heart to tell him I did not figure this one out. I hope he is not disappointed. Cryptic codes were your father's forte. Something tells me they might be yours as well. Maybe you will have better luck piecing it together."

"Would you mind if I take it with me?"

She smiled. "Of course not."

"Thanks, Mum. I'll see what I can come up with. I'll be in touch again soon." Rick leaned in close to her ear and whispered, "I love you."

# Chapter Three

The Elusive Code

The moment Rick stepped out of the car, Eden threw open the front door. "How did it go?"

He approached her with a wide grin. "I got in...and out, obviously." He'd only been at work for nine hours, but God he'd missed her.

Rick cupped Eden's face, kissed her luscious lips then held her hand and steered her into the living room, stopping in front of the enormous window. A panoramic view of the surrounding snow-capped mountains and silver-blue sea stretched out to the horizon. It felt like they'd been thrust into the middle of a 3-D postcard.

He stared into her large, blue-violet eyes, their beauty surpassing the most breathtaking scenery. "I had planned to casually slip this into our conversation, but I can't. I have to tell you now."

"Tell me what?" Her I'm-trying-to-be-positive face didn't quite cut it.

"Don't panic. It's good news." A huge smile exploded onto his face. "I met my mum."

"Your *mum*? Your *real* mum?"

"Yep."

A range of emotions flashed through Eden's eyes — surprise, joy, envy with a tinge of sadness. "Are you sure it's her?"

"Absolutely." Rick pulled the picture frame out of his man bag and showed it to Eden. "Dad sent her this soon after we were married...the first time."

She brought the frame up close to her face and scrutinized the pictures. "These are lovely. What a sweet, thoughtful man."

"Very thoughtful. Check out the back."

She turned the frame over and Rick pointed to the small rose symbol.

"See that gothic rose? Historically, it signifies protection of a secret."

Eden touched the rose key pendant around her neck. "Like this key opening the rose lock in your desk."

"And finding the information hidden about us and Sub Rosa." The magnitude of that secret had definitely required hiding. Whatever his dad had found must be something significant, something equally worth concealing.

She traced the outline of the etchings, like a visually impaired person reading Braille. "So what do these odd letters mean?"

Rick followed the slide of her finger over the indecipherable symbols. "I don't know yet, but I'm pretty sure they're important."

Eden rubbed her solar plexus. "We'll be able to piece things together. I can sense it. I don't know what it is, but since we've been here, I feel like my memory — and yours — are on the verge of...rediscovery."

He took the frame, put it on the coffee table and placed his hand over hers, as though trying to tune in to the same frequency. "I hope so. It's so frustrating knowing that we probably already know a lot of this stuff and just can't access it."

Her determined gaze focused on his. "Yet. We will, though..." She brought his hand to her lips and kissed the underside of his wrist. It was a simple gesture, yet so grounding and erotic. "So tell me, what's your mum like?"

"Sweet, intelligent, beautiful and she only looks about forty-five, if that. But I may be a little biased." He grinned.

"Wow! Did you tell her about Blake and Scarlett?"

"Yep." He ran his palms along the length of her arms and held her hands. "She would love to meet all of you, but I think it's best to hold off...until it's safer."

"Definitely..." A far-away look, a look of daring-to-hope, developed in Eden's eyes. "I wonder if..."

Rick tipped her chin up, until their gazes met. "Mmm?"

Eden kinked her head to the side, like a mini shrug. "It's probably a long shot, but I just thought that...maybe you might come across my family member too. Remember that Salvator said one of my relatives also lived in the compound? I wonder if it's my mother or father or sister or brother?"

"Hopefully we'll soon see. But because they'll be a Violet, I'd better be on my best behavior." He dropped a tender kiss on the top of her forehead where it met her hairline. "I'll investigate some more tomorrow."

They got busy preparing dinner and, later that night after putting the kids to bed, Rick joined Eden in their bedroom, the picture frame in hand. He plonked himself down onto the bed and reviewed the odd etchings. Maybe it might jog an old memory. Rick stared at the unrecognizable inscription, his mind straining to free the imprisoned thoughts, trying to smash the chemical divide between the past and present.

He huffed. "I know I should know this."

"I always find the best thing to do is to not overthink it. Just let your subconscious do all the problem solving. A very intelligent, rather attractive young man once told me that." Eden flashed him a cheeky smile.

He chuckled.

She came to stand between his legs. "All right... Well, I'm going to have a bath." She grabbed his hand. "Join me?"

Naughtiness invaded his smile. "You go on ahead and get the water running. I'll be there in a minute."

The brush of Eden's lips against his was like a wild flame to a wick, sparking his libido. "You'd better be." She walked to the en suite, leaving behind a trail of discarded clothes.

*Mm-m...* His body thrummed, already primed for another night of unbridled passion. And it might just have the added bonus of stimulating his subconscious to problem-solve his father's puzzle.

Rick leaned against the headboard and stared at the squiggles, the mystery of the unfamiliar letters dominating his thoughts. *Again.*

"Rick, are you coming?"

Eden's inviting voice called to him like a sexy siren song. He put the photo frame face down and went to get up, but the gothic rose symbol made him stop. Thoughts rammed his consciousness.

*Gothic Rose... Secret... Come on!* The answer lingered on the tip of his tied-up tongue. *I know I know it. Think harder!* Ah...unknown alphabet... What was the connection? There had to be one...

"Rick, the water's getting cold." Eden's seductive tone tugged at him and he took a step toward her.

"Be right there." Rick unbuttoned his shirt and shrugged out of it.

The rose... Indecipherable text... How could he find out what it meant? Where should he start? He undid his jeans, pushed them to the floor and stepped out of them, sinking his toes into the plush carpet.

Unable to let go of his puzzle-solving fixation, he snatched his mobile phone off the bedside table, tapped the Google icon and typed 'deciphering unknown alphabet' into the search field. A number of entries popped up, and he scanned through the titles.

Halfway down the page he stopped.

*Computer Rosetta Stone*

*Rosetta Stone. Of course!* Why hadn't it clicked earlier? He and Eden had just been talking about how it had helped decode the missionary's records.

Still in his boxers, Rick raced into the bathroom. He slid them off, slipped into the white clawfoot bath and pulled Eden to him, the mass of bubbles bunching up between her back and his chest.

He leaned forward and drank in Eden's delicious damask-rose scent, the foamy congregation compressing, dissipating and relocating. "Seeing you looking so delectable almost made me forget what I wanted to tell you," he whispered into her ear.

She shivered and snuggled into him.

He swept her hair aside and nuzzled her neck. "I think I might know how to find out what it means."

Eden spun around and locked her eyes on his. "Really?"

Rick lifted a loose, wet curl off her cheek. "Yep. I know I said I wouldn't think about it anymore tonight, but my mind just couldn't let it go. So I did a quick Internet search on deciphering unknown alphabets and an entry mentioning the Rosetta Stone came up.

"Then I remembered you explaining about how the discovery of the Rosetta Stone was key in assisting archeologists to decipher the missionary's writings at Ansfrida. That's when I realized that maybe the same principles would work in this case. But I'll look into it more tomorrow. For the rest of the night, I'm all yours."

Eden devoured his mouth with a cock-stirring kiss then slipped back between his legs and rubbed her ass against his growing erection. She caressed his thighs and his breathing staggered. He needed to slow things down, needed a leisurely-paced night of love-making, not a quick fuck.

Rick massaged her back and kneaded her tight shoulders. The tension in her muscles told him she'd put on a sex-kitten front but felt scared. Scared for him, for herself and mostly for their children, which was perfectly understandable, given the circumstances.

And he felt the same. The main difference was that he could turn his worry switch off. Eden couldn't. Ultimately, stressing wouldn't make things better. But try telling that to a person over-ridden with emotion, their body caught in a cortisol-fueled physiological trap. The only way forward entailed him taking action—well-thought-out action—for their long-term best interests.

Rick needed her to relax and to trust him. Words and a little massage weren't working. He needed to go deeper, to start at her naked core of vulnerability.

He nibbled on her sexy little earlobe. "Lean forward on your hands and knees."

She turned her head. "Pardon?"

"I want to pleasure you. Is that okay?"

"Oh-h. Yes." She shifted forward, her fucking incredible ass poking above the sloshing water and giving him the perfect, close-up view of her puckered little hole and hot, hairless pussy. Just drinking in her bare-skinned beauty made him ready to blow.

Rick rose to his knees and slowly trailed his fingers from the base of her neck, down her arched back, through the center of those gorgeous butt cheeks and along her slit.

She gasped and arched against his hand. He leaned forward and kissed along her spine while he reached one hand around and teased her hard nipple. Eden moaned and rocked against him, urging him on. He rubbed his engorged cock along her seam, which was already soaked with her need for him.

She whimpered. "Ple-ease..."

Rick pushed up into high kneeling, keeping one steadying hand on her slim waist, and positioned his cock at her entrance. He slid into her, that initial glide always so deliciously tight.

He had to concentrate so he wouldn't give in to the toe-curling friction, the avalanche of pleasure, and pump hard, or else he'd be done in seconds. He couldn't allow that, especially not for her. Nothing turned him on more than seeing Eden get off.

He ran his thumb between her legs, coated it in her juices and stroked her exposed butt hole. "Trust me?"

"Yes!"

Harnessing all his control, Rick slowly slid his cock almost all the way out of her sex and plunged back in to the hilt. He settled into a solid thrusting rhythm, recoated his thumb in her natural lubricant and pressed against her tight little anal opening.

Her breath caught.

"Touch yourself. Imagine me licking and sucking your clit."

Steam wafted up around them and she moaned and panted and pushed back into him, his thumb breaching her butt to the first joint. Her muscles clamped down, so snug and warm, and all he could think about was fucking her there. He'd fantasized about it heaps but they still hadn't given it a try.

She stiffened.

"Touch yourself. I'm so close and I want us to come together. Can you do that?"

She nodded and reached for her clit. How he wished they had a mirror so he could watch. Every. Specific. Detail. He loved seeing her masturbate, spreading her legs for him, for his and her pleasure. Then, add the view of him sinking into her at the same time and it would be like their own private, full-five-senses adult flick.

Fucking heaven.

Instead of her usual gentle clit caresses, she rubbed like a mixmaster on high speed, stirring up her flesh, the warm water and his desire.

He powered up his pace and played with her back hole, pressing his thumb in, stilling, then easing it out. Her erratic breathing and increased whimpers suggested that she'd almost reached climax.

"Come for me," he said, on the brink of shooting his load.

"Oh, Rick! Ooh-h-h!" Her body convulsed with pure pleasure and detonated his own explosive release.

He fell against her back, spent, and she trembled with orgasm aftershocks.

With each intimate encounter, it seemed as though one of them pushed the boundaries just that bit further, exposing more of their inner selves, deepening the level of trust between them.

Rick pressed his lips to her wet hair. "I hope you know that you and the kids mean everything to me. I'm pursuing this Sub Rosa thing for us...and others like us."

"I know." Eden wriggled free of his embrace and turned to face him, knee to knee. She pressed her wet palm against his thudding heart. "It's just... I don't want to lose you."

He stared into her eyes. A trace of worry darkened the edges of her irises, yet a glow shone through from their emotionally intense lovemaking. "You won't."

*Not this time.*

# Chapter Four

On a Mission

The next morning on the way to work, Rick stopped for petrol. While waiting in the queue to pay, he noticed a white sales tub near the counter, bulging with disposable colored contact lenses.

His brain snapped into gear.

He would be working closely with Sub Rosa staff who were vampire experts. Even though Rick's jade eyes were a watered-down version, one of the scientists could possibly twig to his part-Jade heritage. Salvator had, before he had even met a Jade in person, so it made absolute sense for Rick to mask the true color of his irises to reduce suspicion.

When he reached the cash register, he paid for the fuel, scooped up several packets of the brown contact lenses and added them to the bill. He stuffed them into his man-bag and returned to his car.

Rick scrutinized the 'how to insert a contact lens' instructions on the back of one of the packets. *Finger to eyeball.* He shuddered. *Fuck.* How the hell would he successfully put them in?

Just the idea of his finger in such close proximity to his eye made his eyelids go into a blinking frenzy. How did women apply eyeliner and mascara day in, day out? Rick remained in constant awe of their skill. He closed his eyes and took one, two, three slow, deep breaths.

*Nope. Not yet.*

He put the packet aside, drove about a block away from Sub Rosa and pulled over. With a shaking hand, he opened the box of lenses, peeled the foil off the back of a small pack and pulled one lens out. The concave, brown gelatinous thing looked foreign on his trembling finger.

*I can do this.*

Heart racing like he'd been jabbed with a double dose of adrenaline, he shoved the contact lens at his eyeball and poked himself in the eye.

*Ouch!*

*Fuck!*

The lens dropped, landing on his thigh and bouncing onto the floor. *Perfect.*

He glanced into the rear-vision mirror. Blurry. His eye had turned into a watery, bloodshot mess, reinforcing his failed attempt. *Okay, mini pep-talk time.* Thousands of people managed contact lenses every day, and if they could do it, he could too. Technically.

Though technically didn't always equal reality. He just had to find a way to push past his fear and polish his technique. His life, his family's life and many others' lives depended on it.

Thank fuck no one had stopped him and questioned his Jade genetics-inspired physical appearance on his first day. He'd been naïve and stupidly gung-ho. That exact type of behavior was what had originally gotten him and Eden into trouble. Straight after that, he'd promised her — and himself — that he'd be cautious and think things through before acting.

Rick closed his eyes and did a short mindfulness meditation. He eased his eyes open, picked up a new, pesky brown lens and slotted it into his right eye — no quivering, no flinching, no furious blinking.

Victory. *I can't believe it!*

Could he repeat the effort? A surge of performance anxiety swelled in his stomach. However, his success spurred him on and he effectively re-enacted the same procedure with the second lens.

Rick checked himself out in the rear-view mirror again, and chuckled. *Johnny Depp impersonator. Maybe I should try them out on Eden tonight...* It might add a bit more spice to their already-amazing sex life.

Within a few minutes he arrived at the Sub Rosa corporation car park. His eyes stung like they'd been attacked by a swarm of angry bees. *Settle down.* They ignored the order, though, remaining sore, aggravated and watery. Hopefully he'd adjust to the lenses soon or else risk drawing additional unwanted attention.

Inside, the same flirtatious receptionist sat behind the room-dominating desk, trying to discreetly file a nail. She glanced up, the automatic doors announcing his arrival.

A face-splitting smile spread across her cheeks. "Good morning, Rick."

"You have an excellent memory." Hopefully one day he would again too. He kept his gaze down, searching for a plausible reason for his irritated eyes.

*Ah-ha!* Problems with his contact lenses...and he wouldn't be lying.

"For certain things..." Her reply was rife with innuendo. "Anyway, go on through." She gestured with her elegant arm toward the inner sanctum, like a game show hostess announcing the prizes on offer.

Rick went straight to a small filing room in the main building, just prior to entering the residential area. When he was satisfied that no one was lurking around, he took the opportunity to check out the hardcopy records, hoping to find some information that would lead him to Eden's family member.

He approached the closest gray metal filing cabinet and searched for something to open the top drawer. It had no handle, button, ridge, lock or sign of a key in sight. None of the other storage units lining the wall had a hint of one either.

How the hell would he open the bloody flat-paneled things? Rick grabbed the outside corners of one of the filing cabinets and shook. Nothing. He stood back and stared at the row of unyielding metal, praying the answer would miraculously come to him. He pressed his palm on top of the cabinet and brushed his thumb over the front.

The top drawer shot open and he jumped back. "What the—?"

Rick's gaze stuck to the open cabinet, his heart hammering like he'd run a five-hundred-meter sprint. Then it clicked. *Fingerprint recognition, of course.* He'd read about the technology, but it had been slow to infiltrate the Tasmanian branch.

He waded through the first filing cabinet, which was jammed full of unhelpful old research publications, so he quickly moved on to the second. This one had a policy and procedure theme, including a breakdown of standards for quality research practice spanning from the birth of Sub Rosa. It was all vague, generic stuff so far, stuff the organization spouted to government and potential funders.

In order to find more incriminating information, he had to somehow access the high-security electronic files. If Sub Rosa senior management was smart – and Andy was clever, a conniving prick but a fucking genius – they'd leave no hard copy trace of anything suspect.

However, right now, Rick had to focus on the residents. He needed to take one measured, well-thought-out step at a time if he planned to be successful.

Continuing through the cabinets, he came across nothing on the captives. Maybe their information had all been transferred to top-secret electronic files as well? A weary sigh wrenched out from deep in his chest. *Where to next?* While on site, it made sense to exhaust all the hard-copy file options first.

Rick poked his head through the doorway and peered left, right, left. *Empty.* He snuck out of the room and continued on to the second residential building. At the end of the Jade quarters, he entered an almost blinding, stark white central hub containing the main control room, cafeteria and a number of office spaces and meeting rooms, according to the online orientation package.

He squinted, trying to adjust to the bombardment of artificial and natural light, the aroma of roast pork with crackling tantalizing his taste buds.

A hum of ceaseless chatter competed with the coffee machine in the large canteen. A sprinkling of staff sat around at the tables while many lined up for their morning caffeine fix. Others rushed by solo and in twos and threes, loaded up with books, notepads and envelopes of internal mail. Outside of the labs, this spot was the busiest work area Rick had come across.

Windows on the right showcased the river and the red, yellow, white and brown buildings lined up along its banks. The view, employees, furniture and appliances were the only things adding a spray of color to the space, like some abstract graffiti mural.

Rick tried to absorb the surroundings through slitted eyes. The sensitivity, another indicator of vampirism, he'd blame on the contact lenses to divert suspicion.

The staff he'd passed seemed too preoccupied to even register anything other than their smartphones and computer tablets, *thank fuck*. It made snooping around that much easier.

He kept walking toward the exit leading into the Violet quarters and a sign overhead pointed to the main control room down a corridor on the left and more offices and meeting rooms to the right. He'd have to come back and check those out another time.

Rick stepped from the core into an exact replica of the Jade area, but it was a Violet version. As Salvator had explained, the two clans had to be housed separately to prevent an outbreak of the ongoing civil war.

Apparently, no active conflict existed at present— however, it still simmered away in the background, like a rumbling volcano. Given the right circumstances, the battle could erupt.

Although it was idealistic, Rick really hoped he could encourage the clans to work together. It would make it a hell of a lot simpler to formulate an effective escape plan.

As things stood, he worried about what might happen once the two groups were released. Would they turn on each other and possibly jeopardize their freedom or would they put on a united front to ensure a successful escape?

The glow of violet eyes intermingled with the radiating sunlight bars. Unease slithered up his spine like a cold, slimy snake. Whether they saw him as human or detected his underlying Jade genes, he remained the enemy.

Some residents sat on the couches or in beds, idle, strung out on mind-numbing TV, while others moved around, some agitated, wringing their hands. Others seemed to focus on function, keeping busy tidying up and cleaning, seemingly anything for a distraction. Each indulged in a different form of escapism.

Shades of pale skin and Violet eyes flashed between the bars. All the captives connected in their Violetness, all varying degrees of Eden, just like the Jades were varying degrees of him.

Most of them didn't look up as he passed, as though they were desensitized to the roaming staff, like he represented another invisible worker, which was just how he wanted it. If they recognized him as a Jade and dobbed him in, it would stuff up his whole mission.

At the far end of the building, he stumbled across another deserted archive area. He loitered, feigning interest in his phone until the coast looked crystal clear, then he slipped inside to investigate.

A lot of funds had been poured into the Norway satellite site to provide them with the most up-to-date technology, though at a compromise — skeleton staff. It seemed not even a specialized facility like Sub Rosa was exempt from budgetary constraints and cutbacks.

Rick pressed his hand against the first filing cabinet, then the second and the third, but none opened. *Fuck.* How could he get his security clearance checked and adjusted when Simon, his only high-end tech support option, resided in Tassie?

*Think!* He leaned against the closest inaccessible storage unit and fought against the compulsion to rub his stinging, teary eyes. No matter how much they irritated him, he had to refrain. What if he dislodged one of the contacts? Just the thought of trying to get it back in again was unbearable.

*Buuuuuzzzzzzzzzzzzzzzz!*

Rick jumped, the vibration of his mobile rattling against the metal and thrusting him forward. He snatched his phone from his back pocket and stared at the blurry screen through his inflamed eyes. Simon had sent a message.

How fortuitous. His mind tick-tick-ticked over. Could Simon possibly weave his magic remotely?

Before reading his friend's text, he sent him one straight back.

*Hey, mate, could you please increase my security access?*

Within a minute, he received a response.

*Something must have happened coz they've tightened settings. I'll fiddle around and msg you in about 15.*

At the thirteen-minute mark, Simon's follow-up text came through.

*Okay, I think it's sorted...*

Rick shoved the phone back into his pocket and tried one of the locked filing cabinets. It wouldn't budge. *Fuck.* He should have double-checked his security access with Simon before he left. What a stupid oversight. But everything had happened so quickly.

He took out his phone again and finished reading Simon's reply.

*But there might be a time delay before the changes kick in. Try in a couple of minutes.*

Patience had never felt so painful...that he could remember. After two agonizingly slow minutes, he tried again, and this time the drawer popped open.

*Thanks, mate! I owe you one.*

More than one, in fact. Without Simon's help, succeeding at his mission would be almost impossible.

Upon reaching the sixth cabinet, Rick found an old, handwritten record, listing residents' names against their allocated code names. He scanned the flimsy, faded yellow-tinged document, his eyes burning, watery, and a tear dripped and hit the paper.

"Shit!"

The drop seeped into the fragile sheet and spread. Rick frantically dabbed at it with a tissue, the growing wet patch just about to engulf another name—Ethan Fjelstad.

*Eden's original maiden name... He has to be the one...*

\* \* \* \*

*Violet quarters, Sub Rosa Norway site, 2011*

*Indigo's soft hand throbbed with heat in Hugh's cool grasp. She clasped his hand tighter, looked him in the eye and smiled. So beautiful... The sun's rays penetrated the foliage, the forest glowing with lush, rich green. Hugh led her underneath a canopy of gnarled myrtle beech tree branches and onto a track, his wedding gift to her only a few meters ahead.*

*She gasped. "I can't believe it. It's wonderful! Exactly how I imagined." Her eyes danced with delight and she threw her arms around his neck, the full weight of her slight frame pressing against him.*

*Hugh stroked her mass of springy, caramel curls. "I had a feeling you'd like it."*

*She pulled back, bouncing on the spot, like a champagne cork about to burst free. "I love it! And I love you...more than anything."*

*He leaned in and pressed a tender, adoring kiss to her lips. She glided her warm tongue against his and he cuddled her close.*

*"Let's go inside..." she whispered, her breath like a sultry summer breeze against his skin.*

*He lifted her, carried her over the cabin threshold and straight to their bedroom. They hurriedly undressed, scattering their clothes across the timber floor, and lay on the cozy double bed. She ran her hands over his bare body, sending jolts of electricity through him.*

*"You're heating up." Her big blue eyes filled with concern.*

*"It's you... It's good, all good." He took his time kissing down her neck, to her breasts and flat stomach.*

*He moved his mouth to her inner thighs and she weaved her fingers through his hair and tugged. "Hugh!"*

*His gaze met hers.*

*Her forehead crinkled like a discarded sweet wrapper.*

*"What's wrong? Am I hurting you?"*

*"No, not at all. That's just it. Your touch is the gentlest it's ever been. And your eyes... They've changed color."*

*"Changed color?"*

*"They look blue."*

*He pulled away and inspected himself. Veins bulged in his forearms and the backs of his hands. Was it possible? Could her love have converted him back to human?*

*A rush of uncomplicated arousal coursed through him and he reconnected his lips to hers. They made love for the first time, deep into the night, then lay beside one another, puffing and panting, both their bodies glistening with sweat.*

*Indigo reached across and squeezed his hand. "Amazing! So amazing! See? I told you that you wouldn't hurt me."*

Hugh snapped his eyes open to the dim, dark reality. Indigo's picture stared at him from his bedside table. *Great.* Now not only his conscious but also his subconscious mind played the torture.

Wasn't it enough that she occupied his thoughts every waking moment? Would he have no respite from his grief? He'd noticed that her enthralling eyes seemed to follow him around his cell, like the Mona Lisa, though their color, their depth and their intensity made them so much more beautiful. Unforgettable. Could that be a positive sign? Maybe it meant she was thinking about him too.

Hugh flopped onto his back and clutched at his heart. *Indigo...* Did she still live in Hobart? Had she even stayed single? She'd be thirty-five now, so she'd most likely have gotten married and had someone else's children.

A tear trickled down his cheek and dropped onto his purple pillowcase, spreading into a dark, round wet patch. He propped himself up on one elbow and faced her image again, her expressive cobalt-blue eyes adoring, loving.

Hugh picked up the antique pewter frame and hugged it to his chest. If only he could see her and explain…if she'd let him. He'd sent her reams of gushy, emotive letters during their fourteen-year separation, professing his undying love for her, apologizing profusely for what had happened and begging to see or hear from her again.

But, like a boomerang, all the letters had come back, each with 'return to sender' scribbled across the front in thick red text. Had she even received them? The angry red marker definitely didn't seem Indigo's style…unless she'd had someone do it for her. No, she would have at least read one to see what he had to say and acknowledged it to him, even just to reinforce that she'd moved on.

Hugh brought Indigo's photo to his lips and kissed her. He placed it back onto the bedside table, jumped up and walked in circles around his cell. Why wouldn't the sadness subside, even a little bit?

Her absence brought out the inner masochist in him. Then again, the grief kept her close. What would he have without it? She gave him something to live for, even if the chance of being reunited was remote.

He picked up his breakfast-supplement vial from under the door and shot it. *Blurgh!* His eyes fluttered and his mouth puckered like he'd sucked on a revolting sour lemon. Though, as disgusting as it tasted, at least it stopped the ravenous, all-consuming hunger. He discarded the empty ampule into the nearest bin, under his desk.

His nose twitched. A new human staff member? Hugh walked over to the sunlight bars. No. The man appeared to be full human, with golden brown hair and brown eyes, but his unmistakable Jade scent confirmed his hybrid status.

*What is he doing wandering around the Violet quarters?*

# Chapter Five

## A Relative Find

Rick walked right up to the blazing sunlight bars and stopped. "Ethan Fjelstad?"

The vampire glanced up from his couch, his bright violet eyes spearing Rick to the spot. "Who wants to know?"

Rick felt like a fly stuck in a sticky web of paranoia. "Can I come in?"

Ethan's intense, wary gaze held him immobile, like a spider sizing up his prey. "That depends."

*Does this guy ever blink?* "On what?"

"What you want."

"It's nothing to do with any testing, if that's what you're worried about."

Ethan crossed his arms and leaned against the backrest. "What makes you think I'm worried?"

"Um-m..."

"Assuming was your first mistake and hesitation your second," Ethan said with a smug smile.

*Off to a ripping start.* "O-kay...so are you going to let me come in or not? I need to speak to you about something that I think you'll be interested in."

One of Ethan's eyebrows kinked up. Had Rick actually managed to pique his curiosity? The guy looked him over and gestured for him to enter.

*Breakthrough.*

"Welcome to my humble abode." Sarcasm dripped from his sneering lips.

Up close, Ethan had an uncanny resemblance to Eden, though she looked like a more diluted, exotic version. Everything about her father was full on—his coloring, his eyes, his manner, his presence.

Eden must have gotten her gentleness and warmth from her mother. Sure, she had a fiery side, but not to the same level as her dad.

"Will you need to take a seat?" Ethan's tone said, *make this a short stay.*

*Man, has this guy ever heard the phrase, 'lighten up', 'take a chill pill', 'relax your dacks'...?* "It's up to you. I can stand if you prefer."

Ethan stood, slow, measured and menacing, his gaze like an interrogative spotlight.

*Standing it is then.* "I'm not sure exactly where to start...um-m..." Rick took a step back.

Ethan's steely glare stabbed at him with *don't-waste-my time* daggers.

Rick cleared the nerves clogging his throat. "Eva is alive and well."

A flicker of delighted surprise shot across Ethan's face, and his stare softened. "How do you know her?"

A proud smile lifted the corners of Rick's lips and swelled his heart with love. "She's my wife."

A hardened gleam returned to Ethan's eyes. "Do you work here?"

*Shit.* "Sort of."

Ethan clamped his teeth together and a muscle in his jaw twitched, once, twice.

"So does Eva." *Well, for Sub Rosa.* Rick fidgeted, the grilling heat of Ethan's stare burning his body. "Not here— We met in Tasmania. We both worked at the Hobart office."

A confused look crossed his stony face. "Oh..."

Rick took a step closer. "I'm not like the others. Eva and I are similar, you see..." He looked around, checking that no staff were nearby. "I'm a quarter Jade."

Ethan charged forward, like Rick represented a large red flag to a furious bull. "Then how come your eyes are brown?" he said through gritted teeth.

*Fuck!* Why the hell had he confessed to being a Jade? He'd had the perfect cover. But he'd fucked that up— now he had to come clean. "They're contact lenses. I couldn't risk the Norway researchers suspecting anything."

Ethan crowded Rick and pinned him to the wall. "Leave my daughter alone. Do you hear me?" His breath pelted Rick's face.

What would the guy do, punch him? Now definitely wasn't the time to mention Scarlett and Blake, just in case. Rick's heart slammed against his ribs, his whole body on high alert, but he forced himself to look his father-in-law in the eye. He couldn't show this man any fear. "Please, just let me explain..."

"No Jade is touching my daughter!" Ethan growled, balling his hand into a fist.

\* \* \* \*

In under forty minutes, Rick had extricated himself from Ethan, *thank fuck*, snuck out of work and arrived at Ansfrida.

Eden rushed over to him. "What happened to your eye?"

He shut the door behind him and sighed. "It's these stupid contact lenses..."

She held his face between her hands and her worried gaze locked on his. "I don't think contact lenses cause bruising."

*Shit.* How could he tell Eden that her dad was a bully with a massive chip — no, a five-hundred-kilo-cross — on his shoulder? "Oh, that...um-m...your dad took a swing at me."

"My dad! Really? You found him? I can't believe it!" An ecstatic smile replaced the stress on her face.

*Ah...how about concern for your husband?* "Um-m... Don't you want to know why he hit me?"

She tamped down her excitement and schooled a worried-wife expression. "Oh, yes, of course. I'm sure he must have had a good reason."

"He thinks he does — I'm from the wrong side of the vampire tracks and I work for Sub Rosa. Let's just say he didn't deal too well with finding out his daughter is literally sleeping with the enemy."

She draped her arms around his neck and looked into his eyes. "You're not the enemy. He doesn't know you...or me. Let me speak to him."

Rick placed his hands firmly on her waist. "No. Not yet."

Her bottom lip protruded in a disappointed pout, begging to be sucked.

"You know I'll do my best to make it happen, though at the moment, it's not safe, and there are some other issues that are more...pressing that need to be sorted out first.

"Actually, that reminds me... I need to tell Simon about the writing on the picture frame and see if he can help decipher the message. I tried getting into the electronic Rosetta Stone software and got blocked. Only select university research staff can log in. *Ugh*. But I refuse to give up."

She smiled at him. "I never doubted that. You're a very persistent man — and I love that about you."

"And I love that you get me, trust and support me." Rick kissed his captivating wife then took her hand and steered her to the living room couch. He drew her down onto his lap, the crackling amber flames from the fireplace soothing, regenerating.

He cradled her against him and stroked her soft, silky hair. "Maybe Dad hid some more information in the house, some way to crack his code — possibly in that Nordic history section in our library. I should ask Simon to have a look and see if he can find an ancient Nordic language book while I try to search for some other way to access that Rosetta Stone software."

Eden nestled her head into his neck and he inhaled her signature rose-and-cinnamon scent that never failed to spark his libido.

"That's a great idea. Is there anything I can do? I feel so helpless just sitting here doing nothing."

He kissed her forehead and cuddled her closer. "Actually, now that Simon has increased my security status, I might be able to remotely log into the Sub Rosa database. If that's the case, you could start trawling through the records to look for any discrepancies and save 'questionable' documents as evidence. It'll be a lot safer than me trying to do it discreetly on site."

She stiffened, radiating almost-palpable waves of anxiety. "Won't they be suspicious if you're logged in for a long time, especially if you're at work and not at your computer?"

Maybe she did have some of her dad's paranoia. Given the circumstances, though, her worries were justified. However, when weighing up the whole situation, the threat of being found out was super-slim to none.

"I doubt anyone will question it. I mean, if I have access, there won't be any alerts. And even if I'm still logged in and not at my computer, I may have just locked it and stepped away for a moment. There's no way they'll suspect anything."

Eden lifted her head, her anxious eyes searching his. "What if you've left for the day and some on-the-ball IT guy sees that you're still logged in?"

"I could be working from home or have forgotten to log out. They wouldn't know. But say they don't trust or believe me, without any definitive evidence, the worst they could do is keep an extra eye on my actions.

"So far, I've given them nothing to be concerned about, though. Plus, the majority of the IT guys go home when I do. Usually one is rostered on overnight, in case the shift workers have any issues, but from what I can gather, it's more like a sleepover. I don't think too much work or monitoring gets done."

She laughed—however, the sound had a serrated edge. "Okay, give me the login details and I'll start tomorrow. If I can't get in, I'll let you know." Eden shifted on his lap. "This is so convoluted, isn't it? I've just started to get my head around things, but it seems each day there's something else to consider."

Rick kissed her lush, succulent lips. "It has been pretty full-on, I agree. But if we can get through all this, we can get through anything."

\* \* \* \*

"Where are you going?" Eden asked, still clutching him in semi-sleep.

He kissed her bare shoulder. "The usual. Get some more rest, sweetheart."

Eden turned to face him. "Let me go today instead. Please. It's just one day. We'll only be one day behind. I've been thinking about things all night and…I want to see my dad. I need to explain. I'm sure he can't stay angry if he knows I'm happy, if he knows he has grandchildren…"

Rick palmed her cheek, pushing away a loose tendril of hair. "I told you… I won't put you in danger. And anyway, they expect me. It'll look too suspicious if you rock up now, especially because you're still on maternity leave."

He stared into her eyes with unmistakable sincerity. "I promise I'll get my mum and your dad out of there as soon as I can, and we can have a proper family reunion."

The prickle of budding tears burned her eyes. "What if things don't work out how they're supposed to?"

"We'll deal with it then. There's no point worrying about something that may or may not happen. I swore to keep you and the kids safe, first and foremost, and that's one thing I won't compromise on. Plus, even if you could safely go in my place, I wouldn't allow it.

Those brown contact lenses sting like fuck. It feels like having shampoo constantly dripping into your eyes. And I wouldn't want you to ruin your makeup."

She laughed, sending a tear rolling down her cheek.

"Actually, that reminds me. I better go put them in." Rick swiped away the teardrop that had rolled onto her cheek, pressed a swift kiss to her lips and disappeared into the en suite.

Within seconds, he stood in the doorway, the light glowing behind him as though he was some sort of angel...or superhero. "You've got to see this."

She followed him into the compact bathroom and he pointed to a tissue on the vanity, containing what remained of the brown contact lenses he'd taken out the previous night. He'd never gotten a chance to put them in the bin, not with her impromptu blow job.

Delicious memories of him coming in her mouth, then lifting her up, throwing her on the bed and returning the favor surged into her mind. She indulged, just for a moment, then forced herself to stop and focus on the lenses.

They looked thin, cloudy, patchy, like mini jigsaw puzzles with pieces missing—*a bit like our memories.*

"I realize they're disposable but...what happened to them?" Eden asked.

"Either they're really bad quality, which would explain the price, or my body chemistry has caused their erosion. It's probably a bit of both, though I'm thinking it's more my body chemistry."

She stared at his reflection in the mirror. "Do you think the same thing would happen to me?"

"I wouldn't be surprised..."

"I'm going to give them a try." She snatched a new pair off the vanity and placed them on her irises.

65

"You're right. They're awful. My eyes are burning already."

"I told you."

She removed the offending lens from her watery, irritated eyes, tears spilling onto her cheeks. Then she wrapped the foreign objects in a tissue and headed for the bin.

"Hey, don't you want to see if anything happens to them?"

She stopped and turned to him. "I only had them in for a minute. I doubt there'll be any changes."

"But aren't you curious? I mean, what's the harm in leaving them out for a few more hours? You can throw them away later."

"I suppose..."

He joined her at the bin and pressed a kiss to that super-sensitive spot behind her ear. "Come on. Humor me."

She shivered and handed the scrunched-up tissue to him. "You're such a science nerd. You know that?"

"And a damn sexy one," he whispered, his breath caressing her skin.

She sighed. She couldn't argue with that.

Rick put the tissue beside his discarded lenses and spun her to face him. "I'd better get moving."

Eden wound her arms around his neck. "Just a few more minutes."

"If I stay a few more minutes, I won't be going anywhere." His suggestive smile sent a flare of desire to her sex.

She rubbed her body against his, unable to miss his more-than-ready-to-play cock. "Mm-m... Have the day off and you'll be all refreshed for tomorrow."

"Tempting. Very tempting. But I reckon I won't get too much rest. Just think, with me there and you accessing the database from here, we can get the information we need so much sooner and leave."

She rested her hands on his chest and looked up at him. "I know. But I thought it was worth a try."

"Definitely worth a try. I'll make it up to you later."

"Promises, promises," she teased, right before their lips met.

# Chapter Six

## The Reluctant Return

Stepping through the back door of the Violet living quarters, Rick traversed the rickety timber stairs that led into a frosty meadow, with sections of forest creating natural boundaries around the edge of the agency-owned land. The time had come for an extended exploration of the massive complex.

Ten minutes later he passed a large sandstone and wrought-iron fence and glimpsed a house — *his* house — through the metal bars. He jarred to a halt. It looked like an almost exact replica of his Tasmanian home. He had to get closer and compare the inside.

Rick entered the grounds through a large gate and followed a tree-lined trail that opened up into an English cottage-style garden covered in ice, turning the usually bright colors almost silver. And right there, at the top of the path, stood an Eros-Psyche fountain, just like the one he had at home.

*Unbelievable.* Rick circled it then continued up a set of steps with deep grooves that signified many years of wear and onto a spacious landing. He stopped in front of a grand oak door with black, curvaceous wrought-iron hinging, identical to the door of his house. It felt like he'd been transported to some surreal mirror world.

What did Sub Rosa use the place for? Should he go any farther? What would be his excuse if someone caught him? 'I got lost' probably wouldn't cut it. But the more he stood around and waited, the greater his chances were of being seen.

He eased the door open and stepped into the front foyer. Deathly quiet hung heavy in the air and it smelled dusty and dank, like the place needed a good air-out and vacuum. Hopefully the silent disrepair meant others were rarely around.

He skulked through the top and bottom levels, and the size and layout seemed the same as his home, though the décor appeared to be centuries-old antique. Overall, the place looked more dingy and rundown.

The mansion had been set up like frat-house-cum-hostel accommodation, with shared bathrooms and kitchen. Sub Rosa staff had to board there. Who else would be allowed onto the high security property? From what he'd seen, the space could probably hold up to twenty people at a time.

Rick riffled through the drawers and cupboards downstairs, careful to leave everything as he found it.

A door banged at the back of the house.

Rick yanked his hand from the open drawer and darted his gaze around the open living area, searching for a hiding spot.

Footsteps thumped, growing heavier, louder, nearer. His heart shot into overdrive, pounding so hard that it almost stalled.

*Fuck, fuck, fuck!*

Behind the couch? No, no time. He'd be seen.

Inside the bay window seat? No, too small and likely to be stuffed with storage.

Under the staircase? Only a short sprint away. He had to risk it.

Rick slunk, low, quiet, cat-like, to the door under the stairs and reached for the handle. *No lock, please no lock.* He stared at the door lever and eased it down. *Crrreak!*

*Fuck!* He yanked the door open and shut it behind him, trying to slow his accelerated breathing. Dark and cool, it made a great spot for a wine cellar...and hopefully an excellent hiding place.

The footsteps continued to move closer and stopped right outside where he stood.

*Thump.*

Rick jumped, his heart beating triple time. Was that a fist against the flimsy barrier between them?

"Stupid creepy door. This fucking place is haunted," the stranger said, the sound of his footsteps trailing away then thudding up the stairs.

A door slammed shut overhead.

A cold trickle of sweat slithered down Rick's spine and he breathed out hard. He had to get out of there before the guy reappeared or someone else showed up. Maybe his mum could enlighten him on the origin of the house and confirm who currently lived in it?

He snuck out and, before he left work for the day, he paid his mum a quick visit.

Rhoda's eyes lit up. "Richard! It is so great to see you again," she whispered.

Rick smiled, her genuine joy staking a claim in his heart. "Unfortunately, I can't be too long."

"I understand."

"Do you know much about the house at the back of the property?"

"I did not realize it still stood. I thought for sure they would have knocked it down. I am so glad they have not. It belonged to my family for centuries. You were born in that house..."

"Really? So, what happened?" Rick asked.

Rhoda gestured for him to have a seat. "Sub Rosa set up camp only a few kilometers away and started collecting vampires. That was when your dad and I decided to leave, fearful they would take me as well as you. We ended up fleeing to Australia—back to his homeland.

"We traveled to Tasmania and, with the money we had, bought some land in a lovely spot outside of Hobart called Fern Tree. It did not have the snow-capped mountain range as a backdrop but it still captured our hearts. It had potential. It had the same feel, the same energy as here."

Nostalgia played out in the depths of her jade eyes, like she was watching some internal movie. "Breathtaking myrtle beech and eucalyptus trees and ferns surrounded the block, solidifying it as the ideal spot to build a replica of my family home. Everything seemed so perfect. It would be the perfect start of our new life...together.

"Then one day, while your dad took you down the street to give me some respite, Sub Rosa staff kidnapped me. They had found us. I do not know how. I put up a fight, but they overpowered me with an experimental sunlight stun gun." Her teeth clenched tight and her fingers curled, pressing into her palms. Open close, open close, open close.

"They Tasered me repeatedly during a long plane journey and I woke up here, though it did not quite look like the five-star accommodation it is today. Over the years I broke out many times but never got too far. Then, when they introduced the sunlight bar system in the mid-1980s, I could no longer escape. No one could.

"I had heard Sub Rosa took over a big portion of the land, so I assumed they had torn down any pre-existing structures and rebuilt to suit their purpose. I believe they overspent in the research department, so they must have run out of money for everything else." A sardonic smile crossed her lips.

"As soon as Abe found out where I had been imprisoned, he sent me letters, but it took years before I received them. Sub Rosa held them until the sunlight bars were in place. I am assuming they thought we captives would lose hope and stop trying to flee. Once the sunlight system started, it ended any chance of freedom."

Moisture glistened in her eyes, turning the jade into a deep reflective jewel of sadness. "I finally read every one of your father's messages and he explained what had happened the day I went missing.

"When he had returned with you to the house, I was gone. He knew straight away what that meant and wanted to make sure it would not happen to you. So, he made the most difficult decision of his life and gave you to an orphanage in the hope that no one could directly link you to us, particularly me. I wished he had not done it, but I knew he'd had to...for your protection."

Her voice cracked on the last word and she almost stifled a sob. Even in that small sound, he heard the residual agonizing pain, as though her heart had been ripped from her chest, leaving a deep, scarring wound that had never healed.

"To try to ease the sorrow of losing his wife and son, Abe focused all his energy on recreating our original home, as we had planned. For him, I think it acted as a kind of commemoration of us."

She leaned forward and looked into Rick's eyes, as if to convince him they had done the best they could and had never quit. "Abe never gave up trying to get us all together again, somewhere safe.

"He had this quirky habit where he would try to engage his subconscious to work on a problem his conscious brain could not seem to solve. And he found the best way to do that was to focus on something else, so that is exactly what he did. Abe spent the rest of his life putting all his energy into helping others avoid the same fate, hoping his efforts would prove fruitful, both in saving them and finding the answer to getting us back together as a family."

Disappointment and grief weighed down Rick's heart like a bowling ball in his chest. "I wish I'd had the chance to spend more time with him. He sounded like such a great guy…so generous and selfless. I could have learned so much."

Rhoda intertwined her fingers with his, squeezed and let go. "You are already a lot like him. Do you not see that? He would be so proud—as I am."

Heat rushed to his cheeks. Would she still be proud when she knew what he had put his wife through? Yes, he had had the best of intentions, but his impulsiveness to do the right thing had nearly killed her and himself. He couldn't let that happen again…ever.

He had to be patient, had to be successful this time. His actions had achieved part of his father's goal—to reunite them as a family. Now he just had to fight for their freedom. "Thanks, Mum. That means a lot to me."

"And you mean a lot to me."

* * * *

Rick returned to Ansfrida a couple hours early, and the place as silent as a church. The kids were obviously still napping. Normally they were chattering away with some accompanying clanging from the kitchen as Eden prepared dinner.

In the lounge room, Eden had fallen asleep on the couch, the laptop nestled against her thighs and stomach. Rick slipped the computer out of her loose grasp and placed it on the dining table.

She'd been logged into the Sub Rosa database and had saved a copy of one file...so far. He hovered over it, debating whether to indulge his curious mind or spend some alone time with his gorgeous wife. It was a no-brainer. Gorgeous wife won. Every. Time. He could always check the file later. It wouldn't go anywhere.

Rick sat beside her, slid his arms around her waist and planted a feather-light kiss on her exposed neck. She stirred and pressed her body against him.

"Want to play?" he asked in a suggestive tone.

"What's the time?" Her eyes stayed closed and her voice slurred with lingering sleep.

"That doesn't answer my question."

"Well, that doesn't answer mine either."

He chuckled. "If I tell you the time, will I get a bit?"

Her eyes shot open and she stared at him. "You're a shocker, you know that? Several hours a night not good enough for you?"

Rick put his hands up in surrender. "Hey, I just wanted to know if I'd get a bit of time. I can't help that your mind went straight into the gutter."

"Mummy," Scarlett called.

"Great timing," Rick murmured.

Eden laughed.

"You stay here. I'll go." He held both her hands, brought them, one at a time, to his mouth and planted a kiss on the back of each. "Until later, my love."

Rick jumped up and went to retrieve the kids from upstairs.

"Daddy!" Scarlett squealed.

A big smile lit up Blake's chubby little face and he gurgled with excitement.

"What a welcome." Rick walked over and kissed each of them on the top of their downy heads.

"Blake says he's happy you're home early. And I am as well," Scarlett said.

"Thanks, me too." He scooped the twins into his arms and carried them out of their bedroom and into the hallway.

Rick approached the top step of the staircase and Scarlett's tiny hand touched his eyelid. "Daddy, why are your eyes so red?"

The simple little gesture distorted Rick's vision just for a moment, but it was a moment too long. He lost his footing on the first step and scrambled to hold on to the banister railing to steady himself, catapulting Blake from his grasp.

"Eden!" Rick yelled.

She arrived...too late. Blake hit the third last step and rolled down, slumping in a crumpled little heap on the floor.

Rick charged to the bottom of the stairs with Scarlett screaming in his ear. He reached Blake's broken, bleeding body and froze. Rick tried to move, to tend to his son's horrific injuries, to save him, but he felt trapped, stuck in some intermediary space—a helpless statue able only to stand by and stare.

Then the flow of time recommenced and his stiff muscles twitched, though instead of moving forward, every action rewound in slow motion, until he was standing at the top of the stairs with Scarlett and an uninjured Blake in his arms.

Scarlett held Rick's face in her cool, small hands. "Daddy, be careful."

*What the fuck just happened? And how...? Scarlett.* "Did you do that?"

She dropped her hands and her face tensed, like she thought she'd get in trouble.

"It's okay if you did. More than okay." It was amazing, awe-inspiring, life-saving. In one short moment, his Jade-Violet-human daughter had managed to highlight the incredible positives of a mixed-heritage union that had been founded on love.

Her actions dispelled his fears and demonstrated the great potential gains to an interwoven vampire and human society. It drove Rick's determination to free the Jades and Violets even stronger, reinforcing that he was on the right path.

Scarlett glanced up at him through her long blonde lashes, as if to say, *really?*

"You saved your brother's life." Tears blurred his vision and he cuddled his precious children to his chest, breathing in their sweet baby scent, never wanting to let them go.

When he had steadied himself physically and emotionally, he attempted the stairs once more, this time without incident.

Eden joined them at the bottom of the steps, her eyes red and wet, and wrapped them in a huge hug. "Thank God."

"Thank Scarlett," Rick said.

Eden pulled back, her forehead scrunched in surprise. "Scarlett?"

"It seems she can rewind time."

Eden's mouth gaped.

Blake burbled, his lower lip trembling.

Scarlett nodded at him then glanced at Rick and Eden, her expression concerned, serious. "Blake said, '*I got hurt. Bad. I was so scared...*'"

She turned back to her brother. "I know. I hated seeing you sore. I had to reverse things so you could be better.."

A massive grin pushed the fear and worry out of Blake's plump face and he uttered another sentence, uninterpretable except to his adorable translator twin sister.

Scarlett blushed "He said, '*Scarlett is a superwoman.*'" She shook her head. "I don't think so."

Blake flapped his arms and gurgled.

Scarlett glared at her brother. "No. You can't tell anyone. No one can know."

A big pout puffed out Blake's bottom lip.

Eden caressed Scarlett's cheek. "No one can know what, honey?"

"That I have superpowers. They might take us away from you."

*So spot on... Scarily spot on.* If Sub Rosa found out Scarlett was not only a half-caste vampire but also part

Jade and part Violet, they'd be creaming themselves at the research possibilities. Though, how much did his daughter comprehend? How much could she tune in to? Could she read minds? Could she pick up on his current thoughts?

Rick conjured up his brightest smile and tapped each of the twins on the nose. "Now don't you two worry. We'll keep Scarlett's secret between us and we'll stay safe, together."

In the background, he caught the flicker of fear on Eden's face before she slipped back into her comforting-mother mask.

Rick led them into the living room and he and Eden sat on the play mat with the kids.

*Distraction time. Time for some fun.*

He tipped out a big bag of building blocks, each representing a color of the rainbow.

Blake stacked a couple then waved his arms with excitement and knocked them down, while Scarlett built a red house and placed a purple-white, a green-white, a white-white, and a purple-green-white block combination in a circle.

"Tell us about what you've made, Scarlett," Eden said.

She pointed to the solid red house. "Our safe house." Next, she touched the purple-white block. "That's you, Mummy." *Violet-human.* Then the green-white block. "That's you, Daddy." *Jade-human.* Then the white-white block. "That's you, Blake." *Full human.* She picked up the tallest tower. "That's me." *Violet-Jade-human.* She'd represented their heritage in harmony, something he aimed to do for real.

Rick kissed her soft-skinned forehead. "You're so clever and grown-up, young lady. I forget how old you are sometimes."

A deep frown creased Blake's forehead and he burbled a few words.

Scarlett giggled then turned to Rick and Eden and translated. "Blake's upset you don't think he's smart and grown-up too."

"Awww...sweet boy," Eden cooed, stroking his sad, chubby face. "You're my special little man."

Instantly, the frown disappeared and Blake's characteristic big, bright smile returned. Then he slammed forward on his pudgy palms and gave her a sloppy, wet kiss on the cheek.

"What a little charmer," Rick said.

Eden smirked. "Like father, like son."

They played and chatted for a bit longer, fed and bathed the kids, then tucked them into bed. Once the twins had drifted off to sleep, Rick and Eden returned to the kitchen to eat their dinner.

Eden stopped in front of the stove, her gaze locking onto his eyes. "Oh, guess what? I found something today. I meant to tell you before, but we sort of got sidetracked."

*Yeah, the whole Scarlett superpower thing.* And she was only six months old. As she grew, what other hidden talents would they discover?

"Let me guess... The disposable contact lens you tried this morning disintegrated like mine."

"Yes...but that's not what I wanted to say." She ladled out some steaming Bolognese sauce on top of their plates of beef ravioli.

He took their meals across to the dining table, placed them down and sat opposite her. "I'm assuming it's about the file you saved, then."

Eden speared a couple ravioli onto her fork and glanced up. "How did you...?"

79

"I noticed it when I lifted the computer off your lap. I figured we could talk about it tonight, when the kids went to bed. I'm a bit wary speaking about this stuff, particularly when Scarlett's awake. With her advanced level of comprehension, I'm concerned she'll understand a bit too much.

"She's already anxious about being taken from us and I don't want to exacerbate it. I don't want her unsettling Blake either. Even if she doesn't tell him, he'll pick up that something is bothering her. They're very tuned in to each other."

"Are they ever." Eden put her fork down, had a sip of red wine, then focused her eyes on his. "When I logged in, I started digging around the database and nothing really jumped out at me...until I stumbled into a projects folder and saw a sub folder named 'Norwegian Rose'.

"At first, I didn't take much notice, assuming it formed part of the All Weather Rose project, but when I saw the size of it, I delved a bit deeper. You see, all the other rose-named folders had a range of documents in them not even a tenth as big as this one. I guessed it might be a cryptic cover that was hiding something important—and I was right."

The air in the room thickened and pulsed with their excited, fear-tinged energy.

"I got five documents in when I found it—raw data on a gene eradication agent first used in the late 1930s. Researchers at the time had thought that a concentrated sunlight pill would shock and alter the DNA fabric and reset the 'faulty' gene. Instead, a number of deaths occurred in both the Jade and Violet populations." Eden's eyes widened, as though a bank of barely-contained information battered against her irises, ready to burst out.

"However, in the management report back to the government funding body, it stated that the drug had promise, even though it had shown only mildly effective results, changing one percent of the full-caste test subjects to three-quarter caste. Although their feedback technically had some accuracy, they were withholding some pretty crucial information."

"The deaths," Rick said.

"Exactly. If they'd mentioned that, they'd have broken the government funding contract. They'd have breached the stipulation stating that if any subjects died, funding would be withdrawn. So it seems pretty clear that Sub Rosa management conveniently didn't mention the deaths in order to continue to attract and retain research dollars."

Rick raised his glass in a silent sort of toast and polished off the rest of his wine. "Nice work." *Most impressive.* It totally backed up the evidence he'd found in Tassie.

She averted her eyes and shrugged, the adorable little body language move she did when embarrassed. "I'd planned to save a copy of the contract and management report but all that reading, combined with the warmth from the heater and the sunlight streaming through the window, kind of put me to sleep. Sorry."

Rick reached across the table and held her hand. "That's okay. You've made an excellent start. The stuff you've found so far is exactly the sort of evidence we need, the sort of evidence to finally bring down Sub Rosa."

# Chapter Seven

The Tassie Contingent

*Sub Rosa headquarters, Hobart, 2004*

"Beauregarde, wait!"

The click-clacking of stiletto heels came to a stop and he turned around.

"You were in Norway last week, right?" Indigo's large cobalt-blue eyes studied his.

*When will she give up?* He plastered on his most believable smile. "I was."

She shifted her weight from one foot to the other. "Did you see him?"

Humans were contemptible, but she really took the frosting-topped, cream-filled cake. "Don't you think it's time you moved on? Hugh disappeared on you. Obviously, he doesn't want to be found."

She shook her head, not a single strand of hair budging from the shiny, caramel, slicked-back style. "I can't believe that."

His gaze locked on hers. "It's been seven years. Forget about him. You're doing well without the creep. Look at your career. Who else do you know who has climbed the ranks to senior management in such a short time? You're excelling without him. And you've done it all on your own... Well, except for a little help from yours truly."

Beauregarde pulled at his stiff shirt collar and adjusted his raven brocade waistcoat.

She swallowed hard and loud and looked down. "I know you're trying to be helpful, but...can I ask you a favor?"

*Here we go.*

"I know I probably should have gotten over him and all that but"—she shook her head and refocused her pleading eyes on his—"even though you think he's a bastard and I could do better, could you keep an eye out for him? Please? I just need to speak to him one more time."

Beauregarde forced his perfected caring smile, but the flickering of the faulty overhead fluorescent light mimicking his internal agitation. "Sure. Leave it with me and I'll let you know if I come across him."

Her relieved, joyous smile stretched wide, like she would explode with elation. *Sickening.* He should just make a meal of the pathetic woman to shut her up and put her out of her misery.

She touched his arm. "Thanks."

The warmth of her flimsy little human hand felt as though she'd wee-ed on him, like an anxious, submissive puppy. It took all his self-control to refrain from pulling away.

She continued down the hallway to the lift with a spring in her usually shuffled step. He'd given her hope—and that was all it would ever be. He'd seen the guy all right, knew Hugh well. The stupid, pitiful excuse for a Violet had gotten exactly what he'd deserved.

Beauregarde smirked and continued on to Andy's office for a one-on-one briefing. No way in hell would he help a useless full human, and especially not his Violet 'brother', her ex-lover, given their long, hateful history.

* * * *

*Andy's home, Hobart, Tasmania, November 2011*

Andy sat at his desk, staring at his glowing laptop screen and scrolling through the latest email project updates.

In some ways, he missed Salvator. He could always count on him to stay late and get results. Outside of Simon's recent groundbreaking 'cure' discovery, the period when Salvator had worked at Sub Rosa remained the most fruitful regarding research gains and attracting funding.

After stretching his stiff neck, Andy yawned and glanced at the bottom right-hand corner of his computer screen—*23:48*. He went to log out and a message popped up.

*HartmanR logged into A drive.*

*No. No fucking way.* He leaned in closer and stared at the alert, suddenly wide awake. It had to be a mistake, a computer glitch. How could Rick access his drive? Firstly, the guy was on secondment at the Norway site and, secondly, only someone with administrative rights could get into the CEO's files. Only Andy could grant that level of security clearance.

His pulse thumped in his wrist and neck and temples like a boxing match was slogging away beneath his skin. It had to be a simple error. But he couldn't relax until he knew for sure.

A high amount of sensitive information was on the line and he couldn't afford for it to get into the wrong person's hard drive. It would be a major fucking disaster. There were the select few staff he could trust in the top inner Sub Rosa sanctum, and even then, lots of things could turn a man...or woman.

Money.

Power.

Success.

Retribution.

In his experience, any gender could be corrupted by greed and revenge. All those things had impacted on his decision-making and gotten him to where he was now. However, instead of the strong fortress he thought he'd built, it suddenly seemed like a swaying house of flimsy cards.

He snatched his mobile off the desk and speed-dialed his most senior IT guy, demanding that he investigate and report back as soon as possible. Then he emailed the executive management group, scheduling a meeting first thing the next morning to discuss how to best handle the possible breach.

A purple slime poured down the air conditioning vent in his study and transformed into Beauregarde. "Problems in paradise?"

"Fuck off. I'm not in the mood for your wisecracks."

The egocentric contortionist Violet took a seat, leaned back and propped his black-booted feet on the desk like he owned the world. "Take it easy. What's going on?"

Andy glared at the bastard but couldn't deny his usefulness. Getting someone with Beauregarde's power and inside knowledge off-side would be career suicide — and maybe not just Andy's career.

The guy had a way of sniffing out trouble and unease, like a dog sensed fear in its prey. "One of the research staff may have hacked into my files."

"I can get rid of him if you want." His tone sounded matter-of-fact, yet his piercing, violet eyes bored into him like lasers.

"Thanks. Although I'm very tempted, the last thing I need is to leave a trail of dead bodies behind. It might look a bit…suspect," Andy said with a sting of sarcasm.

"Yes, boss." Beauregarde smirked, not even trying to hide the condescension in his tone.

*Pompous Violet prick.*

"How about I go around to Rick's house instead and see if I can dig up anything of interest?"

"Yeah, whatever." Andy slammed his laptop shut. "What I need is to find out ASAP if he's definitely gotten access and, if so, how to address the issue before we find ourselves splashed across the Internet and arrested."

\* \* \* \*

*Hobart, Tasmania, November 2011*

"Simon, be straight with me. You're having an affair, aren't you?" Grace stirred the half-cooked pasta with choppy, aggressive strokes.

"No! Why would you think that?" He strode across the room to stand by her side.

She braced herself on the bench and stared into the bubbling whirlpool of fettuccine. "You've been so distant lately. It's like you're here physically but not mentally or emotionally."

Simon secured his arms around her waist. "I'm sorry, babe." He nuzzled the spot where her neck curved into her shoulder. "I didn't want to worry you, so I didn't say anything. I promise it's nothing to do with you or our relationship."

She pulled away and spun to face him, dark swirls of fear turning her warm chocolate brown eyes to cold, eighty-percent cocoa color. "Worry me? What do you mean?"

He hesitated. *Shit.* Should he tell her the truth? "Rick isn't in Norway purely for the secondment."

She grabbed a pinch of salt and threw it into the agitated water. "What the hell is that supposed to mean?"

The words butted against his lips, on the verge of breaking free. "Grace…"

She glared at him with a *spill-your-guts* look.

If he didn't tell her now, he'd be relegated to the couch for sure…for days, weeks, possibly forever. "Okay. Rick has tried really hard to keep us out of it because he didn't want to put us in danger, but he needed my help.

"There's some full-on dodgy stuff going down at Sub Rosa and he's gone to check it out. He doesn't have access to all the information so—"

"He needed someone to assist him, someone he could trust."

"Exactly."

She frowned. "You should have told me."

"So I could put you in danger?"

Grace grimaced and shook her head. "No. It's just that we're engaged, and I thought I could have helped you, even by just being a sounding board, someone to debrief to."

He held her face firmly between his hands and caressed her high cheekbones with the pads of his thumbs. "I'm sorry for leaving you out of the loop. I just wanted to keep you safe."

"I appreciate your concern, but it's not just about that. How do you think I'd have coped if something had happened to you? I'd be devastated." Her bottom lip quivered and her eyes turned glassy.

"I'm sorry. I thought I was protecting you."

Large tears spilled from her eyes and he brushed them away. "To be honest, I'm kind of glad you know now. I hated keeping things from you."

Grace wrapped her arms around his waist and held on tight, like he was a buoy, keeping her afloat in the rough sea of worry. "Are Rick and Eden and the twins all right?"

"For the moment. I just hope it stays that way."

"Is there something I can do to help?"

Actually, she possibly could assist. But should he dangle his fiancée like a morsel of meat to a pack of piranhas? "Ah…"

She leaned back and stared into his eyes. "There is, isn't there? Please. I need to do something. I need to feel useful."

"I don't know if it's a good idea."

Grace trailed her palms up his torso and paused on his chest. "Why don't you tell me and I'll make up my own mind?"

A resigned sigh snagged in his windpipe. "Rick's after a book on ancient Nordic language and thinks there might be something in his library at home. The various collections are labelled, so he reckons if such a book exists, it shouldn't be too hard to find. Seeing you've been collecting their mail, I suppose it makes sense for you to go. It might seem suspicious if I turn up instead, though I'm happy to do it if you're not comfortable."

"I'm fine. I want to do it."

They were both lies. He could tell by the way her smile stagnated and she avoided his gaze. Knowing her, Miss Independent, Miss Determined would push herself and do it for him—and her close friends.

Grace had resurrected a non-penetrable outer shell to keep people from getting too close, so most didn't know the depths of her heart except him, the one enduring chink in her emotional armor.

He scrutinized her conflicted brown eyes. Duty of care versus personal safety. "You're sure."

"Yes. Very. I'll call you as soon as I find the book."

Simon went straight to work after their early dinner and spent four solid hours in the lab, experimenting with the most current gold, speckly version of the cure, before he returned to his workstation and grabbed his phone.

A missed call from Grace, and she'd left a message only two minutes prior. She must have gone around to Rick and Eden's early and found *the book*. She really should have waited until daylight, but Grace did as Grace wanted.

Although it could be frustrating at times, her initiative and high drive were a huge part of why he loved her so much. Her confidence, open-mindedness and their incredible sexual chemistry helped too. A broad smile burst onto his lips and he dialed voicemail.

"Simon, it's me," Grace said in a hushed voice. "I hope you can hear this. I've found the book but I'm not taking it with me. I think someone is in the house. I've shelved the book somewhere in the literary section. Whoever it is is getting closer so I need to go. I love y—"

Simon pulled the phone away from his ear and stared at the screen, his heart hammering, his mouth dry, the message bank spiel announcing that was his last message.

He choked on broken gasps of hyperventilated air. *Calm down!* He had to hold himself together. He had to drive straight to Rick's to investigate…and not jump to unsubstantiated conclusions.

The whole thing could be totally innocent. He could be stressing and getting all worked up for nothing. Grace may have mistaken the sound of the house settling for someone being inside, then when she rang, partway through her message, her phone battery died.

*Yeah, right.* He wanted to believe that the situation was harmless, yet he couldn't shake the persistent niggle burrowing into his brain, though worrying and assuming were pointless without facts. He just had to get to Rick's and deal with whatever awaited him.

Before rushing out, Simon stashed several vials of the healing tears in his brown leather satchel, just in case.

He bolted to the car and sped off, drumming an erratic beat on the steering wheel with his fingers, his whole body shaking like a washing machine on spin. Within twenty minutes, he pulled up next to Grace's car at the top of the driveway, ran inside and straight upstairs to the library.

"Grace!"

Framed in the doorway, bathed in silver rays of light, she lay lifeless, blood pooling on the right side of her neck. Simon kneeled beside her and bent down to check her vital signs. A scuffling sound a couple of aisles away startled him. He had to move quickly and get Grace out of there, get them both out of danger.

With a shaking hand, he reached inside his satchel, selected a healing vial and poured the tears over her neck wound. Then in a single, slow, measured movement he stood, slunk past a black gothic desk and down the closest row of books.

A person dressed all in black stood by the window and stared back at him with almost fluorescent violet eyes.

"Hey!" Simon yelled and stepped toward the guy.

The Violet stood firm and sneered. At the end of his raised hand, a steel-gray gun glistened in the moonlight, aimed right at Simon's head.

There was no sound, just the whistling of a bullet, skimmed past his ear. "Fuck!" Simon ducked, his heart thudding, scrambling for a return to homeostasis.

He glanced back up, his breathing quick, shallow, sporadic, but the Violet had gone. Flooded with adrenaline, Simon jumped to his feet and searched the room—however, the intruder had disappeared.

A curtain covering the window flapped. He strode over, pulled it aside and searched for the guy in the garden below. There was no sign of him or anyone else. The Violet had to have reached the surrounding bush, the dim, milky moonbeams unable to penetrate the trees to help pinpoint his location.

Simon raced back to Grace, her breathing wheezy, shallow, labored. *Better than before, thank God!* He grabbed another vial, poured part of the contents over the gash on her neck and the rest down her throat.

In seconds, she went limp. "No-o-o!" He dragged her into his arms and rocked her back and forth. "Grace! *Grace!*" His distressed voice echoed throughout the desolate room. He swiped the tears from his eyes, picked her up and carried her to the car. She had to be okay. She just had to.

On the journey to their house she spoke in delirious half sentences, her eyes still closed. He touched her cheek and her skin burned. *Shit!* He slammed his foot on the accelerator and arrived home in fifteen minutes.

He yanked the passenger door open, collected her in his arms and she convulsed. *Fuck!* Simon struggled to swallow past the block of dread wedged in his throat. He caressed her face in an attempt to settle her and himself. Grace's skin had shifted from hot to blazing, and beads of perspiration broke out on her pale forehead.

"Please be okay," he whispered against her sweat-soaked hair.

He took her inside and lay her on their bed. Still only semi-conscious, she started shivering and jerking.

In the bathroom, he wet a cloth with cool water, then returned to Grace and patted her brow. Trickles of sweat ran down her neck, like an ice cube melting in the sun. He mopped them up and stopped at an odd marking that looked like a branded 3-D image on her skin. A birthmark?

No. He'd have noticed. He'd studied her body like an archeologist examines a rare artifact. Simon leaned in closer, his pulse racing like a time bomb ready to go off.

Two small puncture wounds sat in the middle of a raised circle, like she'd undertaken some strange cupping session. But this blemish, this lesion, hadn't resulted from an alternative medicine treatment. This had occurred by way of non-consensual Violet intervention.

Teeth marks.

Grace had been bitten.

# Chapter Eight

A Bug in the System?

*Trondheim, Norway, November 2011*

Rick looked right, then left. No staff were within view, *thank fuck. Control Room* written in black block letters stood out on the bright white door with no handle. Hopefully entry into the Sub Rosa inner sanctum relied on the same technology as the high-security filing cabinets.

He pressed his palm flat against the cold metal and the control room door swung open. *Yes!* Rick slipped inside, the drone of technology buzzing like a swarm of busy bees. He closed his eyes and plugged his fingers into his ears to block out the annoying hum from his over-stimulated mind.

At the main desk, a black office chair sat idle, spun around as though the previous sitter had left in a hurry. Had a bug infested the system? Surely that could only help his cause.

Rick took a seat and wheeled himself forward until he'd tucked his legs under the huge desk. A myriad of red, black and white buttons and switches covered the vast control panel, sending his brain into overdrive. What did they all do? And how would he ever find out without arousing suspicion?

"Excuse me, sir?"

*Fuck.* Rick's heart stuttered to a stop then jolted back into a fast-paced jog. He whirled around and a beefcake security guard stood in the doorway. Rick had seen the 'bouncers' scattered across the site. They stood out like huge, hairy dogs' balls, the enhanced testosterone brigade. That was a mass generalization, but the signs were undeniable—increased acne, bulging, defined muscles and rounded, bloated stomachs.

"Can I help you?" Rick asked with false confidence.

A fake smile pushed at the guy's lips. "How did you get in here?"

Rick flashed his ID badge. "I'm on secondment and this is part of my orientation. I need to tick off that I've been through each department. I got told if I came here at this time, I'd find a tech who could run me through the system."

The security guard peered at him, as though weighing up the validity of his request. "Usually..."

"Has something happened?"

The security guard folded his Popeye forearms across his barrel chest. "Let me just grab a tech for you." He lumbered out of the room and strode down the corridor.

The guy's departure seemed to steal the suffocating carbon dioxide from the air, leaving it pumped full of oxygen. Rick gulped it down like a fish gasping for life-sustaining breath.

Deflection had gotten him through round one. Could he successfully make it through round two? The security guard hadn't been a real challenge. The tech, however...

A skinny, wiry-haired man stumbled into the room, his face a pale, blank, professional mask, yet worry seeped into his every movement and his stressed mood spread like bacteria, contaminating the space.

Something had definitely happened. But what? If the system had had a glitch, maybe it would provide Rick a chance to enact an escape plan.

"I believe this is part of your orientation to the site." He shoved his trembling hand through his steel-wool hair.

Although the guy maintained a poker-face, the rest of his body language screamed frazzled, so he'd probably believe anything at the moment. "That's right. You seem pretty busy. I can come back another time."

"No, now is fine." The tech walked to the closest chair. "Maybe it'll distract me for a while," he murmured under his breath.

Rick couldn't have been meant to hear that.

The tech wheeled in beside him. "Is there anything in particular you need covered?"

Would the guy be authorized to divulge the workings of such a top-secret setup to a new staff member with supposedly limited security clearance? Then again, the man wasn't thinking straight. Stress had clearly invaded and disarmed his usual defenses. That provided the perfect opportunity for Rick to extract as much information as possible.

"Let me see, ah..." Rick angled himself toward the twitchy guy and couldn't miss the black shadows beneath his eyes. "A general overview of the system would be great—and any key considerations like whether it can be overridden, what happens when there's a power outage, what maintenance is required, if it's had any major issues, if it's considered foolproof…"

Wariness swirled in the tech's washed-out blue eyes. "That's a pretty extensive list. Are you sure they wanted all that covered?"

"I can't remember the exact specs, but that's the general gist."

"Hm-m-m…" The tech cleared his throat and picked at a callus on his finger. "In essence, modified solar panels are used to collect and beam concentrated sunlight rays down into the cells—I mean, residential apartments—and across any other possible exits, including doors and windows. As it grows dark, a dispersal system has sensors that detect the change in light and tap into the sunlight stores to continue the process. It's seamless."

"I thought solar panels collected sunlight and turned it into electricity?"

"Usually, though not in this case. These are a special adaptation. Are you aware of the All Weather Rose Project?"

Rick nodded. His mate Simon had been the lead researcher on that in recent times, so he knew some of the details but not all of them.

"If not for that, we probably wouldn't have this incredible innovation. Everyone knew sunlight was the vampires' greatest weakness—however, in order to use it as an effective control mechanism, it needed to be available twenty-four seven."

The guy stopped picking at his finger, his eyes alive with enthusiasm. "So the research team focused on finding a way to collect and store the sunlight, with the view to somehow using it at night. The breakthrough came when one of the scientists working across both the All Weather Rose and Norway projects experimented with ways to harness sunlight to keep the roses flowering in cooler weather."

With each word the tech spoke, his speech gained momentum, moving faster and faster, like he couldn't wait to finish the story and brag about the research team's misguided, life-threatening achievements.

"He realized its greater potential and put a proposal forward to management to apply the technology to the residential complexes but to use the concentrated sunlight as bars. Andy rubber-stamped it straight away. Prior to that, Jades and Violets constantly escaped. Too many resources were eaten up trying to recapture them rather than working out a way to cure vampirism." Pride shone from the weedy little man's eyes.

Rick forced his fisted hand open and tried to stop his jaw from clenching. He had to appear impressed, not repulsed, if he wanted to keep up the interested, onboard-scientist façade and not come across as a sympathizer — or even worse, draw attention to his part-vampire status.

The guy barely took a breath, spewing out information like he had an acute case of verbal diarrhea. "Most of the research team got reassigned to the Norway Experiment to develop a sound, workable system. Once a prototype became available, it was successfully tested and implemented. Sub Rosa then patented the unique invention. And here we are."

Rick pasted what he hoped passed as a fascinated smile on his face. "Wow. So is there any way to shut it off?"

"In an emergency, only senior management and select staff can override the system. I'm sure you understand why I can't go into detail. What I can tell you, though, is that two people are required to do it."

*Damn!* Rick had hoped the combination of stress and excitement would have made the tech blurt out more revealing information.

The guy tapped his temple. "In terms of a power outage, we have a back-up generator that kicks in within three seconds. Thankfully that's only happened once—and no one got out. Though, in the mid-1990s, the system had to be reviewed and additional safeguards put in place following the successful escape of one of the Violets, who was later recaptured.

"At first, Sub Rosa management put it down to a malfunction. Then, when they investigated further, no errors or issues were detected, leading them to conclude that it had been tampered with. Even though the evidence pointed to an inside job, they could never prove who was involved. So they revised the system to make it harder for anyone to fiddle with it in future."

*Salvator?*

*Yes, Salvator.*

*Bloody Salvator.*

It had to have been him. He'd been stationed at the Norway site right around that time. A smile pushed at the corners of Rick's lips and he fought to keep his expression neutral.

Even though Salvator's actions had ended up making Rick's mission harder, he couldn't help but be impressed. What Salvator had done had taken a lot of courage. Trying something like that would have posed a huge risk to him and the Violet he'd freed. And he'd done it anyway. He'd taken the opportunity to instigate a single escape that could possibly have led to mass exodus.

Although some of Salvator's decisions and actions had been questionable, it appeared he'd tried to do the right thing. Excitement bubbled in Rick's stomach and rose, engulfing his heart and brain, aligning his emotions and rational thinking.

Attempting to override the current system and arrange freedom for all the captive vampires at once would be a lot trickier, though it was not impossible. He just needed to identify and maximize the sunlight barricade's weakest point.

The tech still rambled. "Every component of the system is checked quarterly. As you can imagine, we can't afford to let it run down. In fact, it's going through some maintenance at the moment." A smile hesitated on the tech's lips, as though he realized he'd said too much, and his gaze flicked back to the callus on his finger.

"So no one has escaped since the additional safeguards have been put in place?" The guy had pretty much spelled it out—however, Rick had to double check.

"That's right. You could say the current setup is pretty infallible."

*We'll see about that.* "With the maintenance that's occurring at the moment, is it standard or is there an issue?"

The tech gulped, his Adam's apple bobbing like a raft lost at sea in a wild storm. "Well, ah…" He stopped and stared into Rick's eyes, as though suddenly mesmerized by them. "Are your eyes okay?"

Adrenaline shot through Rick's veins, sending his body into high alert. *Fuck, fuck, fuck!* "Not really. I'm having problems with my contact lenses."

The tech leaned in and scrutinized them. Could he see some jade peeking through? They shouldn't have started eroding yet. He should at least have another hour or two of leeway.

The thud of heavy, hurried footsteps sounded in the corridor. Rick and the tech turned their heads toward the door. The security guard from before stepped into the room.

His grave eyes focused on the tech's. "You'd better come with me."

A reprieve. Saved by the security guard. *Thank fuck.*

The tech jumped up. "Well, that's pretty much it," he said over his shoulder and sped to the doorway. "Excuse me."

Rick propped his elbows on the control panel and pressed his hot face into his sweaty hands. *Close. Too fucking close.* He had to leave now, while he had the chance. Rick slid through the gap left by the slowly closing door and hurried to his car, careful not to make eye contact with anyone.

He planted his foot on the accelerator and didn't stop until he'd driven several streets away. His heart roared like a heavy-duty vacuum cleaner with a faulty off switch.

Rick glanced into the rear-view mirror to take out his contacts. *Fuck!* Instead of the even brown tint, they were patchy, revealing blotches of his jade-green eyes underneath.

Every other time, the lenses had lasted longer. What had fucking changed? Could his immune system be strengthening, breaking down the foreign bodies quicker on each exposure?

While working in a place filled with experts on Jade and Violet vampires, Rick couldn't risk stretching out how long he wore the contacts. He had to try something else, something safer like...*shit*. The only workable option entailed changing to a new pair at lunch time.

The idea of having to take the contacts out and put in fresh ones twice a day was totally cringe-worthy. But the alternative—getting found out—would jeopardize the release of the Jades and Violets, as well as compromise his family's safety.

He couldn't do that, not a second time. Only a total fuckwit wouldn't learn from such a massive, life-threatening mistake. Putting the situation into perspective, a temporary amount of discomfort was a negligible price to pay.

Rick counted to ten then pressed the pad of his finger on the disintegrating lens and lifted it out of his right eye, then did the same with his left. Almost immediately the stinging subsided and the excess moisture cleared from his vision.

He blew out a long, heavy, relieved breath. Thankfully the tech hadn't twigged...at the time. Though, if the security guard hadn't come when he had? The 'problem with my contact lenses' story wouldn't have held up for much longer. A few more glimpses of jade might, no, *would have* been enough to make the vampire connection.

From now on, Rick had to be prepared. He had to be more vigilant and organized, and that meant regular bathroom breaks to check on the integrity of the lenses, just in case they needed changing even sooner.

Rick continued his journey back to Ansfrida, focusing on the windy road ahead. At least he'd gotten some information on the workings of the sunlight bars.

A glow of gold, like an aura, outlined the mountain range with the setting of the sun. Now he just had to come up with a way for the sun to set on the Sub Rosa sunlight bar system.

Deep in thought, he entered his temporary home. Unrestrained, heartrending sobs jolted him back to the present and he raced into the living room. Eden sat on the couch, her gaze glued to the laptop screen, her chest heaving and tears staining her cheeks.

He hurried over to her. "Eden, sweetheart? Are you okay? Are the kids okay?"

She glanced up and more tears streamed down her face. "The twins are fine. They're having a nap, thank goodness."

*Yes.* Whatever the issue, his wife looked far from fine. And with Scarlett's perceptive personality, they couldn't risk her picking up on any trouble and spreading her stress and fear to Blake.

He lifted the computer off Eden's legs and placed it on the dining table. 'Cryogenic', 'memory eraser' and 'trials' jumped out, piquing his interest. He pressed his palms onto the tabletop and leaned heavily against it, devouring the rest of the contents.

*Pre-storage — Y1939 injected with a bright blue cocktail of memory eraser and sedative drugs. His pupils dilated, and he stared blankly at X1944, the researcher and the empty lab. X1944 protested and a tear trickled down her pale cheek. X1944 was then injected.*

*When both subjects' eyes closed and their heart rates slowed to a sedate, steady rhythm, their clothes were removed. Next, the cryonics team replaced the water from X1944's and Y1939's cells with a glycerol-based cryoprotectant mixture – a sort of human antifreeze – to protect the organs and tissues from forming ice crystals at extremely low temperatures. This <u>vitrification</u> process – deep cooling without freezing – claims to put the cells into a state of suspended animation.*

*Once the water in their bodies was replaced with the cryoprotectant, the subjects were cooled on a bed of dry ice until they reached -130 degrees Celsius, completing the vitrification process. Next, they were inserted into individual containers and placed into a large metal tank filled with liquid nitrogen at a temperature of around -196 degrees Celsius.*

*As per the preliminary research, X1944 and Y1939 were stored head down, so if a leak ever occurred in the tank, their brains would stay immersed in the freezing liquid.*

*Day 31 – Y1939 was successfully revived. The researcher asked his name and his forehead creased. His eyes appeared to focus internally as he searched for the answer. He shook his head and replied, "I don't know. Who are you?"*

*The researcher removed his mask. Y1939 stared and stared, his forehead crinkling. "Should I know you? You seem so familiar but I just can't place you."*

*The subject was injected with another dose of the memory eraser-sedative and stored away. Retrieved X1944 after she lay naked for 90 minutes on the heated bed and hooked her up to the nutrition-hydration drip. She came to and stared at the maskless researcher.*

*"Do you know your name?"*

*Her eyes shifted up and to her left and she frowned. "No. Did something happen to me?"*

*"Yes. Do you know where you are?"*

*She shivered and wrapped her arms around herself. "No. But everything looks familiar. Have I been here before?"*

*Like Y1939, her response suggested her mind still held on to memories, hence the researcher administered a further dose of the memory eraser-sedative concoction.*

*Plan – Effectiveness of memory drugs to be reviewed in one month.*

*February 1966 – Injected Y1939 with fluorescent pink memory filler. Subject blinked and closed his eyes. Relocated him into the red receptive room and provided information for him to read and pictures to view, to encourage development of his new identity.*

*Within 45 minutes, attached a nutrition-hydration drip and neuromuscular electric stimulation machine to Y1939 to maintain functional muscle mass. Couched in a state of medically-induced hypnosis, the subject was primed and ready to absorb information about his new, constructed self.*

*Y1939's muscles pulsed in a steady rhythm and his pupils dilated, soaking up the words to create false memories in his vacant mind. After two hours of brain infiltrating and repeated reading, the researcher administered a sedative, detached the subject from the drip and muscle stimulator and stored him away.*

*Next, revived X1944 and injected her with the memory filler. She convulsed and fell to the floor, shaking and writhing. The researcher injected a sedative into her arm and she went limp but continued breathing. Returned the subject to cryogenic storage with the plan to systematically work through what caused the seizure, e.g. start with a lowered memory filler dosage.*

*Plan – Review effect of memory filler drug in two weeks and increase exposure to pictures, watching movies, listening to sounds and music to build strength and depth into new identity.*

A barrage of escaped memories surged into Rick's brain and he stumbled back. Disjointed snippets pushed through—being revived, injected, cryogenically stored.

Intermingled with those were snatches of the red room and his life with Eva—Eden—before and after the experiments, and bits of memories of outings with friends, on his own and with Smokey.

Everything was so scattered, overwhelming. What would he focus his attention on? He attempted to pick through the mental debris, scrutinizing the mix of clear, blurry, half, full, old and new memories. But which ones were real and which had been implanted? How would he ever distinguish between the two?

Then again, maybe the return of information signified a chemical break? Maybe his real memories had never been fully removed. Maybe they had just been hidden somewhere? And now that they'd barged through, they'd begun disintegrating the implanted ones—or were in the midst of the process.

He looked over at Eden, who was curled up in a ball, still sobbing and staring through the window. She had to have remembered as well. Maybe if he compared his thoughts with hers, he'd be able to weed out any false memories?

Her weepy eyes met his gaze and she pointed at the glaring computer screen behind him. "Keep reading," she said between sobs.

Curiosity pushed him to oblige, but Eden's unrelenting anguish tugged at his heart. He desperately wanted to comfort her. Torn between knowledge and emotion, he stood fixed to the spot.

"You need to get to the end," she said, as though reading his mind and making the decision for him.

Rick turned his attention back to the laptop and scrolled through the rest of the document, which referenced an extensive list of experiments conducted on Y1939—him—and X1944—her—over a forty-year period.

Although Salvator had given him a basic rundown of what they'd been subjected to, reading the detached, clinical details slammed it home. No wonder Eden had gotten so upset. Though, at the same time, being a researcher himself, Rick's drive for facts took over.

Once he'd finished skimming the key points, he sat next to Eden, lifted her onto his lap and held her tight, her steady flow of tears soaking into his shoulder.

He stroked her hair and gently kissed her on the forehead. When her crying ceased, she sniffled and glanced up, her dewy, red eyes meeting his waiting gaze.

Rick caressed her wet cheek. "I know this is hard, but in a way it's good to learn the details. I think it's important in terms of monitoring our health—and Blake and Scarlett's as well. The more we know, the better chance we have of combating any weird symptoms that might arise. Plus, reading this just makes me all the more determined to bring Sub Rosa to justice."

"Obviously you didn't..." She started sobbing again, her chest heaving with grief.

"Have a rush of memories invade my brain?" he said, finishing the sentence for her.

"You remember as well, then?" The look in her watery, red-rimmed eyes switched from sorrow and dejection to desperate hope.

"Yeah...well, it's a massive jumble at the moment. I'm assuming they're all my memories."

A deep crinkle formed at the top of her nose, sending more tears trickling down her cheeks. "What do you mean?"

"I'm not sure how much of the info is legit. Sub Rosa did pump us full of memory filler and feed us a bunch of false information."

Her waterlogged, bloodshot eyes were unwavering. "They don't feel false. Losing a baby doesn't feel false."

"What?"

"I was pregnant but" — a heart-wrenching sob broke from her throat—"I miscarried when they caught us." An onslaught of fresh moisture filled her eyes and saturated her cheeks.

He hugged her tighter, the tears stinging his eyes like they'd been wrung from his soul. "I'm so sorry. I wish I could defrag our memories, clear them of all this trauma, heartache and implanted crap and start again." His voice cracked, more memories of that horrific time and his part in it shredding his heart.

After a couple of minutes, her sobbing subsided and she stared up at him, struggling to find her 'strong' face. "There's nothing we can do now except move on. But it's hard when the miscarriage and all the experimental stuff is as real as if it just happened."

"Yeah…it's tough and it's going to be for a while. We'll get through it, though, together. We make a great team."

"We do."

They sat silently for a few more minutes, just holding each other. Something about having Eden so close always created a comforting warmth, making him believe that the strength of their partnership could conquer the ingrained evil at Sub Rosa and create positive change for all.

Using the pad of his thumb, Rick wiped away the lingering snail trail of tears on his wife's cheeks. "You know, I think you're right about the real versus implanted memories. I doubt Sub Rosa would have wanted us to remember the miscarriage and experiments, so those events must have happened…unfortunately.

"If anything, Sub Rosa would have tried to eradicate them, seeing as they serve no purpose in our new identities. That's not to say that some fake memories haven't slipped through with all the others."

"Our experiences together and likes and dislikes can't be made up." Her determined expression was at odds with the doe-like, hopeful look in her big blue-violet eyes.

"Can't they? How can we know for sure?"

She huffed, the air of frustration shooting out her flared nostrils. "Well, it doesn't really matter now anyway, does it?"

"Actually it does, from a scientific perspective. It's essential to know whether the drugs are effective. There are so many possible positive applications. They could be used to treat a range of persisting psychological disorders, for example. This whole journey isn't just about us. It's about making life better for everyone. However, in saying that, I'd like to know that I am who I think I am."

A smile broke through the sadness weighing down the corners of her lips. "Trust you to pull out the scientific-benefits card." She touched his cheek. "You are who you are. I think if the memories are fake and don't seem to fit with you as a person, then they won't continue to shape you in any way. People learn, challenge beliefs, change—or not—and move on.

That's all part of your true character and no false memories will affect that. They can't alter the core of a person. Your true being will reject stuff that doesn't fit."

He pulled back and studied her. "Wow, you're more of a science geek than I gave you credit for."

She laughed and sniffled. "Well, it's hard not to absorb some of the tendencies when you're sleeping with one!"

"Touché." He chuckled. "But, seriously, your assessment makes perfect sense. True character will shine through. Hm-m-m... I wonder if our vampire genetics play a part in that too? They may have impacted on the effectiveness of the drugs."

"Possibly...probably. Though only rigorous testing will work that out and you'd never get ethics approval now. Even if you did, how could you subject people to it after what we've been through? And you have to think that no one in their right mind would volunteer for that sort of experiment. Anyone willing to do it would be from a skewed, insane population, and are they the kind of results you want?"

His wife never failed to amaze him with her insight. "You know I would never subject anyone to testing without full consent. And for the consent to be valid, the person must be of sound mind and have capacity to make an informed decision.

"I don't think there's anything wrong with using the right kind of select population. It depends what results you're after, then you target subjects who meet the eligibility criteria. People with conditions like persistent post-traumatic stress might find that the memory drugs provide massive relief."

She cupped his jaw with her small, soft hand and stared into his eyes. "How about for now we just focus on getting out of here."

"Of course. But it's good to have some focus and future plans. It helps keep me directed and driven."

Eden wrapped her arms around his waist and leaned her head on his chest. "You have this wonderful knack for always seeing positives in really challenging situations. I love that about you. I can always count on you to set your emotions aside and look at things with the clear voice of reason. I wish I could do that, but my feelings get in the way. Thanks for helping me put things into perspective. It does make me feel slightly better."

"Only slightly?" Rick kissed the top of her head, her familiar rose-cinnamon scent calming, centering. "Seriously, I'm glad. I know it can be difficult at times, though like you said, it's imperative we don't lose sight of our end goal. We need to really believe we can pull this Sub Rosa thing off or else—"

She hugged him tighter. "History might repeat itself."

"Exactly. And we can't let that happen."

# Chapter Nine

## In Full Swing

*Trondheim, Norway, November 2011*

At the end of each day, Eden saved an updated copy of the growing list of incriminating evidence onto a USB stick and Rick sent the info to Simon's private email address, just as a back-up.

With every email he'd included a 'delivery' and 'read' receipt and had only received delivery receipts in return. Simon had kept his word...so far. Obviously he'd understood that Rick had set it up that way to protect him.

As had become their weekday routine, Rick rose early and got ready, kissed the kids then Eden and left her busily working away at Ansfrida.

Once he arrived at work, he detoured past his mum's cell for a quick, discreet visit, then headed straight to the control room to start seriously formulating a Violet-Jade escape plan.

After his first control room foray, he'd spent the next few days observing and becoming familiar with the tech roster. A consistent one-hour window opened up mid-morning and early evening when the techs had their shift change handover meetings. Rick used that awesome opportunity to do some scratching around.

According to the large wall clock, it was nine-fifty-five. In less than five minutes, he'd be at the desired destination. He turned the final corner and hotfooted it to the control room door.

"Hey, Rick?"

He stopped, mid sterile-white corridor. *Fuck!*

"It is Rick, isn't it?" The puffed-out man's voice grew closer.

Rick turned, and the silver-haired older guy in front of him, looked familiar. Had he met him during orientation, seen him in a meeting? "Ah, yeah."

"I thought so. I met you briefly during your lab induction," he said, as though reading Rick's mind.

The guy he'd nicknamed 'Oldie'. *That's right.* "I remember." *Now.* Rick twisted his wrist at just the right angle to sneak a subtle glance at the naked gold cogs in his skeleton watch. Two minutes of his precious control-room time had already ticked by. How could he cut the guy short without seeming rude?

"Seeing as you're new, I just wondered if you're interested in joining me for lunch? Fuck, that sounds like a come on. It's not, I swear. Not that you're not a good-looking guy and all, but I don't swing that way and... Never mind. There'll be a small group of us."

Rick angled his wrist. Four minutes. "I had intended to turn you down, seeing as I'm straight and married, but now that you've clarified..."

Oldie laughed and slapped Rick on the back. "You'll fit in perfectly. We meet in the core cafeteria at around twelve-thirty. It looks like you're in a hurry, so I'll let you go."

"Thanks, mate. I'll see you a bit later."

Oldie disappeared around the corner and Rick crept into the control room. He took a seat at the large, recording-studio-mixing-desk-like control panel, its multitude of buttons and switches no longer making him nervous. *The benefits of flooding and desensitization.* However, he couldn't ignore the pressure to come up with a foolproof plan—and fast.

Rick slid back in the chair and tried to get comfortable, though not too comfortable.

Making some 'friends' was a good strategic choice. Not only could he spread his contact-lens problem story so he wouldn't be hassled anymore, but also the connection could help keep him in the loop and allow him to suss out if Sub Rosa senior management was suspicious of him or aware the database had been hacked.

After tinkering for fifty minutes with no spark, let alone a light-bulb moment, Rick snuck out and returned to his desk. Maybe lunch with the guys would give him some fresh ideas?

He resumed typing and got totally absorbed in finishing his latest research article—*The Pros and Cons of Gene Mutation and the Impact of Technology.*

His stomach growled. *Lunch time already?* He dropped his gaze to the bottom right hand corner of his computer screen and, sure enough, it had clicked over to twelve-fifteen.

Rick locked his computer and made his way back to the core. He entered the cafeteria, the air dense with competing roast and casserole aromas, and spotted Oldie sitting near the buffet.

Oldie smiled, and Rick pulled up a chair beside him, with his back to the window. The least amount of glare, the better. Three younger men sat opposite. "I'm so buggered today. You guys kept me up all night. It's like a frat house over there!" Oldie said.

The 'frat house' in question had to be Rick's mum's converted home.

"Well, we did invite you to join us." The tall, lanky researcher said in between mouthfuls of his sloppy, microwaved meat pie.

Oldie popped two pain killers out of their blister pack and into his age-spotted hand. "What's a sixty-three-year-old man going to do with a bunch of guys more than half his age?"

"Have fun?" the quick-witted middle man fired back.

"Ha ha. Thanks, but no thanks. My head's thumping and I didn't even drink!"

They all laughed.

Oldie gripped Rick's shoulder with a sturdy hand. "Anyway, for those of you who haven't met this strapping young man, his name is Rick and he's on secondment from the Tassie office."

The Lanky researcher slurped up the last bit of his pie. "Awesome."

"Are you originally from Tassie?" the shorter bloke asked.

Should he tell them the truth? *Maybe just part...* It would be easier to keep the story straight and reduce the risk of too many probing questions. "No, but my parents moved there when I was a baby, so I consider it to be my true home. I'm a Taswegian at heart."

"Cool. Us three are all from there. Until coming here, I'd never left the island."

The middle guy looked at Rick and smirked. "And you can tell."

The short guy elbowed his mate in the chest. "Look who's talking! Fuck'n smart arse."

The three stooges, researcher style.

Over the course of lunch, Rick got the gossip on the young guys and dubbed them Lanky, Shorty and Ballsy. They'd pretty much come straight out of uni and carried the pub-crawl, party lifestyle with them. They fell into that prime social media age bracket—the stereotypical, entitled twenty-somethings, used to expressing anything and everything to the masses.

Rick learned that, while at uni in Tasmania, the buddies had applied for research scholarships that offered the scientific opportunity of a lifetime—to be recruited by Sub Rosa, one of the leading research institutes, and partake in a classified project based in Norway. Out of the five scholarships on offer, they'd successfully won three.

"We seriously thought there'd be some hot Scandinavian women here and jumped at the opportunity." Lanky's voice sounded sulky, disappointed.

"But it's mostly all blokes or older women, not that I mind an older woman," Shorty said with raised, comical eyebrows.

"We know." Ballsy rolled his eyes at Rick. "Some of us are more desperate than others."

"Hey! Stop giving me shit. I think you guys are jealous."

Lanky laughed, the tone a low, rich Barry White, almost soothing to the ear. "If you say so."

Shorty huffed, grabbed the most current edition of the agency newsletter off the dining table and shoved it in front of his face like a keep-out sign.

The other guys continued their blokey banter.

Only a couple minutes later, Shorty flattened the newsletter on the table and pointed at one of the articles. "Hey, guys, look at this." He kept pointing until all their eyes focused on that very spot. "Sub Rosa has bought the Rosetta Stone software from Cambridge. Must have cost them a fortune."

*Rosetta Stone software?* Rick couldn't believe his luck. He'd tried every possible way to access it online through the Cambridge University site but had consistently gotten blocked. He'd given up and crossed his fingers that Simon would get back to him with something useful from the Nordic history section in Rick's library back home.

But he hadn't heard from his mate either. Not that it stressed him…yet. This new information made Simon's feedback less pressing. It gave Rick renewed hope of solving the puzzle himself — and soon.

Lanky leaned over the newsletter, his eyes scanning over the text. "Awesome! I'll have to find a way to sneak a peek. I originally wanted to major in archeology, you know, though I figured I'd rather work with living females."

Rick chuckled at the mega science-nerd response.

Ballsy plucked the newsletter off the table and flicked through the pages. "Man, are there any key bodies of research Sub Rosa hasn't tackled or bought? Where do they get all their funds?"

*Dodgy dealings and practices, underhandedness and blatant lies.* Rick couldn't blurt that out, not unless he wanted to sabotage his own efforts to save the vampires, himself and his family and shut down the agency.

If these young men were as smart as they seemed, they'd figure it out for themselves soon enough...and leave before they became too entrenched in the corrupt culture.

"Maybe they own the mint too—or at least the research section." Oldie might be close to the guys' fathers' age, but he was equally sharp-witted.

Knowing Sub Rosa, his words had probably held some truth. Rick wouldn't put it past the organization. Something as ridiculous as that no longer seemed so farfetched.

Oldie stood up. "Anyway, I gotta go, guys. Some of us actually do work around here."

A few other staff-filled tables started to clear.

"We can't help it if you drew the short straw," Ballsy said.

Shorty gestured to his senior buddy. "Mr. Big Shot here has just accepted a team leader role."

"Which means *heaps* of meetings." The look on Lanky's face said he couldn't think of anything worse.

Maybe Rick could milk some more information from Oldie, given his management-insider status. Rick laughed. "Poor bugger."

Shorty pulled his chair in closer to the table and made eye contact with Rick. "Okay, this is a little off topic, but I have to know. Have they mentioned the sunlight bullet technology in Tassie?"

"Are you talking about the Taser guns used for capture?"

Lanky moved to sit next to Rick. "Yes and no. There've been some further developments. The Taser guns work on a short burst of sunlight, which only temporarily paralyses vampires. Andy wanted something more potent—a gun with bullets that could actually kill."

"Only to be used if a worker is under threat," Shorty clarified.

Lanky looked around the half-empty cafeteria. No one seemed to be within earshot. "Yeah, right. It gives the workers more options, more power."

Ballsy slapped the agency newsletter down. "And here I was, naïve as all fuck, thinking silver bullets would do the trick."

"It's a total myth. That…and garlic. They're a total waste of time, slight deterrents but that's it. They don't cause any real, and certainly no long-term, damage," Shorty said.

Lanky leaned right in. "From all the testing so far, sunlight causes the most harm. In fact, concentrated sunlight can be deadly."

Ballsy rolled up the newsletter and tapped it on the table. "Trials began a few months ago."

"Trials? What sort of trials?" A coil of stress wound around Rick's windpipe and squeezed.

Lanky stared at Rick with a look that said, *'Are you kidding me?'* "Vampire trials."

Ballsy shoved the newsletter aside and propped his elbows on the table. "A few rebels were selected, and let's just say the results were a hundred percent."

Rick's lungs constricted, as though every last bit of oxygen had been sucked out of the air. How did they choose the 'rebels'? His mum or Eden's dad could have been selected, just by being part vampire… "You mean, they all died?"

Ballsy's pupils dilated, making his eyes look bitumen black. "Yep. Even the ones that were shot in the leg."

"No maiming, just death." Lanky rubbed the bum-fluff-posing-as-stubble on his chin. "The bullets work sort of like a snake bite, poisoning their system."

Shorty crossed his arms. "I think it's bullshit, the whole thing. I know they're vampires, but unethical testing is just...wrong. They still have rights."

"Shut up, man. You're so fuck'n soft." Ballsy snapped back like a cranky, underfed crocodile.

*What the fuck?* Things were even worse than Rick thought. "Is there any documentation around the testing?" Fingers crossed he could add it to his evidence collection.

"Oh yeah, there's documentation, but it's doctored. The stuff they let us and the funding bodies see, anyway. As if they're going to record something like that. If the wrong person got their hands on it, Sub Rosa would be fucked." Lanky's tone sounded quiet, yet sure.

*Damn.*

Ballsy looked around and shifted in closer. "Just between us, I snuck some video footage of their dirty little secret onto my phone. It could be a useful bargaining chip at some stage."

*A blackmailing chip, more like it.* "Would I be able to have a look?" Rick asked.

"I could arrange it, but not here. What time do you finish work?"

"Five o'clock."

"Perfect. Come to our place—an old mansion at the back of the compound. You'll find it, no probs—and you'll get your viewing."

The rest of Rick's day flew and, as planned, he met Ballsy straight after work. The guy wasted no time, ushering him through to the back of Rick's mum's house and stopped on the patio. "Before we go any further, you need to promise you won't mention the footage or where I'm taking you to anyone else."

*Except for Eden and hopefully the authorities, if I can somehow get a copy.* "Yeah, absolutely."

Ballsy's black eyes focused on his. "After today, it's as though none of it exists, right?"

"I understand." Oh yeah, Rick understood perfectly.

Ballsy hesitated, lifted a solar lantern from next to the back doorstep, switched it on and directed Rick onto a path leading into the dark woods. After only a couple hundred meters, they reached a small door and stepped into a cave.

He'd decked it out in ultimate man-cave style. Pictures of scantily clad women adorned the walls, and he'd furnished it with a couch, a bed and included a radio, a TV and tools. Lots and lots of tools. "Wow. Impressive."

"Thanks, mate. It's my equivalent of a shed."

The nerd's equivalent. The room smelled clean and fresh and the temperature felt surprisingly mild, considering the harsh winter conditions. He'd expected cold and dank, chilblain territory. Instead, the cave created a comfortable, hidden den.

"See that bird over there?" Ballsy gestured with the lantern to a picture of a Titian-haired, big-breasted woman with light jade eyes. "I fucked her."

She looked like a quarter-caste Jade. Did the guy realize he'd had sex with a hybrid? "Really?"

"Yeah, picked her up at a mate's bachelor party. She was one of the topless waitresses. Pretty hot, huh? And an incredible fuck too. Kept me up all night. She could run a master class in blow jobs. Fuck'n amazing! I've got a highlights package if you want to have a look."

Had Ballsy made the Jade connection? He'd come across as pretty anti-vampire, but seemed pretty pro himself, so maybe her being part Jade wouldn't affect him. "Does she know you filmed her?"

"Nah, I was discreet."

*Fuckhead.* "Nice work." This guy thought he had the upper hand, though more than likely he and the part-Jade had screwed each other, literally and figuratively. Rick tried to stifle the smirk pressing at the corner of his lips. One thing he knew for sure was that Ballsy couldn't be trusted.

They walked over to the couch, perched on a large carpet cut-off and sat down. A tower of stacked woolly blankets was piled up next to it, with Ballsy's closed laptop balanced on top.

"I use my laptop or phone out here. The reception's actually pretty good, and I don't get bothered." Ballsy opened up his computer and put it on the rickety coffee table. He hovered over one of the mp4 files. "Sure you don't want to have a look at her in action?"

"Thanks, but—"

"You just want to get down to business."

"Yeah, if you don't mind. I need to leave soon or Eden will wonder what's happened to me."

Ballsy gave him an *I-can-see-who-wears-the-pants-in-your-family* look and clicked on the 'vampire shooting' mp4 file. If only Rick could somehow get a copy.

Bluetooth provided the easiest option—however, it still required Rick to activate it on Ballsy's phone or laptop, get through his password protection, pair it with his own phone and select the file for transfer.

122

The more Rick thought about it, the more it seemed impossible. But he had to remain open-minded or else he definitely wouldn't succeed.

The footage looked a little shaky, though clear enough. A group of four vampires—two Jade and two Violet—were led outside into a prison-yard type area. The Violets and Jades taunted and stared each other down. The Violets crowded the Jades, stepping in close and invading their personal space.

The Jades lurched forward, growling, eyes narrowed, and the three-quarter and full castes bared their fangs like alpha dogs ready for a fight. No matter what anyone said, the Jade-Violet animosity remained strong.

They sized each other up, looked around and studied the environment, as though planning an escape route.

*What reason had they been given for being taken outside? Did they suspect something?*

Other than the aggression toward each other, they seemed compliant and non-resistive. Maybe they had just focused on the increased opportunity to break free.

The four guards milled around at the door until a Violet made a run for it. Not even a split-second later, the others followed. Four bursts of white-hot light shot through the air.

All four vampires dropped—one struck in the chest, one in the head, one in the arm and one in the leg. Luminosity traveled through their bodies, bright and glowing, until they lit up like beacons, flashed and convulsed like strobe lights.

The brightness began to dissipate and the full castes morphed into person-shaped charcoal blocks and disintegrated into embers that drifted away in the breeze.

The three-quarter castes writhed and groaned, the deadly light seeming to disintegrate their cells at a slower pace, from the inside out, until they too turned to black dust.

Rick swallowed back the disgust scalding his throat. "So how does the technology work exactly?"

Ballsy shut the laptop and turned to him. "Full vampires have no red blood cells and three-quarter castes very few. What you may or may not know is that they have a very high concentration of white blood cells.

"Studies were done to investigate the strengths and weaknesses, and the researchers found that the vampires' high concentration of white blood cells promoted advanced healing and also conducted sunlight, causing them to overheat and burn. That's why they can't tolerate too much sunshine. All the results so far reinforce that the less vampire genetics, the fewer white blood cells—"

"So there'd be less conductivity to sunlight, making it less dangerous for hybrids." Hence why he and Eden experienced a much milder aversion to the sun.

"Exactly. The sunlight bullet technology has only been tested on a very small sample of full and three-quarter castes to date, and although there's been a one-hundred-percent death rate, with more testing, due to their decreased white blood cell concentration, some three-quarter castes may actually survive. I'd hypothesize that half-castes would be hurt but not killed, unless they bled to death and so on."

It all started to make sense, like pieces fitting together in an abstract jigsaw puzzle. "Ah...now I get how all four vampires were hit at once. Their white blood cell conductivity attracted the bullets straight to them."

Ballsy stared back at him, seemingly impressed with his deduction. "Yep. The pulling power is strong, especially to concentrated sunlight, that the vampires draw the sunlight bullets like a magnet."

Their little meeting soon wound up and Rick drove straight to Ansfrida, eager to update Eden. He strode through the front door, hung his jacket on one of the three brass coat hooks mounted on the wall and called out to her. "Sweetheart, you won't believe this!"

She rushed into the foyer, her finger to her lips. "Sh-h-h! The kids are still asleep…and I'd like to keep it that way for a bit longer."

"Sorry." He threaded his arms around her waist. "I've just got so much to tell you!"

"Well, come on then." She took his hand, led him into the living area and they sat on the couch, facing each other.

He collected his thoughts and looked her in the eye. "Okay, firstly, one of the guys at work has taken footage of two Jades and two Violets shot and killed while testing sunlight bullets."

Shock and disbelief drained the healthy pink hue from her cheeks. "What?"

"Yeah, it's pretty horrible. If I could only get my hands on it—"

"It would be a great piece of evidence to add to the incriminating pile."

He nodded. "I'm not quite sure how or if I'm going to be able to do it, though. The guy is security conscious to the max."

"You mean paranoid."

"Pretty much. But he has reason to be." Rick lifted the abandoned laptop off the coffee table. "There's something else too, something exciting."

He positioned the lightweight computer on his legs and angled himself so Eden could also see the screen. "You know that Rosetta Stone computer program that I mentioned? Well, guess what? I found out today that Sub Rosa has bought it off Cambridge Uni."

Her eyes widened with surprise and she smiled, big and bright. "No way!"

"Yep. So I thought we could try to get onto it through my Sub Rosa login."

Rick scrolled through the alphabetical list of software until he reached 'R' and scanned through each entry. Finally 'Rosetta Stone' appeared on the bottom of the screen and he double-clicked on the icon.

Eden strummed her fingers on her thigh. "This is taking ages!"

"Just be patient. It's a pretty resource-hungry program, and our remote connection doesn't have the strongest connectivity. We could do something else and come back to it later." His gaze roamed over her, slowly, and when their eyes met, he flashed her his *how-about-sex* smile.

Eden blushed, refocused on the computer screen and stared at it, as though willing the page to finish loading. "I don't think I'll be able to relax, let alone pay attention to anything else, until I know whether we can get in."

"You know what they say about a watched kettle."

After five long, dragged-out minutes — where they could have been entertaining each other — the screen changed to a login page.

Eden huffed. "You've got to be joking! Aren't we already in the database? Why do we need a separate password?"

"To stop hackers like us." Rick smirked. "I'll just retype my username and password and see what happens."

The spinning colored ball appeared on the screen, indicating that the computer had gone into information-processing mode, and within two minutes, a new page started loading.

"It looks like we got in!" An exultant smile crossed Eden's lips. But it soon disappeared when 'Site under construction' popped up. "I can't believe this!"

Rick slammed down the laptop lid, discarded the computer on the coffee table and shot to his feet. "Fuck. So close... Argh!"

His wife grabbed his hand and interlaced their fingers. "I suppose we do still have to hear back from Simon." Her voice took on an appeasing, consolatory tone. "Maybe he's found something?"

"I hope so."

Rick took one, two, three long, slow, deep breaths. "Anyway...did you find anymore useful information today?"

"Yes, actually." Her smile returned. "I've added a couple more files to the ever-growing pile. I'm up to eleven now. How about you? Any further movement on the escape plan?"

He sighed. "Not as much as I'd hoped. I thought I might have come up with a reasonably clear action plan by now, but there are still some finer details I need to work out to ensure the least chance of error." Like what it took to interfere with the sunlight bars, even for just a few seconds, long enough for the vampire captives to evacuate their cells.

"It'll come to you."

He hadn't realized how much her faith in him helped bolster his motivation, his determination to see things through, to succeed...this time.

"Eventually, but I kind of need an epiphany now. It's getting close to a month since we arrived and I'm starting to feel the pressure to get things moving so we can leave as soon as possible."

Eden stood and tilted his chin with her free hand so he looked straight at her. "I feel the same, but you need to come up with a clear, close-to-foolproof plan first. We can't afford to just try anything out of desperation. We can't afford to be careless."

"I agree. But that doesn't eliminate the time pressure issue. I have everything crossed that things will fall into place very soon — or else it might be too late."

Eden tugged on his hand. "Come with me." He needed a release and to trust and believe in her and himself and she knew exactly what might help.

She led him upstairs to their en suite and turned on the shower taps.

He raised an eyebrow and smiled in that seductive, asymmetrical, lip-curling way of his. "A shower therapy session?"

"Something like that. Now strip."

He didn't hesitate. In less than a minute, their clothes were strewn across the tiled floor and they stood under the steaming hot water, entangled together and kissing like they'd been banned from it for weeks.

Eden moved her mouth from his lips and traveled along his strong, angular jaw to his ear, down his neck and stopped over his nipple. She sucked, licked and teased each little brown bud with her tongue and teeth, his cock growing hard and poking into her stomach.

With one hand she grasped his taut, muscular butt and, with the other, she stroked his shaft from base to tip, tip to base, over and over, rubbing her thumb over the pre-cum and working it over his skin.

He groaned. "Eden..." It was her cue to continue down, before he pressed her up against the wall and took over. Not that she wouldn't enjoy that, but first she wanted to treat him.

She kneeled before her husband, licked the whole length of his cock and took him deep into her mouth. He sank a hand into her hair, his breathing rough, labored.

Her nipples beaded and her core clenched, his touch, his response to her plucking at an invisible string of desire.

Eden swirled her tongue along his length, using a combination of soft and hard licks, just the way he liked it, and she cupped and caressed his balls.

Rick braced himself against the wall, his legs trembling, his control waning fast. Intent on extending his pleasure, their pleasure, she slowed things down.

He grunted in protest and she let go of him. Squirting some shower gel into one hand, she lubed up her fingers and rubbed against his butt hole. He jerked forward and she eased one finger part way into his tight passage, which now pulsed around the tip.

She returned her mouth to his cock. "Is everything okay?" she asked, knowing how much he enjoyed the vibration of her voice against his aroused flesh.

"Fuck, yes! Deeper." His tone sounded raw, almost a growl. God, she loved his openness.

She took almost his whole glorious erection into her mouth and, with a careful, slow thrust, she pushed her finger to the second knuckle in his butt and stopped while he adjusted.

"More." His voice shook with need and he clutched her head.

She increased her sucking and licking speed and matched it to her finger movement. In seconds he came, the force so strong that her head nearly popped off the end of his cock.

Eden cleaned up the seemingly never-ending spurts of cum with her tongue and kept up the slow finger thrusts in his ass, which appeared to elongate his orgasm. Seeing him let go like that, putting his trust in her to best meet his needs, revved up her own carnal appetite.

Finally, he dropped his hand from her head and slumped against the wall. She removed and washed her finger and kissed his slick shaft.

"Fucking hell." His voice lacked energy, as though the intensity of the orgasm had drained away every last ounce.

She stood and twined her arms around his neck. He pulled her in for a passionate kiss—not surprising, given the joy she knew he got from tasting himself on her lips.

When they pulled apart to take a breath, she said, "So how was—?"

"Fucking incredible. That was one of the best orgasms I've ever had." He held her face between his hands. "So, yes, please add it to our growing sexual repertoire."

He dove in for another heated kiss then continued exploring along her jaw, her throat, her breasts, her stomach and right down to the heart of her sex.

* * * *

On the drive to Sub Rosa the next morning, Simon came into Rick's head again. He should have heard something from his friend by now. A pang of worry stabbed at the pit of his stomach.

Maybe Simon had just been flat-out with work and trying to remain inconspicuous. *Possibly.* However, Rick sent him a quick follow-up text to check in, for peace of mind.

The day passed with still no reply from Simon, which was very unusual—and not in a good way. Normally his responses were pretty prompt. Panic set in like a thick, heavy frost. He couldn't allow it to get the better of him. He had to be patient and give Simon a bit more time before acting. He didn't want to prematurely pursue something that might get his best mate in trouble rather than help.

Distraction always worked best to redirect Rick's thoughts, so he dropped in on his mum for a short visit. Then he swung past the control room for some fresh inspiration and finished up having lunch with his newfound work 'buddies'.

Rick nibbled at his overcooked roast beef sandwich, trying to tune in to the guys' chatter.

Shorty rushed over and plonked down next to Oldie. "Hey, did you guys hear that they're doing some maintenance on the sunlight control system?"

*Still?* It couldn't just be a routine service. They'd have been finished by now.

Oldie glanced up from his green curry. "How did you find that out?"

A *don't-you-worry-about-that* smile spread onto Shorty's lips. "I have my sources."

Ballsy snorted. "Rubbish! You overheard it. You've always been a fuck'n massive sticky nose."

Lanky raised a questioning eyebrow. "How are you always in the right place at the right time?"

Ballsy rolled his eyes as if to say, *duh*. "He works out who to follow."

"He never follows me," Lanky said, a sliver of disappointment tainting his tone.

Ballsy gestured his hand toward him. "Exactly."

They all laughed.

Although Rick would have loved to joke around all day, he didn't have the time or the inclination, not with so many lives at stake. He had to get to the core of the matter, to determine if a system glitch existed and how to best exploit it.

Rick had to get the Jades and Violets out before he could even consider going to the police. He couldn't have them snooping around too early. If they realized the prisoners were vampires, they might side with Sub Rosa out of fear. And that would fuck everything up...majorly. "So is it just a regular check or is something actually wrong?"

Shorty darted his eyes around the group. "Something's definitely wrong. Some of the bars keep dropping out."

Lanky's giant face filled with childlike joy. "If they don't solve it soon, the system may shut down altogether. Can you imagine?"

Shorty leaned in closer. "When I passed the control room earlier, one of the maintenance guys and the senior tech were both fiddling around with a red button and toggle switch, testing for any glitches, apparently."

The inkling of an idea formed on the cusp of Rick's mind. He needed to be physically present in the control room so the burgeoning thought could sprout like a spring bud.

He checked his watch—one p.m. A few hours remained until the late afternoon handover. He needed to distract himself in the meantime, so he headed back to his workstation and knocked out his latest research report.

When he finally reached the control room, he sat at the massive desk and attempted to absorb the environment without attaching any conscious thoughts.

His gaze wandered over the control panel until he'd almost reached a meditative state, his subconscious trying to piece things together, trying to determine if he could somehow rig up the environment so he could deactivate the sunlight system without involving another person.

"Rick?"

*Fuck!* He jolted his head up. The tech from the other day, stood in the doorway with a maintenance guy. The sunlight bar debacle had definitely created a bigger problem than they'd anticipated.

A dubious smiled extinguished the distress on the tech's face. "Back for some more information?"

"Yeah, I'm still trying to get my head around the brilliance and ingenuity of the system. It's really impressive."

"When it works," the maintenance guy murmured.

The tech not-so-subtly rammed his elbow into the guy's stomach. "Ah...sorry, Rick. He needs to get in there and do a final check. Just standard procedure stuff."

*Standard procedure, my arse.* Rick tried to disguise his chuckle with a cough. "No worries. Hope you don't have a long night ahead."

On the drive to Ansfrida, a plan began to take shape. If maintenance couldn't fix the problem, all he'd need to do was maximize on the fault and cause a bigger outage in the sunlight streams. Could he realistically make that happen?

While the maintenance guys posed a positive diversion, they could equally be a hindrance, possibly even restrict his access. No, he couldn't think that way. He had to remain confident and optimistic if he had any chance of succeeding.

In the morning, he'd inform his mum and Eden's dad of his intention to free them and the others. And he'd ask for their assistance to get the word out to the rest of their communities to be ready to leave as soon as the sunlight bars disappeared, reinforcing that, worst-case scenario, they'd only have a few seconds to act.

Thanks to Shorty's revelation, Rick was pretty sure the two red buttons and toggle switches near the front but on opposite ends of the control panel, had a part in switching off the bars. Unfortunately, he hadn't been able to figure out a way to disengage them himself.

Hence he'd cycled back to the original sticking point. He had to choose a trustworthy second person to help him shut down the system. He'd been mulling over potential options since he'd left the office, but only one person kept coming to mind.

# Chapter Ten

Breaching the Comfort Zone

It got to seven-thirty p.m. and Rick still hadn't returned home. Every other night he'd arrived by six-thirty at the latest. Eden's hematite ring seemed to grow with heat until it almost singed her skin. She checked her mobile to confirm that she hadn't missed any of his calls or texts. She willed the phone to buzz or ring—something, anything to let her know he was safe.

Eden called him for the tenth time but got diverted to voicemail. *Shit! Shit! Shit!* Rick never turned his phone off. Maybe the battery had gone flat. *As if.* Rick always kept his mobile charged. In fact, it caused most of their arguments—him always being so accessible.

Headlights slashed across the window. *Rick?*

Eden threw open the front door just as her husband stepped onto the patio. "Thank God. I'd started to worry. I tried to ring you but your phone went straight to voicemail—"

He brushed his lips against hers. "Sorry, my battery died. Though I reckon you might forgive me when I tell you the good news."

Her eyes searched his, her hematite ring now back to a steady, humming warmth. "Have you worked out how to shut off the sunlight bars?"

"Sort of." Rick guided her to the couch and pulled her onto his lap. "I've developed a plan. It's not ideal, but I think it'll work." He hesitated.

He clamped his hand on her thigh and looked her in the eye. "Tomorrow morning, I'll pay a visit to your dad and my mum and let them know what I'm going to do and ask them to spread the word to the others. Then, at midday, you and the kids will drop by under the pretense of taking me to lunch."

Worry flooded her veins like the aftermath of a stress tsunami. Her and the twins at Sub Rosa, the epitome of evil.

Rick's Adam's apple bulged like he'd swallowed a ping pong ball. "I had hoped to keep you and the kids away from the compound, but now I have no choice. You're the only person I can truly trust to help me override the system."

She stared back at him, speechless. What could she say to that? No? She didn't really have a choice.

"Eden, tell me what you're thinking."

"I want to help you..."

"I hear a *but*."

"I don't care about me so much. It's the twins. I couldn't live with myself if something happened to them."

Matching worry whirled in his green eyes. "Me either. I don't want anything to happen to any of you."

"But —"

"I can't think of any other way. I've weighed up every option and, believe it or not, this one seems the least risky. If I had longer, I would have sussed out how to construct a concealed rigging system to help me do it all on my own or find who else I could trust and ask them to assist instead. But our time *is* running out. If we don't do something now, we might not have another chance."

"You're right." Even though it twisted her stomach and tore up her heart to admit it. "It makes perfect, practical sense. I'd rather us all be together than you put your faith in a stranger."

Rick stroked her cheek, his hand smooth, soothing, strong. "I really wish it didn't have to come to this."

"I know." A resigned smile relaxed the tension she hadn't realized had etched into her forehead.

Rick kissed her hairline, temples, tip of her nose, mouth, then nuzzled into her neck. "Let's go upstairs." They needed some couple-strengthening passion time. If they were going to be triumphant with this Sub Rosa thing, they needed true unification.

He kept hold of her hand and steered her up the steps, straight into their bedroom, and shut the door. If what he had planned came to fruition, there'd be some serious noise. And he didn't want to disturb the twins.

Rick walked her toward the bed, kissing her the whole way, until the backs of her knees hit the mattress and she dropped down into a sitting position. He switched on the lamp, took off his top and unbuttoned his jeans. Eden's breath hitched and her pupils dilated so wide, only a small blue-violet ring remained visible around the edge of her irises.

He shrugged out of his remaining clothes and stood bare before her. "Like what you see?" he said, with his most mischievous grin.

Her gaze went straight to his erection, which was bobbing proudly, not far from her face. She licked her lips. "Very much."

"Someone has way too many clothes on."

She glanced down at herself and snapped into action, as though she hadn't realized she'd just sat there and ogled him like he'd performed a private striptease, straight out of a *Thunder from Down Under* show.

She removed her T-shirt and bra while he kneeled between her legs and yanked off her leggings and panties, exposing her smooth, sweet pussy. It already glistened with her juices, her intoxicating arousal creating a heady libido-boosting scent.

"Lie right back." He hardly recognized his desire-husky voice.

As per his command, she lay flat, and he grabbed just below her knees and lifted her spread legs until they bent against her chest. "Hold them there." On display like that, she looked mouthwatering, an erotic feast ready to be devoured.

They'd been so intimate together and yet sometimes a blush still crept across her skin, like now, deep and ruby red. So damn adorable...and sexy.

With his hands on her ass cheeks, he dove between her legs and gave her clit one quick flick with his tongue. She moaned and he licked along her seam, lapping at her moist folds and dipping his tongue inside her sex.

*Honey.*

*No. Nectar of the gods.*

*Pure, sweet, addictive.*

He thrust repeatedly into her core and caressed her butt with his hands. She whimpered and gripped his head, pressing his face farther into her hairless flesh.

When he slipped from inside her, she mewled, but instead of sliding his tongue back in, he trailed it to her rear hole, licked around the edge, then pressed the puckered center.

Her ass lifted off the mattress and she gasped. He massaged her butt cheeks and up along the backs of her thighs with sensual strokes. "Everything okay?"

"Yes," she said, all breathy. "You just surprised me."

"In a good way or a bad way?"

"Good. Very good." She tugged on his hair, drawing him back between her legs.

He rimmed her some more then dragged his tongue along her drenched folds and sucked on her clit.

She gripped his hair tighter, sending pleasure-pain tingles along his scalp and right down his spine to his already-steel-hard cock. "Rick. Oh yes!"

He teased her with licks and sucks, changing up the pace until her panting and little moans suggested she was hovering close to climax. Rick lubricated his thumb and two fingers with her juices, then inserted the fingers into her sex and pressed his thumb against her asshole.

She arched her back and pushed against his thumb, and it slid inside her back passage.

They groaned together.

Rick continued to work her super-swollen clit with his tongue and thrust into her with his fingers and thumb.

"Come in my mouth," he said, and she did, bucking and calling his name.

Rick continued his pleasure onslaught until she'd fully ridden out her orgasm. He eased her legs down, climbed on top of her and kissed her hard on the lips. She responded with such passion that it surprised him they didn't set the sheets on fire.

Eden flipped him onto his back, her luxurious dark hair draping forward and framing her flushed face. "Your turn. What would you like?"

They'd successfully moved past round two of his anal campaign. Would they make it to round three? "To hold you from behind and play with your beautiful breasts, while you rub your clit and I stick my cock in your incredible ass." There, he'd said it. Out loud. His darkest desire was now out in the open.

"You want us to have...anal?" The seductive huskiness had fled from her voice and been replaced with...uncertainty.

"Yeah."

"Why?"

He tucked a twirl of her hair behind her ear. "To explore each other further, to engage in total, intimate trust."

"Not to try something new?" Her eyes searched his, as though they'd reveal the honest answer.

"That too. What do you think?" *Please say yes.* He'd been working toward this very point to build on their relationship, to deepen it, and he was beyond willing. He wouldn't push her, though. He'd just keep chipping away at her fear until she felt ready to join him...assuming they survived their bring-Sub-Rosa-to-justice mission.

"I think...that if you think we should try, then let's do it."

He pulled her down for a deep, gratitude-filled kiss. "You're sure?"

"Yes. I trust you."

It was just what he needed to hear.

She rolled onto her side and lay stone still.

Rick nestled into her back, swept her hair aside and nipped and kissed her nape. That always got her going. She pushed her butt up against him and rubbed his granite-hard cock. He groaned then bit and sucked the sensitive spot on her neck, creating a big red love bite.

Eden reached behind, grasped his hand and curved it over her breast. "Touch me. Make me come."

His cock throbbed. If she kept talking like that, he'd lose his load all over her back before he even got close to her ass.

Rick cupped and caressed the satin-like skin of her breast and gave her nipple a tug. She whimpered, pushing her chest against his palm. Every inch of her felt so fucking amazing. She glided her hand between her legs and stroked her clit while he rubbed his aching cock along her slit, coating it in her wetness.

Eden rocked her pelvis between their hands and his erection, and her desperate little moans nearly sent him into premature-ejaculation territory, like an inexperienced teenager.

One more tweak on her nipple then he reached around and snatched the tube of lube off the bedside table. He squirted a generous glob onto her puckered hole and she gasped and shivered, but it didn't stop her playing with her clit.

Fuck, she looked so damn sexy, all flushed and panting and wanton. He pressed the head of his cock against the cool liquid.

Control. He prided himself on exercising restraint and he normally managed it well—except now, when all he wanted to do was ram himself home. However, joint trust and pleasure remained his number one goal, not getting his rocks off at the expense of her enjoyment.

He applied gentle pressure, and the head of his cock slipped inside. "How's that?" His voice sounded shaky, breathless.

"Tight. Full. But okay."

He eased out then pushed back in with a single, cautious thrust. "Tell me if you need me to stop."

"Don't stop."

Rick gritted his teeth and pulled nearly all the way out, then pressed in a little deeper each time.

Eden rubbed her clit harder, quicker. "Oh yes. Yes!"

Her sphincter's grip on his cock loosened and he slid in all the way. "Fuck." He stilled, allowing her to adjust, then he picked up speed.

In just a few more thrusts, she cried out a sequence of garbled words, her body thrashing with an endless orgasm. Her asshole clenched and released his cock, over and over, and he shattered, shooting out stream after stream of cum in the climax of a lifetime.

The flood of endorphins transported Rick to another dimension, and he lost all sense of time passing. One moment they were in the throes of unbridled passion, sharing the incredible connection, and the next they were cuddled together, kissing, caressing, murmuring sounds of love and affection as they floated back to reality.

He kissed the pulse point below Eden's ear. "You okay?"

"Mm-m-m..."

Rick smiled against her skin. "Is that a *yes*?"

"Mm-m-m..."

He lifted the quilt over them and rolled her relaxed body to face him. Her eyes had a dreamy, just-been-thoroughly-fucked look, boosting his ego and making him so very proud. He'd made the right decision and it had panned out just how he'd hoped.

*Better.*

"Eden?"

"Mm-m-m..." She snuggled into him like she'd hit subspace.

He swept her hair off her face and massaged along her spine with long, gentle strokes. They'd conquered the fear holding back their intimacy and strengthened their relationship. Now they just had to utilize the trust they'd built and work together to conquer Sub Rosa.

* * * *

*A white room, sitting in a pram in the corner next to Blake, with Mummy and a purple man. Purple and green people rushed in, yelling and banging their fists against the thick white wall. Sunlight fire in front of the windows and doors, made purple and green people jump back like they'd been burned.*

*Two men held Daddy and a small group of others shouted at him. He tried to pull his arms free but the big, muscly men held him tighter.*

*More and more purple and green people filled the room, the noise getting louder and louder. A big thump made the muscle men turn around. Daddy got free and ran.*

*"Rick!" Mummy called out.*

*He saw her and smiled and kept running toward her.*

*Bang!*

*Daddy dropped to the ground, blood all over his chest and coming out his mouth.*

Scarlett's eyes flew open, her heart beating hard. "Daddy!" she screamed.

Silence.

"Daddy!"

In just pajama pants, he stumbled through the doorway, his eyes half closed. "What's wrong, sweetie?"

She could hardly breathe. So many words came into her head but she couldn't make a sentence.

Daddy walked over, picked her up and hugged her. "Did you have a bad dream?"

She nodded and snuggled into his strong, warm chest. "You got shot and bled."

"Shh-h... It's okay. It was only a dream," he whispered.

She moved back and stared into his eyes. "It felt so real!"

"Nightmares can be pretty scary sometimes, but they're not real. See? I'm fine."

She cuddled him again. His heart pounded against her ear. His words didn't match how he felt inside. Did her dream scare him too? Or was it something else?

"Do you want to come into bed with me and Mummy?"

"No, it's okay," she said against his salty skin.

He kissed her hair then looked into her eyes. "Are you sure?"

"Yes. I don't want Blake to worry if he wakes up and I'm not here."

Daddy gently lowered her into her cot and gave her his *I-love-you-so-much* smile. "You're such a sweet, special girl. Do you know that?"

# Chapter Eleven

## On Tenterhooks

*Oslo, November 2011*

Dull echoes grew louder, clearer, and he emerged into glaring bright light. A gasp of sharp, icy air grated his lungs and awakened his hibernating hunger. Smothered in shadows, he lay wrapped in warmth. A blurry fair face smiled.

"Rune — my magical creation." Her soft lips branded him on the forehead.

He latched on to a pink nub and suckled. Drained dry and starving, he took a bite. Metallic heat flowed into his parched mouth and down his throat. He sucked and sucked and sucked, but it still didn't satisfy his thirst, his hunger.

"What is he doing?" a shadow screamed.

Torn away by foreign hands, he sucked the air, desperate for more. The lady lay limp. Rune cried and cried and couldn't stop.

His biological mother was dead, within hours of his birth. How could he live with that? He wasn't supposed to know. Then he'd overheard his surrogate mothers talking—the one downfall of having three loving mums—and his strange, vivid memories had suddenly made sense.

They had looked after him in shifts, scheduling regular handovers since that moment, the moment when he'd sucked the life out of his own mother. Yes, he'd been a newborn baby and hadn't known any better, though that didn't make what he'd done excusable.

"If you want to blame anyone, blame your father," they'd all said when he'd spoken to his mothers, both alone and together.

But how could he? His supposed deadbeat of a dad had never been around. Rune had never seen the guy, not even in a photo. And all he knew of his personality he'd pieced together through his mums' snarky comments. Maybe they blamed Rune for his father's absence? Though, by the revolted tone in their voices at the mention of the man, it had to be something more sinister.

"Hey, birthday boy, are you still with us?"

Rune snapped back to the present.

"Push that dark brown mess of hair out of your eyes. How do you even call that mop a style?" Mother three, the youngest and most outspoken, constantly hassled him since he'd let his hair grow...more like gave him crap.

He tried not to smirk, raked his 'messy mop' out of his eyes and blew out the fourteen candles on his raw beef mince cake.

"Did you make a wish?"

Did he ever—that his mums wouldn't freak out at what he was about to request. He glanced up, his hair falling back across his face, and made eye contact with each of his mothers—well, the best he could through the thick dark brown strands—his heart racing, his mouth desert dry. "Yeah. I want to meet my dad. Where is he, anyway?"

Mother one sighed and fingered her long, golden braid. "I knew this day would come."

Mother two's piercing jade eyes pinned him to the spot. "Your 'dad'? Out gallivanting, searching for new conquests."

Mother three glanced at one and two and shook her head, her silky white-blonde hair whipping her shoulders. "The bastard. How could we have been so gullible?"

They hated him. They'd made that punch-to-the-face clear. Rune had psyched himself up all year to ask to see him. The demand went against their wishes, but he couldn't ignore it anymore. The incessant drive to know at least one of his biological parents had become all-consuming.

Rune's stomach tensed and he swallowed the churning nausea from the impending argument. "I still want to meet him—and make up my own mind."

The mothers looked at each other, clearly weighing his request.

Sadness filled mother one's deep green eyes. "All right, we'll arrange it. You can see for yourself."

Mother two walked over to him and touched his cheek. "I hope you won't be too disappointed."

The look in mother three's eyes said, *though it's highly likely.* "A reality check will be good for you. As soon as you meet the dickhead, you'll finally not just realize but believe you're not responsible for Demi's death."

Rune's wish must have been granted, because there were no more arguments, no more freak-outs after his birthday or in the week leading up to his dad's visit. Though the time seemed to shuffle by in slow motion, each day dragged out like it was a year.

He marched up and down his bedroom in his black boxer shorts. What would he say? He had so many questions. They had so much to catch up on. Where would he start?

Tension gripped his stomach like the Terminator's cold, robotic hand. *Chill.* Rune gripped the handle of his wardrobe, closed his eyes and breathed. Slow, deep in, slow steady out, repeat. He'd always considered the meditation crap his mums went on about to be total rubbish, but it actually seemed to be working.

When his heart rate slowed and his muscles relaxed a bit, he yanked the closet door open. Hangers upon hangers of 'teen' styles. That word so sucked but it fit, unlike three quarters of the gear he'd recently outgrown.

What did a son wear when meeting his father for the first time? Should he go formal or casual? Suit and shirt or jeans and T-shirt? He desperately wanted to make a good first impression, while remaining true to himself. *I have to be me.* And if his dad didn't like him...? He didn't want to think about that.

He pulled out a pair of black jeans and a tight black T-shirt and slipped them on. Calm descended over his skin and seeped into his jumpy nerves. Rune's mothers, especially mother three, gave him a hard time for falling into the stereotypical rebellious goth phase and he consistently reminded them it wasn't a phase. He embodied true goth. They all did. Though the Violets fit the feel more than the Jades.

Rune stood in front of his full-length bedroom mirror, his deep violet eyes staring back at him, their green flecks catching the light like chips of emerald. He adjusted his V-neck T-shirt and straightened up his shoulders.

Slouching had become a habit, revealing his lack of confidence. He had to slash that from his being, from his life. He needed his dad to be proud of him. Rune rummaged under the bed for his runners and squeezed them on. If he didn't hurry his dad would —

"You must be Rune."

He shot his head up and craned his neck. A tall, stylishly-dressed dude with waist-length, flowing black hair and full-on violet eyes stood behind him.

"How did you—?" Rune stammered and turned to see him properly, to prove his flesh-and-bloodless form.

His dad smirked. "I thought I'd just sneak in and surprise you." He blew the tips of his fingers and rubbed them against his chest. "I slipped under the door."

"What?"

"Didn't they tell you anything about me?" He balked like that couldn't be possible, not for someone like him—someone special, important, God-like.

*Only that you're a selfish, arrogant loser.* "Not really."

His dad looked him over, his expression as easy to read as invisible ink, and joined him in front of the mirror. "Where do I begin?" He drummed his long, pale fingers against his chin. "You must call me Beauregarde. No sentimental 'Dad' references, please.

Just uttering the word makes me cringe." He shuddered.

*Warm, loving, affectionate* — the perfect antonyms for his father.

"What else? Let's see… My Violet parents changed me against my will close to eight hundred years ago, and I've been doing whatever I want ever since. I may as well make the most of it, right?" A sneer curled onto his lips.

"I suppose…"

Beauregarde's mesmerizing stare sank into him like some strange hypnosis. "If you're smart, you'll make the most of it too. You can have however many women you want, from here to Australia."

*You mean, if you're a lying, manipulative user?* "Really?"

"Yes…how old are you now?"

"Fourteen."

"And still a virgin."

*How did he know?* Heat rose in Rune's cheeks and his gaze fell to his feet. It wasn't like he didn't think about doing it. It had been on his mind heaps in the last six months, since his first wet dream. He just hadn't found a girl he wanted to go there with…yet. Thank the fucking universe for his hand and the Internet or he probably would have exploded.

"I thought so. I can fix that."

"No, that's okay," Rune mumbled and kicked a non-existent mini ball between his big toes.

"Oh…you like men?"

He shook his head. "No!"

"Then we need to sort this out. That's the problem with being raised by women. They stifle a boy's growth and make him soft. No son of mine is going to be a frigid wuss of a vampire."

How could he and this guy possibly be related? They were as similar as heaven and hell. Rune forced a smile through clenched teeth. "Thanks for the offer, but I'll do it in my own time, when the situation's right. At the moment, I want to get to know you—and understand how you can slip under doors."

Beauregarde's intense eyes peered at him as though he couldn't quite believe sex hadn't secured the number one spot on *his* son's top priorities list. "Some of us have special powers. Mine is the ability to transform my body to move in and out of tight spaces."

"Wow!" *Could I possibly have a special power?* "What else can you do?"

"Fuck as many women as I like."

Back to that again. *Urgh.* The guy was fixated, rigid and egotistical as all fuck. His selfish, chauvinistic sense of entitlement made Rune sick. Rune's mums were right. This man was a jerk of the highest order—and his father, unfortunately. "So, do I have any brothers or sisters?"

"Plenty, I'd say."

*I'd say?* How could he not know? "Can I meet them?"

Beauregarde's laugh scraped like fingernails clawing a blackboard. "I'm sure you can, and you probably already have met some of them."

"Won't you help me?"

Beauregarde stared at Rune like his question, his caring, his interest in family indicated a sure sign of weakness. "I don't know where they are."

"You don't know where they are? You helped create them. They're part of you. Aren't you interested?"

"Not really."

Man, this guy epitomized 'asshole'. "Did you ever even love my mum?"

"I hardly remember her. You've got to understand. There have been more than a few." *Said like a true narcissist.*

"You're a total fuckwit!" The words shot out like a misfired gun. Were his mums sure this...*person* was his biological father? Maybe his mum had been with someone else as well...hopefully.

Beauregarde smirked. "I love you too, son."

Anger rose in Rune's throat like a raging fire. "No wonder they hate you."

"There are always plenty of others."

Rune clenched his hand into a fist and threw a punch at his father's fuck'n smart mouth.

Beauregarde grabbed Rune's wrist before it made contact and twisted it behind his back.

Rune doubled over and gasped for oxygen, black blotches splattering his vision. "Ouch! You're going to break my arm!"

"I should, too, just to teach you a lesson, you insolent little shit." He tightened his grip and held, then released it, dropping Rune to the floor just before he passed out.

Rune gulped down massive mouthfuls of air and rubbed his throbbing arm.

"Just as I thought—a fucking waste of time. That is exactly why I have nothing to do with any of you. You don't deserve to be recognized as my son."

Rune stared up at him through moist eyes. Although not a big fan of the man, it didn't stop his dad's words from cutting into his heart like a blunt knife. "But—"

"I knew this was a mistake." Beauregarde shook his head, as though super pissed at himself for ever agreeing to come.

He focused his cold violet eyes on Rune, freezing him to the spot. "From now on, you don't exist to me. If I see you again, I'll make sure you're thrown in the Sub Rosa compound along with your mothers. You'd be the perfect test subject, you little Jade-Violet mutant."

"My mothers?" Rune jumped to his feet. "What do you mean?"

He reached for Beauregarde's brocade vest and missed, the selfish bastard disappearing like a switched-off hologram, his laugh an evil, lingering echo, bouncing off the walls.

Rune ran into the living room. His mothers were gone—and all because he'd pushed to meet his horrible father. Was he cursed? First he'd killed his biological mother and now he'd put his surrogate mothers in danger.

Deep belly sobs shook him and he fell to his knees. He squeezed his eyes shut and a river of tears cascaded down his face. He had to get his foster mothers out of Sub Rosa. But how? Rune couldn't risk fronting up there. He'd be no use to them if he got captured as well. The only way around it required him to somehow find his father and beg for his assistance.

His stomach tensed so hard he could have shit diamonds. He *really* didn't want to see the arrogant, chauvinistic pig again—however, he had no choice. Beauregarde was the only one who could get his mothers out. And Rune would risk his own safety to do it. Now how would he find the slimeball? *Think.*

A glowing purple dot pulsed in his brain. Great... Either it marked the start of a migraine or a meltdown. *Perfect timing...not.* He shook his head to try to shake the blinking bright spot from his mind, but it stayed there, more prominent than ever.

And now a green flashing dot with purple center joined it. *This has to be a migraine.* He went straight to the medicine cabinet and poured himself a special purple wine.

"Sorry, Mums. It's an emergency," he muttered. He drained every last drop from the heavy pewter cup and wiped his mouth with the back of his hand. Lightheadedness whirled around his brain and he gripped the sink. *Oops!* Maybe he should have had fifty, not a hundred milliliters. *Too late now.*

Rune lay down on his bed and calm soaked into his body. He closed his eyes but the pulsing dots persisted. Maybe if he slept, they'd go away. He flopped onto his back and within minutes began to doze. The purple dot throbbed, zipping from spot to spot, like a spirograph, while the green, purple-centered dot pulsed in soothing rhythm with his heartbeat.

He focused his eyes inwardly and an island floated to the surface beneath the dots. Scandinavia? He sat up. No, a world map. He scrutinized the flashing dots — both crowded into Norway. What did they mean?

Rune ran his fingers through his rebellious hair and racked his brain. What were the glowing pulse points trying to tell him?

All day he tried to solve the dots puzzle, with no luck, and went to bed just as perplexed. In the morning he woke up surprisingly refreshed. *Must have been the wine.*

He yawned and stretched then padded into the kitchen with bare feet. The dots hadn't moved, remaining camped out in his Norway mind map, and his subconscious had come no closer to deciphering their message.

He opened the fridge door and stared at the near emptiness. Grocery shopping now took the number one spot on his list of priorities. Maybe a decent feed would help him concentrate, work out what to do, what all this dot stuff meant.

Although stressed, he didn't feel like he'd had a nervous breakdown. Then again, he'd never had one before, so he had nothing to compare it to. He'd just have to be patient, do the required research, make the most practical decisions and the answer would come to him...hopefully.

During the day, the purple dot moved, and not just a little bit. It crossed countries, while the jade-violet-centered dot remained stable and steady. By the next morning, the purple dot had traveled across the world to Australia. *Australia? What the fuck?*

Rune shoveled the last few spoonfuls of raw, bloodied beef mince into his mouth and leaned back in his wooden dining chair. *Hang on.* His dad had mentioned Australia. Did the purple dot denote the prick? If so, Rune could track him like a GPS. *Weird, but cool.*

Though, if the purple dot represented his dad, who was the green dot with the purple center? Another relative? A brother, sister? He'd have to wait to investigate until his mothers were freed. For now, he needed to get to Australia, find his father and convince the conceited jerk to make his wish a reality.

Under his bed, Rune dug deep and pulled out his 'treasure chest'. His mums had filled a carved wooden box with survival essentials, just in case they had to relocate quickly. It was sort of a vampire first-aid kit.

Vampiric life remained nomadic, full of risks, danger, uncertainty. Nothing had changed in the last few thousand years. His mothers had warned him never to get too comfortable in one place. When that happened, it increased the likelihood of a significant change. And their prophecy had eventuated.

Rune lifted the lid off the box and rummaged through fake birth certificates, medical records, credit cards, bank accounts...

"Ah-ha!" He pulled out a stack of passports, held together by two brittle rubber bands that snapped with the slightest movement. Rune laid the selection of passports across the timber floorboards and went through them one at a time. Baby, toddler, *out*, child, *out*, teenager, *too young, out*, early twenties... He scrutinized the picture.

Could a fourteen-year-old half-vampire pass for a twenty-one-year-old human? He did look mature for his age, and if he took along a selection of supporting documentation...

Yeah, he could do it. He just had to look confident. He just had to apply some of the method acting techniques his mums had taught him and truly play the part, believe it...at least until he got out of customs in Australia.

* * * *

Thank the fucking universe, he'd succeeded. Rune had followed the purple dot to Hobart, Tasmania without a hitch and stood outside the Sub Rosa office building. It wasn't the smartest, safest move, but he needed answers.

With Beauregarde somewhere inside, Rune hung out, risking his own capture, ready to confront the fuckwit. He hid behind the bushes at the edge of the car park and glared at the black, shiny façade, waiting for the bastard to leave.

The time dragged, like each second ticked through quicksand. His dad had to come out for something. He couldn't be in there all day and all night, could he? How many meetings could a person attend?

The sun set, the sky streaked with ribbons of gold, purple and pink. Rune stretched and yawned. Jet lag sucked. But he refused to relax, worried he'd doze off in the bushes and miss this prime opportunity.

It grew dark, with only artificial streetlamps and the large moon offering splashes of light.

Movement. *Finally.* The purple dot grew closer and approached him. Rune's stomach clenched. What exactly would he say? His pre-planned speech had vanished, leaving behind only a couple of key words.

Rune focused on the dot, using it as a form of meditation. Five hundred meters, four hundred meters, three hundred meters, two hundred meters, one hundred meters. Every muscle in his still-developing body tensed, preparing to fight.

Beauregarde strutted through the automatic front doors, head up high, like a member of some arrogant, old-fashioned aristocracy, his long black hair and coat tails flapping in the breeze. His striking style and presence could fool people...initially, though not for long. Anyone with half a brain would soon realize he came up empty in the personality department.

More than empty. Could a person possibly have a character filled with minus traits? Selfish, paranoid, aggressive…yet, his dad saw himself as smart, strong, powerful.

At the corner of the building, Beauregarde turned right and almost flew toward the nearby hills. Rune followed, surprised at his ability to keep up with his dad's speed-of-light pace. They reached a sandstone gothic mansion positioned high up off the road. Could the awesome place be his dad's house?

Beauregarde scaled the side of the building and slipped through a tiny gap in the upstairs window. Nope, not his place…unless he'd forgotten his keys. *Hmm….* What had brought him here?

Without his dad's full-Violet climbing skills, Rune waited for him outside. At least his inner GPS wouldn't lose track of him. Time seemed to stagnate while Rune's anxiety built.

Needing to release some pent-up energy, he started to pace, wearing a path through the luxurious garden and around to the front of the property, past a parked car. Someone was home. Did his dad know that or would it be a surprise?

A large marble fountain bubbled away and he walked over to it. Water splashed and gurgled over a lovey-dovey statue, surrounded by cupids, hearts and roses, and an inscription ran around the base

*Deep inside the chambers of my cavernous heart lay secrets, truth and eternal love.*

Rune slid his hand over the smooth marble. "Cool." *Crunch, crunch, crunch.*

159

A car? Coming up the driveway? *Shit!* His heart back-flipped once, twice. Where could he hide? His gaze ping-ponged around the yard, searching for a suitable spot, and stopped on a small alcove off the side of the house. It provided the perfect position to hole up and still keep watch. He sprinted over to it and slipped inside.

A car pulled up next to the parked one, engine running, headlights blaring and a man jumped out, a full human man. He ran up the front steps of the house and disappeared through the door.

"Grace!" a male voice cried out.

Silence, some shuffling sounds and then...

*Bang!*

Rune jumped, his heart slamming against his sternum. Was that a gunshot? Should he go inside and check things out? He wanted to but the purple dot — his dick of a dad — moved toward the same window he'd entered earlier. Rune didn't want to try to track him down again when he was this close.

Rune hightailed it to the side of the house and arrived right as his dad leapt from the ledge. Beauregarde landed on his feet, quiet and agile as a cat, ran a couple hundred meters and stopped.

"Why are you following me?"

Rune's breath caught in his throat, like choking on a fishbone. *How did he know?*

Beauregarde turned around, a sneer on his moonlit face. "I told you that I don't want anything to do with you."

Rune stood tall and firm. "I'm not here for me."

"Then why are you here?"

"To ask you to release my mothers." Rune injected his voice with a confidence he didn't feel.

A mocking laugh boomed from Beauregarde's mouth. "You're kidding, right? You're having me on."

Rune gnashed his teeth together to stop from telling the guy to go fuck himself and ruining the last hope he had to save his mothers.

Beauregarde laughed harder, stumbling back and clasping his chest. "That's the most hilarious thing I've heard in a very long time."

Rune clenched his hands into fists, his nails cutting into his palms.

"You came all the way here just for that?"

Rune nodded, forcing his gaze to remain on the cruel bastard in front of him. *What did Mum ever see in the guy?*

"Well, you've wasted your time."

"So you're not going to help me?"

The fuckwit scoffed. "No."

Rune shoved his bleeding hands on his hips. "Why not? I haven't done anything to you. You don't even know me!"

Beauregarde stepped forward and stood over him. "And I don't want to. Now back off or I'm going to hand you over to Sub Rosa myself."

Rune didn't want to beg, but he'd tried the Mr. Tough Guy routine and failed. Although his whole body protested, he had to plead, grovel or else risk never seeing his mums again while they rotted away in Sub Rosa jail. "Please! Can't you just do this one thing? Then I'll never bother you again."

Beauregarde backed down, swept his shiny black hair over his shoulder and sifted through the ends with his manicured fingers. "I don't know how to tell you this, kid, but they're dead."

"What?" No. He must have misheard.

"They died in transit." Beauregarde shrugged, not one ounce of remorse in his eyes. "Sorry."

Rune glared at him, refusing to get sucked into his mind games, refusing to believe his bullshit. "You're lying."

"Am I? Why would I do that?"

"Because it's how you roll." The black-hearted bastard couldn't help himself. Spreading misery everywhere he went seemed to be his main goal in life. And so far, he'd done an outstanding job.

Beauregarde didn't even try to contain a laugh. "Not in this case. They're dead, dead as rusty, distorted, useless doornails."

Tears bled from Rune's eyes and he ran at his tormentor. "You fucking pig!"

Using every bit of force, he rammed into his dad's brick-wall stomach, eliciting a pained groan from the cocky asshole, and they both fell onto the dry, rough grass. They tumbled and rolled down the hill toward a babbling stream and came to a stop on the embankment.

Rune pinned his dad down and threw a punch. Beauregarde didn't even blink, grabbing his hand and squeezing it like a car crusher.

"Ouch!" Rune cried out, his eyes watering, and hit the ground, cradling his hurt hand.

Beauregarde loomed over him and grabbed his neck in a choking hold, stifling his breathing.

"You're strangling me!" Rune croaked, his arms flailing, trying to dislodge his father's deadly grip.

He smirked and sat on Rune's chest, keeping his palm pressed against Rune's throat. "Good, then it's working."

Taking a breath felt like sucking air through a squashed straw. With his strength dwindling fast, Rune attempted to whack his father's arm, but the asshole wouldn't let go.

Blotches of black and purple filled Rune's eyes, distorting his sight. Would he die or just pass out? His eyelids fluttered, and he struggled to keep conscious.

*Smack!* His dad slammed forward, loosening his grasp and smothering Rune's face. Using his last stores of energy, he pushed Beauregarde off him and the bastard landed with a thud on the dry, dusty earth. Oxygen whooshed into Rune's lungs and he coughed, his chest stiff and aching.

An elderly white-haired man appeared overhead, with a glowing moonlit aura. Was it God? *Am I dead? Am I in heaven?* Rune tried to make eye contact, blurriness warping his vision, and his eyes slipped shut.

* * * *

"Ugh," Rune groaned. His head pounded with a full-blown, skull-splitting headache. *Not a dream. Definitely not a dream.* He rubbed his temples and attempted to sit up.

A warm, gentle hand pressed on his shoulder. "Lie still."

"Where am I?"

"In a safe place."

A downpour of memories gushed into his mind — leaning on the man, stumbling down stairs into a tunnel, his dad trying to kill him. Rune snapped his eyes open. "Where is he? Is he dead?"

The white-haired man smiled down at him. "I left him by the stream. He'll be fine."

"Oh." Rune wasn't sure whether to be happy or sad about that.

"Would you like something to eat?"

The man had wise eyes, like Moses in one of those old movies. "Yes, please."

"Is fresh beef mince all right?"

Better than all right—perfect. Rune's favorite. He nodded.

The man smiled and left the room. A full human who understood Rune's needs... How could that be? From everything he'd heard, most humans had no idea about the existence of vampires.

Rune sat up in the cushiony double bed and studied the compact but cozy space, lit by large candles. There were no windows, only a small wooden wardrobe and matching bedside table. His jeans and T-shirt hung neatly over the back of a chair near the vanity mirror.

The door creaked open and the man entered, carrying a tray with a glass of special wine and a plate of raw beef mince, as promised. He placed it on the bed.

Rune stared at him, still trying to get his head around where the guy could have gotten his vampire knowledge. "How do you know what I am?" *Shit.* He shouldn't have asked that. Not yet, not before knowing the old man's agenda. He had to be concussed or something.

The man's reassuring eyes eased his stress. "My wife is a half-caste."

"Really? Can I meet her?" Rune picked up his plate, scooped a big mound of meat onto his fork and shoveled it into his mouth.

A sad smile tugged at the man's paper-thin lips. "Unfortunately not...but maybe one day."

Obviously she'd been captured and held prisoner in the Norway compound, or had she met the same fate as his mothers? It sounded like the man still held out hope. And Rune didn't want to be the one to dash his savior's dreams.

The old guy sat on a chair by the bed, his movements stiff and slow like Tin Man.

"How did you stop my dad?"

The man's eyes filled with disgust and disbelief. "*That* was your father?"

Rune gobbled down some more meat and had a big gulp of special wine. "Yeah. It's kind of complicated."

"I see." He said it like he totally understood Rune's need not to give any further explanation.

"So how did you do it, knock him out? He's a full vampire and you're a human. Humans don't have the strength..."

The man pulled out a gun from a holster at the back of his belt. "We have resources."

"Bullets don't kill us."

"I know. And this won't kill either, unless it's misused." The man angled the weapon in the candlelight. "It isn't a regular gun. It's a stun gun, of sorts. It uses short bursts of concentrated sunlight."

*That must be how Sub Rosa manages to catch and control the vampire population.* Rune stared at the shiny black pistol, too scared to touch it. "No way..."

"It's true." The man re-holstered it. "I don't want it to accidentally go off."

"How did you get it?" Rune hoed into the remaining two mouthfuls of his meal.

165

"Some previous Violet visitors disarmed a Sub Rosa guard and brought it to me as a gift, a thank you for providing them with protection. They understood that I'd need to protect myself from some vampires, just as I protected them from some humans."

Rune put the tray on the bedside table and polished off his goblet of special wine. This guy had real hero traits, the exact sort of man he wished he had for a father. "Cool."

"So tell me… What are your plans?"

"I don't have any…anymore. I came here to find my dad and ask him to release my mothers from the Norway compound. They helped me meet him and he screwed me over. He arranged for their capture and" — Rune sniffled and wiped his nose with the back of his hand — "now they're dead."

The man squeezed Rune's arm, his touch warm, soothing, caring. "I'm so sorry to hear that. You're welcome to stay here until you work out what you want to do."

"Thanks, but — "

The man raised his hand in a stopping motion. "You look mature, though you seem young, too inexperienced to be wandering around on your own."

Rune puffed out his still-developing chest. "I can look after myself."

"Maybe. But for now, it's in your best interests to remain hidden. I don't imagine you want to meet up with your dad again just yet."

*Yeah…* He had a point. It made total sense to stay far away from Beauregarde, forever if possible. Although Rune didn't know his dick of a dad well, their brief meet-ups had shown him to be a dangerous combination of unpredictable and vindictive. "I suppose I can hang around for a little while."

A mega smile turned the man's face into wrinkle city. "Excellent. I'll enjoy having the company. I haven't had much since I died."

"Died?" The guy looked pretty alive to him. Unless Rune had fallen into the depths of unconsciousness, delirium or was living out his own personal *The Sixth Sense* moment.

"I figured 'faking it' would allow me to safely continue my work without being disturbed."

*Phew.* So he hadn't imagined the conversation or been talking to a ghost. *Good to know.* "What sort of work? And how did you fake your own death?"

The man mirrored Rune's position. "In answer to your first question, many years ago I made it my mission to save you lot from Sub Rosa and find a way to free those who were captured. The saving part has gone well, mostly, but not the freeing part so much…yet. But I won't give up. I'll never give up." The man might be physically frail but his eyes shone with inner strength, self-belief and fierce determination.

"In terms of my death, I had a heart attack about four years ago. I'd been living upstairs in the main house and hiding the Jades and Violets down here. An unexpected visitor gave me some information about my missing son, and soon after he left, my heart stopped. It was a result of delayed shock, I suspect.

"My housekeeper found me and I got rushed to hospital by ambulance. When I came to, I thought, *what if I were dead? What would happen to my mission? What would happen to my wife?* Then I realized, maybe there could be some advantages to people thinking I'd died. My heart attack gave me the opportunity to pretend it was true." A scheming smile spread across his lips, almost straightening out the wrinkles around his mouth.

"What *if* I were 'dead'? I started weighing up all the pros and cons of faking my death and the idea took root. It really resonated with me. The more I thought about it, the more it reinforced the many positives. So I rang the Jade who had been staying with me at the time, and she helped me escape one night, altering the computer records to list me as 'deceased'."

"That's pretty cool. And no one questioned it?"

The man smirked. "Well, if they did, they would have soon given up, seeing as I got 'cremated'."

Rune laughed. "Nice one."

"I thought so. She also dug me a short-cut emergency exit, leading straight into the bush to help keep me hidden when I needed to venture out. That has helped significantly." The man almost vibrated with pride for the huge feat he'd accomplished. And so he should. Today's technology made it hard to stay off the grid and almost impossible to successfully pull off something so huge.

"Anyway, I should let you have more rest. I'll wake you up when I bring you breakfast. What would you like?"

A diet high in raw beef mince was the vampire-human hybrid equivalent of eating fast food. Nutritionally speaking, he should mix it up...and include options with a broader range of vitamins, minerals and fiber. *Nah...* Stuff that. He'd get back to a balanced diet once he recovered. "The same again would be awesome."

# Chapter Twelve

## A Taste of the Future

*Hobart, Tasmania, November 2011*

*A cherub with rosy cheeks and golden hair grabbed Rune's hand and led him up a winding path out of the woods. They emerged into the sunlight, and she transformed into a hot blonde with enticing jade, violet-flecked eyes.*

*At the front of her mansion, she stopped beside a large marble statue, her white, almost see-through dress billowing in the breeze. Rune touched her cheek, but his hand was no longer that of a fourteen-year-old boy.*

*He had morphed into a man dressed in a tight black T-shirt and cargo pants, his dark brown hair short and styled, the long top layers hanging forward as he leaned in for a kiss.*

*Her gaze flicked to his, and with a cheeky grin, she turned and flitted up the stairs. Rune chased after her and found her lying naked on a double bed, with white chiffon and red rosettes draping around the four-poster frame. Her pure fair skin glimmered in the late afternoon light, spilling through the window, casting a lustful spell on him.*

*Rune threw off his clothes, his heart hammering, his breathing erratic, and joined her on the bed. His body crackled with high-voltage electricity. He scooped her into his arms, brushed her pouty lips with his and pressed against her skin.*

*Tingles zipped between them, like their energy and excitement fed off each other and escalated. Tongues and bodies entwined and they became luminous, their brightness blinding.*

Rune's eyes jolted open, his heart banging against his sternum like a battering ram, his cock swollen and aching with the need for release. *Where am I? Where is she?* Darkness. His super-sharp vision zoomed into focus and he glanced around the small, familiar room.

*That's right.*

He lay in bed, in the safety of the white-haired man's bunker. All the candles had burned right down, so he must have slept through to mid-morning. Possibly longer.

Actually, where was the man? He said he'd be back and wake him up for breakfast. Maybe he thought he'd let him sleep? A shiver of unease rippled along his spine and lodged in his stomach. Something didn't feel right.

Throwing the blankets off his legs, Rune jumped up and searched through the rabbit warren of rooms. He reached a larger, lounge room-kitchen area and the kind old guy lay sprawled out on the floor, his ashen, clammy skin the blue-gray shade of near death.

Rune dropped to his knees beside him and put his ear to the man's chest. His faint heartbeat fluttered and his chest rose and fell in an irregular rhythm. He held the man's shoulders and gently shook.

"Are you okay?"

No reply, just more loud, gurgling, abnormal breaths.

Rune ran his palms along the man's arms, assessing for any injuries, looking for even the smallest response, and clasped his hands. "Squeeze my hands if you can hear me."

The man's fingers tapped Rune's skin. Could he hear or was the movement just a reflex, a spasm? Rune repositioned the man into side-lying. "You'll be okay," he said, over and over, like the repetition would make it real.

*What should I do?* He couldn't take a registered dead man to hospital.

The old guy coughed and wheezed and slumped onto his back, air expiring from his lungs like a popped balloon.

"No!" Rune yelled. No one else could die because of him or he'd never recover. He cradled the man's head and shoulders and rocked back and forth, trying to stifle the sobs scraping his airway. He hardly even knew the guy, yet the sorrow cut right to his soul. Tears poured from Rune's eyes, bathing the man in salty grief.

"Please be all right."

The man remained limp within his arms.

"Come on, please. I can't lose you as well. I just can't." He hugged him close, his tears soaking into the old guy.

When they were both drenched, Rune pulled back and studied the man's face through blurred vision. Had his eyelids flickered? Rune wiped his watery eyes with the back of his hand and leaned in closer.

The man gasped and his eyes flipped open. "Rune?" he croaked, trying to regain focus.

"Yes, I'm here." *Stay with me. Please stay with me.* "I'm just going to move you to somewhere more comfortable."

He groaned in what sounded like agreement.

Rune gently lifted him onto the closest three-seater couch and propped up the man's back with pillows. "What do you need?"

"Water." Even with Rune's supersonic hearing, he had to strain to make out the man's soft voice.

Rune grabbed him a full glass and helped him take a couple of sips. "I think you should eat too."

"Can't."

He lit a candle, kneeled beside the man and their gazes locked. "You have to. I'll make you chicken soup."

The man's eyes still looked glazed and heavy, and his forehead scrunched up like a crinkle-cut chip. "You can cook?"

"I had three mothers. Of course I can."

The old guy chuckled and Rune had never heard a better sound.

He continued to play nurse to the man and, within a few days, the guy had not only fully recovered but also looked younger. Younger and fitter. How could that be? Vampire genes were known to ward off old age, but the man was full human.

Rune had never heard of anything turning the clock back for mortals, especially after illness. If anything, they went the other way. He could only put it down to one thing—his tears. They were the only vampire substance the man had absorbed, ingested.

"It makes sense," the man said, after Rune explained his theory. "You're a very smart and kind boy."

*Boy?* "Thanks." Rune half smiled and sat opposite him at the wobbly wooden table.

The man shuffled forward in his seat, the warm LED lighting giving his skin an extra healthy glow. "Can I ask you a favor?"

"Sure. Anything."

"Can I bottle some of your tears?"

When he'd said 'anything', he hadn't anticipated *that.* "Why?"

"For medicinal purposes."

*For fountain-of-youth purposes, more like it.* "Are you going to sell them?" Rune searched his eyes for an honest answer.

The man balked. "No. What makes you ask that?"

"Because you could make a killing off an anti-aging tonic."

"It'll be purely for personal use, I promise." The man's serious, unblinking eyes suggested he meant what he said.

Should he trust the guy? He still didn't know him well enough to be sure. Though the man had put himself at risk to save him without knowing what Rune could offer. Would a scumbag do that? Not likely. "All right, I'll do it. But you'll have to put on a sad movie or two, because I can't just cry on demand."

The man smiled. "I've got *West Side Story*. It makes me cry every time. Will that work?"

Rune hadn't heard of the show. *Finding Nemo* was the last film that had caused him to squeeze out some tears. Of course, he'd only just turned seven at the time. "I don't know. But I'll give it a go."

While the man put the movie on, Rune got comfortable on the couch. Two-and-a-half hours later, the story of the star-crossed lovers had successfully wrung out twenty vials of tears.

The man touched Rune's wet face. "Now that's impressive."

Rune sniffled and laughed at the same time. "What do you plan to do with the tears exactly?"

"Drink them."

"Drink them?"

The man levered himself up off the couch and furniture-walked to the kitchenette. He poured himself a glass of water, then turned and propped his elbows on the bench. "Well, it's either that or inject them. I can't say I'm a big fan of needles. You?"

"Nope. Needles suck."

"They certainly do." He gulped down the water and refilled his glass. "I'll start with having a couple of teardrops a day and see how I go. I don't want to overdo it. I just want enough to keep me well, at least until I see my wife and son again."

Rune swallowed the lump of dread wedged in his throat. "Do you know where they are?"

"My wife's in the Norway compound—or at least she was up until 2007. I had to stop writing to her when I 'died'. As for my son, the last I heard, he's supposedly safe." The man averted his weepy eyes. "I've spent so much time looking for him and his wife. And I won't give up. I won't ever stop."

"So what's the plan?"

The man's expression said, *isn't it obvious?* "Keep searching, look for leads and try to find a way to shut down Sub Rosa. It should be easier with two of us."

Rune stepped back and held up his hands in a *just-a-minute, don't-get-too-excited* gesture. "I still don't know how long I'm sticking around."

The man smiled like he could forecast the future. "You're free to leave whenever you want. You won't go, though. Not yet. Maybe not ever."

\* \* \* \*

Rune shrugged on his black woolen coat. "I'm just going to grab something for dinner. Do you need anything?"

The man held a torch and shoved his Taser gun into the holster hanging at the back of his waist. "Hang on. I'll come with you."

Rune stopped in the dark corridor and turned to him. "Are you sure you should? I mean, you're still recovering."

The man did a James Brown spin. "I'm fine. Better than fine. In fact, I feel good. Great. Better than I have in years!"

Watching the age strip off him as each day passed was so cool. He'd gone from a white-haired, frail old man to a gray-haired, fit-looking sixty-year-old. "There's that other small detail too. You're meant to be dead. What if someone sees you?"

"I doubt it. No one will see me, because they're not expecting to. If anything, they'll just notice a guy with his grandson." Rune couldn't say no to that self-assured smirk.

They followed the tunnel and used the short-cut emergency exit the man had spoken about, and finally showed him once he'd stabilized. Climbing the flight of stone steps, Rune pressed the obscured exit button on the wall. The trap door opened overhead, sending streams of moonbeams through the foliage and adding extra light to their path.

Rune had to check with the man one more time before they stepped outside. "Are you sure you're strong enough?"

The guy stared back at him with a *you're-not-talking-me-out-of-this* look. "Yes. Remember, up until you came, I'd been going out alone with no adverse effects. Plus, now I'm fitter, appear younger and have you to protect me."

Rune raised his eyebrows. "So you're putting all your faith in a fourteen-year-old bodyguard?"

"Not just any fourteen-year-old bodyguard. You're special and you know it."

*Special, really?* He'd always seen himself as different, but that didn't quite mean the same thing. His mums had valued him, loved him unconditionally, though they were biased. They were his parents. That was their job.

This guy had no reason to talk him up or to even like him, but he did and he didn't hide it. It made Rune all warm inside, like the man's words were a heat bag, comforting his injured soul.

"Come on. Let's go." The rejuvenated man switched off and pocketed the torch, snapping Rune back to the moment.

They stepped into the open and the man swept his gaze across the dappled, moonlit area like an experienced professional spy, then focused in on Rune. "Right, well, you go off and do your hunting and I'll keep an eye out for any strays."

Rune stood firm on the mossy forest floor. "I'm not leaving you out here on your own. I'm your bodyguard, remember?"

The guy pulled out his Taser gun and cocked it, ready for firing. His roguish grin made him look like a cowboy from an old-school western, ready to tear up the town. "I'll cramp your style."

"You mean, I'll cramp yours."

The man laughed, rich and full and deep. "Seriously, I'm too heavy footed. I'll scare all your dinner options away."

He did have a point. Full humans seemed to have missed out on the silent stealth gene.

"I'll just wait right here. How does that sound?"

"Hmm-m... Promise me you won't wander off."

The man gripped the gun sideways over his chest and held up his other hand, palm out, like some sort of military salute. "I swear."

Rune sniffed the air. *Deer, close by.* He tracked the scent to a nearby creek and found an adult male drinking from the edge of the bank, its antlers a sharp bone sculpture curved into the shape of a heart.

*Beautiful, too perfect a specimen to kill.* Saliva sprang into Rune's mouth, opposing his thoughts. He needed to eat. Survival overrode beauty. Rune pounced, leaping high and fast through the air.

"Rune! Quick!" The man. Had he gotten in trouble?

Rune landed with a heavy thud, splashing his prey and himself with cold, sobering spring water. The deer bucked and took off, like a plane charging down the runway. Rune ran back to where he'd left the man. *Please be okay.*

In less than two minutes he found him, crouched down among some fluorescent green ferns, a decent distance from where they'd agreed he would wait.

"Are you all right? What are you doing all the way out here? You promised —"

"Shh-h-h... Come here." The man's whisper sounded harsh, no-nonsense.

Rune walked over to him without making a sound, and a Jade woman lay on the ground, unconscious. "Is she okay?"

"I'm not sure. I don't think she's eaten for several days. Can you kill something for her?"

"How about a rabbit? It'll be easier and quicker than a deer."

"Yes. Just hurry."

Rune searched the forest. Where had all the animals disappeared to? It felt as though they'd scattered, knowing he was on the prowl. His nose twitched. Wombat? He'd only ever read about their scent, dank and musty. They were an Australian vampire delicacy, apparently. Maybe he'd have a little taste himself.

A rustling in the bushes just ahead drew him forward. He peered into the tangle of leaves and roots and spotted a large, fat wombat, waddling back to his underground home. They had a bit in common—hiding during the day and coming out to feed at night.

He crept up close until he could almost touch the wombat's fur, feel the heat radiating off its chubster body, taste the tang of its hot blood. Before he could grab the fat little thing, it disappeared down a hole in the ground.

*Shit!* He dove in after it, grabbed one of its hind legs and yanked. They shot backward out of the burrow like a cannon ball and thumped onto the moist earth. The wombat scratched and scrambled but Rune refused to let go.

He sank his teeth into the largest throbbing artery and guzzled a mouthful of blood. It was an odd, gamey taste, though good enough.

Holding the carcass in his arms, he ran at triple speed to where the man kept watch over the starving Jade. Rune dropped to his knees and angled the wombat, ready to drain the remainder of its life force. "Open her mouth."

The man held the Jade's lips open and the blood drip, drip, dripped onto her tongue.

Rune couldn't see past the beefy brown beast. "Is she swallowing?"

"Not yet, but her mouth is watering, which is a good sign."

Rune craned his neck to see around the carcass. "She just licked her lips and gulped." With aching arms, he held the wombat in place, squeezed out the last few drops of blood, then put it aside and scanned over the weary Jade. "Do you think she'll be okay?"

The man patted Rune's back. "Thanks to your life-saving efforts, yes."

The Jade coughed and her eyes sprang open.

Rune plastered on his most dazzling, you're-safe smile.

Her pupils dilated until her eyeballs were murky black pools. She edged away, out of Rune's reach, jumped up and took off before he could blink.

Rune turned to the man. "She must have seen my Violetness and freaked out." He slammed his palm against his forehead. "Uh! Sorry. I should have thought of that."

The man touched his arm and a current of reassurance flowed between them. "Don't worry about it. You saved her life and that's what's most important."

* * * *

*Hobart, Simon and Grace's place, December 2011*

The vampire tears had repaired the wound on Grace's neck and stabilized her vital signs, but they couldn't cure her affliction. Though Simon knew what should. He sped to Sub Rosa, snuck into the lab and stuffed four vials of the gold trial serum into his brown leather satchel.

No human trials of the cure had been done yet, but he didn't have time to wait. The rat experiments had been a great success—however, he couldn't guarantee the results would translate to humans. There could be unforeseen side effects. The pressure of the situation meant he'd just have to take that risk. Grace had already been infected for two days, leaving only one day until she fully transformed.

Simon dashed home and raced back up to the bedroom.

Empty.

She'd gone.

Hyperventilating breaths sent his head into an oxygen-deprived spin. Where was she? Simon stumbled into the corridor and searched right and left. Where could she be? He'd have to find her, and quickly. He couldn't let her run loose. The damage she could cause... His heart pounded a punishing post-run pace. He couldn't think about that. One thing at a time.

Pipes lurched and water gushed. *The bathroom down the hall.*

Simon peeked through the open doorway. Grace was bent over the basin, cupping her hands and filling them with cold water to refresh her face. Her hair shone with raven flecks. *Fuck.* His body shook with uncontrollable stress.

She looked up, her muted violet eyes staring back at him in the mirror, a pained smile tugging at her mouth, revealing her incisors part way to becoming fangs, poking over the top of her bottom lip. She fucking needed a feed and he was the easily accessible, tempting human morsel.

Simon's breath caught in his throat and scalded like acid corroding his flesh. He had to do this. She would want him to...if she were in a suitable state to give consent.

"I'm burning, like fire's in my blood." Her eyes, her voice begged for his assistance.

"I know." Simon approached her, slow and cautious, and thrust a vial into her field of vision. "Drink this. It'll help."

Her pale forehead buckled, like faulty venetian blinds, but she accepted the cure. She chugged it back, and he slipped in close and poured another vial over the bite.

Grace shuddered, flicking ice-cold water and glittery gold fluid across his white top. "What are you doing?"

"I promise I'll explain later." He held her hand and directed her back to their bedroom.

Simon lay down and Grace burrowed into him. She smelled as though she'd bathed in high potency frankincense and myrrh. As the seconds passed, the scent faded and the soaring heat from her skin began to dissipate, her fever subsiding. Either the cure had kicked in or he'd intervened too late. Only time held the answer.

Grace's breathing slowed and she fell into a deep, hopefully restorative, sleep. Exhaustion hit Simon like a head-on crash with a bus full of airborne valium. He roused, several hours later, with Eden's cat Thornton curled up in Grace's place.

"Grace?" Lethargy lingered in his groggy voice.

No answer.

That kicked him into high alert. He charged through the house, checking every room. She'd disappeared. Simon stopped and bent forward, bracing his hands just above his knees and taking a long, deep breath. *Fuck.*

Rick's cat, Smokey, jumped onto the windowsill and sat in the weak, cooling rays from the setting sun.

*Meow.*

Simon went over and patted him. "You're such a lush." He stopped mid-stroke. A space in the driveway could only mean... Grace's car was gone.

"Fuck! Fu-u-uck!" He thumped his fist on his thigh. Was the vampire venom too strong for the cure to take effect?

Smokey stared at him and tapped his arm for more pats.

"If she's a newborn on the loose, Hobart's fucked!"

# Chapter Thirteen

An Introduction into the World

*Sub Rosa, Norway site, December 2011*

Rick thrummed his fingers on the desk and glanced up at the clock in the open-plan office—eleven-fifty-five. Eden and the kids would arrive any minute and he still hadn't had a chance to tell her dad about the escape plan. Now she'd have to do it while he made his way to the control room. It wasn't ideal, not ideal at all. He fingered his lanyard ID, his pulse pounding, and stepped into the corridor.

Just before he reached reception, five security guards approached him with *don't-fuck-with-me* looks on their hard, chiseled faces. *Fuck.* His heart stammered but he tried to muster his most convincing, poised demeanor.

The guard he'd met in the control room took the lead. "Sir, you need to come with us."

*Not a question, a demand.* Rick subtly wiped his sweaty palms on his pants. "What's this about?"

"Everything will be explained." The guard's tone and stance said *but not now*.

Rick smiled at the stony-faced group. "Can't we just get it sorted here?"

"No." The same burly guy grunted.

Didn't the others speak English? Maybe they were mute, giving control over to their leader. Two of the pack edged in beside him, interlocked their arms through his and dragged him forward. They marched down the passageway and Rick struggled to keep in step. Where were they taking him? How would he get away? And what about Eden and the kids?

* * * *

Eden concealed her eyes with the disposable brown contact lenses, packed Scarlett and Blake into a taxi and traveled to Sub Rosa.

Twenty minutes later, Eden pushed the twin pram through the entrance of the Norway site and right into a revoltingly sweet, floral-scented reception area.

The receptionist eyed her with undisguised suspicion. "Can I help you?"

"I hope so. I'm Eden Hartman and I'm meeting my husband for lunch." Her stinging, teary eyes squinted to read the woman's name—Rochelle.

The woman looked her up and down. "You're Rick's wife."

"That's right." Eden forced a relaxed, cheerful smile onto her face and hoped it looked believable.

Disappointment marred Rochelle's controlled expression, like she'd just found out her day spa appointment had been double-booked. *What is that about?* "You must wear contacts as well."

"Sorry?" Eden subtly dabbed at the descending teardrop on her cheek.

"Rick has a lot of problems with his and it looks like you do too."

Looked like she'd paid *a lot* of attention to Rick.

The woman's smile hardly touched her lips, let alone her eyes. "Please take a seat. I'll let him know you're here."

Eden sat on one of the uncomfortable, neutral-colored couches and kept an eye on the woman and the kids. Rochelle pressed a button on the switchboard and continued typing. Twenty seconds passed without her speaking into the headset. Why hadn't Rick answered?

A niggle wormed its way through her stomach, leaving a trail of worry. Maybe he'd stepped away from his desk for a minute. But he knew they'd be arriving at midday. Eden fidgeted with the pram handle and glanced up at the bold black-and-white clock. Two minutes and nothing.

The receptionist tried again. After thirty seconds she made eye contact with Eden. "He's not answer—"

"Is it possible to buzz me through? I can wait in his office and surprise him." Did that sound too anxious, too forceful, too desperate?

The receptionist stared, seeming to consider the pros and cons of Eden's proposal.

How could she get her to let her through? *Ah yes!* "I'm on maternity leave at the moment but I work at Sub Rosa too, back in Hobart. So I have security clearance, if that's what you're concerned about. Go ahead and check." Eden wiped her weepy eyes with the back of her hand.

Rochelle's gaze shifted to her computer monitor and she started typing.

Eden stood and pushed the pram over to the reception desk.

After the longest minute in history, the woman looked up and handed her a visitor ID tag and security pass. "You'll have to find your own way through to his office. I can't leave reception—"

*Perfect.* "That's okay. If you give me directions, I'll be fine. If I get lost, I'll just ask someone."

"If you have a mobile phone, I can give you the WiFi password to access an online campus map and orientation tutorial, which takes you through the building a section at a time."

"That would be great, thanks." Eden dove into her handbag and pulled out her phone.

"The password is 'Sub_Rosa-TheCure'"

*The cure for what? Trouble makers? An elixir to eliminate anyone or anything standing in the way of lining the pockets of power-and-money-hungry bigots?* The branding made her sick. "Thanks so much for your help."

Scarlett and Blake chatted away to each other, seemingly oblivious to the danger. *Thank goodness.* She really didn't need scrutinizing eyes focusing on her trying to settle two screaming children. The less attention they had, the better.

Eden pushed through the first security door and proceeded past a corridor lined with labs and a section of empty, ghost-town-like offices. Which one was Rick's? And where were all the staff and the imprisoned Violets and Jades?

She stopped and logged in to the online orientation program to get her bearings. Her blurred vision made her phone look like a glowy, vomited mess of colors. She blinked a few times to clear her eyes and refocus.

How had Rick managed to wear the damn lenses every day for the past six weeks?

The desk allocation plan showed Rick's designated office, up on the left. The bland, gray, open-plan space had a handful of people buzzing around…with no Rick in sight.

Eden went to push the pram over to the closest group, when an older guy approached her with a warm, friendly smile. "You must be Eden."

"That's right. Is Rick around? We're supposed to be having lunch together."

He glanced at the others. "Do any of you know where Rick went?"

A short, young guy sidled up to them and smiled at Blake and Scarlett. "I saw him speaking to some security staff earlier on his way to greet you guys in reception. He probably got caught up sorting out something for them."

Panic clutched at her stomach and her hematite ring burned into her skin.

"Your husband's in demand around here." The guy said it as though he could sense her concern. "I'm sure he'll be back soon."

Her eyes welled up—and not just because of the contact lenses.

The older guy jumped in. "Why don't you make your way down to the core and wait in the cafeteria? It's nicer down there. You'll probably run into him on the way."

Eden glanced at her mobile—twelve-thirty. The security guys had obviously found something out and taken Rick somewhere for further questioning. She'd scour the whole site until she found him.

She faked her cheeriest smile and bent down in front of the kids. "We're just going to go for a little look around."

"Is everything okay, Mummy?" Scarlett whispered.

At times like this she really wished her daughter wasn't so damn perceptive. "Yes..."

Blake looked at Scarlett and burbled a few words.

Scarlett's concerned eyes glanced into Eden's. "He wants to know where Daddy is — and so do I."

Eden caressed their chubby cheeks, gulping back the tearful sob threatening to betray her. "He's been held up. He's very busy. We'll see him soon, though, okay?"

Blake smiled and kicked his legs, while Scarlett studied her with skeptical eyes.

"Okay, let's go!" Eden swallowed the mass of worry growing like an out-of-control tumor in her throat and pushed the pram up the hallway.

A couple of staff rushed by her without even a glance, like they lived in a parallel universe, on the other side of one-way glass. Most people were usually drawn to the twins. They made quite the conversation starter...in the real world.

But this was Sub Rosa, land of the surreal. In this instance, she'd take lack of attention as a blessing. The less interaction she had with the staff, the better their chance of success.

They approached a door with a frosted-glass panel. Eden peered through it and could only make out distorted shapes on the other side. She reached for the handle, her hand trembling. What would she be walking into?

# Chapter Fourteen

## Lost and Found

Eden pushed the door open just enough to check out the new section for safety.

*Jade territory.*

*With no immediate threat evident.*

*Thank goodness.*

But it still didn't stop her heart from almost beating right out of her chest. She wouldn't be able to calm down until she found Rick alive and safe.

Sunlight streams divided up the area, giving the space a feeling of false freedom, just as Rick had described.

It looked like a large airport lounge with eager yet restrained passengers biding their time, awaiting the commencement of their journey.

She pushed the pram inside and quietly closed the door. Outside of the odd announcement over the loudspeaker and a handful of staff scurrying about like lost ants, the pleasant surroundings made it hard to believe they were in such a miserable place.

Eden hurried the kids through the Jade quarters and reached another door. This one supposedly led into the central hub, described by the orientation package as the physical and intellectual core of the organization. *So that was what Rick's colleague had been referring to when he'd said 'core'.*

Light glowed around the edge of the door, as though they were about to be abducted by a landing UFO. She reached for the handle and a staff member pulled open the door from the other side. Glaring white scorched her eyeballs, and left smoldering spot fires burning black blotches into her vision.

"Mummy! It hurts!" Scarlett cried.

Eden bent down and tried to attune her already-stinging eyes to the brightness. She'd thought the brown contact lenses would act like window tint, providing some protection. They camouflaged the true, telltale, blue-violet color of her irises but didn't do anything to reduce the glare or discomfort.

Scarlett squeezed her eyes shut, her lip trembling.

Eden stroked her daughter's scrunched-up face. "It's okay, honey. Keep your eyes closed."

Streams of tears trickled down Scarlett's cheeks.

Eden glanced at Blake, her own eyes raw and watery.

He smiled, eyes wide, and flapped his arms—his signature excited move. He didn't share their sensitivity, confirming it had to be a vampire responsiveness thing. Eden blotted her eyes with a tissue. Thankfully, she had her contact-lens, hay-fever story to cover her reaction.

"Blake said we should keep going," Scarlett whispered, without opening her eyes.

Ahead on the right, a table of workers chatted in between munching on sandwiches and a range of hot meals, backlit by sunlight pouring through the large windows. The mingled pasta and roast meat scents smelled like a hospital cafeteria. Eden kept her eyes lowered from the blinding natural and artificial light blasting her from all around.

She passed by and pretended to sneeze to keep up her allergy cover story. A couple of cursory glances, a few brief smiles and the workers went back to their lunchtime conversations. Thankfully. It was a small win, but she'd take it.

Eden continued toward the end of the corridor. Still no sign of Rick. Her heart rate tripled and her breath came in short, shallow bursts. Where had they taken her husband?

"Stop!" Scarlett said, her tone firm and certain.

Eden moved to the front of the pram and squatted down until she was at eye level with her daughter. "What is it, honey?"

With her outstretched little hand, she signaled to a hallway on the right of the green-and-white exit sign, glowing overhead. "Daddy!"

Another sign pointed to the control room down a passageway on the left and offices and meeting rooms to the right. Eden pushed the pram in the direction Scarlett had indicated and scanned along the corridor.

"Stop, Mummy!"

Eden obeyed her daughter's confident instruction, put the brakes on the pram and peered through a small viewing window in a closed metal door. Sure enough, Rick sat on a sole wooden chair inside the desolate, sterile room, elbows on his knees and leaning his head against his clasped hands.

She turned to the twins and smiled. "Good work, Scarlett!"

Eden searched for a lock, a knob, a handle. "How do you open this thing?" Gliding her palms over the shiny steel surface, she felt for any bumps or hidden activators.

*Nothing.*

She pressed her shoulder up against the door and nudged. It didn't even show a hint of movement.

"Arrggh!" Eden planted the sole of her shoe against the impenetrable metal, put all of her weight behind it and pushed. The bloody thing didn't creak, let alone budge.

She turned and leaned her back against the unbreakable barrier. What could she do? She had to do something before someone noticed, before whoever had locked Rick away came back to collect him.

*Simon.* Didn't Rick say he'd increased his access privileges?

She had to call Simon...before Sub Rosa management worked out that she was onsite and they started searching for her.

Eden scrolled through her contacts, her hand shaking so much she could hardly hold her phone. Somehow, she selected Simon's number and dialed.

*Please answer.*

On the second ring, the line connected. "Eden? What's up?" Simon's strained voice leached stress, like something was wrong on his end too.

Eden cupped her hand and whispered into the phone. "I need your help. I need you to increase my settings to high-level access. *Now.*" She felt like a bitch not asking about him and Grace but—no time.

"Sure. What's going on?"

"Sorry. I can't go into it at the moment. How long before the changes take effect?"

"Once I've upgraded you? A few minutes."

*A few minutes.* Her stomach clenched and her heart and breathing stuttered then banged out a frantic pace, like she'd been jabbed with adrenaline. A lot could happen in a few minutes. Anything could go wrong.

"Okay, done."

"Thanks so much. We'll be in touch again soon." *Hopefully.*

She disconnected the call, stared at the time on the screen and waited. And waited. And waited.

Scarlett poked her head out. "What are you doing, Mummy?"

How would she explain? "Waiting for Simon's help to get Daddy out."

Fear swam in her jade, violet-flecked eyes. "But he's far away."

Eden tried to conjure up what she hoped looked like a confident, reassuring smile. "It's okay, honey. He's helping through the computer."

She checked the time again. Not even two minutes had passed. But she might as well try. If staff noticed her and the kids hanging around that same spot too much longer, they might alert security.

Eden pressed her trembling hands on the door.

Nothing.

*Shit.* How much longer?

A couple of staff walked past and she held her phone to her ear, talking in hushed tones as though on a call, and rocking the pram. The multi-tasking-mother act usually worked as an excellent suspicion diversion. Would the trend still be successful with switched-on, hypothesizing scientists?

The workers disappeared into a room at the end of the hall and she checked the time on her mobile again. Three minutes. Eden ran her hands along the length and breadth of the door and...

Nothing.

*Shit!*

Her heart thumped in her throat, her lungs constricted and her head spun with dizziness. She swayed, grabbing for the door to steady herself, and closed her eyes.

*Click.*

The door gave way and she jumped back.

"Eden?" Rick's steps ate up the distance between them and he reached her in seconds.

Blake burbled and Scarlett cheered, "Daddy!"

Eden threw her arms around Rick's neck, tears welling in her eyes. "What happened? Are you okay?"

He cupped her cheek, his touch, loving, relieved, grounding. "I'm fine. I'll fill you in later. Right now, we need to split up."

"Split up? But—"

He held her face between his warm hands. "It won't be for long, I promise. You need to trust me on this."

She tried to ignore the resistance tying knots in her stomach and nodded.

"Take Scarlett and Blake and continue out through the exit into the next building. Your dad is about three quarters of the way down on the right. Tell him we're going to deactivate the sunlight shield, and he'll only have a few seconds to move. And ask him to pass the word on to the others as well, so they're ready.

"Hopefully the glitch will give them longer, but who knows. I'd planned to give your dad and the rest of the Violets a heads-up myself but ran out of time. I only just got to tell my mum and some key Jades before coming to meet you and getting detained."

He stroked her cheekbones, stimulating acupressure points and inducing a receptive, almost hypnotic state. "When you're done, meet me at the control room, down the opposite corridor."

Her gaze remained glued to his. "What about the twins?"

"I think it's best they stay with your dad."

A wave of fresh tears filled her eyes. How could she possibly leave her babies? Yes, Ethan was her dad, but he was a stranger to her and the kids. And if he didn't approve of her marriage to Rick, would he even accept them?

She'd re-evaluate whether to leave the kids in her dad's care, depending on his response once they met. "How will we get anywhere near the control room? They're going to be looking for us soon, if not already."

"I'll find a way." Rick's stare said, *We can do this.* Then he kissed her, infusing their connection with love, affection and an indescribable tenderness. "I love you." Those three special words had never held so much meaning. Their genuine sentiment stamped a permanent mark right onto her heart.

Rick clasped Eden's hand and walked over to Blake and Scarlett.

Blake gurgled and kicked his arms and legs.

"Hi, Daddy!" Scarlett squealed.

Rick put his finger to his lips and kneeled in front of the pram. "Sh-h-h."

Scarlett stared at Rick, her little face puzzled. "Your eyes look funny, Daddy."

"It's okay, sweetie." Rick removed the patchy brown contact lenses. "Much better, see?" His eyes had returned to their natural light jade color, though they were watery, bloodshot and red-rimmed. *Far from better.* But then he smiled his irresistible Daddy smile and kissed Blake and Scarlett on the forehead. "Make sure you're good for Mummy."

The twins' little heads bobbed up and down like nodding novelty dogs in the back window of a car on a bumpy road.

Eden discarded her own partially disintegrated contact lenses and, although her eyes were still irritated, thanked God that the stinging stopped.

Rick rose to his feet and held Eden's hands. "Now go — and hurry."

"Be careful." Eden couldn't say all she wanted to, not without worrying the kids and possibly alerting Sub Rosa security. So she spoke silent words of love, encouragement and don't-risk-everything-to-be-a-hero through her pleading eyes.

"You too."

"Good luck, Daddy, from both of us," Scarlett said in a quiet little voice.

"Thanks. I'll see you soon, okay?" Rick's smile looked solid, steady, self-assured, but was it all for show?

* * * *

Andy charged down the gray corridor, his teeth clamped shut like a triggered bear trap. "Where is he?"

He'd just spent thirty hours in transit with his senior management team — Worried, Distressed, Interested — now trailing behind him as he powered ahead to interrogate Rick in person, only to find out that his chief suspect had disappeared.

Jetlag and frustration had pushed him right past the knife-edge of anger into vein-popping, finger-stabbing, wall-punching rage. How could the elite of the security-guard service let this happen?

The head of security tried to keep up with Andy's blistering pace. "We're not sure, sir."

"You told me you had him. What the fuck happened?" Rick had better be close by and cooperative or there'd be painful ramifications for him and Andy's so-called top-notch staff.

"Um... He, um... His w-wife, um..." The big burly guy suddenly looked like a primary school kid in the principal's office.

Andy stopped and glared at him. "His wife *what*?" His tone could crush bone.

"S-she um-m...f-found him and ah...o-opened the door and...he ah-h...escaped. But he can't have gone too far. His security access and pass have been deactivated."

"And what about *her* pass?"

"Ah-h..." Not done. Another dumb-as-fuck oversight. Did he have to spell out every single fucking step?

Andy had been ready for a fight for hours, his hands fisted for so long that they spasmed and cramped. He stretched out his aching fingers and curled them back up until his knuckles turned white and his nails dug into his palms. "What the fuck are you waiting for? Do it *now*!"

# Chapter Fifteen

### Turning the Tide

Power-walking with the pram through the Violet quarters, Eden darted her eyes from cell to cell, scrutinizing each Violet male. Would she recognize her own father?

The only image she had of him came from an aged, sepia photo taken when he'd married her mother over sixty-five years ago. Time pressure pounded at her temples. *Come on, Dad.*

"Mummy, over here!" Scarlett had somehow gotten out of the pram and toddled off ahead.

"Scarlett! Wait!"

She ignored Eden and kept on going.

Eden gripped the pram handles hard. "Hold on, little buddy," she said to Blake, and chased after her daughter.

Within arm's reach, Scarlett stopped. Eden swerved to the right, just missing her.

"Here he is, Mummy." She pointed her tiny finger at the solitary man behind the sunlight bars.

He stared back at them, his violet eyes aglow, his black eyebrows drawn down into a scowl—or was it wariness? The man looked like a mid-forties, color version of her father on his wedding day. It amazed her how little time had affected him. The vampire gene really did have youth-retaining properties.

She opened her mouth to speak but the words got lost between her brain and her lips.

He crossed his arms and tapped his foot. "Can I help you?"

"I hope so. It's me. Your daughter."

"Eva?" He studied her like a treasured relic he'd just discovered. "Come in."

She hesitated at the sunlight bars, but Rick had assured her they could breach them with no dangerous side effects. Eden pushed through, the bars hot and sending a rubber-band-snapping sensation across her skin.

Then the heat stopped.

She'd made it.

Moisture swam in her eyes and she hugged her dad.

*Zap!*

Eden broke the embrace and jolted her head around.

Scarlett jumped back, her pale face frightened. "Mummy, I can't get in."

"Just wait there. Okay, honey?"

Scarlett pouted, her lower lip sticking out in protest, but she nodded.

Eden turned back to her dad. "I go by Eden now. It's kind of a long story. And here are Scarlett and Blake, your grandchildren." Fear clawed at her heart. How would he react? Scarlett clearly had some Jade qualities.

"My half-Jade grandchildren." He shook his head in fatherly disappointment. "Of all the men you could have chosen…"

Eden shoved her hands on her hips. "Rick's a good man. A great man, actually. And you'll see that too when you get to know him better."

"A Jade's a Jade." His lips were tight, rigid.

She stamped her foot. "Come on, Dad. That's so narrow-minded and discriminatory. You need to take each person on their own merits. Give him a chance. He's going to disable the sunlight bars to get you and the others out of here."

"It can't be done." He crossed his arms, blocking out the idea, a smug smile on his lips, like he'd rather see a Jade fail, proven wrong, than gain his own freedom. Her dad had chosen not just to cut, but to saw off his nose to spite his face. *Yeah, smart move. Not.*

"Rick has found a way. You just have to be ready. No stuffing around. You've only got a few seconds' grace before the back-up generator kicks in."

His gaze held firm on hers, like a heavy hand pressing her down. "It's not possible."

*Negative. So damn negative.* And all because Rick came from Jade stock instead of Violet. No wonder the clans had gotten stuck in the Sub Rosa compound. They wouldn't even work together to save themselves when they had the opportunity. "Yes, it is! We can't muck around. We have limited time."

He grasped her arms, his violet eyes listen-to-your-father stern. "You may as well forget it. It's not going to happen."

She yanked her arms from his hold, glaring at him with a retaliating, listen-to-your-daughter stare. "Dad, give him the benefit of the doubt. There's no harm in being prepared, is there?"

He mulled over her comment, as though debating whether agreeing to a Jade plan—even one that benefited him and the other Violets—could be considered treason. "I suppose." His tone sounded reluctant, weighing down his words. "Tell the others. We'll discuss your Jade sympathies later."

She huffed. Her dad was so closed-minded. But they had no time to stand around and argue the point. Instead, Eden sprinted from cell to cell, explaining an express version of the escape plan to the other Violet captives. Part way through, one of the Violets told her she'd get the word out to the rest of them, using her powers of telepathy.

Relief washed over Eden and she rushed back to her father. The pram sat right up close to the sunlight bars and he smiled, actually smiled, and even laughed with Blake and Scarlett. However, as soon as he saw her, the dour mask returned and he stepped away from the twins.

Eden fought back the grin pushing at her lips. "All done. Now, I just need to ask you a really huge favor." The stress at his possible rejection erased the short-lived smirk. She straightened up and stood tall. "I need you to look after Blake and Scarlett while I find Rick."

"No."

She couldn't believe he'd actually flat-out refused. She had to find a way to convince her dad or his negativity would win out and Rick's plan would fail. Then all their lives would be in serious danger.

A hint of tenderness softened his defiant violet eyes. "It's too dangerous." He said it like he couldn't live with losing her again. And the realization that he cared, really cared, about her and was afraid for her safety hit her right in the center of the heart.

Tears burned like a blowtorch to the back of her eyes. How she'd longed for that sort of parental love. But she couldn't bask in it, couldn't let the emotion delay her from the greater goal. She'd already wasted more time than she'd intended, getting around to some of the other Violets. She had to keep moving. "He needs me. He needs a second person to override the system."

The diamond-hard glint returned to Ethan's eyes. "There has to be another way. Only a Jade would put his wife and family at risk."

*Back to that again. Ugh.* "What other alternative is there? Who else could he totally trust? Hm-m-m?" Her dad had really started to get on her nerves, anger shunting through her veins and making her blood boil. But maybe fury and frustration were a good thing, maybe they'd help her feel less stressed and more focused.

"Given the predicament he's put us in, I don't have time to come up with an alternat—"

"Enough. Like he'd rush back to you and ask for your assistance after you punched him." His eyes flared, priming for a retaliation, but she beat him to it. "I'm going. Look after the kids."

Eden hugged Blake and Scarlett and kissed their soft, precious cheeks. "Granddad's going to look after you for a bit, okay? Mummy's got to help Daddy."

They nodded in unison. She kissed them one more time then took off down the corridor to rejoin Rick.

In the central hub, she found him hovering in front of the control room.

Rick's face looked grave. "I can't get in. They deactivated my pass and security access."

"Let me try mine." She moved past him and pressed her palms to the door.

*Nothing.*

She moved their position.

Not even the hint of a click. A lightning bolt of panic struck her and blasted through her jangled nerves. "They must have deactivated mine too."

"Fuck!" He slammed his fist against the impenetrable glass window.

A head jutted out from under the control desk. "Someone's in there!"

Rick followed Eden's pointed finger to the startled man. "It's the maintenance guy from the other day."

Rick smiled and waved the guy over.

The man's dark blue overalls hung off him, droopy and tired, reflecting his facial expression.

He opened the door and stood in the threshold.

Rick's megawatt, charming smile made its appearance. "Hey, mate, for some reason my security access isn't working, so could you do me a favor and let us in? Apparently there's some corrupt worker on the loose and we've been asked to man the control panel as a precautionary measure."

"I don't know. I don't have authorization..."

The high wattage smile faded, replaced by Rick's serious, high-pressure sell. "Do you want to be responsible for a hacker gaining access and totally fucking up the system? There'll be angry Violets and Jades everywhere!"

The guy hesitated a second, two, three, four, then pushed the door open to let them past.

Rick gave a solid pat to the man's upper arm. "Thanks, you're a life saver." Potentially. Assuming she and Rick could stop the sunlight bars.

"I better go get the tech."

Rick looked so calm and matter-of-fact that most people would have bought it, except Eden. The pulse point at the base of her husband's neck throbbed, giving away his anxiety. "Sure."

More like fantastic. They'd be alone and finally able to set things right, make a positive difference, eliminate the fear.

The guy disappeared down the hall, and Rick turned to her. "It looks like the sunlight system maintenance is still happening. Fingers crossed that the fault works in our favor and holds him up long enough to ensure that we have everything sorted before he gets back."

Rick sat at the control panel and directed Eden to the far end of the room. Right in front of each of them a red toggle switch jutted up next to a red button.

She glanced at her husband's face and their gazes locked.

"When I say 'go', pull the lever toward you with one hand and press the red button down with the other. It has to be done simultaneously or else it won't work. Ready?"

"Yes." *For more than forty years.*

"One, two, three. Go!"

No clank, no buzz, no flicker.

No change.

The steady background hum almost seemed louder, more persistent, as though taunting them with the system's infallibility.

A muscle twitched in Rick's jaw. "Our timing must be a little off. Let's try again." He stared into her eyes. "Ready? One, two, three. Go!"

Same, steady hum.

Rick slammed a hand on the control panel. "Why the fuck isn't this working?" He scanned the numerous buttons.

Eden's stomach churned, turbulent with rising waves of stress. If they didn't work this out soon... She stared at the rows and rows of red, black and white buttons and switches, not quite sure what to look for. Her heart boomed, rattling her ribs like a hardcore drum beat in an edgy underground club.

She bent down to check underneath the desk—for what, she had no idea. More than likely her subconscious had decided to give her a break from the overwhelming display.

In among the shadows, a shaft of light beamed down and highlighted a cut-out panel. Had she found something of significance? "Hey, Rick, there's a little trap door under here. Maybe..."

Rick dove under the desk and crawled toward the back. "There's one up here as well. Nice work, sweetheart."

His approval warmed her right to the core, making her feel proud, valued, appreciated. Under pressure, she'd delivered. In the past, she had relegated that role to her husband, the man of the family. That thinking was definitely a throwback to her 1960s self, a self she had now shed and replaced with a strong, progressive, adaptable woman, taking responsibility and making changes for the better.

Rick reached into the gap, fiddled around and, with a creak and thump, something fell into place. "Eden, stick your hand inside the gap at the back of the desk and there should be a shiny red pedal. I need you to pull it down," he said, crawling out from under the desk.

She did as he asked, returned to her chair and re-established eye contact, waiting for further instructions.

"Okay, put one of your feet on the pedal, reposition your hands on the button and lever — that's it — and on the count of three, we're going to simultaneously activate them. One. Two. Three."

A jolt, a flicker in the overhead lights, followed by a metallic groan. Had they shut down the main generator?

A couple of Jades dashed past the control room. *Yes!* "We did it!" A flood of euphoria doused the fear in Eden's gut and she raced over to Rick.

Out of the window, a mass exodus of staff, maintenance crew and techs charged across the grounds — and who could blame them? They'd be crazy to hang around now that the Jades and Violets were free.

A whirring, clanging shudder shattered the calm. It had to be the second generator kicking into gear. Rick slipped his hand around Eden's and they joined the steady flow of Jades moving through the building toward the nearest exit. However, with all the jostling, pushing and shoving to escape, Eden lost her grasp on Rick's hand and he disappeared into the sea of green and gold.

\* \* \* \*

Hugh sat in the corridor, his head in his hands, right in front of his cell, while the odd Jade and Violet scampered past, searching for another exit. However, hurrying wouldn't get him or them anywhere...yet. His escape in the mid-nineties had made sure of that. The security had been upped one-hundred-fold.

The guards had reveled in telling him all about how the sunlight bars had been extended to cover windows and all possible exits. So until someone shut down the sunlight system—permanently—they remained trapped.

Patience... He just had to have patience. Being out of his cell took him one step closer to finding Indigo—not that he had any idea where to start, other than her parents. But he doubted they'd help him after he'd left her at the altar. Although it hadn't been his fault—not entirely—they didn't know that. They didn't know he'd been captured and imprisoned against his will.

Even if he got lucky and they did steer him in the right direction, she might not want to see him. She might not want to be found.

No. She'd want to at least hear his side. His Indigo, the sweet woman he knew, would want to hear his explanation, would need to. With his determination, he'd find her and tell her the whole story or die trying.

"Hugh?"

*Indigo?*

It couldn't be her, could it? He had to be imagining her voice, dreaming up her presence, like he had every day since they'd shoved him back in his cell. Either that or he'd not just lost the plot, he'd shattered it into a million pieces, making it almost impossible to put back together.

"Hugh." She touched his arm, her fingers light, her sweat combining with her distinctive Indigo scent. She wasn't a dream or mirage. She was real.

His ravenous gaze ate up her elegant designer slacks, her tucked-in white shirt, her tailored jacket. She'd slicked back her caramel hair, tying it in a low pony tail highlighting the loss of youthful fullness in her face. And yet, somehow, she looked even more beautiful. "Indigo?"

She kneeled beside him. "You recognize me?"

"Of course!" He caressed her cheek, still not quite believing they'd found each other. "I've memorized every detail of your face. I've thought about you every day, every night, every moment." Thick, hopeful tears oozed out of the corners of his eyes. "You're as breathtaking as ever."

She slid out of his touch and stared at the floor. "Then why did you leave me?"

He lifted her chin up and looked her in the eye. "I didn't. They found me and spiked my drink with the IVD tranquilizer. It knocked me out, made me unconscious for two days and I woke up here. In hell. I tried to get in touch to explain but all my letters came back to me unopened...if they were ever sent in the first place."

"I thought—"

"That I'd changed my mind."

Tears rolled down her pretty pink cheeks. "I was so hurt. Devastated. I didn't know what to do with myself." She swiped her eyes with the back of her hand, black mascara staining her skin. "I ended up staying in Hobart, hoping I'd see you. Then I met Beauregarde and that's when things changed."

*That's right.* The bastard had tormented him about recruiting her, about her turning anti-vampire. "Beauregarde." He spat out the name like it was poison.

"Yes. Do you know him?"

Did he know him? *That was the absolute understatement of the year.* He'd been the bane of his centuries-long existence, a pebble in his shoe that he couldn't shake. "Yes. Long story. Keep going."

She hesitated, as though the pressure of waiting would force him to elaborate. No chance. Not yet, not until she finished explaining her side.

"After a few drinks one night, I blurted out what had happened between you and me and that's when he told me about the Norway Experiment. He said he thought it might help me heal, help me finally get over you. I had other ideas. "I applied for a job at Sub Rosa, hoping to track you down. I kept wishing I'd been wrong, that you hadn't changed your mind and they'd caught you instead. Not that I wanted you in here either, but—"

He held her face like a fragile, delicate flower. His delicate flower. "I understand." He wanted to remove her weak, wounded smile, to remove all the hurt.

"I worked up the ranks until I made it to senior manager of organizational culture, but I still couldn't get access to the Norway Experiment files. I applied for a secondment here and got rejected because I didn't have research experience. So with every avenue shut off, I gave up."

She stared, as though willing him to understand something she still didn't. "Yet, in my heart, I kept wishing we'd be reunited, that I could at least find out the truth...and see you again. I kept telling myself that if we were right for each other, it would happen."

"And now it has." Hugh grasped her hand, brought the back of it to his mouth and kissed each knuckle. "I've missed you so much."

"I've missed you too."

Using the pad of his thumb, he stroked her supple skin with reverence. He didn't want to ask—however, he had to know. "Did you ever get married?"

She looked at him as though he'd asked the craziest question in the world. "No! How could I, when all I thought about was you?" Indigo lifted her left hand, the violet diamond engagement ring he had given her all those years ago sparkling on her finger. "I've never taken it off."

"So...I'm assuming you don't have any children then?"

"Definitely not. I haven't been with anyone else since you. I've been free physically, but not emotionally. Emotionally, I've been a prisoner, just like you...until now."

Hugh had thought he'd experienced joy, though it had never felt like this, like every single cell in his body expanded with elation until he almost burst. "You're as sweet and adorable as ever." He kissed her, and it transported him right back to the last time, her softness, her warmth, her intoxicating feminine scent, eliminating the misery of the cold, dead years in between.

A handful of scurrying Violets rushed by and she jumped, tearing her lips from his. "We have to get you out of here."

"Unfortunately, it's not that simple. Until the sunlight bars are turned off, I can't leave."

She frowned, dialing her face back to her twenty-one-year-old self. "We can't stay here, either. We have to hide. If any of the senior management group see me with you..." They'd both be hanged, dried and pulverized.

Hugh stood, extended his hand to help her up and led her into the closest abandoned office. He went to shut the door and a shiny black shoe wedged the gap,

210

thrusting the door back, revealing a young, arrogant man holding a gun.

A sardonic smile slithered onto the guy's lips. "Where do you think you're going?"

Indigo grabbed Hugh's arm and tugged. "I'm just moving him on."

"Into a deserted office?" The smug bastard pointed his gun at Hugh.

"He'd hidden out here on his own and I wanted to make sure he couldn't escape." Her voice trembled in that nervous way, like when she'd confronted her parents about their relationship.

The full human man raised his manicured eyebrows and shoved the gun into Hugh's chest.

Hugh coughed, the air serrating his throat like razor blades.

Indigo sucked in a sharp breath and flinched. Did the man notice her discomfort, see through her hardline businesswoman charade? "Come on. Do you really think I'd do something stupid, something that could jeopardize my career, my life?"

The guy's gaze shifted between her and Hugh, as though to assess whether the body language signs matched her words. "I didn't think so, but now I'm not so sure."

She stepped forward, right into the man's face. "Drop the gun or I'll call Andy."

His grasp tightened around the trigger. "Go ahead."

Her face turned deathly-ghost white. "What?"

He pulled the gun from Hugh's chest and waved it around the confined space. "Go ahead. He won't come. He can't even hear you in here."

Indigo yanked on Hugh's arm and dragged him back.

The sick bastard squeezed the trigger.

Indigo jumped in front of Hugh, the concentrated sunlight bullet penetrating her chest at close range, and she fell to the floor.

"No!" Hugh dropped to his knees, by her side, the blood pouring from the burned-out hole in her heart.

Her breathing became jagged, uneven, building fluid burbling in her lungs. "Run!" Her vocal chords sounded severed, the word an almost inaudible whisper.

He couldn't leave her. Not again. Not ever. Hugh hugged the only woman who had set his heart aflame, connected with his soul, the only woman he would ever love.

Tears brimmed in his eyes and spilled like a broken faucet, coating his cheeks, and bathing her cavernous wound. "I'm so sorry. I'm so sorry."

*Crack!*

A shot shattered the stagnant air and speared his thoughts.

Hugh jolted his head up. Had he been injured?

No, but the gunman hadn't been quite so lucky. He lay in a crumpled pile on the floor with Ethan, a half-caste from Hugh's clan, standing over him and, in the doorway, a couple of wide-eyed kids sat strapped into a pram.

"Thank you." Unrelenting tears cascaded down, drenching Hugh and Indigo.

Ethan put a comforting hand on Hugh's shoulder. "Is there anything I can do to help?"

"No. Unfortunately." Hugh stroked Indigo's shiny caramel hair. He scanned over her body with blurry eyes. The bleeding had ceased and she had passed out, her breathing still labored, her pulse thready.

His tears had helped stabilize her, but could they save her human life? The severity of the lesion meant her condition could get worse at any moment. He had to make a life-changing decision, and soon.

Either he left her human and took the risk that she'd pull through or bit the fast-approaching bullet and change her, with the possibility that she still might die. Pressure built in his brain like an over-pumped tire.

What should he do? If her heart stopped beating, she'd have no chance of survival.

# Chapter Sixteen

## Cracking the Code

*Hobart, Tasmania, December 2011*

A car pulled up in the driveway and Simon rushed to the window, half expecting it to be Andy or the police. He held his breath until his lips must have turned cyanotic, and peeped through the blinds.

The sensor light blared, illuminating Grace's car and her in the driver's seat. However, he couldn't quite make out her coloring. She reached across to the passenger side, grabbed something and stepped out into the brightness

He raced to the front door and threw it open. "Grace!"

She sauntered over to him, her hair a rich, glossy, warm brown, her eyes like mouthwatering melted chocolate. It had worked. The cure had worked. *Thank fuck.*

"You called?" She planted a kiss on his parted lips, as though nothing huge, life-changing, had occurred over the past seventy-two hours.

"Where were you?"

"Don't you trust me?" She was the same old Grace—flirty and fun and full human.

"Of course I do, but I was worried. *Very* worried. I don't think you realize how sick you were."

"Sorry. Though I think you'll agree that my, ah...short departure was worth it." She pulled a book from her bag. *The* book. It was the one on ancient Nordic language that Rick had requested.

"You didn't... Do you understand how dangerous that was?" Fuck, she could've... He could have lost her...permanently.

"Yeah. But Rick and Eden are like family, and if we can help them, even in the smallest way..."

Simon couldn't argue with that. He held her face between his hands. "You're incorrigible. You know that?"

A proud smile slid onto her lips. "That's part of my charm."

He laughed. *So true.* It formed part of the reason he loved her so much. He clasped her hand and led her into the lounge room.

They sat on the couch and Grace put the book down beside her.

Simon grabbed his phone off the coffee table. "Rick still hasn't called." He'd spoken to Eden, increased her access privileges, then...nothing. She'd said he'd hear from them shortly, and he thought he would have by now unless... "If they don't contact us soon, I'm ringing the Norwegian police."

"How long has it been since you heard from them?" She tried to disguise the tremble in her voice, but he knew her so well that it was impossible to miss.

"A couple of hours. I know it doesn't sound like long, but when I last spoke to Eden, it seemed like things were...a bit off."

"Oh..."

Simon stared at his mobile. His heart chanted, *call the police, call the police, call the police,* but his rational mind intervened, like a consciousness coup, and dictated that he hold off. "I'll just give them a bit more time. I don't want to raise a false alarm. It might cause them more problems. So, what do you say that in the meantime we try and make sense of this code?"

"Okay." Since when did Grace give one-word answers? She had to be hugely stressed. Like him, she wouldn't want to sit around all helpless and wait. However, it didn't pay to be over-reactive.

Simon tried to distract himself by scrolling through the close-up photos Rick had sent him of the unusual alphabet on the back of his mum's photo frame. Then he opened up each picture, one at a time, compared each odd squiggle to the alphabet in the book and created a conversion table.

Bit by slow bit, he pieced the words together into a meaningful sentence. He glanced up at Grace, unable to wipe the ecstatic smile off his face. "We fucking did it!"

He selected Rick's number from his favorites but, instead of ringing, the call went straight to voicemail. "Fuck!"

Simon tried Rick's and Eden's mobile five times over the next hour with no success. "Something's not right."

"Have you checked the time difference? Maybe they're asleep." Hope. It glittered in her eyes. Though it was obvious that she, just like he, didn't truly believed it could be such a simple explanation.

He angled his watch to read the time. "It's three-thirty-five a.m. here and they're ten hours behind, which makes it just after five-thirty p.m."

"Oh."

*Uh-oh, more like it.* Unease sat heavy in his stomach like a curdled tub of sour cream. Sub Rosa management was dodgy, no question about it. But would they really risk disposing of two staff just to protect the project? Given the high stakes, anything was possible. Desperate times often pushed people to act in ways they never imagined.

So how long should he wait to take action? If Rick and Eden were in trouble, they needed help — and soon, possibly now. But if they weren't, sending the police prematurely could put them in grave danger.

Should he give Sub Rosa the benefit of the doubt or jump the proverbial gun and go with his fear?

# Chapter Seventeen

### Finding the Jackpot

*Sub Rosa, Norway compound, December 2011*

"Where do you think you're going?"

The abrupt, authoritative voice was unmistakable. Rick stood still among the rushing throng of Jades, closed his eyes and tried to tune in to the mindfulness practices he'd struggled to adopt.

A million thoughts swirled around his brain like a category five cyclone, competing for attention in his head. Was Eden safe? The twins? How about his mum and Ethan? Had they been quick enough to flee their cells?

Rick turned against the tide to face his nemesis. Andy stood before him, flanked by the security guard brigade, all carrying sunlight bullet handguns.

"Home. Excuse me." Rick kept his voice cool, collected, in contrast to his hammering heart, and attempted to rejoin the exiting Jades.

Andy stuck his arm out. "I don't think so." Two guards, packing semi-automatic pistols, bulldozed through the mayhem and restrained Rick.

He struggled against his captors, trying to break free, but their grip tightened like a ratchet.

"So, where's your lovely wife?" Andy asked, obviously fishing to find more leverage.

Rick wanted to smash the smug smile off the guy's face. "Eden visited earlier. She left a while ago now. She'll be sorry she missed you."

Andy's steel blue eyes glinted in the light like the sharp edge of a knife. "You need to stop lying to me..." *Or else there'll be far worse consequences.* He didn't have to say the words. They were clear in his cutting tone.

The CEO stepped right into his personal space, his smile growing even cockier. "We both know she's still here."

Rick's jaw tensed, a muscle jumping right next to the pounding pulse in his neck. He had to hold it together. He had to find a way to break free and find Eden before they did.

Andy kept talking, a rising din blocking out his voice and making it phase in and out like an untuned radio station. The guy's lips moved with bursts of broken noise but Rick couldn't decipher the meaning above the racket.

The entourage spun around in the direction of the disturbance. Ahead, a growing group of Jades and Violets pressed against the walls, avoiding the exits.

Extra vibrant sunlight shields blasted down the front of the windows and doors leading out of the complex, preventing their departure. The sardine-like mob of vampires shouted, nudged, rammed, which escalated into infighting, reigniting the centuries-old war.

One hundred percent of Rick's captors' attention focused on the combat between the clans, their grip on his arms slackening. Like a slick, wet fish, he slid out of the burly men's grasp and ran, weaving a path through the crowd, searching for Eden and his family.

"Rick!"

He stumbled to a stop at the adjoining door leading into the Violet residential area. "Eden?" Rick turned, his eyes skimming over the crowd.

*No...*

*No...*

*No...*

*No...*

*Yes!*

His gaze zeroed in on his wife and kids, and he raced toward his most treasured target.

*Boom!*

A gunshot splintered the air and searing heat bulleted through Rick's chest. He gasped, lurched forward and hit the ground at Eden's feet. Wheezy breath caught in his windpipe and hissed from his lips. The excruciating pain felt like someone had taken a shovel to his heart and dug a tunnel deep, deeper. He fought against it and raised his head, his eyes focusing on his wife's.

She reeled backwards, shock plastered across her pallid face.

Rick took massive mouthfuls of air but no oxygen filtered down into his tight, aching chest. Dizzy, he fell face first onto the cold floor. Short, sharp, shallow breaths refused to pass his throat and his lungs gurgled with rising blood.

Eden screamed. "Rick! No!" She dropped to her knees, rolled him onto his side and brushed his hair from his cheek, her teardrops raining down onto his blood-drained face.

He coughed, spraying the sterile white floor with bright red mist. "Go." His whispered voice had lost all power.

She pulled her hair back and leaned her ear close to his mouth.

"Get out" — his wet, raspy breath spattered against her skin and she sobbed — "while you still can."

*What?* She couldn't leave him. *Ever.* Sobs shredded her airways and she held him tight, defying his request, refusing to budge.

This couldn't be happening. Everything was supposed to work out this time.

"Eden." The air hissed from his lungs like a slow leak in an air mattress.

Her gaze connected with his glassy, pleading eyes.

"Please." He seemed to lose focus and coughed, bigger drops of blood spewing out. "For me."

A delirious glaze swept over his eyes and he slumped against her.

Eden shook him. "Rick. Come on, Rick. Please. Look at me. Say something. *Please.*" Anguish clogged her throat and she choked on hyperventilated gasps of air. Tears poured from her gritty, waterlogged eyes and bathed the large gash in his chest.

A man's hand, her dad's, touched her with loving tenderness. "Ev... Eden, we have to move. There's nothing more we can do for him."

*Nothing more we can do for him?* How could he say that? How could he think she could discard her husband, the love of her life, like a useless piece of trash? Suddenly her dad's hand felt more like a weapon, creating more damage, more destruction. She shrugged him off. If Rick were a Violet, would her father have been so quick to give up? "No!"

Ethan persisted and tore her away.

"No-o-o-o!" She resisted, returning to support Rick beneath the weight of her grief.

Ethan kneeled in front of her, tipped her wet chin up and looked her in the eye. "Sweetheart…"

She batted his hand away. "Don't ever call me that! That right is reserved for Rick and Rick alone. And now he's…" Eden couldn't breathe, the contaminated air inflaming her windpipe and corroding her lungs, her heart, with poisonous emotion.

She slumped forward, rasping, gulping, sobbing and rocked, unable to turn off the tap of sorrow. Her dad didn't walk away, didn't leave her. He stayed, silently placing his palm on her back. Instead of inciting more anger, it induced a soothing, Reiki kind of calm, clarity.

*The children!* She shot her head up.

The twins had cuddled together, consoling each other. Blake's watery, frightened eyes stared at her, like she symbolized the boogie man. Eden followed his gaze to her top, covered in Rick's blood.

No wonder they were so scared. They'd seen their dad shot and she looked like she'd stepped right out of a slasher movie. She took off her top, leaving on the camisole underneath, and forced herself onto shaky legs. She had to pull it together…for them.

Scarlett suddenly remembered her dream. It had come true! *No.* It didn't have to be that way. She could change things.

"It's okay," Scarlett whispered into her crying brother's ear. "I'll fix it...like when you fell down the stairs. Remember?"

Blake looked up, tear trails on his round face, and nodded.

Scarlett bit her lip and stared hard at her daddy, who was lying in a large red puddle.

She stared and stared, putting all her sadness, anger and love into one single thought.

The seconds passed and she went into a trance, blocking out the yelling, fighting, crying.

Then it happened, just like before. Everything reversed in slow motion, like rewinding a show on TV, picking up speed until her daddy was being held between the two scary men.

Blake clapped and babbled, bringing her back into the new present. This time, instead of the Jades and Violets punching and shouting, they stood and watched with big eyes and their mouths hanging open.

She looked at her mummy. She'd stopped sobbing and her gaze moved between Scarlett and her alive-again daddy. Mummy hugged her and Blake and cried, but they were different tears. Tears of happiness.

The Jades and Violets started getting noisy again, and Scarlett looked up over her mummy's shoulder. This time, the vampires weren't fighting with each other. This time, they ran toward her daddy.

The two beefy guards let go of Rick like his arms were venomous snakes and started to run, but a swarm of seething vampires surrounded them. Rick weaved through the growing horde of Jades and Violets, saw Eden, Blake and Scarlett in a little huddle across the room and raced over to his family.

Rick snaffled the kids into his arms and kissed them, then set them back down in the pram and turned to his teary wife. "Are you okay?" they said at the same time.

He cupped her cheeks and kissed her forehead, then her lips, and counted himself so goddam lucky to be alive. "Yes," they replied in unison.

He skimmed his thumbs along her delicate jawline. "Where's your dad?"

"He went to round up any strays and direct them back here."

"Excellent."

"How about your mum?" Eden's blue-violet eyes searched his, concern etched into her tone.

He surveyed the room. "I'm not sure."

"We have to find her then."

"Not yet. First we have to shut down the sunlight system, once and for all." Rick grabbed the pram handle with one hand and Eden's hand with the other and steered them around a rush of Violets and Jades.

"Is that even possible? What if there's another back-up system?"

Rick glanced at Eden and straight back onto the path ahead. "We knocked out the main generator, so there has to be a way to override the second one, as well as any other back-up mechanism. They're machines, and all machines have some sort of off switch. All machines can break down and require maintenance, which means they can be stopped."

At the control room, the door hung open and Rick ran inside. He scanned the area for something he might have missed — another button, another hidden panel...

The din from the amassing Violets and Jades grew, like a long-overdue vampire revolt. *Think.* Supposedly only certain staff knew the code to shut off the sunlight bars permanently, but surely there had to be a system disable switch as a backup somewhere.

A dark, sinister laugh weighted the air with dread.

The twins whimpered.

Rick spun around. In the doorway stood a full-caste Violet with a satanic gleam in his glowy violet eyes.

Rick held his hands out in a placating, *I'm-not-the-enemy-here* gesture. "I know you've probably been in here a long time and are dying to get out, but please just bear with me for a little bit longer. You'll be free in no time. I promise."

The pure Violet laughed harder, his menacing tone slashing through the noise of the desperate Violets and Jades slamming into walls, trying to break out. "I don't think you understand. I work with Andy."

A man who despised vampires had allowed this one into the trusted top ranks of Sub Rosa? It didn't make sense on so many levels. "With Andy, *CEO* Andy?" How could a vampire turn against his own persecuted kind and work for the enemy?

"We agreed to meet each other's needs. You could say it's been a…reciprocal relationship." In a flash, the Violet hovered right over Rick. "I should have gotten rid of you after Salvator, but Andy didn't want any more dead bodies. That was a tremendous fuck up of epic proportions. I'll fix things, though. I always fix things." The fluorescent light glistened off his ready-to-feed, fully-displayed fangs.

Rick's pulse galloped like a spooked, wild horse. He had to get away, but how? The vampire's violet eyes hypnotized his, transfixing him like a fly in a sticky web. The Violet swooped in, grazing his ice-cube-cold lips against Rick's skin.

Eden gasped. "No!"

"Daddy!" Scarlett screamed.

Blake bawled like he'd wrung the tears straight from his sensitive little heart.

Rick couldn't move, terrified the Violet would turn his attention on his family. He closed his eyes in anticipation of the inevitable bite. How would it feel? Would his vampire heritage prevent him from death by exsanguination? If he lived, would the venom convert him into a half, three-quarter or full-caste vampire?

The Violet inhaled, as though getting hard off Rick's scent.

"Beauregarde! Stop."

Rick snapped his eyes open. The older, nervy senior manager stepped past a shaking Eden and distraught kids.

The smirk on Beauregarde's face made Rick want to smash the guy's lips right through to the back of his head. "Ah...just in time. You can help me get rid of these two."

The manager's jaw ticked and his arm hung by his side, his trembling hand holding a revolver.

"You're Mummy's uncle." Scarlett's sure, confident tone tore Rick's gaze away from the older man to Eden.

"No, honey." Eden caressed Scarlett's blonde curls, her voice soft.

The man's eyes filled with what looked like remorse, or maybe regret? "She's right."

William Darnel was Eden's uncle? *What the fuck?*

Eden stared up at the distressed, gray-haired older man, surprise plastered across her face like a horror movie billboard. "What?"

"It's true."

"You..." she shook her head. "You must have known." She pointed her finger at him. "You must have known what happened to us...all these years...and you did nothing."

His gaze fleetingly connected with hers. "What happened to your mother—my sister—made me so angry. You have to understand." Air rasped in his chest with each labored breath. "Your birth... It killed her. I thought controlling the vampires, including you, was for the best."

"Enough with the family reunion." Beauregarde bared his teeth and pressed the razor-sharp edges to Rick's exposed neck.

Rick squeezed his eyes shut and braced himself for the puncture into his carotid artery.

Shouts and stomps from the imprisoned Violets and Jades escalated, pressure building like gas behind a champagne cork.

*Thump!*

Rick's eyes flew open and Beauregarde lay unconscious on the floor. "What the hell...?"

"Sunlight Taser...triple strength. I've been wanting to do that for such a long time." A small smile created extra creases on William's crinkled, maze-like face.

"Thank you." Rick exhaled a gush of pent-up breath, his body in post-stress relief. "How long will he be out?"

"At least three hours." William raised his croaky voice over the rising commotion.

Rick pinned him with a let's-get-this-sorted stare. "Good. Now, how do we disable the generator?"

William glanced at Rick, Eden and the kids, holstered his gun and sat at the control panel, wheezy and out of breath. He sucked in several greedy gulps of air, then logged in to the system.

Rick, Eden and the twins crowded around him as he scrolled through the extensive menu. When he reached the security settings, several windows opened up and he entered a sequence of passwords.

William pushed the chair back and stood. He moved aside, broke into a hacking, congested coughing fit and gestured to Rick. "Sit."

Rick took his place, while William braced himself on the desk with one hand and covered his mouth with the other. In a short break between violent coughs, he pointed to Eden. "Up there." He waved his hand toward the spot she'd sat at before.

Eden took her place, looked at Rick then at William. Rick followed her gaze. Her uncle had stopped coughing and just managed to stand, his lips tinged with blue and his skin a grayish hue, except for his stained yellow smoker's fingers.

He looked up, his eyes weary, his rattled, labored breathing like he'd inhaled someone's coin collection. He tried to talk but instead, just panted and hissed. His quivering hand reached inside his jacket and pulled out an asthma inhaler. Two puffs, pause, two more puffs.

Who knew when the guy could next utter some intelligible words? They didn't have time to wait around and see, so Rick took the lead. "Eden and I need to simultaneously pull the red toggle switch and press the button and pedal, right?"

William nodded, his lips transitioning from blue to purple-pink.

Rick stared at his wife. "After three. One, two, three."

The computer monitor changed to a blue screen — the blue screen of death. Lights flickered, the computer shut down and a hiccupped whirring signaled the generator chugging to a halt.

"We did it!" Eden jumped up from her chair, ran over and threw herself into Rick's arms.

*Thwack!*

Holding hands, they ran into the main corridor just in time to see a mass of Jades and Violets pour outside, rejoicing in their freedom...with each other.

Rick hugged Eden to him and kissed her hair, cheek, lips. They'd won. And just like the rest of the vampire community, they were finally safe, free.

William struggled over and patted Rick's shoulder. "Well done."

Rick released Eden and shook the man's hand. No matter what his past actions, today he had helped make a positive, life-changing difference. "Thank you. Without your input, this couldn't have happened."

His gaze returned to Eden, who still looked dubious, like she didn't fully trust her uncle. And that made total sense. After his part in their predicament, it would take some solid time to decide whether to let him into their life. But at the moment, they had other family to find. "Let's go round up your dad and my mum and get out of here."

Eden chewed on her bottom lip. "What about Andy? We can't let him get away."

"Fuck!" Rick rammed his hands through his hair. "Of course we can't. Eden, you stay here with the kids and I'll check out the Jade section."

"That leaves me with the Violet section then." A smudge of reddy-pink had returned to William's face, yet the wheeze still lingered in his speech.

"Look what I found."

"Ethan?" William's face went as white as Hollywood-actor-bleached teeth.

"William?" Ethan's tone sounded curt, yet heavy with a core-deep sadness.

"Andy," Eden and her uncle said in unison.

Rhoda appeared behind the sullen CEO. "Mum!" Rick couldn't contain his joy at seeing her free and working together with an anti-Jade Violet for the greater good. "Perfect timing."

Ethan scowled. "What would you like us to do with him?"

If Rick left it up to Ethan, he'd tear the guy to pulled-pork-style shreds. Going by their first encounter, he was surprised that his father-in-law's explosive temper hadn't overridden his rational brain. "Hand him over to the police so he can rot in jail."

"You don't have any evidence against me. Whatever you saved on your phone and laptop is gone. They'll laugh you out of the station." Even surrounded, with no chance of escape, Andy still clutched to his cocky, pompous persona.

Rick stepped past the unconscious Beauregarde and stood in the rogue CEO's personal space. The tables hadn't just turned, they'd flipped right over. Rick had never felt so pleased, so vindicated. "Hmm...I don't think so. You might have heard of a little thing called back-up. And I still have a couple of key witnesses." Rick motioned toward his mum and Ethan. "Sorry to disappoint you."

Andy's arctic blue eyes turned glacial and he jerked forward, attempting to yank his arms loose.

"Come on. Let's get him arrested and charged." Rick shoved past the CEO and smiled. Ethan had done a military-approved job with Andy's necktie, going by the complex army knot he'd used on the prick's wrists.

William shuffled over to Beauregarde, a hand on his holster. "How about *him*?"

Ethan reached out and placed a reassuring hand on William's forearm. "You escort Andy, and I'll take care of the double-crossing bastard."

"With pleasure."

Rhoda stood by Ethan. "I'll help you."

Rick walked over to Eden and, thank goodness, the kids had fallen asleep in the pram, understandably exhausted—like him—but he couldn't afford to take a nap. Not yet. "Sweetheart, take the twins back to the car and I'll join you shortly."

Blue-violet flames of fear flared in her eyes. "Where are you going?"

"I just need to check something out quickly."

She pressed her palm to his chest, her eyes pleading. "Please be careful."

"You too." He brushed her hair off her face and kissed her with an infusion of love, respect and longing. When he finally pulled away, her half-mast eyes looked like she'd been drugged with passion. But he'd have to explore that later.

Rick dashed through the empty buildings and out into the extensive rear yard, where some Jades and Violets still hung back, speaking. Civilly. To each other. Without raised voices or fists.

He smiled and ran to the back of his mum's old house, followed the path to Ballsy's hideout and broke in through the small doorway. Rick propped the door open, allowing the last struggling streams of natural light to penetrate the cave's interior. Ballsy's laptop sat idle on the coffee table, so he nicked it and left.

The forest was quiet. Too quiet. Oppressive quiet. There was no bird song, no skittering wildlife, only the sound of his footfalls and labored breathing.

"Where are you going with that?"

*Fuck.* Ballsy's voice. Why had he stayed?

"It has evidence the authorities need to see," Rick replied.

Ballsy stomped up to him, dry dead leaves crunching under his feet. "Really? Do they?"

Rick stood firm, the frosty wind sawing his airways and slicing right through to his bones. "Yep."

"And what about me? I'm not going to jail."

"Who said you were?" Rick tried to stifle the involuntary chatter in his teeth.

"Come on. Do you really think I'm that stupid?"

He had to find a way out with the laptop. He clutched it tighter, the metal drawing the last ounces of heat from his flesh, making his joints ache as though stabbed with shards of ice.

Ballsy tried to look tough but oozed desperation. Making a deal with him would be as easy as negotiating with a kamikaze pilot or a suicide bomber. "You'll be giving evidence, so how can that get you in trouble? It's Andy who's going down for this."

"You don't know what else is on that laptop."

Ah... The unrevealed yet clear reason behind the take-no-prisoners approach.

Ballsy motioned for him to hand it over. "Give it to me."

Rick stepped back. "Not until you tell me what's on it." Which was absolute bullshit, because no way would he relinquish such crucial evidence. But he'd stall until he could successfully break free, laptop in tow.

Ballsy studied him, as though weighing up the sincerity of Rick's request. "Sex tapes. Not all the girls are human or of consenting age. Plus some...sensitive correspondence with Andy."

Ballsy grabbed for the computer and Rick lifted it out of his reach.

"What sort of correspondence with Andy?" He quickly gelled, not requiring a response. "Oh... blackmail."

"So you better hand that over." Ballsy tried to snatch the laptop again—however, Rick moved too fast.

Rick shook his head. "Sorry." He really wasn't, though. Not one bit.

Ballsy's dark eyes looked injected with black ink, anger swirling in their depths. "If you don't give it to me, you will be."

Rick went to bolt past Ballsy, tripped on the prick's outstretched foot, and crashed to the ground, the computer still safely tucked up under one arm.

Ballsy kicked him in the side and pounded on his shoulder to try to loosen his grip, but Rick clamped down harder, like a provoked Venus Fly Trap.

"Give me the fucking laptop!" Ballsy's voice cracked like a rock hitting a windscreen and he booted Rick harder.

Rick curled into a tight ball and groaned. He had to do something. He had to stop him from stealing back the additional evidence.

Ballsy went to kick him again and, drawing on every last bit of adrenaline-fueled strength, Rick grabbed his foot, dropping his adversary to the forest floor. While the guy gasped for air, Rick pushed into standing, his body throbbing with pain like he'd been hit by a speeding Mack truck. He had to try to ignore it, couldn't dwell on it. Excruciating pain or not, he had to go.

He hobble-ran back to the compound and around to his car, parked at the front.

Eden stood by the open back door and had the kids all strapped in. "What took you so lo— Rick!"

"Just drive!" Rick collapsed into the passenger seat.

She touched his face, the only part of him that didn't hurt like fuck. "Are you okay?"

"Yes." *No.* He couldn't let on, though, couldn't let her worry. Worry caused mistakes. Worry led to disaster. "We need to leave."

"How about the others?"

*Fuck.* None of them had a car.

"I said we'd wait until their taxi came...in case of any more trouble."

She was right. They couldn't just take off, especially now with Ballsy on the loose. Not that he posed much of a threat with Rick's half-caste mum and father-in-law around.

Ethan stalked over to them, looking like a big, broad, don't-fuck-with-me warrior. "Is everything all right?"

He had to answer honestly. With Ethan's inbuilt bullshit detector, holding back from him would be pointless. "Not really. I stole a worker's laptop with some pretty damning footage and documents. And now he's—"

Ballsy emerged from the woods at the far end of the carpark, and the moment he spotted Rick, his body shook and his face went red with rage.

He broke out into a sprint...toward Rick.

With his gun pointed at Andy's back, William nudged him across the carpark to join Rick and family.

Ethan and Rhoda banded together and made a protective wall in front of them.

Ballsy stopped as though he'd slammed into a solid, invisible forcefield. All color drained from his skin, like a discarded vampire conquest. And in some ways, he was.

He darted his gaze around him, as though assessing the best escape route, and ran back the way he'd come, disappearing into the forest.

"Should we chase after him?" Ethan said, in a *please-let-me-deal-with-the-prick* tone.

"No. I'll hand over his laptop to the police and let them track him down." The guy wouldn't be able to get too far. His human abilities were limited, but a rogue vampire... "How did you go with Beauregarde?"

A satisfied grin brought sunshine to Ethan's stormy face. "All taken care of."

# Chapter Eighteen

## Confessions

After a couple of hours with the authorities, giving statements and providing carefully vetted evidence, Rick, Eden and the kids returned to Ansfrida. They put the exhausted twins to bed, and Eden stayed and read them a story to make sure they settled. Rick returned downstairs, collapsed onto the couch and checked Eden's mobile.

Several missed calls from Simon filled her phone screen. Had he cracked Abe's code? He had to find out…and update him regarding what had happened.

Simon answered after one ring. "Eden?"

"It's me, mate."

"Rick. Thank God." Simon breathed out a long, relieved sigh. "Is Eden okay? The kids?"

"Fine and fine."

"Good. I started to panic. I was just about to call the police."

Such a great, reliable, switched-on friend. "How are you and Grace?"

"Okay." Simon sounded nervous, like he was holding something back. "So tell me, where were you guys? I've been trying your phones for the last few hours!"

*Deflection.* His mate's key strategy, his modus operandi when withholding information. Rick would have to probe further when he and his family returned to Tassie. Right now, Simon needed an explanation of the Sub Rosa situation.

"We were hauled up at the Norway site, then the police station. Somewhere along the way my phone died a violent death at the hands of Andy. Thankfully, Eden survived. Thankfully, *we* survived."

"What the hell happened?"

"I'll explain the details when I see you, otherwise we'll be on the phone for ages. The most important thing you need to know is that Andy has been arrested."

"No way! What did they get him on?"

Rick grabbed his glass of straight Scotch off the coffee table and lifted it to his lips, his hand shaking. Shock. It was inevitable, really—no matter how strong he thought he was, no matter how together, no matter how in control. "Misappropriating funds, imprisonment and inhumane treatment of test subjects and falsifying research results."

"So…they know about the Jades and Violets then?"

The alcohol warmed his throat but did nothing to alleviate the chill still lingering in his veins. "Not exactly. Let's just say we spun a certain story and angled the evidence a certain way, based on facts.

"The police believe the captives were humans with a particular type of heritage and coloring who were targeted for experimentation for genetic cleansing reasons, sort of like what Hitler tried to do with the Jews. We thought it would be best for everyone not to publicize the whole 'vampires live among us' thing. Can you imagine the public panic?"

"Yeah, it would be a disaster. The knowledge needs to be weaved into society, slowly, gently, drip-fed to eliminate or at least reduce the fear."

"Totally. It's the only way to have any hope of achieving equity."

"Speaking of fairness, will Andy be extradited?"

Rick polished off his drink and cleared his throat. "Not at this stage. From what I understand, he'll remain in a Norway prison while the case is being investigated. Then I guess it depends on what the Norwegian legal system decides.

"The irony is that he became obsessed with eradicating the vampire gene because he thought his parents had been killed by Jades. It turns out they got changed to Jades and ended up imprisoned in the Norway site. He saw them, softened his approach, improved compound conditions and got fixated on finding the cure to change them back. But they don't want to revert to human."

Simon sighed and Rick imagined his mate shaking his head with frustration and disgust. "So he did all that only to fuck up his whole life and the lives of so many others."

"Yeah… I know it's taken a long time — however, I'd like to think we ended up saving a few lives too." The alcoholic buzz started to kick in — and just in time. The floatiness helped prepare him to go with the fast, slow or stagnant flow. "So…do you still have the classified emails we sent through?"

"Sure do. All safe and secure."

A whoosh of relief rushed out of Rick's lungs and he dropped his head against the backrest. "Good. You see, my laptop came to an untimely end as well."

"Shit. Though an upgrade's as good as a tropical holiday — or so I hear."

Rick chuckled, deep and hearty, seeds of joy sprouting in his soul. A robust plant this time, long-lasting, enduring. Unlike his and Eden's Richard-and-Eva, cut-flowers version of a life.

"So when do you guys get here?"

The cold, damp chill, like sleet in his blood, began to lift. "Soon. We just need to get a few things sorted first. There might be a few extras tagging along."

"Extras?"

"Yeah, Eden's uncle and dad — and my mum."

"Whoa! That's great, but didn't you say you both had no family?"

"Add that to the list of things I need to explain when I get back."

"Well, hurry up! I want to hear all the gossip." And Rick couldn't wait to tell him. However, he wasn't sure how his best friend would take the news about Rick and Eden's heritage.

In his dealings with Simon, his mate had always been fair, practical, open-minded. But being fair and having a part-vampire as a friend were two different things. Rick hoped he'd be accepted.

"So, ah, now that Andy's in custody, what's going to happen with Sub Rosa?" Simon asked, interrupting his thoughts.

"The Norway site has been shut down while the investigation's happening, so I imagine the Tassie site will be next. Given the circumstances, I'd say it'll be the death of the organization. I mean, who's going to want to continue to fund a corrupt, unethical business?"

"True. I'm surprised we haven't heard anything over here yet. But it is only five a.m."

Rick slapped his forehead with the palm of his hand. "Sorry, mate. I should have checked."

Simon chuckled, all signs of nervous apprehension now gone. At least for the moment. "No worries. I couldn't sleep anyway."

"You should be able to now, so I'll let you go. I'll be in touch when we have a return date."

"Sounds good. I'll pick you guys up, seeing I'm likely to be officially unemployed by then."

Simon's tone held humor, but the comment whacked Rick like a medicine ball in the gut. Job losses were the one negative side effect of what Rick had done. Not everyone employed at Sub Rosa was dodgy, so that meant good, hard-working people would not only lose their positions but also potentially their lifestyle and the safety of a secure home.

While he'd set some people free, others were now financially shackled. He'd been so fixated on seeking justice that the full fallout hadn't registered in his one-track mind. "I'm so sorry. I didn't even think."

"Don't be sorry. The place had it coming. I don't know how much longer I could have stayed, knowing about the ingrained, high-level crooked shit going on. The apple rots from the core and I didn't intend to be the sour, toxic, cast-off skin. I see it as a blessing."

Would others? Maybe once they knew the story. Maybe he could work out how to help them in some way? "Thanks, mate, for understanding and being such a great, reliable support. Oh hey, just quickly, any luck decoding my dad's message?"

"Yep."

*What?* And he hadn't said a thing. Then again, Rick hadn't given him much opportunity. "And?"

"I'll fill you in when you get here."

*Bugger.* It looked like they'd be keeping each other in suspense. "Touché." Rick chuckled, hoping Simon couldn't hear the barely-masked edge of frustration.

Resolution. It had eluded him for over forty years. And he was tired, fatigued and burned out from all the fighting. Rick needed all the frayed, loose ends tied up like he needed food and water and air. He'd gotten close, so close to piecing it all together, yet the final fragments still remained just out of reach.

\* \* \* \*

Beauregarde switched on the scrambler device voice encryptor and dialed. "May I speak to the inspector in charge of the Sub Rosa investigation?"

"Of course, sir, and your name is?"

"Let's not worry about that for now."

"But, sir, we need —"

"Would you like to hear what I have to say or not?" Even his distorted voice sounded as clipped and short as a buzz cut.

Silence.

Paper shuffling, whispered snippets.

"Just one moment, sir."

Beauregarde marched up and down the corridor of his Violet harem, his long dressing gown tangling around his legs, his phone call eating into his fucking time, literally and metaphorically. However, he had no other choice. It had become a matter of self-preservation.

With Andy in custody, Beauregarde had no doubt the guy would sell his lily-livered, weak-ass soul in exchange for freedom. When things went the CEO's way, he acted tough and in control, but it was all an act. In reality, he'd show his wussy true colors, his cowardice, just like the rest of the humans. Saving himself would be his number one priority. So Beauregarde had to get in first.

"Can I help you?" This voice had a deeper, firmer, more commanding tone. *The Chief Inspector, perhaps?*

"No. I can help you, though. I believe you have Andy Falon in custody."

"We're not able to give out that information."

*The Western world and its privacy and confidentiality crap.* "Let me rephrase then. I know you're holding the Sub Rosa CEO and I want to make sure justice is served." *In my favor.*

"You'll need to make an official statement. When can you come in?"

*Fuck.* "I can't. However, I have some information I can tell you over the phone that should help..." *Ensure Andy stays in jail.*

"In order to proceed, we need you to come down to the station and complete a signed declaration."

Beauregarde twirled a long strand of hair around his finger, the moans and mewls from his orgying bevy of Violets beckoning him from the other side of the wall. "Looks like I can't help you then. Sorry for wasting your time..."

"Sir, please wait." A pause, with hushed, muffled voices chattering in the background. "All right, go ahead."

*That's better.* "I'm a former employee, but not the kind you'll find on the books. I got contracted under the table, along with many other deals, during Andy's time as CEO. I saw some horrible, appalling things but I couldn't speak up. I knew the dire consequences if I did. The silent threat kept me gagged.

"I didn't want to end up like Salvator Aalem, an employee who supposedly died in an innocent accident. I know for a fact he found out some sensitive information and started searching for more evidence to expose Andy and the agency. So Andy arranged for the problem to...disappear."

He stroked his dick. Between the teasing whimpers and pleasure-filled groans coming from the next room and off-loading his skewed, incriminating story, Beauregarde was about to go off like a shaken-up bottle of champagne, spurting out flagons of celebratory fluid. "I was present when Andy gave the order to dispose of Salvator, and the next morning he was found dead.

"The police determined he'd had a simple but fatal fall. I assure you, Salvator had been pushed. Andy bragged about calling in a favor from a coroner friend who glossed over the scene, reporting no suspicious circumstances." He stifled a groan and slowed the rapid hand stokes along his swollen cock, savoring the pre-orgasm state.

"I see. And outside of a verbal report, do you have any hard evidence to corroborate your story?"

"No, however, I'd suggest speaking to the senior manager of business services, William Darnel. He's been with the company over forty years, so he would definitely know about some of the illegal dealings." If William could help stitch up Andy and maybe get a bit of prison time too, it would be perfect. Just the thought made him ready to blow. Now he needed a Violet's hot, dirty mouth wrapped around his dick.

"Beauregarde..." A chorus of seductive voices drifted from the bedroom.

*Fuck!* He dropped his cock and stabbed the 'end call' button on his phone. Fingers fucking crossed that the cop hadn't heard. But even if he had, it didn't really matter. He couldn't identify Beauregarde by his distorted voice, and the diverter on his mobile meant he couldn't be tracked.

Beauregarde rifled through the disorganized filing system in his brain. His details had never been recorded at Sub Rosa. *Had they?* He'd always been employed as a silent, paid-under-the-table consultant. That was what Andy had consistently reinforced. But he was about as trustworthy as a snitch on death row.

If any trace of Beauregarde existed, it would be in Andy's office at the Tasmanian Sub Rosa site. They'd agreed that any electronic communication between them would be erased. Knowing Andy, he'd probably kept a copy for insurance. Then there was still the Rick problem he had to eliminate. A clamp of tension gripped his stomach like an angry fist. He had to check out Andy's office then find Rick. First, though, he needed a release.

Beauregarde discarded his robe and strode into the bedroom. One quick fuck and he'd be on his way.

\* \* \* \*

Starlight shone, dispelling the darkness. Rick loaded his family's luggage into the car, in preparation for their early morning trip to the airport. They'd be home in the next thirty-odd hours.

He closed his eyes. *Home.*

It felt like forever since he'd last been there. A few times during the Norway stay he'd questioned whether he'd ever be able to return. Thank fuck everything had worked out. Thank fuck it was second, not third, time lucky.

He gazed up into the night sky, as if to say a silent prayer of gratitude, and staggered back against the boot. The spectacular guiding star that had led them safely to Ansfrida at the start of their Norway journey had reappeared.

*So tell me, bright star, are you going to lead us safely home?*

Rick could almost swear the heavenly body gave him a twinkly little nod.

He went inside, collapsed into bed and proceeded to sleep well, the first fully restful sleep he could remember in…as long as he could remember.

Before he knew it, he, Eden and the kids were on the plane and on the way back to Australia.

They touched down in Hobart, with both Scarlett and Blake miraculously still sound asleep. Eden had become an expert at slow, gentle, steady movements and successfully placed the twins in the double pram without them waking.

"Impressive." Rick brushed his lips against the shell of her ear. "As always."

She shivered, giving away the impact of his whispered words and light touch on her arousal.

"You're already wet for me, aren't you?"

Eden spun around to face him, acting all horrified, but he could tell by her flushed cheeks that she was super turned on. "Rick!" She shot him her best attempt at a glare, but couldn't hide the desire dancing in her eyes. "We're in the middle of the airport."

Her blue-violet irises had turned an almost amethyst, lust-darkened purple, making his cock cricket-bat hard. He pressed it against her stomach, his silent promise of hours of adult pleasure. "As soon as we get home and get the kids settled, I'm taking you straight to bed, Mrs. Hartman."

A seductive smile spread across her lips and flooded his brain with X-rated images. Her sucking him off, him sucking on her breasts, stroking along her seam, spreading her bare legs and using his mouth to take her to paradise.

A wave of sultry heat licked up and over every inch of his skin, setting his heart racing in anticipation. He subtly adjusted himself and focused on getting control of the erection situation or he'd struggle to walk, let alone concentrate.

Once he'd somewhat tamed the sexual beast, he held Eden's hand, and together they pushed the pram up the ramp to the gate lounge, where Simon and Grace waited. The stricken look in Grace's normally bubbly brown eyes was unexpected. Rick had never seen her so stressed, so serious.

Grace ran over and threw her arms around Eden. "Thank God you're home!"

Simon reached out to shake Rick's hand and pulled him into a bear hug. "Mate, it's so good to see you."

"What a sweet little bromance." A wet-eyed Grace stared at them with a cheeky grin. Now that was more like Eden's fun-loving friend.

"What, so only women can show emotion?" Simon scowled, but the corners of his lips twitched in his poor attempt to hold back a smile.

"I think it's...progressive," Eden said, joining in on the teasing.

Finally having the freedom to smile and laugh and joke without the underlying threat of danger felt so fucking fantastic.

The ladies walked ahead with the pram—catching up on gossip, no doubt—while Rick and Simon followed behind with the luggage.

"Where are your parents and Eden's uncle?" Simon asked, over the trundle of their suitcases and the overhead announcements.

"The CIA ended up getting involved and wanted to ask them some more questions, so they won't be arriving for at least a couple of weeks. The agent explained that they knew about the whole vampire thing and were doing a bit of crisis management and containment. Eden and I spoke about staying until our parents and her uncle were done so we could all travel together but thought it'd make more sense to get the kids home and into a routine."

They walked out into the warm night air and strolled toward the well-lit, multilevel car park. A bright, violet- jade light twinkled overhead, as though the Norway star had followed them home. Was that even astronomically possible?

In the car on the journey to Fern Tree, Rick sat in the front passenger side in silent awe. The star remained in sight, illuminating a path all the way to their front door. Rick shook his head, trying to make sense of the vision.

Were his eyes playing a prank on him? The emotionally intense past few weeks, plus the mammoth flight, had sapped his energy and left him deliriously tired. It had to be that—or maybe a similar star existed in the southern hemisphere.

They arrived at the house and Rick unlocked the door and switched on the light. Fuck, it felt good, stepping across the familiar threshold and back into the loving home he and Eden had forged together.

They left the luggage in the front foyer and, while Eden put the kids to bed, Rick showed Simon and Grace into the conservatory. He grabbed them all a drink—a stiff one to prepare them, him mostly, for what he would share—and embarked on the elaborate tale of his and Eden's background and the resulting quest.

Stunned didn't even describe the looks on Grace and Simon's faces. They both sat on the couch opposite him, staring in a sort of dazed wonder.

"Wow," Grace finally said, with not even a hint of fear or rejection.

Simon studied Rick, as though trying to spot the Jade signs he'd missed. "'Wow' doesn't even come close to what I'm feeling. I'm still reeling from the fact that my best friend, his wife and daughter are vampires!"

Rick grinned with delight and relief. Simon still referred to him as his best friend. He couldn't have asked for a more positive sign. "Part vampire, to be exact."

"Remind me never to sit too close to you when you're hungry." Simon slipped him a sly smile and swallowed the rest of his single malt Scotch. He put his empty glass on the coffee table and fixed a sincere gaze on Rick. "But seriously, there's an antidote now, so there's nothing stopping you from becoming full human...if you want."

Rick had toyed with the idea, the way a cat pawed and batted a dead mouse. "I'd be lying if I said I haven't considered it. But you know what? I am who I am, and I'm comfortable with my identity.

"I was born with vampire genes and so to me, my Jade heritage is just as important as my human one. I don't see either as superior or inferior to the other...unlike some people. A lot of their fear is based on ignorance, just like it is with any different race or culture. Ultimately, if a person is good, that's all that matters. Don't you agree?"

Simon glanced at Grace then smiled at Rick with unconditional love and acceptance. "Yep."

Grace squeezed Simon's hand and sent Rick the same warm vibes. "Absolutely."

"So, I believe a person should have freedom of choice in terms of taking the anti-venom, unless they're deemed not of sound mind or dangerous by law. Then I reckon there's a case to administer it without consent. Though, even that needs further discussion and debate."

"Right up to the law-making level." A cynical spark flared in Simon's eyes. "But a lot of what happens, what's agreed to, will depend on who gets the rights to the drug, who has the money and hence the power to provide input into developing the accompanying legislation."

Rick grabbed the bottle of Scotch and poured another shot into their glasses. "Well, funny you should mention that, because I have a business proposition."

Simon's confused expression resembled the one he got when his experiment results didn't turn out as planned. "A business proposition?"

"Yeah. I thought you and I could start up our own company with a focus on health and wellbeing research and treatments, which would include the patent to the vampire anti-venom and soulmate serum. We both have the drive, experience and passion."

Simon's broad smile looked the same as the grin he sported when his scientific endeavors had exceeded predicted outcomes, which was exactly what had happened in this case. "Sounds brilliant. But how about funding, especially for the vampire products—if vampires supposedly don't exist?"

Rick had thought heaps about that, and as long as they pitched their idea to the right person at the top, they'd be set. "Once we get the patents, I don't think we'll have any problems attracting funding. Those in high-level government positions are well aware of vampires. They just don't want to publicize that we live among human society…yet.

"In the end, they'll do whatever's needed to keep the knowledge contained and society as safe as possible. But we'll work on spreading the word about Violets and Jades, and achieving successful assimilation. If, by some chance, we run into any issues in the meantime, I can use my grant-submission writing skills to try to obtain more funds to support our other work, which will, in turn, support the business as a whole…and us."

Eden appeared in the doorway. "Did you guys want another drink? How about a celebratory champagne?"

"Well, I won't say no to that!" Grace angled herself toward Simon, squished his hand between hers and gave him the most hardcore, *you-would-have-to-be-the-biggest-prick-around-to-deny-me* puppy eyes Rick had ever witnessed. Even the most heartless, self-absorbed man couldn't say no to that look. "Please say you're driving."

"Anything for you, babe." The way Simon stared at her solidified that the poor bastard was totally under her spell. Going by Simon's past comments, she'd more than make it up to him in the sex department. They were insatiable…a bit like him and Eden.

Simon's gaze didn't shift from Grace. "Just half a glass for me."

Eden returned carrying a tray with four champagne flutes and handed one to each of them.

Simon accepted his half-full glass, breaking the Grace spell, and snapped his attention onto Eden. "Thanks. Oh, we'll drop Thornton and Smokey off tomorrow."

"No problem." Eden cozied up to Rick on the couch. "So, what have I missed?"

"I've given them the CliffsNotes version of events." Rick shone his thousand-lumen-spotlight stare on Simon. "So now, partner, I think the time has come for you to enlighten us about my dad's code."

"I wondered how long it'd take for you to bring that up. You've done well. We've been back nearly an hour already."

Eden shot to the edge of her seat, her leg bobbing in an attempt to relieve her pent-up stress. "Oh, before I forget, would you mind looking after Scarlett and Blake when we pick up my uncle and dad and Rick's mum from the airport?"

Grace shifted forward and put a steadying hand on Eden's knee. "Not at all. I'm looking forward to meeting the rest of your family."

"Hopefully they won't bite each other's heads off on the plane ride over," Rick muttered, concerned about residual human-Jade-Violet rivalry. "How were Smokey and Thornton, by the way?"

"Great. I think I've nearly convinced Grace we should get a pet of our own." Simon patted her thigh.

Grace slapped her hand over Simon's. "I told you. It's either a pet or a baby."

Eden's eyes went so wide they nearly bugged right out of her head. "Ooh, is there something you're not telling us?"

"No!" She paused then a pink flush rose up her face. "Well, actually..."

"We've set a date" — Simon glanced at Grace then back at Rick and Eden — "for the wedding."

Rick jumped up and shook Simon's hand. "It's about bloody time."

Eden shuffled in next to Grace and gave her a hug. "That's fantastic news! When is it?"

"January twenty-first. It's just a registry thing..."

"There's no such thing as 'just' when it comes to marriage. No matter what the ceremony, a marriage is sacred." Eden pulled back and bounced in her seat, as though the full impact of the news had only just sunk in. "That's only a few weeks away!"

Grace intertwined her fingers with her fiancé's. "Yeah. After everything that's happened, we decided it was stupid to hold off any longer. I mean, what were we waiting for? We both know we want to be together."

Simon's gaze shifted between Rick and Eden. "We hadn't planned to tell you tonight, but now that the subject has come up, we were wondering whether you guys would be our witnesses?"

"Of course!" Rick and Eden replied in unison.

Rick raised his glass. "I propose a toast. To new beginnings."

Simon, Grace and Eden lifted their crystal champagne flutes to his, setting off a harmonious little tinkle. "To new beginnings."

# Chapter Nineteen

## The Nordic Code

Simon pulled his phone out of the back pocket of his jeans. "All right, I suppose it's time for me to finally reveal this code, huh?" The screen lit up, his gray-blue eyes turning almost turquoise.

He scrolled and scrolled then stopped and glanced up. "We found an old Nordic language book in your library, as you predicted, and successfully used it to translate your dad's inscription."

Simon cleared his throat. "Deep inside the chambers of my cavernous heart lay secrets, truth and eternal love."

They were nice, poetic words, words that sounded super familiar, though what did they mean? And where had he heard them? Obviously the phrase hid something important, or else why had his dad gone to the trouble of coding something so complex, so obscure? "It's lovely, but what's it trying to tell us?"

Eden rejoined Rick on the adjacent couch. He wrapped his arm around her and held her close, so close their heartbeats almost synchronized. "Maybe just that," she said.

"No, it's too simple." Rick tapped his fingers on his lips. "There's something cryptic in there. I just need to work out what it is."

"Daddy!" Scarlett's cry sliced through Rick's solution-focused thoughts.

"Looks like someone's not sleeping again." Hopefully the twins wouldn't be plagued by night terrors. They'd seen so much, been exposed to way too many frightening things in their short little lives.

Simon gave him a what-do-you-expect stare. "I'm not surprised. It's been excitement central. It's probably going to take both of them a while to get back to normal."

Whatever normal meant these days. That was something he and Eden and the kids would need to explore.

"And you know this from experience?" Rick said with a smart-alecky smile and moved toward the door.

"Well, no. But I'm a scientist and I've read all the studies."

They all laughed, the sound soothing, healing, natural.

"Daddy!" Scarlett's voice rang out louder and more desperate.

"I'll be back shortly." Rick took off upstairs and entered the twins' bedroom. Scarlett stood in her cot with a beaming smile on her face. He did a double-take. He'd expected a stressed response, not a cheerful one.

"Shh-h... You'll wake up Blake."

"Blake? Uh-uh. He's out of it. He's really tired from the trip."

"And you're not?"

"I am but…I wanted to say goodnight and…"

He touched her small, sweet face. "Is everything okay?" In other words, *you're not scared, are you?*

She beckoned him to come closer and clutched her chest. "I feel someone close by."

Rick studied his daughter. She didn't seem upset or rattled. In fact, a gleeful glow emanated from her, almost like she was in love. *Odd.* "What do you mean, *feel someone?*"

"Like how I feel you and Mummy and Blake, but a bit different."

Rick searched her eyes. "Scary different?" It didn't look like it — it looked like the total opposite. However, he had to check.

"No. Exciting different."

Rick smiled and kissed the golden curls stuck to her damp forehead. "A lot has happened and you're probably just happy to be home."

His words were like a pin to a party balloon, the elation draining from her face and leaving it deflated. "Oh."

He tipped up her sad, pouty chin. "It's not a bad thing. It's normal…totally normal."

"If you say so."

Rick had intended to calm and comfort her…and hadn't quite succeeded. She lay back down, the turmoil and disappointment in her jade violet-flecked eyes screaming *you-don't-believe-me.*

He wanted to believe her, but what did her words mean? They stumped him, just like his father's code did. Not knowing what else to say, what could improve the situation, he did the dad thing and covered her with her quilt. He kissed her on the cheek, hoping his actions at least offered some support. "Now get some sleep, okay?"

She gave him a watery, wounded smile and closed her eyes.

\* \* \* \*

Rune bit into the throbbing artery of the deer's neck, sucking down every single drop of blood, then tossed aside the lifeless carcass. *Ugh. Full.* He rubbed his rounded belly and slow-mo-ed to his feet. His dad's purple dot blipped, getting close…again.

His heart thumped like the dirty bass at a rock band's stadium show. Had Beauregarde come back to find him and finish him off? Or did he want to collect him and hand him over to Sub Rosa as a prize specimen to be tested and prodded and poked?

The green, purple-centered dot flashed like a laser light in his mind's eye. He squeezed his eyes shut. *Look at me!* the bright dot demanded, like a rescue flare drawing him to a secret spot. Whoever the dot represented had traveled from Norway and now lived super close by.

He jogged back to the underground hidey hole, a sparkling star shining overhead, nature's air traffic controller, guiding his way. Maybe he'd finally meet the mystery person.

The no-longer-white-haired guy opened the door into the concealed chamber. "Any stray Jades or Violets about?" The weak, mid-nineties man he'd first met had morphed into a strong, middle-aged warrior, matching his mental toughness—and all thanks to Rune's revitalizing tears.

"None so far…though my internal GPS is working overtime tonight." Rune stretched out on the couch.

The man perched on the edge of the seat, next to Rune's hip. "What do you mean? Is your dad here?"

Rune swiped the hair out of his eyes and met the man's concerned stare. "Yeah, looks like it. But it's not just that. Remember the other dot I told you about? That person's close by now too." The green, purple-centered dot pulsed at a steady tempo, slowing down and syncing with his heartbeat. Each pulse warmed his blood with affection, as though the person sensed Rune was speaking about them…and liked it.

"Are you going to track them?"

Rune refocused his eyes on the guy beside him. "I don't know."

"Aren't you curious to find out who it is?"

"Yes…and no. What if they're working with my dad?" The vibe from the green, purple-centered dot pulsed with love, not hate, but it could be a ploy. A more mature Violet with strong manipulative powers could totally be setting him up.

The man went into full father mode—not an absent, sperm-donating dick of a dad, a real, caring one, wanting the best for his son. "What if they're not?"

Rune's chest swelled, as though pumped up with love. "I'll think about it."

"Make sure you don't wait too long or you might miss the opportunity."

# Chapter Twenty

Discovering a Hidden Treasure

Keys in hand, Rick strode out to the car.

"You're very quiet this morning. Is everything all right?" Eden's voice caught up to him just before she entwined their fingers together.

He stopped in front of the Eros and Psyche fountain and looked into her eyes. "I'm just a little preoccupied. My dad's code is doing in my head. I thought that once I knew what it said, I'd have the answer. Instead, I've got more questions. What could it possibly mean?"

"That he loved your mum very much?"

He smiled and propped against the circular outer edge of the statue. "Yes... I keep trying to convince myself that it might just be another one of his love notes, where he'd upped the criteria for a bit of a challenge, and ended up making it too difficult for Mum to decipher...but there's this persistent gnawing in my gut that refuses to let me believe it's that simple. Why go to so much trouble with this particular message? And what's with the 'secrets' and 'truth' reference?"

Eden shifted closer until she stood between his legs and placed her hands on his chest. "Rick, it's been two weeks already. How long are you going to persevere?"

He slowly rubbed his palms up and down the back of her hands. "Until I'm convinced that I know what it really means. While my mind continues to work overtime and the little metaphorical dog keeps treating my stomach like a bone, I can't let the code meaning go."

She speared him with her sensible-Eden stare. "Not to sound negative, but you might never find out. Don't let it eat you up inside. The kids need you. *I* need you."

He lifted curled fingers to her beautiful, concerned face and caressed her cheek. "I know. I promise I won't let it consume me. I just feel like I'm really close."

She stepped back, grasped his hand and tugged him toward the car. They drove straight to the airport and waited in the international arrivals area, his brain still working through code meanings in the background.

Not long after they had arrived, Rhoda and Ethan strolled out of the center of three doors. Eden rushed over, hugged her dad and kissed her mother-in-law hello. "Um...where's my uncle?"

Rick hugged his mum then hesitated in front of Ethan.

"He's been called in for more questioning." Ethan jutted out his hand, grasped Rick's and did something Rick never thought he'd see—he pulled him in, a Jade, for a brief but genuine man-hug.

When they parted, Rick stood, stunned, like he'd been jolted out of a surreal dream.

Rhoda ushered them into a loose huddle. "They think Andy was involved in Salvator's death. Apparently someone told the police your uncle might know something, because he worked at Sub Rosa for so long."

"Do you think they'll arrest him?" Eden's voice jittered and Rick could almost sense the worry plummeting to the bottom of her stomach.

Ethan put a comforting hand on her arm. "It's hard to know. It'll depend on what information he can offer."

Eden stared at Rick. "I doubt he had anything to do with Salvator's murder. He did do some awful things to you and me, in particular, though he seems remorseful. I'm willing to forgive him."

Ethan's lips lifted into a rare, unexpected, approving smile. "You really are a very sweet girl, just like your mother Eva..."

Eden had been named after her mother? That must have been such a difficult, heartrending decision for his father-in-law, given the circumstances.

She wrapped Ethan in a hug. "Thanks, Dad." Tears bulged in her eyes. Of course she'd be sad about never knowing her mum, having lost her soon after childbirth, but she had her father. And from Rick's in-depth conversations with Eden since they'd returned, he was certain that she couldn't be more grateful.

Ethan swiveled to face Rick, his father-in-law's eyes swimming with nostalgia and regret. "Oh, and they caught that corrupt full human who followed you to the carpark too."

*Ballsy. Excellent.*

Rick deposited the airport trolley and it rattled and clanged, securing a spot in the growing metal conga line. Then he rolled their parents' suitcases over to Eden.

One had a violet tag and the other a jade. Heaven forbid their luggage got mixed up. It was so, *Errr Jade germs! Yuck, Violet germs!*, just like kindergarten kids. Rick clamped his teeth together to stifle the full-blown laughter threatening to spew from his lips.

Eden tried and failed to suppress the *you've-got-to-be-kidding* grin pushing at the edges of her mouth. "Let's go."

They walked to the car, loaded it and made it to Fern Tree in less than thirty minutes.

"Oh, Rick, it is beautiful, just like my family home in Norway." Rhoda pressed her face to the back-passenger side window. "Every detail... It is just... perfect."

Rick parked at the top of the driveway, his gaze meeting his mum's in the rear-view mirror. "I told you it looked identical. Hopefully, once the Sub Rosa investigation is done, you'll get the Norway house back."

"Yes, that would wonderful, but I think it will take some time."

"Now, with Sub Rosa shut down, we have all the time in the world." A celebratory smile seized Rick's lips whenever he spoke or even thought those astounding words.

"Oh, a reproduction of our special statue." Rhoda pointed at the Eros and Psyche fountain through the glass.

Eden swiveled in the front passenger seat. "Your special statue?"

His mother's smile turned wistful, bittersweet. "Yes. Abe proposed to me right in front of it. It will always be a special place for me, for us."

"Us too!" Eden held out her hand to Rhoda. "The lady who sold us this soulmate ring swore Eros gave it to Psyche. Before I even knew about the statue, the story drew me in. I connected to it."

"It solidified..." *No. No way.* Rick threw open the car door, jumped out and sprinted across the yard to the fountain.

"Where's he going?" Ethan's voice trailed behind him.

Rick circled the statue, looking for the inscription. *Ah-ha!* He bent over and caught his breath. The familiar words ran along the base of the fountain, etched into the stone like the ten commandments. *Unbelievable!*

Eden raced up and stopped beside him, her breathing ragged. "Are you" – *puff-pant, puff-pant* – "all right?" She glanced at him, then at the fountain and gasped. "It's the –"

"Yeah, I know. I knew I'd seen or heard it before...somewhere." It wasn't quite 'X marks the spot', though not far off.

"Would you like to enlighten us?" Ethan asked.

Rick stood tall and turned to his mum and father-in-law, trying to control his excitement about as well as a kid on Christmas morning. "Sorry. Basically, my dad sent Mum a message in code and...this is it."

Rhoda bent down and traced the engraving with her finger. "Do you think he wanted to let me know that he had recreated our special fountain here?"

"Yes, but it has to mean more than that, or else why send you the message in complicated code? I'm thinking this fountain is more than just a fountain. It holds a secret, something he didn't want just anyone to know about."

Ethan's brow developed its signature cynical crease. "Like what?"

Rick ran his hands along the cool, smooth marble and scanned it from top to bottom, right to left. "I'm not sure...yet." He completed a slow, clockwise circuit. Outside of the quote, nothing else stood out. He stepped back and scratched his head. There had to be something — an indent, a small symbol, a button.

On Rick's second revolution, instead of sweeping his hands across the surface, he poked and pressed.

"Hey, Rick, come and have a look at this." Not even the gushing of the fountain could drown out the excitement in Eden's voice.

Rick hurried around to join her, his mum and Ethan at the front of the fountain.

Eden pointed to a raised love heart, couched between two roses on the base, located directly under the Eros and Psyche statue. "It's your parents' initials."

Sure enough, 'AH + RH' was etched into the heart in Gothic script.

"So Abe..." A sentimental smile stirred on his mum's lips.

Rick bent down and studied the heart. Several of them had similar squiggly designs but only this one had the special dedication. Unsure exactly what to look for, he stared and stared, analyzing every microscopic detail. He reached up as though to caress the carving and shivered.

*A cool draft.*

He dropped his arm by his side. The air caressed his skin, showing not even a hint of a southerly breeze.

*Weird.* Slowly, he lifted his hand until it hovered over the raised heart.

Cold air blew, but it wasn't coming from outside. It came from within the fountain. His heart rate went from steady jog to full-pelt sprint. He glanced at Eden, his mum and Ethan, their expressions showing their eagerness for an explanation. "There's an opening under there." Containing what, he had no clue.

Ethan held his hand over the heart and crouched beside Rick. "It's probably structural."

Definitely structural, possibly hiding a secret, underground compartment. Could it be a cellar, a bunker, a bomb shelter? "I felt a breeze, only coming from here." He touched the heart again, then pressed hard on it.

Nothing. No shifting, not even a slight shake. Rick sighed. He'd thought for sure it would activate something.

He leaned into the heart and lifted his hand off it to release the pressure. The heart sank. Literally. Rick jolted back before he lost his balance, and the water stopped flowing. The fountain creaked open, revealing a stone staircase leading down into a dim, dark chamber.

Rick's mouth gaped like a faulty trap door. He flicked his gaze to the others. Their eyes bugged out and their mouths formed shocked, open 'O's.

"Wait here." Rick ran to the car and returned in under a minute, torch in hand. His gaze shifted from his mum to his wife to her dad. "I'm heading down there to have a look. Does anyone want to join me?"

"Definitely," Eden said.

"I'm in." Ethan's tone had a military-captain edge.

Rick turned to his mum.

"I am too curious not to come."

"Great." Rick sent a beam of torchlight along the stone stairs into the blackness.

The small team followed behind him down the seemingly endless steps. Finally, he reached the bottom, the ground flattening out into a sandstone path within a narrow corridor. The thick, damp air clogged Rick's lungs with fine, floating particles of dust.

He coughed, setting off a spluttering chain reaction. He'd never had asthma, but his chest tightened as though a steel belt had surrounded his airway and squeezed. It had to be nerves — or post-traumatic stress. He *had* been submerged in a claustrophobic storage unit for over forty years.

*Slow calming breaths. Slow calming breaths.*

At the back of the small investigative party, Ethan was last to step off the staircase and onto the flat path. Not even a second later, a loud, scraping, body-shaking slam shook the space.

"We're trapped in here!" Eden's voice sounded breathless, panicked.

Rick's stomach clenched and his pulse pounded in his ears. *Settle down.* Freaking out wouldn't help anyone. "I doubt it. Where there's a way in, there's a way out." The calm confidence of his tone surprised him. He almost even believed himself. "I'd say it's a safety feature, built in to the design, for when my dad hid the Violets and Jades."

"When we planned the house, Abe did speak about a bomb shelter. This must be it. He must have converted it into a refuge instead," Rhoda said.

"Clever." *Ethan, a believer? Wow.* Rick would never have thought it possible.

"Very," Eden said, the tremble now gone from her voice.

*Phew!* His air of self-assurance had worked...as well as his mother's words. "Let's see where the tunnel leads."

The trail wound down, and they walked for nearly forty-five minutes before reaching a large, semi-camouflaged steel door. Rick shone the torch over it, illuminating a circular lock.

Did the secret lie on the other side? "Anyone good at breaking and entering?" Rick said, hoping like hell one of the others could suggest a way in.

"Maybe. Don't ask." Ethan slipped past the ladies and stood beside Rick. He pulled out a couple of toothpicks from his back pocket and prodded the lock, like a skilled surgeon attempting to remove a lodged bullet.

Seconds stretched out to agonizingly slow minutes, as though they were trapped in some warped time zone where two seconds ticked forward and one back. Rick struggled to stand still, his foot scraping against the sandstone, straining to hear the click of the lock. "How's it going?"

"It's not," Ethan grumbled. "Whoever designed this knew the tricks and made it impossible for people like me to break in."

"Maybe we should just knock." Rhoda's slightly-accented, sensible voice cut through the one-way thinking.

Rick stared into his mum's steady green eyes. "Do you really think if a person's on the other side, they'll answer?" Could it really be that simple?

"Probably not, but it is worth a try." Rhoda stepped up and struck her knuckles against the door. *Tap tap tippity tap.*

They waited.

No noise.

Nothing.

They looked at each other, the last flare of hope in their eyes snuffed out like a candle in a windstorm. Other than dynamite, they were out of options.

Rhoda knocked again, louder this time, each strike echoing down the passage.

Nothing.

A giant dump truck of disappointment tipped its load on top of Rick and his body slumped. He'd really thought all the answers would finally be revealed. Now he'd just have to be patient...until they found a solution.

Patience—the story of his life so far. "We may as well head back. Maybe there's some info in the house on how to open that lock." Rick tried to inject some optimism into his tone...and didn't quite succeed. He pointed the torch beam along the tunnel and started to walk away.

*Ca-clunk. Whuooosh.*

Rick whirled around and stared at the partly open, mammoth door, a bright wedge of light slicing into the dim space. He blinked and squinted, trying to see through the blinding gap.

"R-Rhoda? Is that you?" A man's voice. A familiar man.

Rhoda moved into the light. "Abe? But—"

A middle-aged man threw his arms around her, hugging her so tight that they looked interconnected. But the guy wasn't just any middle-aged man. He looked exactly like Bram...really Abe, Rick's supposedly dead dad.

"I knew it. I could tell your knock anywhere." Abe pulled back, reached for Rhoda's hand and held it.

Rick's mum and dad, both alive, back together and they looked incredible. *Hang on...* His mum's youth he understood, but his dad's? It made no sense. Abe would be in his nineties, and with no vampire genes, he should look ancient. "Dad? What's going on?"

Abe waved them all inside. "Come in. I'll explain."

Rhoda brushed a kiss across Abe's lips. "I have missed you so much."

"I've missed you too. Terribly."

"Thank God we are together again now."

He caressed her cheek. "Just as I had always hoped."

Her smile clearly contained a complexity of stored emotions — nostalgia, relief, love. She kissed him again, let go of his hand and continued through the doorway.

Rick gave his teary-eyed dad a hug before following Rhoda into the hideout. He stopped just inside the door and shunted his gaze back and forth between his parents, *his parents.* He was still in a state of shock.

"Ah...Eva. It's lovely to see you again." Abe gave Eden a kiss on each cheek.

"I go by Eden now. It's a long, convoluted story." She smiled, big, bright and beautiful. "Lovely to see you too."

"Mr. Hall, I presume. I'm Ethan. Ev— Ah...Eden's dad."

They shook hands. "Abe, please. Good to meet you, Ethan."

Once everyone found a seat, Abe shut the door and sat beside Rhoda on a carved, decorative loveseat.

Her wonder-filled eyes met his. "It is just like..."

"Your parents' couch... Where you first kissed me."
She smacked his hand. "Abe."

If Rick's mum could fully blush, her face would be neon red.

Abe's mischievous smile reminded Rick of himself. It seemed he'd inherited his father's teasing behavior. It was amazing how much he'd picked up from his dad, given how little time they'd spent together, how little he knew him.

DNA. Genes. They had power.

Abe leaned in and whispered in Rhoda's ear — something scandalous yet enticing, going by her gasp and the wide-eyed expression on her face.

"Right." Abe inhaled deep and exhaled slow, then glanced at everyone in turn. "Time to fill you in." He cleared his throat and held Rhoda's hand in his lap. "In November 1939, my dear, sweet Rhoda got taken from me, and I had to give up our beloved son, Richard, for adoption...for his safety. After that, I lost my motivation to stay in Tasmania and build a family home. We were supposed to do that together. But after several months of moping around, feeling sorry for myself, I decided it had to stop.

"I needed to change my mindset. I needed to think differently, optimistically, if I wanted a positive outcome. I needed to believe that one day we would be reunited." Abe raised Rhoda's hand to his lips, kissed it and returned their joined hands to his lap.

"The Second World War had started, and air raid and bomb shelters were all the go, so I included one in the architectural plans...as a precaution. I forged ahead with building a replica of Rhoda's centuries-old family home in Norway, with a secret entry through the fountain and under the stairs of the house into what would become the vampire safe haven."

Ethan, Eden and Rhoda sat statue-still and silent, listening. They all looked as riveted as Rick felt.

"My brain constantly churned away in the background, trying to think of how I could get Rhoda out of the Norway compound while, from a safe distance, I kept an eye on Richard.

"When he started working at Sub Rosa, I grew concerned. But the more I thought about it, the more I realized it could be a blessing. Having the right person working from the inside, although potentially dangerous, could be extremely handy.

"I passed myself off as Richard's uncle, eager to find out information that might help me free Rhoda and also to get close, to develop something akin to a father-son relationship without putting either of us in danger. I really wanted to tell the truth but worried about the consequences if anyone at Sub Rosa found out about Richard's origins."

Abe focused on Rick with a *please-forgive-me* look in his eyes. "When you and Eva married in 1965, I still had no useful information on Rhoda. I gifted you the house and used the opportunity to travel to Norway to attempt to break her out. Then I planned for us to retreat down here for a while, to keep Rhoda out of sight and safe and give you and Eva some privacy."

His dad scrubbed his face with his hands. "Unfortunately, my trip turned out opposite to how I'd hoped and I returned full of frustration and despair. I had failed to free Rhoda and found out you and Eva had disappeared. My gut told me Sub Rosa was behind it, but I couldn't prove anything. I couldn't go to the authorities on just a hunch. Plus, I worried that if the police got involved and started poking around, *missing* could soon become *dead*."

Rhoda squeezed Abe's hand. He turned to her and smiled, a resigned, remorseful smile. "I stayed in limbo, waiting, listening for Sub Rosa news to help me develop a new plan of action. I made sure to keep myself busy or I'd have gone insane. I concentrated on shielding Jades and Violets and wrote to Rhoda to stay connected, to keep the romantic fires burning and ensure she remained in the loop...without giving too much away."

He caressed Rhoda's cheek and ran the pad of his thumb across her lips. "I sent the picture frame with the Nordic code, hoping that one day it would lead you here and we could be together again. I never gave up hope.

"In 2007, a researcher named Salvator, a friend of Richard's back in the sixties, visited me and I found out he'd met you in the Norway compound. He looked older, of course, but I recognized him straight away."

He switched his gaze to Rick. "We shared stories and everything was fine until he left. Something just didn't sit right. When he'd spoken about you, he'd gotten all fidgety and struggled to maintain eye contact. He'd definitely held back, kept something from me. I got up and tried to catch him before he drove off, but suffered a heart attack in the front passage."

Eden gasped and Rhoda clutched Abe's hand tighter.

"I came to in the hospital...and decided to fake my own death. One of the Jades staying with me at the time helped. She altered my records to 'deceased' and built me a shortcut, emergency exit out of here and straight into the bush to decrease the chances of drawing attention to myself.

"Given my age, no one questioned my passing. Being dead allowed me to carry on with my work, with my scheme to somehow, some way, be reunited with my family, while decreasing the danger."

Abe glanced at Ethan, Eden, Rhoda and finally his gaze reconnected with Rick's. "Everything went well — or as well as it could for a frail man in his nineties hiding from society and harboring vampire fugitives." That twinkle in his eye returned, the never-give-up persistence and fight-for-fairness Hall trait Rick had inherited.

"This past November, I rescued a Violet-Jade-human boy named Rune and it happened again." Abe rubbed his breastbone. "I'd left him to rest when a pain shot through my chest and radiated down my left arm. I tried to call him but no sound came out. He found me barely conscious, broke down, wept and continued crying until he had literally bathed me in his tears."

A look of pure wonder sparkled in Abe's eyes. "Within a week, I'd fully recovered and looked and felt younger than I had in a very long time. I couldn't believe the man I saw in the mirror. I could only attribute the changes to the vampire tears. They seemed to have both healing and age-reversing, fountain-of-youth properties.

"With Rune's permission, I bottled some and began ingesting a couple of drops daily. As you can see, it has shaved forty years off me. I look and feel middle aged — and I have him to thank for it. He didn't just save my life. He allowed me to live long enough to realize my dream — to finally be reunited with my wife and son."

Rhoda hugged Abe and he kissed her forehead like she was a priceless cherished gift.

"Wow." Eden's eyes widened with a look of awe, wonder.

"Incredible." It was the first word Ethan had uttered since the introductions. Rick had never seen him so silent. It seemed that all of them had been moved by Abe's amazing story, even a hard-ass, anti-Jade Violet.

"Big time!" Rick moved to sit on the other side of his dad. "You know, we were living in the house for the past year. What a shame neither of us realized."

Abe kept one arm around Rhoda and angled himself toward Rick. "I agree. Several times I nearly ventured back up there. However, my frailty and the fact that I was supposedly dead meant I couldn't afford to be out and about too much.

"My vampire boarders informed me that people were living in the house but I never even dared to think it could be you and Ev...Eden. I thought the real estate sharks had decided to make some money off an as-yet-unclaimed, deceased estate."

"Yeah, sadly, it's not too far of a stretch." The more Rick studied his dad, the more memories of Bram infiltrated his mind. It helped that Abe looked around the same age as Bram when Rick had last seen him.

Maybe with time, more real memories would trickle through and he could gain back more of his life. Although it would be great, he'd learned the importance of living in the present. "Speaking of vampire boarders, what happened to Rune?"

"He's still here. Well, close by. He should be back soon. He's such a sweet, caring boy."

Rick smiled, joy spreading through his body like a hit of high-quality MDMA. He'd found his dad alive and had Rune to thank for it. "I'm looking forward to meeting him."

"Me too." Eden approached Rick and he drew her down onto his lap, her euphoria absorbing into his skin and notching him up to a state of pure bliss.

Rick wrapped his arms around Eden's waist and made eye contact with his dad. "Being tucked away down here, I'm assuming you haven't heard the news about Sub Rosa?"

Abe's forehead furrowed, deep grooves denting his middle-aged appearance. "What news?"

"It's been officially shut down and Andy, the current CEO, has been arrested. All the Jades and Violets are finally free and can now live a relaxed, peaceful life…together. No one needs to hide anymore." Rick could hardly contain the huge smile stretching his lips.

Eden looked up to Rick like an adoring star-struck fan. "And who do we have to thank for that?"

Heat rushed to his cheeks like she'd held a bare-flamed torch to his skin. He never had taken compliments well, especially when broadcast in front of a group. "We all played a part."

Ethan walked over, slammed a firm hand on Rick's shoulder and looked him in the eye. "You're too modest. If it wasn't for your bravery, intelligence and quick thinking, this uprising wouldn't have happened. We're all indebted to you."

*Whoa.* Had he heard right? Flattery from grim, gruff Ethan? "Thanks, but—"

"No buts. He is right." His mum's praise didn't surprise him—however, the feeling of pride it stirred up absolutely did.

Abe slapped a warm hand on Rick's arm. "That's my boy!"

Eden stared at her gold marcasite watch. "Look at the time! Simon and Grace must be wondering what happened to us!" She stood and tugged on Rick's hand. "We should make our way to the main house..."

Rick glanced at Abe. "And you can meet our twins — Blake and Scarlett."

"Twins?" Abe jumped up from his seat, grabbed a set of keys off the antique coffee table and strode toward the door. "What are we waiting for?"

# Chapter Twenty-One

Surprise!

Rick emerged from a hidden trapdoor under the main stairs of the house, while the others followed behind. Light chatter floated down the hall. There were more voices than just Simon and Grace. Some others must have arrived. Could one of the guests be the elusive Rune?

He continued to the conservatory, and in between Grace and what appeared to be a full Violet, sat Indigo, Eden's boss, the senior manager of organizational culture. *What the hell is going on?*

Simon carried a tray of drinks over to the coffee table and glanced at Rick. "We wondered where you'd gotten to."

The chatter ceased and they all turned around to look at him.

"Um…we had an unexpected detour…"

Grace shot Rick a tell-me-the-truth stare. "Is everything all right?"

Rick smiled and the tension in her face eased. "More than all right. Are the kids asleep?"

"Yeah, I put them to bed about ten minutes ago. They couldn't keep their little eyes open."

The Violet rose and walked toward Rick, his eyes unexpectedly warm and gentle. "We haven't met. I'm Hugh. I believe you already know my wife, Indigo."

*How the fuck did they get together?*

"They had only just gotten married at the top end of Norway, with the Northern lights as a backdrop. You should hear their story. It's so romantic! A researcher called Salvator created a sunlight bar glitch back in the mid-nineties that helped Hugh escape. He met Indigo while on the run. But I should let them tell it." He hadn't expected such gushiness from Grace, someone who was usually so…liberated, carefree, free-spirited.

*Salvator…* Had Hugh heard what had happened?

"We will, later. Seems like there are a lot more important things to catch up on first." Indigo averted her large, cobalt blue eyes, strings of caramel curls falling across her flushed cheeks.

*Sweet and switched on.* Hugh had done well. Indigo and a pure Violet? A match made in heaven.

Hugh's gaze reconnected with Rick's. "I hope you don't mind us barging in. We came straight from the airport. We wanted to thank you and Ethan for helping us. And Salvator… Do you know where I can find him, by any chance?"

"Unfortunately, Salvator was another Sub Rosa casualty. Andy had him killed when he found out that he'd tried to log in to classified files remotely. Eden and I had only just gotten in contact with him. It's a long story, but basically he planned to help us bring down Sub Rosa."

"I am so very sad to hear that. If not for him, Indigo and I never would have met." Tears swelled in Hugh's eyes and tumbled down his cheeks. He swiped at his face with the back of his hands. "I'm sorry about this."

Indigo joined her husband, put her arm around him and rubbed his back with long, soothing strokes.

Rick could almost feel the love bond between them. "There's nothing to be sorry about. I'm sorry to have upset you."

Hugh's tears slowed down and he smiled with a mix of grief and gratitude. "It's okay. I'm fine. Thank you for telling me."

"So…how did you know where to find us?"

"Oh, Ethan mentioned you both and this place – and that he planned to visit."

The more Rick looked into Hugh's eyes, the more he couldn't look away. Now that the tears had stopped, they had a calming, meditative, almost hypnotizing quality. "Well, you're in luck. He's right behind me."

As if on cue, Eden and Ethan entered the room, followed by Abe and Rhoda, holding hands.

Simon nudged Rick's arm. "You didn't tell me you were having a party."

Rick chuckled. "I didn't realize I was either."

"I'll get more glasses."

After Rick introduced everyone, Hugh went straight over to Eden and reached for her right hand. He raised it, as though to plant a kiss on it, but stopped short of his lips. "Unbelievable." His gaze moved between her hand and her eyes.

Eden glanced at Rick with a 'what the – ?' expression on her face.

"Oh, I'm sorry." Hugh lowered her hand to her side. "I should explain myself." His violet eyes glowed with wonder and sparked with barely restrained excitement.

"It's your hematite ring. I made it...a very long time ago.

"I gave it to my Violet brother, David, to support and protect his forbidden relationship with a Jade named Oriel. It helped them stay together in a non-conventional way, to be as one when the whole world rejected them. You see, it's a soulmate ring, attracting couples who are in danger of being separated."

The bright guiding star flashed into Rick's mind. Could a heavenly body like that be what Hugh meant by non-conventional, by David and Oriel being as one? Were they up there in the sky helping protect other forbidden lovers from separation? Before what he'd experienced, he'd never have believed it. Now, he wouldn't be surprised.

"That is so...freaky." Eden stared at the ring on her hand. "Rick bought it for me when we started dating, before all this happened." She looked at Rick then at Hugh. "We gravitated toward it, like a magnet."

"Actually, it started before that." Everyone turned to look at Abe. "I came across the ring on my travels, and out of desperation I bought it, hoping it would help me free Rhoda. However, I soon realized we needed to be together and under threat of separation for it to work.

"I held on to it anyway, part of me still wishing it would help. Then when you and Richard announced you were engaged, back in 1965, the ring—it sounds crazy, but it spoke to me in a non-verbal way. An indescribable pressure built in my brain, almost forcing me to hand it over to you."

Rick stared at his dad, awestruck and totally rapt. "I'm so glad you did. Coming across the ring at the market helped get us back together—me and Eden, you and Mum, me and you two, and Eden and Ethan—back to the truth."

Hugh smiled, his lips spread wide and beaming with pride. "I'm glad to see it's done its job."

The conversation seemed to stimulate everyone's appetite and they chatted more over dinner.

Soon after they had finished eating, Simon and Grace stood, hand in hand. "Sorry to break up the party, but we should go," Simon said.

Rick kissed Grace on the cheek and shook Simon's hand. "No worries. Thanks again for babysitting the kids...and playing host."

"Any time." Grace cast her gaze across the group. "It's been lovely meeting you all."

"We must arrange another get-together soon." Abe's smile radiated warmth and enthusiasm.

Rick escorted Simon and Grace to the front door and stopped halfway down the hall, blinded by ultraviolet-jade light. He raised his arm to shield his squinted, fluttering eyes and tried to focus.

"Where's Abe?" A young man's voice simmered with tension.

Rick stepped forward. "Rune?"

The light ratcheted up to high beam. "Where's Abe?" The kid's teeth clamped together in a bone-crushing grind.

Rick held up his hands in a gesture of surrender. "He's right here. Dad?"

Abe entered the passageway and stood with Rick. "It's okay, Rune. Rick is my son."

Rune dropped his head, the violet-jade light sweeping in an arc across the timber floor. "Sorry. When I got back you weren't there. I waited and waited and when you didn't come..."

Abe went to Rune and slung his arm around the young man's lean, muscular shoulders. "You were worried. It's totally understandable. But everything's fine. How about you come in and meet everyone?"

He nodded in that shy, universal teenage way.

"Daddy!" Scarlett's little cry drifted down the stairs.

Rune jolted his head up. "Who's that?"

Rick smiled. "My daughter, Scarlett."

Rune darted his now powered-down gaze across to Abe. "She's it— She's the green-purple dot." Whatever the hell that meant.

The young man's intense eyes focused on Rick's, his gaze softening further to a warm, violet-jade glow. "Scarlett is like me."

How did he know that? He hadn't even seen her yet. And what was this green-purple dot business? Maybe he also had a heightened sense of feeling similar to what Scarlett had described.

"We can't go now. I've got to see what happens," Grace said, and dragged Simon back into the conservatory.

Rick went to collect Scarlett and Blake and brought them downstairs, where they were showered with kisses and hugs. They smiled and giggled in that contagious toddler way, lapping up the attention.

Rune stood back from the crowd, his hands in his pockets, and stared at Scarlett, but not in a creepy way. He seemed to study and compare her to him, as though trying to make sense of things.

She glanced up and froze, her gaze locking on Rune's. A shiver of excitement rippled through her little body.

Blake looked at her and gurgled. Had he sensed it too? She blushed and averted her eyes from Rune's scrutiny. They definitely had some kind of special, shared connection. Only time would tell what sort.

"My precious grandchildren." Abe's eyes glistened and he reached out to them. They went willingly and he kissed and cuddled them tight.

Rune approached Scarlett, his stare resolute. They had a plug-in-socket bond, creating electricity, not only between, but also around them. Rick's skin pulsed with warm positivity.

Scarlett touched the young man's cheek. "Can I play with Rune?"

Rick looked at Eden. The relaxed joyfulness on her face indicated she felt it too. "Of course."

A shy smile pushed at the corners of Rune's lips and he held her awkwardly in his arms. He gave her a hesitant hug and patted the top of her head.

Scarlett turned to Rick and Eden. "I'm going to marry Rune."

Grace clapped her hands together and smiled. "Aww...that's so cute!"

Rick gave his daughter his best stern-father stare. "I think you might be a bit young for that."

"When I'm bigger, I mean." Scarlett's voice sounded newscaster serious, like she knew it would happen.

Rune's angsty teenage face transformed to gentle and boyish. Maybe Scarlett was right. Maybe they were soulmates, meant to be together. Strangely, the fourteen-year age difference didn't feel disturbing, probably because by the time Scarlett reached adulthood, she and Rune could act on any residual attraction and the age gap would be negligible, given the vampire gene's youth-retaining properties.

A sudden chill frosted the air. Rune shivered, panic pouring from his eyes.

"That's if you both make it, you little mutants!"

Rick spun around, his heart in his throat, desperately searching for the intruder.

Blake cried and scrambled into Eden's arms.

In the doorway, Beauregarde appeared with a snide, fiendish smile on his face.

"You were dead. We disposed of you." Rhoda's disbelieving voice sliced through the hysteria.

"Sorry to disappoint." Beauregarde entered the room with not even an ounce of apology evident in his swagger. "Ah, Hugh, Indigo... What a lovely surprise. I didn't expect to see you here." He slapped his hand against his heart and shot a dagger-filled stare at Hugh. "Things just keep getting better and better."

In an instant, Beauregarde had Rick in a chokehold. Rick gasped, fighting to suck in some oxygen. How had the prick moved so fast? "I think I'll start with you. I don't like leaving unfinished business." His cold breath pelted against Rick's neck, like ice shrapnel.

"Rick!" Eden screamed, triggering memories of the moment he'd been shot. Scarlett's rewind-time powers might be required, but would they have enough potency to reverse this situation? She'd be competing against Beauregarde, an experienced Violet, his special ability honed and strengthened.

Rune deposited Scarlett on the couch and zipped to Rick's side. "Dad, no." His tone sounded don't-mess-with-me firm.

*Beauregarde? Rune's dad?* A father and son couldn't be more different.

A booming, guttural laugh rumbled from Beauregarde's chest. "Dad? That's hilarious. I disowned you. Remember?"

Rune glowered and stepped right into Beauregarde's face, his jaw tensing.

"Rune!" Scarlett sobbed and Rick could almost hear her bottom lip quivering.

Dark blotches marred Rick's vision and he wobbled, his legs like semi-set jelly.

"It'll be okay." Rune stared down his dad but kept his voice steady, gentle in response to Scarlett.

Beauregarde snickered and Rune charged forward, yanking his dad's arm from around Rick's neck. They stumbled backward and Rick dropped to his knees, gulping down large lungfuls of air.

Hugh and Ethan rushed to Rune's side. Beauregarde attempted to throw them off—however, Hugh shoved a balled-up serviette into Beauregarde's mouth while Rune and Ethan pulled the bastard's hands behind his back.

"I've been dying to shut that big trap of yours for centuries." Pure satisfaction infused Hugh's every word.

They dragged Beauregarde toward a dining chair and he went limp, the white linen napkin falling to the floor. He morphed into a violet oil slick and slipped from their grasp.

"What on earth?" Eden murmured, shocked into statue-stillness, as the Beauregarde puddle slithered away.

Indigo grabbed Grace's hand and they retreated into the back corner of the room.

Beauregarde popped up right next to them and they screamed. "You can't catch me, so you may as well stop trying." The arrogant prick didn't even flinch.

"Never!" Hugh catapulted himself like a cannon ball and slammed into Beauregarde. They hit the timber with a loud thud and tumbled out into the corridor.

Ethan and Rune dove into the scrum and, within seconds, they'd restrained the cocky, evil dickhead.

Rick ran to the kitchen, grabbed a large clear container with a lid and returned just as Beauregarde transformed. He rushed over, collected Beauregarde's molten, violet body and sealed the lid. Carrying the container back into the conservatory. It jolted and shook in his hands, so he slammed it onto the floor and sat on top.

Abe's grin reflected Rick's sense of triumph. "Well done."

"What will we do with him?" Rune's eyes twitched with worry. "It won't take him long to work out a way to escape."

Hugh pressed a reassuring palm against Rune's back. "I have a solution." He glanced at a dumbstruck Simon, sitting at the table. "You mentioned before that you've come up with the cure for vampirism, correct?"

Simon nodded.

"Beauregarde always complained about how he'd been changed without a choice and grieved for his humanness so, why don't we give it to him? It'll be a happy ending for everyone. He gets what he supposedly always wanted and it renders him harmless."

The container jumped and shuddered under Rick's butt, as if in protest. "Sounds perfect." He directed his gaze at his stupefied friend. "Have you got any vials handy?"

"Ah…" Simon stammered and swallowed once, twice, three times. "I do. I-I've still got some left from when Beauregarde bit Grace."

*Beauregarde bit Grace?* When the hell did that happen? Simon had conveniently omitted that juicy piece of information.

"What?" Eden said, her voice shaky, shocked.

"I'll explain later. My satchel's in the car." Simon ran out of the room and returned, after a couple of minutes, with a vial containing a glittery gold substance. "Who would like to do the honors?"

The lid shook under Rick's butt and nearly bucked him off, like a cowboy on a raging bull at a rodeo. "Ooh, he's a feisty little slime, isn't he?"

Hugh chuckled, collected the vial from Simon and joined Rick. "I'm more than happy to do my part in bringing Beauregarde to justice." His vibrant violet gaze swept across the room and connected with Rune's. "But only with my nephew's help."

A deep crease split Rune's forehead. "You're my uncle, as in…my dad's brother?"

"Not by human blood. We share the same vampire parents. They passed on their Violet DNA to both of us."

Studying the similarities between Hugh and Rune, it made sense. Thankfully, Rune had inherited Hugh's strain of the Violet DNA and not his father's.

Rune smiled, large, relieved and radiant. He loped over to Hugh and Rick, stopping on the way to ruffle Scarlett's wavy golden mop of hair.

She giggled, a hearty belly-wobbling little laugh.

Hugh raised the vial to Rune, as though in toast.

Both of them had a resolute gleam in their eyes. "Ready?" The lid jerked and pounded and rattled, but Rick didn't budge.

Hugh removed the stopper and he and Rune held the vial between them. Then they glanced at Rick and nodded.

Rick moved aside, lifted off the rumbling lid and together, Hugh and Rune poured the cure over the mass of violet goo. The golden, glittery substance folded into the churning slime until it melded together. The potent scent of frankincense and myrrh filled the air and the fluid agitation subsided. The violet substance sparkled and thickened, morphing into a solid.

"Stand back!" Rick tipped the changing mass onto the floor and stepped aside.

Eden cuddled Blake close. "Are you sure that's the right thing to do?"

Rick's eyes met her worried gaze. "Trust me."

The small group crowded around Beauregarde and the slimy sludge took shape, like smelted bronze setting into a fully formed statue. He writhed and groaned, his black hair stripping to blond and his eyes from violet to a dull, mud brown.

"Urgh." The reverted Beauregarde sighed and went limp.

Rhoda surveyed his flaccid human body. "Is he dead?"

Rick kneeled down and lowered his ear to Beauregarde's mouth. "Nope. He's breathing just fine." He smirked up at his mum. "I think he's just adjusting to his humanness."

"Let's see how much he enjoys getting what he wished for." Hugh's contagious smile infected everyone in the room, bar Beauregarde.

After several minutes, Beauregarde's eyes struggled open. "Urrgh. I feel like death, like I've broken every bone in my body."

Hugh crouched beside his ex-Violet brother and patted his arm. "You're human again, just as you always wanted. So get used to the pain."

"Human? No. No-o-o!" He tried to sit up, but Hugh held him down.

"You probably need some rest and recovery time…before they cart you off to jail."

Rick forced back a chuckle. Hugh was making the most of it—and deservedly so.

Rune sat cross-legged on the floor in silence, his thick, dark brown hair hiding his face.

Scarlett crawled to the edge of the couch and poked her head around the side, her jade, violet-flecked eyes wide with worry. "You okay?"

His violet, jade-flecked eyes focused on hers, and he ruffled her hair again and smiled. "Better than ever."

# Chapter Twenty-Two

Unity at Last...

Hugh held Indigo's hand and led her into a quaint stone cottage in the Tasmanian woods.

"Where are we?"

"You'll soon see." He pushed open the heavy wooden door, the *creeak* competing with the rowdy resident kookaburras.

His blindfolded wife tugged on his hand and tentatively tapped her foot on the ground in front of her, as though checking for steps. Hugh guided Indigo into the open-plan living room and removed the blindfold.

She blinked and squinted, her eyes adjusting to the bright sun beaming through the sash windows. "Beautiful." She released his hand, stepped toward the light and did a slow, one-hundred-and-eighty-degree turn, taking in the surroundings. Her awe-filled eyes met his. "This is so beautiful, breathtaking."

He released the pent-up air in his lungs. "I hoped you'd say that. I bought it for us. I furnished it with just the basics for now. I thought we could both go shopping and pick some new things for our new life...together. I hope you don't mind. The place was too perfect to pass up."

Her cobalt-blue eyes shone with gratitude and love. "It's exactly everything I've ever wanted. I can't believe you remembered."

"Of course, I remembered. I remember every detail when it comes to you."

Indigo flung herself into his arms and held on like she never wanted to let go. "You're the sweetest, most loving, considerate man."

Love. No other feeling measured up to it. To be truly appreciated and understood was an absolutely priceless living gift. Hugh trailed his hands over the curve of her waist and he tightened his grasp on her hips, plastering their bodies together like space was the enemy.

He had nearly lost her. Those first few days after she'd been shot had been harrowing. Hugh had teetered on the edge of a massive life-changing decision—transform her into a Violet to keep her alive or risk her pulling through as a human. He couldn't lose her again, not when they had just found each other.

They had camped out in Rhoda's abandoned family home on the Norway Sub Rosa site, and he'd only left her bedside long enough to refuel. Hugh's tears wouldn't stop, bathing her in his hope and despair and love.

On the third day she'd sprung to life, like she'd never been hurt, and he'd whisked her off to the Northern Lights for an impromptu wedding, one they should have had fourteen years prior.

And that was when he'd decided. They'd been lucky this time. His tears had healed. But what about in the future? What if he couldn't get to her soon enough? The fragility of life— He wanted to share it with her, equally. To be in sync, to grow.

"I want us to start a whole new life together. And Rick and Simon have been kind enough to help me with that." Hugh took a small vial out of his jeans pocket. "I think you know what this is."

"I know exactly what that is, and you don't need to take it." She pushed the vial aside, the sincerity in her eyes almost his undoing. "I love you for who you are."

"I know. I want to do it, though. I want us to have children. I want to age with you. I want to be able to make love to my wife without fear of hurting her."

She held his face between her hands and brushed the soft pads of her thumbs across his cheekbones. "You won't hurt me."

"I might, by accident."

"It won't happen. You won't let it."

"Even if you're right, what if you become pregnant? Your life will be in danger. I can't take that risk. I can't bear to be without you."

She pressed her palms against his chest, her warmth seeping into his skin. "I don't want to lose you either. What if you have a reaction to the cure and something happens to you?"

"Nothing is going to happen to me except that I'll be human again, like Beauregarde, but hopefully not as miserable." That teased a smile from her lips. "Oh, and my coloring will be a little different too—olive skin, light blue eyes, brown hair. I hope that's acceptable."

Her smile grew to breathtaking proportions. "More than acceptable. I love blue eyes. But violet are amazing too."

He laughed, still not quite believing he'd gotten everything he'd ever hoped for.

The cheer leeched away from her face and her lips flatlined. "You really don't have to do this."

Hugh held her hands over his heart. "I want to. I've never felt so strongly about anything before. Actually, that's not true. Nothing can compare to how I feel about you." Then, with his lightning-fast reflexes, he removed the airtight stopper from the vial of glittery gold liquid and drank the drug before she had a chance to stop him.

Nothing happened. Every sensation felt the same since he'd transformed hundreds of years ago.

A niggle, a twitch, a rush. And all at once it seemed he had millions of invisible surgeons working inside his body, stripping and reassembling his DNA, pulling and stretching, stinging and stabbing, rubbing and pressing. The flood of sensations overwhelmed him, like being in an operating theatre without anesthetic.

A waft of frankincense and myrrh scented the air and the discomfort stopped.

His body hummed with new and vaguely familiar sensations, reprogrammed like restarting a computer in 'system restore' mode.

"Are you okay?" A blurred Indigo stood before him, her voice far away.

*Yes! I'm fine...sort of.* Caught in a trance-like, catatonic state, he couldn't answer her. How long had he been in transition?

Fatigue sank into him and he stumbled toward the closest couch. He slumped onto it and had a sudden urge to breathe, regularly. Did that mean the conversion was complete? "A mirror?" His husky, raw voice scraped his throat.

Indigo dashed off and returned, holding an open compact. Hugh studied his reflection and smiled, suddenly shy and nervous, exposed. "Here I am."

She dropped onto his lap and threw her arms around him, her glorious caramel curls tickling his neck. "Thank God! I started to worry. You've been under for nearly half an hour! I tried to talk to you but you wouldn't respond."

Hugh pulled back and stared into her beautiful blue eyes. "I tried to reply, to let you know I was okay. I just couldn't shift the words from my mind to my mouth. I'm sorry."

She scooted closer. "You don't need to be sorry. How do you feel?"

He squeezed her to him, enjoying the freedom to touch her without the risk of inflicting pain. "Tired, which is kind of nice, actually. It makes me feel human again."

Fatigued or not, Hugh couldn't hold off anymore and kissed his wife, human to human, man to woman. His heart raced, heat radiating from his revived, hot blooded skin. Touching her felt like the first time, though somehow more connected.

He stood, holding her against him, and took her to bed, where they could finally, truly unite.

# Chapter Twenty-Three

Offering Forbidden Fruit?

*Hartman residence, 2028*

"How's Rune doing?" Eden draped her sheer black dressing gown over the nightstand and joined Rick under the doona.

Rick swiped the air, shutting down his holographic computer tablet, folded the mini-projector base and placed it on the bedside table. Then he repositioned himself so he faced his sexy wife. "Fine. Why?"

"He hasn't come around for ages, so I just wondered…"

"Wondered what?"

"Whether he might be seeing someone."

"I doubt it."

"Then why has he stopped visiting? Have we upset him in some way?" Her eyes tracked back and forth, as though scanning her brain for possible incidents.

Rick reached up and caressed her cheek with the back of his fingers. "Sweetheart, he's not upset with us."

Her eyes searched his, not convinced. "Then what is it?"

"Why are you so concerned?"

Eden touched his chest, playing with the smattering of hair and sending tingles of longing to his cock. "I don't know if you've noticed, but Scarlett's been...sad. She really misses him."

"So what are you saying?"

If she didn't stop her distracting strokes soon, he'd press her down and...

"I think you should encourage him to come around."

"You know what that means, right?" The knowledge of the likely consequences tore him from the edge of desire right back to reality.

"That he's going to visit again?"

"Yes, and that we have to be prepared for their relationship to move to the next level."

Her hand froze mid stroke. "You really think...?"

"Yep. It's only a matter of time."

Eden frowned, as though not realizing the full ramifications...until now.

Rick swept a few loose strands of hair off her face. "I know Scarlett is only seventeen in human years, but she's always been advanced for her age. Physically, emotionally and mentally she's more like a twenty-one-year-old. And although Rune's thirty-one, he only looks twenty-five. They're well matched in character and appearance and I don't see why we shouldn't foster their relationship."

Her face turned whiter than white, as though all traces of red blood had been drained. "So you're all right with them possibly having sex?"

"Whether I am or not, do you think it would stop them? If they really want to do it, they'll find a way. We can't have them chaperoned every minute of the day.

Ultimately, they're both pretty sensible, so we just have to trust their judgment."

Eden dropped her hand and scrunched and unscrunched the doona, staring at the creased fabric. "I suppose."

He tipped her chin up and looked her in the eye. "I'm not excited by the prospect of our daughter being sexually active in the near future either, but they seem destined for each other. The most important thing is that they're careful. Although I love the twins more than anything, it would have been nice for us to have a bit more time alone together before they came along, don't you think?"

"Definitely."

They both lay down and Rick wrapped his arms around her, molding her body to him, skin on skin. "A strict, *do-as-I-say* approach might work on Rune, but it'll push Scarlett to rebel. The best way to get the message across is by leaving the lines of communication open and encouraging them to talk to us."

"So what's the plan?"

"What makes you think I've got a plan?"

She drew light, desire-inducing lines on his bare chest. "Because you're Rick and you always have one."

He laughed, forcing himself to stash away his cock-throbbing, heart-racing need to make love to his wife...for the next couple of minutes, anyway. "Well, I thought..."

\* \* \* \*

*The black knight galloped up the driveway on his raven horse. He tied her to the Eros and Psyche fountain, scaled the side wall of the house and slipped into Scarlett's window. He landed on her bedroom floor, quiet as a stealthy panther.*

*Scarlett snapped her eyes open and stared at the Adonis-like male specimen, bathed in pale rose moonlight, his black cape billowing in the cool night breeze. She sat up, her translucent white negligee hugging her skin.*

*"Rune?" She couldn't hide the breathy, undisguised want in her voice.*

*He strode over to her, his violet, jade-flecked eyes flashing with desire. Rune discarded his cape, pressed his strong masculine palms down on either side of her and leaned in, his hot lips melding with hers. Playful kisses teased, taunted, made her ache and pine for more.*

*Then he pulled back, his gaze following a scorching path along every curve, caressing her almost-naked body.*

*Rune kicked off his black, silver-buckled boots, undid his black shirt and pants, whipped off his black boxers and kneeled before her. He grabbed her bunched-up slip, lifted it over her head and pulled her onto his lap. She clung to him, locked in a frantic kiss, Rune using his fingers to undertake a slow explorative journey right to the heart of her.*

*One more swipe of his thumb across her clit and she came, glowing like a jade neon sign with a violet aura. He lay her back against the bed, pressed the head of his cock to her entrance and eased into her wet opening.*

*They set a smooth, sexy rhythm and soon the glowing light traveled over his body and he orgasmed. His raspy groans sent her over the edge once more and she climaxed. They remained joined, riding out every last bit of pleasure, engulfed in one big circle of brilliance.*

*They collapsed against the bed, still entwined, and continued to kiss and caress in their cocoon of bliss, the jade and purple aura starting to fade on their return to earth.*

*Scarlett shifted to cover them with the quilt, and a jade ball of light shone in her eyes, pulsing just above her pubic bone. She rubbed her hand on the hot spot...*

"Rune!" Her eyes flew open and she sat up, her heart hammering, air grating her windpipe. She slammed her hand against her lower stomach. *Just a dream.* Scarlett lay back down. What did it mean? Her subconscious nighttime images had a way of connecting to real life. Maybe she would see him again soon. That had to be it.

Her heart fluttered like a lovestruck, gushy teenager, which she was. But she couldn't just put it down to her raging pubescent hormones. She'd reacted to Rune from the first moment they'd met. Even before.

All morning her stomach twitched with unexplainable excitement that heightened in the afternoon. She hung out with Blake in the conservatory, trying to distract herself, trying to sit still when a delicious rush surged through her body and swirled around her heart. "He's here!" She clutched her chest with one hand and her navel with the other.

"Who's here?" Blake flicked virtual buttons and swiped his holographic mobile phone without even glancing at her.

"Rune, who else?"

That got his wayward attention. "What's he doing here? Mum and Dad are going out..."

"Maybe he wanted to visit us." *Me in particular, hopefully...* She jumped up from the couch and skipped toward the door leading into the kitchen. "I'll get dinner ready."

Adrenalin coursed through her veins, making her almost lightheaded. Rune had finally returned. Had he missed her as much as she had missed him? Was that even possible? If he had, wouldn't he have dropped by earlier?

She braced herself against the dark granite bench top. Did he have a girlfriend? No. If he did, wouldn't her dad have told her? And if Rune had started seeing someone else, why come and visit her now? Unless he felt he owed her the truth, no matter how hard.

*Stop it!* Speculation wasted energy and time and caused unnecessary worry. He would arrive any minute and she would have her truth radar ready.

# Chapter Twenty-Four

Sweet Seventeen?

"You're sure you don't mind staying home with the kids tonight?" Rick grabbed his jacket and hovered in the front doorway.

"Dad, we're like...seventeen. We don't need a babysitter. No offense, Rune," Blake yelled from down the hall.

Rune didn't blame the guy. He and Scarlett were more than old enough to look after themselves — or was Rune just trying to convince himself of her maturity? Give himself permission to feel and accept the growing, unrelenting attraction to the gorgeous young woman? No, not just feel and accept. Act on.

"No worries, Rick. Happy to help." Rune waved him off, along with his inappropriate thoughts for the man's daughter, who he had agreed to babysit. *Shit.*

Rune found Blake in the conservatory and the guy greeted him with a trademark teenage semi-scowl. "I'll make sure I keep out of your way. Just pretend I'm not here."

Blake rolled his eyes. "Uh-ha." He scrolled through a message on his holographic mobile. "Scarlett's in the kitchen," he said, already refocused on his bloody phone.

Technology had seemed to infect the younger generation like an addictive disease, creating a worldwide epidemic. Rune got it. He too had become attached to his mobile like a third arm, but he'd been vigilant about putting it away and socializing, rather than succumbing to the obsession. It all came down to control.

Rune walked toward the adjoining door, trying to keep his steps even, carefree, his heart racing like he'd just completed a high-impact cardio session. "Oh, and don't worry about sneaking your girlfriend in. I won't say anything."

"How did you...?"

Deflection, and it worked a treat. Rune grinned. Blake couldn't be any more transparent if he were a clear pane of glass.

Rune eased the kitchen door open and froze. Scarlett stood at the open fridge, her golden hair flowing down her slender back. He had watched her grow into this breathtaking young woman. Each day she'd become harder and harder to resist, a forbidden temptation, like an illicit drug craving.

"Rune!" Scarlett spun around, her irresistible jade, violet-flecked eyes and lithe, sexy body flooding him with a soul-deep yearning. She ran over and hugged him, her white cheesecloth dress clinging to her womanly curves. "It's so good to see you! It's been ages! You should come around more often. I miss you."

*Don't bar up, don't bar up, don't bar up.* "It's been a bit hard with work." His voice sounded strained, harsh even to his own ears.

She stepped away, a frown marring her sweet, stunning face. "Since you moved out, we hardly see you anymore."

Scarlett had no idea how much he wanted to spend time with her. He thought about her every day, several times. Who was he kidding? Fifteen minutes didn't go by without her invading his thoughts. But with Scarlett still only seventeen and Rick as his boss, he didn't want to overstep the distinct, delineated mark. He had to be patient. "Sorry…"

She thrust her hands onto her hips, highlighting her narrow waist. "Is that all you can say?"

"What do you want me to say?"

She huffed and shook her head, her glorious hair caressing her exposed shoulders. "Nothing. Don't worry." Scarlett stomped to the fridge, selected items from the fully stocked shelves and shoved them on the bench. "Do you want something to eat? I'm making rare steak and steamed veggies for me and Blake."

Did he want something to eat? Oh yeah, but not of the food variety. *Fuck.* He had to stop his deviant thoughts before she discovered he felt as crazy about her as she did about him. "Yeah, that would be nice, thanks. Can I help?"

"You can chop the veggies. You know where everything is." Her clipped voice sounded as sharp as the knife she handed him.

They finished making dinner in silence and retreated into the conservatory to eat.

Rune sat at the head of the table with Scarlett on his right, Blake on his left, and Smokey and Thornton lazing at their feet, just like the non-complicated—okay, less complicated—old times. "So where's this girlfriend of yours?"

Scarlett's eyes bugged and her gaze locked on her brother. "*What* girlfriend? How come you didn't mention her to me?"

Blake stared at his plate and his leg shook, rattling the glasses and cutlery on the table. "Will you guys just leave it alone."

A knowing, semi-smug smile spread onto Scarlett's lips. "Oh, I see. Nothing's happened yet."

"And you were hoping tonight would be the night." No wonder the poor guy didn't want a chaperone.

*Bzzzzz.* Blake's holographic phone projected next to his half-empty plate. He glanced at the notification, blushed and snatched his mobile off the table. "That's it. I'm going upstairs."

"Are you hiding her in your room?" Scarlett used her trademark sisterly teasing tone.

Blake scraped his chair back and stood, swiping his phone shut and shoving it along with his miniscule projector point and fidgety hands in his pockets. "Hilarious."

Rune stared at him until he caught his eye. "You know we're just joking, right? Look, I'm totally fine with her visiting for a bit—just leave your bedroom door open."

Blake's gray eyes flared and his jaw clenched and unclenched. "As if she's going to come if we have a babysitter." His voice went all teenage tantrum and he took off upstairs, leaving Rune and Scarlett alone.

*Shit.* He shouldn't have joined in on the ribbing and scared him off. Blake was his buffer and now he had none. Maybe his subconscious had planned it all along.

Scarlett's gaze latched on to Rune's and wouldn't let go.

He gulped down the remaining red wine in his glass. "So, your dad said Ethan, Abe and Rhoda have been away for a while. When do they get back?"

"Grandpa Abe and Grandma Rhoda in about two weeks. I'm not sure about Grandpa Ethan yet. You know what he's like— He's always got some cause to fight."

Rune chuckled but it sounded forced, nervous. "So, are Abe and Rhoda having a good time?"

"They're loving it, especially Grandma. The Norway trip's been really therapeutic for her, getting back ownership of her family home. They're staying there while they have restorations done, which she's really enjoying."

He fidgeted with the pure white napkin in his lap. "I'm so happy to hear that."

"Yeah, it's great seeing people so in love and supportive of each other. They're true soulmates, like Mum and Dad. Most of my friends think it's gross when they see their parents and especially their grandparents kiss and hug and hold hands, but I think it's beautiful, special. Don't you?" She slid her hand over his thigh and a lightning bolt of lust shot straight to his cock.

He recoiled like she'd poured boiling oil over his leg. "Scarlett, what are you doing?"

She retracted her hand and stood, pink exploding from her chest up to her forehead. Then she turned and ran upstairs, closely followed by Smokey.

*Fuck!* Thornton rubbed against his feet, as though to console him, and he reached down and patted the fluffy little purr boy. For a twenty-one-year-old cat, he still strutted around like a youngster half his age, which shouldn't be a surprise, seeing as Rune had added the odd few tears to Thornton and Smokey's drinking water over the years.

Rune cleared the table, cleaned the dishes, then slumped onto the couch in the conservatory and tried to watch TV. After five minutes, he still couldn't concentrate. Did he really want to push Scarlett away? Because that was what he was doing. He had to think hard about how to best handle the situation.

His mobile buzzed and the charcoal metal, pea-sized projector point in his front pocket transmitted the phone into his hand. Scarlett had sent a visual message. "Sorry about running off before. Can you please come upstairs? I need to speak to you about something." Her eyes were bloodshot. She'd been crying. Guilt sank like a rock in his stomach.

He swiped his phone shut and made his way up to her bedroom. Being alone with her, next to her bed, probably wasn't the best idea, but he prided himself on his control. However, his heart didn't seem as convinced of his ability to uphold his moral standards, pounding against his ribs like the cops at a criminal's door.

He reached her bedroom and tapped on the door's central wood panel, the last remaining barrier between them...other than clothes. And didn't that just send a barrage of naked images tumbling around his brain. He kept his voice quiet. "Scarlett?"

"Come in."

He swung the door open and hesitated on the threshold.

"Can you close the door behind you, please," she called out from her en suite.

The latch clicked shut and he stood, waiting. An enticing mixture of rose petals and exotic spices scented the air. "What did you want to talk to me about?" He tried for an apologetic tone—however, his voice came out all husky, desperate.

Hopefully he hadn't totally fucked things up. If she sent him away and requested never to see him again, how would he cope? What would he do? *Anything and everything to get her back.*

The en suite light flicked off and she stepped into the dimly lit room, wearing a red, almost see-through negligee and sky-high stiletto heels. *Whoa! No.* He tried to take deep, measured breaths. "Scarlett..."

She sauntered over to him and stopped, her full, pert breasts only millimeters from his chest. Had he managed to successfully hide the blaze of desire in his eyes? Going by her forward behavior, he'd failed. Big time.

He squeezed his eyes shut, blocking out the tormenting view of Scarlett, his one true temptress. What if holding on to her meant physically demonstrating his feelings? Could he really go through with it tonight? He wanted to, fuck, he wanted to, but should he? Conflict warred inside him—mind versus heart.

"Rune?" Her whispered voice was laced with vulnerability, uncertainty.

He honed his gaze on her spectacular jade, violet-flecked eyes.

"Do you think I'm attractive?"

"You're beautiful." He couldn't deny it.

"Then why do you keep avoiding me? You won't even hug me anymore. Is there someone else?"

"No." *Never.*

Her eyes searched his, mirroring the confusion of his emotional state. "Then what's the deal?"

"Scarlett, you're seventeen and I'm thirty-one."

"So? You can't compare us to full humans. We're different. We age differently."

She was right. They'd quickly reached mature adulthood, him a strapping man by sixteen and her, a voluptuous woman by fourteen. Then everything had slowed down. Once an adult, the more vampire genetics, the slower the aging. "Still...."

"Don't you love me anymore?" Her words insinuated that he'd loved her all along—and he had. Although she was fourteen human years younger than him, she had sensed their connection just as strongly, possibly more. So not answering truthfully would make him an idiot and a liar.

He touched her upper arms—the supposed safe zone. *Yeah, right.* His skin already tingled with hypersexual awareness. "That's just it. I love you more than ever. It's too tempting being around you, near you."

The vulnerability and uncertainty disappeared from her face and she smiled. "I'm old enough to know what I want, and I want you." She pressed her palm to his black-T-shirt-covered chest and rubbed. "I always have and I always will."

He enclosed her hand with his and held it against his thumping heart. "Although we have feelings for each other, it doesn't mean we should act on them. Not yet. We really should wait."

"For what?" Her question bordered on begging.

"For you to be a bit older."

She pulled her hand from under his and he immediately felt the loss, the disconnection. "Why?"

307

"Because it doesn't look good for a thirty-one-year-old to be dating a seventeen-year-old."

Scarlett stamped her foot, her stiletto heel just missing his big toe. "Stuff what anyone else thinks. Human chronological aging doesn't apply to us. Plus, Mum, Dad and Blake love you. I love you, I'm in love with you and that's all that matters."

"Others will judge…"

She stared at him, her eyes turning into fiery green balls of defiance. "I don't care. I can't wait another year."

"Try waiting sixteen."

Scarlett trailed her hands up over his bare arms and secured them around his neck, flaming need heating his blood. "I can't even imagine what that's like, how frustrating. So why hold off any longer if you don't have to?"

"I don't want to, but I should."

"No, you shouldn't."

"Scarlett…" Rune's resolve almost crumbled.

She dropped her gaze, as though studying the small space between their bodies. After a short silence she glanced up, a spark of excitement flickering in her eyes. "How about this— If you kiss me, I promise I won't hassle you again until I'm eighteen."

His cock perked up at the prospect. "I can't. I have to be responsible. Your parents asked me to look after you and your brother, not make a move on their daughter."

"Come on, please." The pleading look in her eyes made her even more irresistible. How he'd love to hear her beg and scream his name in ecstasy, though that was strictly for another time—in the future.

"Just one kiss, for my seventeenth."

Every bit of lust in his body cranked up to one hundred out of ten on the I'm-so-fucking-turned-on-it-hurts scale. Should he, or shouldn't he? Only a simple, single kiss. Nothing more. That couldn't get them in too much trouble.

His mind's stance shifted more strongly toward *yes* than *no*. What had happened to his moral compass? It seemed to have deserted him. "Just one kiss."

She nodded.

His gaze slid from her sparkling, eager eyes to her succulent parted lips. Eyes, lips. Eyes, lips. Eyes, lips. *Just one kiss...* He stroked her cheek, curving his fingers over her high cheekbone and down, around her jaw. Tipping her chin up, he brushed his lips over hers. Light, gentle contact, yet potent as hell.

She tightened her arms around his neck and molded against him, joining her mouth to his, hot and feverish.

Rune slid his palms along her back and planted his hands on her slender waist, every nerve fiber pinging with desire, like a whole-body climax. He deepened the kiss, their breath intermingling, their tongues delving, caressing, exploring...

She jumped back and pressed at her kiss-swollen lips with the back of her hand, her eyes wide with panic. "My parents— They're nearly home. Quick, go downstairs!"

He didn't move, he couldn't, still recovering from the passion they'd shared. If she hadn't pulled away... "I thought you said they'd be supportive."

"Come on, Rune," she begged, though not in the way he fantasized, and nudged him toward the door. "You need to hurry."

The front door latch clicked and footsteps traveled along the foyer.

He held her worried face between his hands and gave her a quick kiss on the lips, his body protesting the short-lived contact, desperate to continue where they'd left off.

They'd only agreed to one kiss and had shared much, much more. And he didn't just mean physically. The experience seemed to drill right down to his DNA, changing him forever, for the better, so he shouldn't be so greedy. "What am I going to tell them?"

"Nothing."

"I have to."

"No, you don't." She stared up at him, worry transforming her striking face. "What if they don't let you see me anymore?"

"They may not let us be together alone, but I'm sure they'll still let me come around. I mean, I work with your dad...assuming he doesn't fire me."

"He won't fire you. He might ban me from seeing you, though."

"With high risk comes high reward...for the most part."

Her eyes searched his, the violet flecks like chips of amethyst, floating in a jewel-green sea. "What do you mean?"

"If they're okay with us, you'll get your wish. We won't have to wait any longer." And it would give him permission to pursue her, touch her. A shiver of longing rolled up his spine and spiked in his heart. Now that they'd kissed, he wanted her more than ever.

Her forehead crinkled with confusion, surprise, hope. "I thought you said..."

He ran his hands along the length of her trembling arms. "I've changed my mind. You're right. We love each other, and if your family is supportive that's all that matters."

"Rune?" Rick's voice shattered their little love cocoon.

Scarlett jumped, her pulse pounding in the base of her neck.

"Wish me luck!" Rune flashed her his most charming smile and rushed out of the door before she could stop him.

"Oh my God! Oh my God! Oh my God!" Scarlett squealed and slapped her hand over her mouth. "Oops!" she giggled and bounced on the spot. *Wait till I tell Asta!* Her best friend would freak out.

She should have known something amazing would happen after her full-on Rune dream. Scarlett closed her eyes and relived the kiss. Kisses. A wave of pleasure swelled between her legs. Now that they'd broken through the invisible barrier, how could she ever go back? Hopefully they wouldn't have to.

It all depended on how Rune phrased it and her dad's response. Her parents were pretty open-minded and easy going, but she'd never tested them when it came to a romantic relationship. The one positive was that they knew and loved Rune. Would that change when her parents found out they'd kissed? She should take the opportunity to physically re-experience it one more time, just in case.

Scarlett stared at a spot on the thick wooden door and focused. Time stuttered, stagnated, then started to rewind. She stopped the reversing flow just as Rune dipped his head to kiss her.

However, instead of leaning all the way in, he chuckled. "Using your powers wisely, I see."

Heat rose from her chest and flared in her cheeks. "I just wanted to make the most of it. Don't you?"

A wicked grin spread across his gorgeous face.

"That's a yes, right there."

Rune pressed his lips hard against hers, and she thrust her tongue into his mouth, desperate to taste him, to explore the depths of their desire. He groaned and lifted her up, pulling her in tight, the friction of her erect nipples rubbing against his chest and her clit against his hard cock driving her close to coming.

She rocked against him, chasing an orgasm, when gravel crunched in the driveway. Her parents were back already. *Damn. Double damn.* She should have timed it better, ravished Rune a couple minutes earlier, then she'd be writhing and screaming his name right now. But that was probably not the best way for her parents to find out about their revamped relationship.

The front door latch clicked and Rune put her down, breathless. "Scarlett, you're driving me crazy, in the best possible way." His smile radiated naughtiness, like he couldn't stop imagining all the naked fun they could get up to. Or maybe that was just her.

Scarlett squeezed her thighs together, in a pathetic attempt to settle her craving for his cock. Inside her. As well as other places. She wet her lips. "We did agree we wanted to make the most of it."

He laughed, rich and sexy and so do-able. "They do say practice makes perfect. And we shouldn't aim for anything less than expert."

Scarlett slowly walked her fingers down his chest. "We should sneak in another one then."

After their fifth and hottest *close-to-sex-with-their-clothes-on* kiss, Scarlett reluctantly set time back into forward motion. Once Rune had left her to go talk to her parents, she flopped onto her four-poster bed and stared at the intricate canopy centerpiece.

Her mum and dad had to know how much she loved Rune. She'd never even tried to hide it. And he had shown an interest in her too. Nothing sexual, up until now, but there had always been something extra-special about their connection. So their new relationship status shouldn't surprise her parents, shouldn't come as a shock.

Though, maybe their human ages would have an impact on her parents' decision, as Rune feared. Maybe she should have waited until she'd turned eighteen to come on to him. But she couldn't. Her hormones were like petrol flowing through her veins, and him, a struck match.

Not seeing him for the past few months had been torturous. She'd had to take the risk and it had been worth it. Not only had she experienced her first, long awaited, thrilling kiss with the man of her fantasies but also, he'd confessed his love.

The jade flecks in Rune's violet eyes had glowed with intensity right before he'd kissed her each time, the white-hot memory sending a rush of heat from her toes to her fingertips. She traced her hands along the path his had taken, reigniting the ache in her sex. "Rune." His name was a prayer, a vigil, a whispered plea for his return, and not just in the sex sense. She wanted him, needed him, wholly.

Scarlett reached down between her legs and rubbed her swollen clit, desperate for relief. She'd often imagined Rune, using the images to fuel a full-blown orgasm. But this time felt different, better. This time she had some real sensations to add, like a secret ingredient, speeding up the happy ending. "Ah... Ah-h-h-h!" she moaned, coming all over her hand and wishing it was his mouth.

\* \* \* \*

Rick hung his jacket on the coat stand and faced Rune. "How were they?"

Rune swallowed the lump of guilt in his throat. "Fine."

"Are they in bed already?"

Two teenage night owls in bed early would surprise any parent, set off a warning light blinking in their head. And in this case it would be totally justified, spot on, considering what had happened.

Rune shoved his fidgety hands in his front pockets. "Yeah... Ah-h... Can I speak to you about something?"

"Sure." Rick gestured toward the conservatory.

They walked into the back room and Rune sat in his usual spot facing the window, the large pink-tinged moon showering them with rousing rays.

"Would you like a drink?" Rick went to the liquor cabinet and poured himself a Scotch, like his dad-radar had signaled danger ahead and he needed to be ready.

"No, I'm fine, thanks." Not fine exactly. Nervous. Gut-clenching, heart-racing, pulse-pounding nervous.

Rick sat on the couch opposite him. "What's going on?

Rune straightened in his seat. Success was all about confidence and sureness. "I kissed Scarlett."

Rick raised his eyebrows. "You kissed Scarlett?" Surprise tinged his tone, but there was no anger...yet.

*A few times.* "Yeah, sorry. I should've been more responsible."

Rick sank the rest of his Scotch and leaned forward, bracing his elbows on his knees. "When she rewound time more than once, I figured something had happened that she'd wanted to change or, in this case, relive. So how did the kiss come about exactly?"

His breath stuck in his throat, like a fishbone gone down the wrong way. "Um... I tried to keep my distance and she got upset with my *disinterest* and stormed off to her bedroom. About half an hour later she messaged me and apologized and said she needed to speak to me. So I went upstairs and—"

"She came on to you." It wasn't a question, more a clarification. The man knew his daughter. Even so, Rune couldn't let her take the blame.

Rune's gaze crashed to the floor. "It's no excuse. It doesn't matter whether she started it or not. I should have resisted."

"But you couldn't." Rick said it with not even a hint of malice, like he understood the feeling from firsthand experience.

He had to be honest in order to move forward positively. "No."

Rick levered himself up off the couch and Rune startled. Had the guy's calmness masked his true intentions? Would he hit him? Teach him a physical lesson about keeping his hands to himself?

Rick said nothing, walked back over to the liquor cabinet and poured himself another stiff drink, a double this time, the amber fluid filling up half the Scotch glass. That couldn't be a good sign.

Rick returned to his seat, gulped down a large mouthful and stared at Rune, studied him like he'd placed him under a high-powered microscope. "I see."

He had another big swig, without even a blink. "I have to admit that I'm surprised it's taken this long."

"What?"

"It must have been very difficult not to act on your feelings."

More than *very difficult*—that was the hugest understatement of the century. It'd been like trying to convince himself he wasn't hungry, like he didn't need food to survive.

Had Rick's reply been strategic, in order to bait him? Had he adopted the good-cop-style interview tactic to lull Rune into a false sense of security, to make him think he understood, but didn't, and held back ready to pounce?

Rick's calm tone and interested, open posture seemed genuine, like he had no such agenda. Ultimately, even if he did, Rune had to be truthful and prepare to suffer the consequences. "It was."

Rick shifted forward, his scrutinizing gaze like a spotlight, exposing his behavior. "So why did you?"

"What? Wait?"

"Yes."

Rune gulped, his throat raw and scratchy and dry. "She's only seventeen, so I thought I should hold off at least another year."

Rick moved to the edge of his seat, his knees only millimeters away from nudging the coffee table. "But she doesn't want to wait." Although not a question, Rick's words still felt like an interrogation.

"No." His reasoning needed to be clear if he wanted Rick to make a fair judgment.

Rune leaned forward and mirrored Rick's position, their reflections staring up from the glass-top table. "She assured me that I'm the one for her and I know she's the one for me. I've known it from before I even met her, so I'm pretty sure we're meant to be together."

Rick smiled as though Rune had answered correctly. "Then why delay things any longer?"

"Are you saying you'd support a relationship between us?"

Rick finished his Scotch and put the empty glass on the coffee table. "Scarlett's been miserable since you've been away. She loves you very much and I can see you feel the same about her."

"So...the age difference doesn't bother you?"

"Not at all. Eden and I knew it would only be a matter of time before you'd be a couple. Your connection is almost palpable, a living entity."

Relief washed over him like cool-change, summer rain. "Yeah, it feels like that sometimes...most of the time, actually."

Rick scrubbed his hands along his thighs—back and forth, back and forth—his facial expression turning courtroom-judge serious. "I do have one request though. Promise me you two will be careful. Vampire sperm is very persistent and resilient."

Rune squirmed in his seat. "This is weird."

"Why? Sex is a natural thing, a natural need. I just want you to both be prepared. The attraction between you is strong and that, combined with the urges arising from your vampire genetics, means that if you're physically intimate, the chances of it ending in sex are extremely high. So unless you're both wanting a baby straight away, I'd suggest using these."

Rick retrieved his wallet from the back pocket of his pants, dug inside and handed him a couple of packaged condoms. "They're sun-infused and are ninety-nine percent guaranteed to kill off vampire sperm."

Rune had seen them at work but felt awkward asking for details, given that Rick, Simon and Hugh were well aware of the attraction between him and Scarlett. He stared at the condoms in his hand. His future father-in-law had effectively given him the green light to make love to his daughter? He definitely hadn't seen that coming. "So, you're okay with us..."

Rick snatched his glass off the table and returned to the liquor cabinet. "Are you sure you don't want anything?"

"No. Thank you." He had to keep his mind alert, sharp. Being uninhibited would only lead to trouble.

Rick poured some soda water into his glass, swished it around and sculled it, then returned to his seat. "I can't say I'm thrilled by the prospect of you two... But I'm not averse to it. It would be naive to think it's not going to happen, and whether I condone it or not won't make a difference. It won't change your feelings for each other. The thing is, Rune, that if I had to pick anyone for my daughter, it would be you. You're a great guy and we all care about you very much."

Not only had he gained Scarlett's love, which was pretty awesome all on its own, but also the love of a family. Having that sort of connection was something that had always been super important to him. Rune's cheeks burned. They had to be as red as a Santa suit. "Thanks. I really care about all of you too. You guys and Hugh mean everything to me."

Rick smiled, the sincerity reaching his eyes. "If you ever want to talk to me about something, anything, please come and find me, okay? I try to be as fair and non-judgmental as possible."

Rune curled his fingers over the condoms and squeezed them into his hand. "Thanks. I appreciate it."

"I suppose you should go and tell Scarlett the good news... Oh, and you're more than welcome to spend the night any time you want."

Ascending the steps back up to her bedroom felt like walking on billowy clouds on a path to heaven. Had the conversation with Rick really happened? One minute he'd forced his feelings into hiding like a vampire fugitive from Sub Rosa, back in the bad old days, and the next he could express his true emotions like a lovestruck boyfriend serenading the subject of his desire.

Rune reached Scarlett's bedroom and pocketed the condoms. Even with Rick's blessing, he decided to take things snail-pace slow. He and Scarlett had known and understood each other for a long time, but as friends. Now he wanted to savor their getting to know each other as romantic partners, lovers.

Scarlett swung the door open and pulled him inside. "How did everything go?"

Rune pressed a soft kiss to her brow. "Close your eyes and hold out your hand."

"What?"

"Humor me."

"Can't you just tell me?" Impatience radiated off her like heat off a brick on a scorching-hot day.

"I think this will explain everything."

A puzzled smile quirked up the corners of her lips, but she did what he asked.

He placed the condoms onto her outstretched hand. "Check these out."

She opened her eyes and her gaze fixed on the degradable-plastic-coated contraceptives. "Where did you get—?"

"Your dad gave them to me."

Scarlett's cheeks turned as red as her name. "No way!"

"Yep. So I'd say you were right. Your parents are *very* supportive."

Her mouth formed a perfect sex doll 'O'. "He encouraged us to have sex?"

"Not exactly... It's more risk management."

"I knew my parents were great — but not this great!"

Rune chuckled.

She refocused her gaze on the condoms, like the world had twisted on its axis, creating a new gravitational force. "Hm-m-m... Maybe Dad's using reverse psychology? Maybe he thinks by being upfront and supportive, we'll think twice about it and hold off?"

"I don't think so. I think he understands our situation and wants to help."

She curled her fingers over the square packets. "I get what Dad's saying, but when we do it the first time, I want to feel just you inside me."

*Fuck.* Her seductive words made his cock ache. "I'd love that too, but prevention is the priority. There's no easy cure for pregnancy."

"I only ovulate every second month, though, so wouldn't one month be safe? How long can vampire sperm survive?'

*Good question.* "I'm not sure. I'll need to test it."

"When?"

"I'll get straight onto it tomorrow."

Scarlett wound her arms around his neck and pressed the full length of her body against his. "And in the meantime?"

*I guess not everything needs to be off limits.* Rune traced his hands over her thinly-veiled, curvaceous hips, every cell in his body screaming, *I want you.*

The fevered look in her eyes said, *I want you too.* Scarlett sashayed backward, drawing Rune to her double, four-poster bed. She dropped the condoms onto the bedside table and tapped the touch lamp until the light went off, the room remaining bathed in bright rose moon rays.

Scarlett's flaxen hair flowed across the red satin pillowcase, her body on display like a tray of scrumptious desserts. Where would he start? He wanted to try everything at once, a glutton for her beauty. Desire swirled in her eyes, the jade-purple luminosity like Fourth-of-July fireworks.

Rune kissed his way from her lips to her ears, to her neck, to her nipples and right down to her mound. The pulsing green, purple-centered dot in his mind's eye swelled, and a shaft of light spiraled around the outside like an aura.

He stopped, hovering his lips over her pubic bone.

She whimpered. "What's wrong?"

He locked his gaze on hers. "You know how you're a green, purple-centered dot in my internal tracking system?"

"Yeah…"

"Well, something weird just happened. Inside your dot is a pulsating green-purple pinpoint."

"What do you think it means?"

"If my gut instinct is correct, there's only one thing it can mean. If we have unprotected sex, you'll get pregnant."

"Really?"

He placed his palm on her lower belly. "I think it's showing me you've got a viable egg."

Her eyes widened like she'd spotted a huntsman crawling on the wall behind him. "No way!"

He lay alongside her and held her in his arms. "Yep. It looks like my internal tracking system monitors person, place and…conception."

Hope and carnal hunger fought for prominence in her eyes. "So it'll probably tell us when we're safe too? It must pick up on your studliness."

He chuckled. "And the stage of your eggs…" Another sign to hold off on sex. But that didn't mean everything had to wait.

Rune tilted her chin up so their eyes met. "Marry me?"

# Chapter Twenty-Five

The Big Day

*Hobart, Tasmania, December 2029*

The pink dawn crept into the night sky, the early morning light catching Scarlett's beaded wedding dress and sparkling like a brilliant-cut diamond. Rose-gold patterns projected onto the walls and ceiling reminding her of the cherished kaleidoscope toy Rune had given her as a child.

She reached across and ran her palm over Rune's side of the bed. Cold, empty. God, she missed him. Since that amazing April night when he'd first kissed her, they'd been inseparable. He'd pretty much moved back in, with the added bonus of them sharing her bed. The way Rune looked at her, the way he spoke, the way he touched her... Tingles raced over her skin and she sighed.

It had been a little over eighteen months since that incredible, life-changing night, so people probably thought they were having sex. But no... The threat of pregnancy proved to be an excellent contraceptive, though it didn't stop them spending long nights exploring each other's bodies with their eyes, hands and mouths. A thrill, like a surge of electricity, sizzled low in her belly.

Tonight would finally be the night, assuming Rune's internal tracking system backed up the test results. She reached down between her legs and closed her eyes. "Please let it be tonight," she whispered.

\* \* \* \*

Alone. It felt weird. Rune had gotten used to waking up with Scarlett in his arms. Though last night, he'd been relegated to his old silver-and-black-themed bedroom. A teenage time warp meshed with late twenties, frustrated singledom.

Tradition dictated that the bride and groom should be separated, that it would be bad luck for him and Scarlett to set eyes on each other the morning before their nuptials. Hugh was adamant, after what had happened to him and Indigo. Rune considered it superstitious nonsense, but he'd ended up agreeing.

Why tempt fate? And it would only be for one night. He stretched, the black cotton sheets cool and caressing against his naked body. Rune shivered, though not from the cold. He rolled onto his back and folded his hands behind his head, his erect cock tenting the top sheet. In just a few hours he would be reunited with his beautiful bride and they would become husband and wife in every sense.

He took matters into his own hands, stroking himself to orgasm, hoping the release would help him get back to sleep. It didn't. He couldn't lie still, hyperalert and agitated as though he'd ingested twenty cups of strong black coffee. No longer able to rest, he got up and showered, ready for the support crew to arrive.

By eleven a.m. all the guys had invaded his old bedroom, including Simon's fifteen-year-old son, Trent, already dressed in his usher's suit and ready to go. "Hey," he muttered, then slouched onto the double bed and zoned out into a game on his mobile phone.

Rune shook out his sprung-tight shoulders. "Why am I so nervous?"

Hugh walked over and adjusted Rune's violet-jade buttonhole corsage, his lips curving into his trademark reassuring smile. Even after returning to full human, he seemed to retain his emotive power. "It comes with the territory. You'll be fine."

"I still can't believe you and Scarlett are getting married already." Blake fiddled with his tie in the free-standing, gilded-silver mirror. He glanced up, the reflection of his steel gray eyes connecting with Rune's. "Don't get me wrong. You guys are great together. It's just—"

"She's only eighteen. I know that it's not ideal." Guilt and desire warred in Rune's gut. He'd wanted to wait until she'd turned twenty-one, but he'd never convince someone as headstrong as Scarlett. Although frustrating at times, overall he loved that about her. She'd reinforced the strength of their love, that even their families agreed they were meant for each other, and anyone who had issues with them must be mean, ignorant or closed-minded.

Hugh put his hand on Rune's shoulder, his calming blue eyes smoothing out more kinks of tension. "Your circumstances haven't been straightforward boy-meets-girl, but you're making the most of them. You're doing the right thing. Don't ever question that."

His reassuring words made total sense. Though, when had Hugh ever been wrong? Rune had never seen him make a massive mistake. However, Hugh didn't agree. His heart still hadn't fully healed after leaving Indigo at the altar all those years ago.

Forget that no one blamed him, that everyone knew standing her up hadn't been his fault. Sub Rosa had recaptured him, prevented him from fulfilling his promise. But perfectionist Hugh constantly strived for excellence, so he couldn't totally let it go.

A love of people formed Hugh's true essence, demonstrated by the wonderful warmth he radiated, like sitting in front of a fireplace in a cozy cabin. He had a way of putting everyone at ease...except Beauregarde. They were like a split, ex-Violet version of Jekyll and Hyde.

Beauregarde still had a way of hurting, upsetting and polarizing people, even in jail, whereas Hugh brought people together and made them feel calm, heard and appreciated.

Rick appeared in the doorway, all suited up and father-of-the-bride serious. "Ready?"

Rune had been ready and waiting all his life for Scarlett. The impending ceremony and finally making love to his bride were what made him nervous.

Rick led the mini male procession into the back garden of the Hartman gothic mansion, and Rune took his place at the top of the aisle and waited with Hugh and Blake by his side and the celebrant ahead.

He tugged at his black fitted jacket, re-straightened his already aligned black and ivory waistcoat and breathed in slow and deep, out long and hard. Anxiety about the wedding and the wedding night fought for supremacy in his mind.

The act of lovemaking didn't concern him. Scarlett's pleasure rated number one on his priority list. The issue came down to whether unprotected sex would be safe. He'd had all the tests done, as a backup, and according to those, they were well and truly in the extremely-unlikely-to-get-pregnant zone. However, he couldn't stop the stress from simmering in his mind like a brain stew.

His tongue pressed against her pubic bone would be the ultimate litmus test, assuming it had one hundred percent accuracy. But he couldn't be totally sure. His breath sawed against his windpipe.

*Calm down.* If his internal tracking system result matched the sperm potency findings, then the chances of conceiving had to be super-slim to none. So if the two tests aligned tonight, it should confirm it as the best time for them to take the risk.

Soft music played, redirecting his attention down the violet and ivory rose-petal-covered aisle. Hugh's fifteen-year-old daughter Faith led the procession, her shiny Titian-color hair cascading over her shoulders and her violet chiffon dress flouncing around her legs. Behind her, Asta, Scarlett's best friend, looked a picture of willowy elegance, decked out in jade chiffon.

When Faith reached the violet climbing-rose-covered arch, Scarlett appeared, her arm tucked through Rick's. Violet and ivory roses adorned her flowing, golden hair, and perfectly accompanied her figure-hugging ivory lace wedding gown. She glided toward Rune, his soon-to-be wife a breathtaking, sexy angel sent from heaven. He had truly been blessed.

The ceremony flew by, with Rune so mesmerized by Scarlett that he surprised himself by not only remembering his wedding vows but also timing his responses correctly. The whole thing felt surreal, a utopian dream, her betrothal kiss like a princess awakening her prince in a reverse fairy tale. And the best thing of all—none of it was fantasy.

They got whisked away for photos and before Rune could catch his breath, he and Scarlett were directed onto the cozy dancefloor for the bridal waltz.

When the song finished, she grasped his hand. "We should do the rounds."

Her great-uncle sat alone at the guest table, the warm afternoon light doing nothing to soften the cavernous wrinkles on his weathered face. He'd somehow survived into his early nineties and looked every day of it.

Years of chain smoking, drinking and stress had eroded him into a frail, shriveled husk, a sort of man-prune. He fumbled for a cigarette in his shirt pocket, saw Rune and Scarlett approaching and placed it next to his lighter on the tablecloth.

Scarlett and Rune pulled up a couple of chairs next to him.

William rammed his wrinkled, translucent hand through his mass of yellow, cigarette-stained hair. "Congratulations."

"Thanks." Concern sandbagged Scarlett's smile. "So…"

Rune voiced the question that had stalled on his wife's lips. "How are things?" Such a simple, non-threatening query…normally, though not in this case. This came with complexity.

William coughed, the distinctive smoker's rattle clanging in his chest. "I've been better. I'm a living advertisement for how not to lead your life." The words were harsh, but humor twinkled in his eyes.

Scarlett touched her great-uncle's arm. "Don't be like that."

He dropped his gaze to her hand, to the cigarette, then back up to meet her eyes. "It's true. I put your grandfather and mother through hell. Your father too. I still can't believe how forgiving they've been, considering—"

"That was in the past. People make mistakes. We all do. You've got to remember that you've done a lot of great things too. You helped save us and, don't forget, your crucial testimony put Andy *and* Beauregarde away."

William patted her knee. "You're a lovely, very understanding young woman." Then his gaze flicked to the cigarette on the table and across to Rune. "You two are very well suited." With a shaky hand, he picked up the cigarette and lighter. "Some habits are too hard to break."

She clamped her hand on William's feeble forearm. "Why don't you try Rune's tears? They're healin—"

"I know. Thank you, but I don't deserve them."

"Come on." Her eyes pleaded with him to reconsider.

"No, I'm going to be firm on this. I was anti the vampire gene." He shook his head, the stench of stale cigarette smoke tainting the air. "If there's one thing I try my best not to be these days, it's a hypocrite."

Scarlett dipped and angled her head until she regained eye contact with her great-uncle. "You're not. You accept us now."

Rune shifted his chair in closer. "And you have for a long time."

"Yes…" William put one hand on Scarlett's knee and the other on Rune's. "Still, I just can't. Please respect my decision."

She took a deep breath, as though to counteract William's wheezy, labored response. "Of course. We just don't want you to suffer."

"I know. You're both very kind." Her great-uncle rocked forward, and after three attempts, he levered himself up and broke into another coughing fit. "I need some fresh air." He chuckled, the cigarette poised between his gnarled fingers.

The moment he stepped outside the marquee, he lit his cigarette and puffed away, a greedy man sucking up a nicotine feast, smoke drifting lazily toward the sky.

Ethan took William's place beside Scarlett, a glass of special red wine in his hand.

Scarlett kept her eyes on the fading decrepit figure. "I can't help but feel sorry for him."

"Don't."

Scarlett spun to face Ethan. "Granddad, that's a bit harsh!"

"What I mean is that he wouldn't want you to. He's…resigned to his fate."

She shook her head, as though determined not to give up on William. "Anyway, how have you been? What have you been up to?"

"Still ironing out some things in Norway."

Scarlett stiffened, worry oozing out of every pore. Rune reached for her hand and held it. "I thought everything was sorted."

"Not exactly. Even when great things happen, often a few spot fires still need extinguishing. People tend to pull together in a crisis, then revert back to old ways in stable times. It's cyclical. It's animal behavior. I've seen it a lot over the years."

Some people found Ethan too abrupt, too clinical, too honest, whereas Rune appreciated it. He'd always preferred to know the facts of a situation rather than assume. "Are you talking Jade versus Violet or vampires versus humans?"

"All the above. They've nicknamed me 'Switzerland' over there. I'm neutral, the mediator... Who would have ever thought?" Ethan laughed. "I was quite the rabble rouser in my day."

"Wow, great work, Granddad!" Scarlett kissed Ethan on the cheek without letting go of Rune's hand. "But um-m...when do you plan to move back here permanently?"

"When my work's done."

"Please don't take too long. We all miss you. _I_ miss you. I feel like there hasn't been much of a chance for us to spend quality time together."

"You should watch what you wish for. I'll end up being around so much you'll be begging me to leave." A bright smile cracked Ethan's usual surly expression.

"Never!" The violet in Scarlett's eyes flared, as though aligning with her Violet genes and creating a deeper sense of empathy.

Rune joined in on the Violet love. "Impossible." Ethan was a huge asset, with his strong, passionate, honest take on situations, ideas, systems.

Ethan smiled bigger than before, finished his glass of red wine and stood up. "You two are good kids. I'll catch up with you both again later."

He went to the bar and joined Hugh and Simon in conversation. Indigo and Grace chatted nearby, keeping a watchful eye on the bridal table where Faith and Trent whispered and giggled.

Abe and Rhoda cut up the dancefloor like a couple of professional ballroom dancers, while Rick and Eden moved from guest to guest, like the perfect hosts.

"Have you seen Blake and Asta?" Scarlett said, her voice breaking into Rune's observations.

He scanned the surrounds — not in the marquee, not on the dance floor, not in the garden. "They've sneaked off somewhere."

"I doubt it. What would they have to talk about in private? I've known Asta since prep and she's always sworn she'd never be romantically interested in a full human, especially my 'annoying' brother."

"Yeah, but things change. Maybe she's carried an inextinguishable torch for Blake for ages but worried about hooking up with him in case it affected your friendship?"

Scarlett's brow furrowed, as though focused on trying to piece things together and make sense of the situation. "Blake's never even hinted at liking her. You'd think he'd tell me if he had the hots for my best friend."

"Maybe he didn't think he had a chance, considering her stance on full humans. And like her, he probably didn't want it to affect your relationship."

Scarlett squinted her eyes at him in concentration, with a hint of disbelief. "Hm-m-m…" She clasped Rune's hand and whispered, "Let's go check out your theory."

She steered him along the winding backyard path, through vibrant flowers in full bloom, the music from the party growing faint.

A melodic laugh carried like a warm summer breeze from over the other side of the stone-walled garden.

Scarlett eyed Rune, her cheeky smile inviting him to do naughty things to her. *Patience.* It wouldn't be too much longer until they made love. And he wanted to make sure their first time was special, not a quick fuck against a wall. Though that might be fun in future...

He nodded his head toward the opening in the stones. "Shall we?"

The violet flecks glowed in her jade eyes and she nodded.

In the far corner of the secret garden, partially obscured by vivid, rambling, cottage-style plants, Blake and Asta stood entwined in a lip-locked embrace.

"Should we say something?" Scarlett's sultry breath stroked Rune's ear.

He shivered, overwhelming desire challenging his ability to think straight. "Yeah, we should warn them. Better us than someone else." Rune not-so-subtly cleared his throat.

Asta and Blake jumped back and stared up at them, redness creeping from their necks right up their faces.

"We were just..." Blake stammered.

"Getting to know each other better?" Rune couldn't contain the sly smile curving his lips.

"Ah...yeah," Blake said with a nervous stutter.

"I think you guys better go back before anyone else notices you're missing, unless it doesn't bother you." Scarlett's soft, encouraging voice had a no-nonsense edge.

Asta's deep jade eyes twinkled with tenacity in the afternoon sunlight. "It doesn't bother me."

Blake turned to her with a conflicted look of hope and disbelief. "Are you sure?"

"Absolutely. If Scarlett can get married at eighteen to a thirty-two-year-old, they'd be massive hypocrites to question our relationship." Asta glanced at Scarlett and Rune. "No offense."

"None taken," Scarlett and Rune said in stereo.

"How long has this been going on?" Scarlett asked.

"Mentally and emotionally, for years. Physically, not until today. We'd both tried to fight it." Asta's tone combined with the expression in her eyes said, *we've wasted so much precious, irredeemable time.*

"Is that why you kept telling me you could never be interested in a full human?"

Asta held Blake's hand and walked toward them. "Yeah. I thought if I said it enough, I'd actually believe it. For too long I let my parents discourage me from even considering getting involved with your brother because of the differences. You can't help who you fall for though, right?"

"Exactly." Rune smiled and wrapped his arm around his wife's waist. "I think you guys make a great couple."

Scarlett snuggled into Rune's side. "Me too."

Blake's gaze zoned in on his sister. "Really? You mean that?"

Asta's stare flicked from Blake to Scarlett. "It doesn't bother you?"

"Of course it doesn't. I can't think of anything better...outside of Rune being my husband."

They all returned to the party and, as the sunlight dimmed to dusk, Rune and Scarlett farewelled the last of their guests. Finally, they made it upstairs after a long but brilliant day, and lay naked, cuddled up in the dark, not that darkness was a barrier. With his excellent vampiric night vision, he could see his new wife almost as clearly as if she were in pure daylight.

Rune kissed her temple. "You know we could have gone to a hotel tonight."

She rubbed his chest and it felt like being massaged with passion oil, lust pinging in his blood and swelling his cock. "I know, but it's more comfortable here, and we won't have to worry about getting up early to check out. We can stay in bed all day, if we want. No one will disturb us. Plus, we're going on our honeymoon at the end of the week anyway."

"Mm-m… I'm looking forward to it. It'll be nice to have you all to myself for a while."

She retracted her hand and the flow of euphoria stopped like a plug pulled out of a socket. "Nice? Is that all?"

"Okay, amazing then. How's that?"

"Much better!" Scarlett kissed his lips and resumed rubbing. "You know, I'm still a bit freaked out by Blake and Asta…but in a good way. I love them both. I really hope things work out for them."

"Me too. They do make a cute couple. I suppose they could always have a sip of the soulmate serum and check it out."

"They could…though it kind of takes the fun out of finding out for themselves and seeing if they can make it work." Scarlett kissed his bare shoulder, her hot breath extra enticing on his skin.

"Totally." His breathing short circuited. "The success of a relationship comes down to physical attraction, working as a team and having the same philosophical outlook on life. Someone doesn't necessarily have to be your soulmate for that...but it helps."

Her soft lips traveled along the length of his neck. "The connection would have to be stronger between soulmates though."

*Fuck.* If she continued, he'd blow before they even got started. "For sure. Look at us...and your parents and grandparents."

She teased his mouth with light, sensual kisses and licks. "Maybe the ability to connect with a soulmate runs in my family?"

Rune's mind fogged with desire, too misted over to think rationally, which wasn't a surprise, given that ninety percent of his attention had diverted to his dick. "Possibly. I can't say it's that way in mine...except for Hugh. I suppose it has to start somewhere."

"So, ah...is it safe for us tonight," Scarlett whispered, her voice full of hope, "to physically seal the deal?" Her jittery laugh sounded part nervous, part excited.

"So the tests say. I'm not one hundred percent sure yet. I need to double check."

"Double check?"

"Yeah, just to be certain." *Well, more certain.* Rune rolled her onto her back, devouring her scrumptious body. He slid along her, the shear and friction of their skin electrifying every nerve ending.

Rune kissed her pubic bone and inner thighs and dipped his tongue between her legs. *Soaked. Already.* And such a fucking turn-on. He licked the length of her slit and thrust his tongue inside her. Her juices flowed, sweet and succulent, and she arched against him.

He traced a path back to where she wanted him, exploring and sucking on her folds and finally flicked her swollen clit. She clutched his head, her nails lightly scraping his scalp and he groaned. Rune lapped at the erect little nub, eliciting a sequence of moans, and sucked her into his mouth.

She climaxed and he kept licking and sucking and eased a finger inside her. She whimpered and bucked and panted. He pushed a second finger into her core, curled both until he found that special little bunch of nerves he'd read so much about and she screamed his name, coming again and again and coating his hand and lips in her juices.

Rune moved back up her slightly sweaty, sated body and she crushed her mouth against his and sucked on his tongue. Much too soon, she pulled back and searched his eyes. "So what's the verdict?" Her desperate, breathy voice slammed against his lips.

"You're delicious." His cock throbbed with the need for release.

"Not that!"

He nibbled the sensitive spot where her jaw joined her neck. "Oh, you mean whether we can *do it*."

She grabbed his face between her hands. "Yes! Come on, stop teasing me!"

He chuckled, unable to miss her restrained edge of control about to snap. "Nothing's coming up so —"

Scarlett locked her lips on his like a vacuum seal, pushed him onto his side and curled her leg around his waist. He caressed her satin-smooth back, and she reached down and stroked his cock, aligning the head between her legs. If he didn't get inside her right now, he'd come like a horny teenage boy.

It took every last shred of self-restraint for him not to slam into her tight channel. Rune guided himself into her and kissed her hard to distract himself, and her, from the well-documented first-time pain. Not that his Scarlett was fragile. She thrust down onto his dick, taking him deep inside, proving her fiery, feisty, passionate nature. It was one of the things he loved about her so much.

"Ugghh!" he groaned, out-of-this-world pleasure flooding his synapses.

They moved in rhythm together, a violet-jade glow growing around them, and they climbed and climbed until they detonated. Orgasmic shrapnel flew through his body, reigniting the lustful fire — over and over and over.

Scarlett's hot lips consumed his again and he held her snug against him, floating in a cloud of ecstasy. Would he ever come back down? Could he ever return to earth? Normality? Hopefully not. The physical-emotional release transcended reality. She'd instigated a tangible change in him, a completeness.

Their breathing resettled and the pulsating violet-jade aura began to fade. Scarlett lay back against the white satin sheets, her eyes vibrant. "Wow!"

Rune nuzzled her flushed face. "I agree. Amazing. Beyond words. The incredible chemistry, the connection...so much deeper than I thought possible."

Scarlett slid her searing skin along the length of him. The more they touched, the more he craved. "So...we should make the most of it while we're in the baby-free zone."

He kissed her forehead, nose, lips, his cock almost recovered and ready for the next round of lovemaking. "Mm-m...definitely."

# Epilogue

Double Trouble

*Hobart, Tasmania 2032*

"So are you staying with me tonight?"

Rune interlocked his fingers with Scarlett's. "Definitely. Unless you need some time on your own to recuperate."

Her gaze met his, her jade, violet-flecked eyes shining. "No, I want you here." She leaned across to hug him. "Ouch!"

"Waaah!" Both babies broke out in a chorus of wails.

"You need to take it easy, young lady. That's an order."

Scarlett nodded but attempted to get up.

Rune held her in place. "Uh-uh. You stay right where you are. I've got it."

She crossed her arms and huffed. "Trust them to play up as soon as Mum and Dad leave."

He chuckled, reached into the double cot and patted Asher and Tegan's nappy-clad bottoms.

Scarlett lay down and closed her eyes. "Much better."

Within seconds, the twins had settled and drifted back to sleep. *Interesting...* He shouldn't be surprised. Scarlett always told him he had the magic touch. And didn't that just stimulate an avalanche of erotic memories, like replaying the favorite snippets of their own, homemade adult film collection.

Rune rubbed his temples to ground himself. There would be plenty of time to indulge in his imagination later. Currently, he had a theory that he wanted to test with Scarlett and the twins. As much as he'd love to take all the credit for settling them, the facts pointed to a stronger bond with his wife.

Not that it was unusual for kids to connect more with their mother, according to the multitude of studies he'd read, but this registered at a much deeper level.

He perched himself on the edge of Scarlett's hospital bed and her eyes fluttered open.

"Can I try something?"

She looked groggy, exhausted, sleep-deprived. "Um...sure."

"Can you sit up and lean forward again...please?"

That woke her up. She glared at him. "Are you a sadist or something? It bloody hurts!"

He put his finger to her lips. "Just for a moment, I promise."

Her face twisted into a wary, what-the-hell-are-you-up-to expression but she did as he instructed, levering herself into sitting and slightly folding forward. "Arrrrgh!"

The babies cried, as though tripping an invisible sensation wire, connecting them to Scarlett.

Rune slapped the mattress. "I thought so."

Scarlett cradled her abdomen. "What? What's going on?"

He repositioned and puffed up a mountain of pillows behind her and she rested against them. "The babies, don't you see? They're tuned in to you. When you're relaxed, they're relaxed. When you're in pain, they're in pain."

"Isn't that kind of normal?"

"Not to this extent, no."

She shifted one way then another, as though seeking the perfect comfortable spot. "What does it mean?"

He cupped her cheek and she leaned into his hand, like a bunting cat in a reciprocal pleasure exchange. "I don't know. It could be a vampire special ability thing. I bet Rick will be on top of it. We should run it by him when he gets back."

By the time Rick and Eden returned, Scarlett had fallen asleep.

Rune met them at the door. "How was dinner?" he said, keeping his voice low.

"Lovely," Eden whispered. "We brought you back some rare beef salad, with extra rare beef. We thought you could do with some energy." She placed a white cardboard takeaway box on the overbed table, then glanced at sleeping beauty. "How is she...and the twins?"

"She's fine, though a little tender with certain movements. Bizarrely, the babies seem to tune in to it."

"What do you mean?" Eden asked, her and Rick joining him at the double crib.

"They match her mood. When Scarlett's in pain, the little ones act up, and when she's relaxed or resting, they're totally settled."

Rick rubbed the goatee bristles on his chin. "Intriguing…"

Excitement gushed up inside Rune like a burst water pipe. "Isn't it? Do you think it's a vampire special power thing?"

"Sounds like it. I'd be interested to test whether they're in tune with you too. Are you up for that?"

"Totally."

Eden pressed light kisses to her grandchildren's heads. "Are you sure you should disturb them? They look so peaceful."

Rick snaked his arm around his wife's waist, holding her close in a trust-me embrace. "Sweetheart, it's fine. If my theory works, they'll only be upset for a second."

Eden stepped back and scrutinized her husband, then Rune. The stern, wary expression on her face screamed, *I'm not convinced.* But she didn't try to stop them.

Rick slapped an eager hand on Rune's back. "How do you want to do this?"

"Um-m-m…yeah…ah…"

Rick's eyes seemed to scan internally, as though reading scrolling text in his mind. "What about a firm handshake? Or an elbow to the stomach?"

"Let's try the handshake first."

Rick grinned and stretched out his arm, an ominous glint in his eye.

Rune clasped Rick's hand and his father-in-law—only a mere quarter vampire—clamped on like an old-fashioned nutcracker. And that wasn't the worst of it. With his hand trapped, paralyzed into place, Rick increased the agony. He introduced an undulating movement akin to some torturous chiropractic treatment, shifting Rune's knuckles in and out of position.

"Fu-cowch!"

Rick loosened his grip for less than a second, but long enough for Rune to yank his hand free. "Where the hell did you learn to do that?" He opened and shut his hand and massaged his aching joints.

The babies' faces screwed up and they started bawling. Rick, Eden and Rune peered into the crib and both Asher and Tegan held their tiny little right hands against their tummies.

"Ethan demonstrated it on me once." Rick's voice sounded faint, distracted, his gaze focused on the twins' reaction. "Just as I thought — They're attuned to both of you, even to the point of sensing physical pain in the same spot. Based on the evidence, I'll take a speculative punt and predict they'll be in tune with each other as well.

"Scarlett and Blake certainly were — and still are, to a degree. I imagine it'll be even stronger in these two, given they both have the vampire gene. I'll need to conduct some more tests, though, to check the extent of the connection and prove the theory."

Eden swatted her husband's arm. "Rick! They're not some experiment for work. They're our grandchildren!"

"Sorry, darling. You know what I'm like. I can't help myself. This whole area fascinates me. Just when I think we've worked out the breadth of the vampire gene's abilities, I learn there's so much more. I'm starting to believe that the knowledge we have is a screw and from there we've got to build a car."

She touched his cheek and their gazes met. "Remember what happened to us?"

Technically neither Rick nor Eden remembered all the specifics of their time spent in the Sub Rosa basement, being guinea pigs for memory drugs and cryogenics, as far as Rune was aware. But that didn't mean they didn't get the enormity of it—the possible side effects, the risk to their lives.

Rick framed her face with his hands. "I would never let that, or anything like it, happen to anyone. I'm just talking about some simple, non-invasive research."

"Oh, Rick." She smiled and shook her head.

Eden's concern made absolute sense. No matter how small the experiment, it always included risks. It didn't have to be physical, it could be mental, emotional. However, life itself was about taking measured risks in order to grow, prosper, succeed. "I must admit, I'm pretty interested in sussing things out a bit more too."

Eden stroked the now snoozing twins' backs. "Let's get Scarlett's opinion about it first, shall we?"

Scarlett stirred, her eyes fluttering open. "Did I hear my name?"

"Yeah…" Rune used the opportunity to launch into an explanation of the robust discussion he'd had with her parents. The twins woke up, as though they knew they were being spoken about, and Eden handed them over to Scarlett for a feed.

"I don't know. I don't want to psychologically scar them." Scarlett positioned Tegan and Asher on the U-shaped pillow, so they could both suckle on her breasts, and a nurse brought in a couple of bottles of cow's blood to top them up afterward.

Rune sat on the edge of the bed and kissed her worried forehead. "Your dad reckons they'll be pretty resilient, seeing as they both have the vampire gene."

Scarlett's gaze shot to her dad. "How do you know for sure they won't be negatively affected, long-term?"

"I don't, though we're talking simple little things, nothing invasive, so it's extremely unlikely."

"Extremely unlikely but possible." She turned to Rune, eyebrows raised. "So you thought hurting yourself to see if it affected the twins was okay?"

"I didn't get hurt...exactly."

Her eyebrows just about raised past her hairline.

If the studies were to be of any value, he and Scarlett had to both be on-board, comfortable. And she wasn't. Clearly. "All right, we won't carry out any testing. It'll just be pure observation."

"I'd prefer that, for the moment. I'll re-evaluate once they're older and I have a better idea of how they cope with adversity."

Disappointment weighed down Rick's heavy sigh. "Fair enough. But you're missing out on a great opportunity. The whole vampire community is missing out. The vampire gene seems to have some real plasticity. It's adaptable, flexible... However, it would be useful to know the broader applications and possibilities, to have quantifiable results. Results help with funding to support current and future projects and improve lifestyle."

"Don't try and guilt me, Dad. I admit the whole idea is interesting and the data could be useful. I just don't want my babies to be research subjects, to be put in possible danger. When they're at an age where they can choose for themselves..."

"Good for you, honey." Eden sat on the other side of the bed, facing Scarlett, and soothed the babies with loving strokes to their heads and little bodies.

Rune contemplated the conversation. The complexities and joys of the vampire gene. "You know, I understand why Hugh took the cure, but I don't know if I'd be able to. My vampire heritage means as much to me as my human heritage. I don't think I'd be able to choose between the two."

Asher and Tegan suckled steadily — their babies, the amazing little lives he and Scarlett had created. Being a husband to such an incredible woman was awesome enough. Add being a dad to that and his life had become practically perfect.

Scarlett stared down at their little miracles. "I know what you mean. Though we're lucky because we're the same mix." Her eyes met Rune's stare. "If one of us was full vampire or full human, maybe things would be different. Either the vampire partner would have the cure or the human partner would drink the healing, fountain-of-youth tears, assuming they were still in regular supply."

"True. It does depend on the circumstances. Speaking of my tears, did I mention your dad's got Simon working on how to replicate them?"

Her gaze darted across to Rick, a proud smile plastered across his face. "No. Wow! That would be awesome!" She turned back to Rune with the cheekiest grin. "Then there'll be a lot less pressure on you to perform."

A chuckle rumbled in Rune's throat at the sex-laden insinuation.

The twins stopped feeding, smiles curling up the corners of their tiny mouths, as though they got the joke, then they latched back on to her nipples.

"We've come close to developing a mimicking agent. Simon's still slogging away at it. He's a pretty unbelievable scientist, so I have faith he'll come up with something successful soon." *Rick and his one-track research mind.* But Rune admired his passion. Without that, there wouldn't be any new discoveries, any innovation.

It was hard not to absorb some of his father-in-law's excitement. "Anyone who can come up with the cure and an antidote to the soulmate serum can almost do anything!"

Asher's jade and Tegan's violet-tinted eyes intensified and they seemed to suck harder on Scarlett's nipples.

Scarlett pressed at the twins' heads, a prompt for them to ease up, but they kept on going. She glared at Rune. "They're picking up on your enthusiasm. Tone it down. Please."

"Sorry, Scar." Rune took a slow breath in then long exhale out. Slow breath in, long exhale out. "Any better?"

Asher and Tegan's eyes closed and their grip seemed to soften.

Scarlett leaned into the mountain of pillows behind her back and sighed. "Much. Thanks."

Rune took over from Eden and stroked the twins on the forehead until they looked totally relaxed.

"I think they're almost done." Scarlett nodded to the cow-blood-filled baby bottles on the bedside table. "Could you —?"

Eden picked up the bottles. "We'll take them and top them up."

* * * *

Only a day later and Scarlett and the babies were discharged home. Rune charged ahead with her bags and came back for the twins. Upon entering the front door, her dad's framed poem to her mum greeted her in the foyer.

*Freedom of Love*

*Capture,*
*Discover,*
*Reckoning.*
*Finally completing the journey*
*for freedom*
*Grateful and privileged*
*to travel that life-changing path with you,*
*My forever love.*

It felt so good to be home.

Scarlett started up the stairs with Smokey and Thornton rubbing against her legs. Were they keen to see her or the new additions or both?

She entered her old, redecorated nursery. A few licks of dark cream paint and rearranging of furniture had made all the difference. The walls were adorned with colorful prints of cute baby animals and, in the far corner of the room, next to the sash window, a large stuffed toy giraffe and teddy bear overlooked a mahogany toy box.

A matching dark wood dresser, wardrobe and changing table completed the rest of the space. The room had a fresh and new feel without losing any of its warmth. She kissed the sleepy duo in their baby capsules and Rune placed them into the crib.

"Come on, little stickybeaks, out you go." Scarlett ushered Smokey and Thornton out of the twins' room and shut the door.

Rune switched Bluetooth on the baby monitor, activated the projector pea in his jeans pocket, paired the Bluetooth signal with his holographic mobile and swiped his phone shut. "All righty, chill time."

Once they reached their bedroom, they undressed, snuggled up in bed and, in seconds, she drifted off to sleep.

"Scar..." Rune's soft whisper brushed her ear.

"Mm-m," she grumbled and rolled over.

He tightened his arms around her waist and she pressed against his muscular stomach and unmistakable erection. "It's nearly dinner time."

Did he mean that in the literal or blow job sense? Maybe she could have both. She eased her eyes open and her gaze bounced around the room. Twilight? Already? Her growling stomach went into worried-mummy lock down. "Where are the twins?"

"They're still asleep in their room but are probably due for a feed soon. It's nearly seven."

"Seven? Far out!" She went to sit up and clutched her stomach. "Owww!"

Dual shrieks pierced the silence.

Rune assisted her into sitting. "Careful."

With slow and cautious movements, Scarlett shifted her legs to the edge of the bed.

"What do you think you're doing?" Rune jumped up, threw on his short black robe and stood before her in full protector mode. "I'll grab them and bring them to you. You stay put, okay?"

Stay put? How did a mother with a still intact, invisible umbilical cord feel the pull and not act?

She nodded. Reluctantly. For the next few weeks, she had to find a way to be at peace, delegating duties to Rune and her parents and try to relax.

She'd gone into labor early and Rune had rushed her to the closest public hospital. Thanks to all her dad and Simon's hard work and persistence, vampires had been integrated and fairly well accepted into human society. Before that, she dreaded to think how many babies and mothers had died.

Women with even a hint of vampire heritage would have avoided human hospitals, fearful of Sub Rosa snapping them up for testing, of the barrage of questions from hospital staff and how to explain their differences without drawing unwanted attention. Fearful that the blissful birth event would turn into a horrid research-focused nightmare.

Over the last few years, the healthcare system had been revamped to cater to a wide variety of humans and vampires. Vampire health and wellbeing had now become part of the curriculum for those studying to become health professionals. Doctors could also go on to become specialists in the field. The advances had been brilliant, life-saving.

So she should be grateful that her greatest issue was having to rest up. But Scarlett had always been active, used to doing things whenever she wanted. She'd rarely had to deal with restriction. She'd never had a sick day—well, since her parents had realized she'd needed some blood in her diet when she was still a baby—and that had set up false expectations, a false perception of the real world.

Pining for Rune up until the age of seventeen had given her a small taste of limitations, but she'd finally worn him down. She couldn't wear the healing process down, though. A dose of unwanted reality sure had a way of tearing the happiness from her heart. Patience, she had to be painfully patient.

"You must be feeling bet—" Rune stood in the doorway, the quiet babies strapped to each side now turning niggly.

Better. She was, sort of—however, Scarlett didn't want to be just better. She wanted to be back to normal. Rune jiggled and rocked the twins in his arms. Rune. Maybe he could help her—and not just by taking charge of the children. "I've been thinking. I wonder if your tears will heal my cesarean wound? They worked on Granddad's heart."

"Yeah, but Abe's full human. They might not have the same impact on a hybrid. They might not work at all or have side effects. We haven't done testing on a Jade-Violet-human heritage person like you. Not yet."

"They might be even more effective. I think it's worth a try, don't you?"

Asher and Tegan stopped whining, alertness and expectation replacing the tears in their eyes. "It sounds good in theory but...I don't know. What if the tears create added complications?"

"I doubt it. If anything, they'll help me heal faster. I'm willing to give them a go."

He stared at her, conflict contorting his handsome face. "Even if I agree, I can't just cry on command."

"Oh. Yeah." She flopped back against the bed, disappointment draining her enthusiasm.

Rune approached her, exuding empathy. "But I'll try for you. Here, take these two and I'll do my best to squeeze out some of my special healing brew while they feed."

She scooted into sitting, careful not to pull the stitched cut on her tender stomach, propped her back against strategically placed pillows and positioned the U-shaped cushion to help support the twins.

Rune assisted and lovingly watched her feed their babies, happy tears bulging in his eyes.

Asher and Tegan seemed to sense her eagerness and Rune's joy, beating their suckling time record and sporting contented, sleepy smiles. As soon as she and Rune had burped and changed the babies' nappies, Rune returned them to their cot and rejoined Scarlett.

He raised a small glass, a quarter filled with a clear syrupy substance. "Ready?"

"Go for it." She lay back and exposed the small incision on her abdomen.

Rune trickled his tears over the red line and they bubbled and fizzed. He stopped pouring and searched her eyes. "Do you want me to continue? It looks like it hurts, like acid eating into your skin."

It was the total opposite. Appearances could be misleading. "It's soothing, believe it or not."

He blinked like a camera on continuous mode. "Oh." He appeared surprised. He obviously hadn't expected her response. It always amazed her how just one word could convey so much. "Okay, um...you should drink the rest." He handed her the shot glass with the remaining sambucca-looking fluid. "You need internal healing too."

Scarlett swallowed the silky substance. It formed a protective coating in her mouth and slipped down her esophagus, leaving a light, salty aftertaste. A wave of nourishment rolled through her body, boosting her energy.

Her wound stopped bubbling and fizzing, only a fine line remaining where the cut used to be. It looked more like a skin fold now than a lesion.

Scarlett sat forward "No pain. That's awesome! Thank you." She threw her arms around her husband and hugged him close.

He pulled back, a warning look in his eye. "Promise me you're still going to ease into things. Your body needs time to repair on its own, physically and emotionally—healing tears or not."

"Okay, okay, Mr. Bossy."

"You love it when I'm bossy." She did, especially when he had that dark Dom tone in his voice, like now. She pressed her sex into the mattress to stem the growing need.

Rune placed his palm over the incision spot. Warm energy flowed like Reiki from his hand and her breathing slowed, deepened.

She closed her eyes. "Mm-m..."

The stream of energy ceased and she snapped her eyes open.

Rune's assessing gaze greeted hers. "Enough for now. You need to eat."

They threw on some clothes and he held her hand as they headed downstairs. Her mum and dad had already set the conservatory table. Glasses sparkled and the silver cutlery shone in the low, welcoming light. Gleaming white plates were topped with bloodied, rare steaks. Her mouth watered at the raw metallic sight and scent.

"This is perfect! Thanks, Mum."

Her dad pulled out a chair for her in her regular spot. "It's what the doctor ordered, literally."

Scarlett sat, with Rune by her side and her parents opposite, as always. Creatures of comfortable habit. She cut into the bleeding meat, saliva pooling in her mouth, and gobbled down a large piece. "When are Blake and Asta getting back?"

Her mum's smile burst with knowing. "Soon..."

Scarlett hadn't really needed to ask. She could feel Blake already — and her grandparents. They were close by. But she'd play along. "When's soon?"

Her mum had a sip of red wine, still trying to keep up the façade. "They booked their flights the moment they heard the news."

Scarlett shoved another slice of steak into her mouth, trying not to let on that she'd worked out their little surprise. "I can't wait to see them."

"I'm so glad to hear that, Sis."

"Blake! I knew it!" Did they really think they could hide him from her? Although she still felt a little out of sorts after having the twins, it didn't impact on her innate vampiric, person-proximity sensing abilities. She swiveled in her seat and her brother stood with Asta by his side, only a few meters away.

Enormous grins split their faces.

Scarlett jumped up and hugged them, joyous droplets rolling down her cheeks.

"How about us?" Grandma Rhoda's voice.

Scarlett's gaze shot to the doorway and her three grandparents sauntered in. Her feeling powers, when it came to close family, never failed. She hugged them all too and returned to Rune.

She squinted her eyes at her husband, the guilty expression on his face giving her the answer before she even asked. "Did you know about this?"

"Maybe. I'm surprised you didn't pick up on it."

Scarlett leaned into his ear. "I did...sort of. The pregnancy and birth knocked me around, but not that much."

Her mum collected their empty plates and stopped beside her. "Oh, and your great-uncle, and Hugh and Simon and their families want to visit too. I said I'd see how you are and let them know later in the week."

Her parents disappeared into the kitchen and returned carrying plates of savory and sweet finger food.

Blake's gray eyes danced with mischief. "Look, sis... I think I'm speaking on behalf of everyone here when I say, it's lovely seeing you both, but, ah...we're kind of hanging out for the main attraction."

Before she could formulate a smart-ass reply, Rune slung his arm around her shoulder and said, "Well, you'll just have to be a little more patient. They're asleep, and waking them prematurely is like invoking the wrath of God. So if anyone wants to go there, I won't stop you, though you'll be nominating yourself to spend the rest of the night trying to settle them."

Grandma Rhoda's sparkling jade eyes drew Scarlett's gaze like priceless jewels. She still couldn't get her head around someone so young-looking, vibrant and progressive being a great-grandmother. "Can I at least have a sneak peek? I promise I will be as quiet as a field mouse."

"Hey, don't try and push in, Gran," Blake protested. Then he glanced at Scarlett and winked. "How about the rest of us?"

Her brother—from the moment he could talk—had always been a shit stirrer, but in a harmless, fun way. He'd started off so cute, mute and charming...until he'd found his voice. She'd missed him and his sharp tongue so badly since he and Asta had left to travel overseas twelve months before. Three-D Skype and visual messaging had helped—however, it wasn't the same as having him within touching distance.

Her dad had developed some interactive touch software with Simon but it was still in the experimental stages. Scarlett sighed. "All right, follow me."

The visitors crowded around her and she led them up the stairs, like a motherly pied piper. She eased the nursery door open and peered inside. Asher and Tegan lay on their sides, their eyes open, facing each other and gurgling, as though having a private conversation.

Scarlett rushed over to them, gatecrashing their little chat.

They both stopped babbling and smiled, like they comprehended. How could that be? They were newborns in tiny onesies, just over two days old. No way could they be that advanced yet. Then again, she had been advanced for her age and, she and Rune had a similar genetic make-up, so a high chance existed that their offspring would also smash their milestones. They would probably exceed what she'd achieved.

"You two should be asleep," she whispered.

They stared up at her, an unmistakable glint in their large, bright eyes.

Scarlett turned toward her family, hovering in the doorway. "Come on over. They're awake."

Grandma Rhoda pushed to the front. "Ooh, they are so sweet!" She lifted Tegan out of the crib, her sad stare landing on Blake. "I did not get to enjoy you and Scarlett at this age."

Granddad Abe stroked Tegan's cheek. "Me either." He looked at Scarlett, a warm, proud smile on his face. "They're beautiful."

"They really are adorable." Asta reached into the crib and picked up Asher. "I almost want one myself."

Blake's face went bleached-out white. "Oh, really?"

"I said almost." Asta's sassy response and accompanying smile earned her a chuckle.

"Hey, little guy!" Blake tickled him under the chin. "Welcome to the family." Then his assessing gaze targeted Scarlett. "He's super alert, isn't he?"

*And that's not all...* "Yeah, they're both pretty on it."

Grandpa Ethan stood back quietly and observed, as though assessing potential army recruits. "Yes...their eye contact is like that of an experienced soldier."

After a few more minutes, Scarlett rounded up the family posse and returned downstairs, anxious to update her husband on their babies' behavior.

She took Rune aside, her skin burning with pent-up stress.

"Is everything okay? You look flustered."

"It's the twins."

Grandma Rhoda and Blake stood out of hearing distance, cuddling Asher and Tegan.

"They seem fine. What's going on?" Rune lifted a long curl off her face and tucked it behind her ear.

She leaned in close and, in the softest whisper, relayed the interaction between the children. "I don't know whether it's purely genetics or what, but Dad's going to love it!"

Rick pushed a tray between them, holding a couple of blood-filled bottles for the babies. "Love what?"

She swallowed, eyes wide.

Rick's gaze shifted back and forth between her and Rune as if to say, 'someone tell me something, anything.' "What's going on?"

"Nothing, Dad. We'll talk later, okay?" Scarlett said, shutting down the budding conversation.

Rick scrutinized her. "Scarlett?"

"It's nothing urgent. I promise." She grabbed Rune's hand and tugged him away from her detective dad. "We should mingle."

Rick reluctantly continued past them and gave a cow-blood-filled bottle to Grandma Rhoda and one to Blake. They topped up Asher and Tegan until they looked dosed up on sleeping pills, then put them back to bed.

By the time it reached ten p.m., Scarlett had hit the wall. She yawned. "I hate to crash on you guys but I really need to get some sleep."

"I think I might join you." Rune slid his arm around her waist, his voice a seductive whisper.

Scarlett smiled and snuggled into him, pressing her palm to his chest. "I look forward to seeing you all again tomorrow."

Rune saluted the small gathering. "Goodnight, everyone."

"Goodnight," the small group sang out.

Halfway up the stairs, Rune pressed her against the balustrade and kissed her like a starving man hoeing into a succulent rare steak.

She broke away a few minutes later, desperate for some air. "What's that for?" Her breath came out in choppy pants.

"Just an appreciation of my stunning wife. Is that okay?"

She touched her fingers to his chest and followed the path over his ribs to his six-pack stomach and down to his twitching cock. "Absolutely." Her gaze moved from his eyes to his lips, and she pushed up on tip toes and kissed him back with heart-pounding passion.

"Mm-m... I can never get enough of this, enough of you."

"Me either. But the sooner we get the kids sorted, the sooner we can continue."

That was all he seemed to need, clasping her hand, entwining their fingers and continuing up the rest of the stairs, like she'd thrown a lead around his cock and assured him a trip to the promised land.

They entered the twins' room and the cot was empty. Scarlett turned to Rune, her breathing stilted and shallow, gaining speed toward hyperventilation. "Where are they?"

He held her face between his hands, the move he always used in an attempt to center her. "Don't panic. Maybe your parents have them."

She grabbed fistfuls of his T-shirt. "I didn't see them go upstairs, did you?"

"No, but maybe they slipped past us. Until we know what's going on, we just need to stay calm. We'll find them." He held her hand and steered her to their bedroom.

"You can't seriously be thinking about sex."

Muffled synchronized crying came from behind their bedroom door.

Rune barged in and the twins lay side by side, cuddling each other on their bed.

"How the hell?" Scarlett dropped his hand and rushed over to them. "How did you two...?"

"I think they sensed our desire to be together and wanted to make sure they were cuddled and fed again first."

Scarlett jolted her head up to meet his gaze. "What?"

Rune joined her and stared at their babies' innocent-looking faces. "You two are little buggers." He wound an arm around Scarlett's waist. "I think they can teleport themselves."

"Teleport?"

"There's no other explanation, is there, you cheeky little things."

How could she stay mad at the small, curled-up pink and blue bundles?

Asher and Tegan smiled then winked at Rune.

He snapped his head around to Scarlett. "Did you see that?"

"Unbelievable!"

What had they bred? What other surprises did they have in store for them?

Rune rubbed his hand affectionately up and down Scarlett's back. "Well, one thing's for sure. There's never going to be an ordinary moment in this house."

# Want to see more like this?
# Here's a taster for you to enjoy!

# The Royal Gordanos:
# A Royal's Touch
## Makayla Roberts

### *Excerpt*

*Humans are such mundane creatures. They carry on with their lives, unaware of just how vast the world truly is.*

*They're unconscious of the immense number of demons roaming through their cities, living secret lives among them. Demons hide behind magical glamour spells to make themselves invisible to mortal eyes, but many of them just blend in with only the subtlest indications of their natures. Vampires have stunning, heart-wrenching beauty – shifters, the sweltering heat of their skin that is far hotter than a human's and trolls have impenetrably thick skin and a brief flash of red in their eyes when they grow angry.*

That was one of the things Ava loved most about humans. They were simple-minded. Where her world was filled with danger, darkness and children of the underworld, humans were oblivious to the mystical existence around them.

She envied that about them. To be able to live their lives with no clue that they were always surrounded by creatures that go bump in the night. It was miraculous how blind they were.

Yes, envious indeed. Yet, at the same time, she couldn't help but admire them.

To have a demon strolling past them every day, even serving the food at a restaurant they frequented — *cough, cough* — yet never even knowing... She only wished to trade places with them. Maybe then she'd be able to get a full night of sleep.

"Don't tell me you're daydreaming again, Ava," a friendly, yet gruff voice called out.

Ava turned a smile on her boss, who was raising a bushy gray eyebrow at her through the small square window separating them. Though he was a rough-looking old man with a perpetual scowl, he had a heart of gold. He'd give the clothes on his back to someone in need.

A trait lacking in the majority of demons.

"Sorry about that, Mr. Tommy," she said. She picked up a thin white rag and tasked herself with wiping down the countertop. The diner she worked in was fairly empty at this time of the morning. The early morning rush had ended, but there were a few customers seated at the tables, finishing off their meals.

Tom's Place wasn't anything special, but there was a certain charm about the diner that made Ava feel comfortable working there. A gray-and-white checkered tile floor complemented baby-blue booths and metal tables. The walls were the same blue, with aged pictures from the diner's first opening in the twenties hanging on the walls. The windows had a faint tint on them to keep the inside cool and shaded, which was perfect for Ava.

She had a mild allergy to the sun's rays.

In all honesty, she didn't need this job. She'd managed to save up a considerable amount of wealth over the years to keep herself comfortable for a while.

However, as a waitress, it was a great way to interact with humans. She enjoyed studying them, learning more about their ways. She'd been sheltered from them until she reached adulthood. When she'd gone off into the world to discover for herself what was out there, she'd developed a substantial fascination with the fragile beings.

It had quickly become her small bit of joy in life — *which is rather...bizarre, isn't it?*

They were a puzzling race. The smallest of incidents could be fatal for them, and they were foolishly driven by their emotions rather than their minds. She didn't understand it in the slightest, but she wanted to. It was intriguing.

But no matter how much she enjoyed watching humans, she couldn't get involved with them any more than that. She'd never forgive herself if anyone was hurt because of her carelessness.

Especially not *that* human. There was one in particular her body craved like no other, which was a very, very dangerous thing in her predicament.

The bell above the diner door rang and the delicious scent of sandalwood filled her nose. *Speak of the devil...* She frowned to herself and looked up at the two men who took a seat at the diner bar, right in front of her. As always.

They were both dressed in uniform and both as handsome as could be. However, it was the one to the right who made her heart skip a beat. The human cop was so good-looking it was almost painful. In all her hundred-plus years of living, she'd seen her share of handsome men. But this one? He took the cake.

He had a crew-cut hairstyle, his hair cut close to his head on the sides, while the remaining dark hair on top was longer and neatly brushed backward. His eyes were a bright golden color, framed by thick, dark lashes that were long enough to make any woman seethe with jealousy. He had a thin, straight nose and a chiseled jawline so sharp that only a master craftsman could have sculpted it with such perfection. And his lips? Full, flawless and made to please a woman.

And when he smiled…

*Good gods, when he smiles.* His teeth were even and white, his cheeks bearing the deepest set of dimples she'd ever seen. Add to that his six-foot-three muscular build and he was a walking sexual invitation affecting women within a five-mile radius. And Ava was no exception.

Which was what frustrated her more than anything. She couldn't get involved with anyone right now—least of all a human—no matter how much her body ached for his touch.

"Good morning, Aaavaaaa," Marc drawled, those dimples flashing when he grinned.

Ava kept her face blank at the lazy way he drew her name out, but inside her heart was pounding. Even his smooth voice had her shifting her feet as heat began to pool in the pit of her stomach.

She gave him and Duncan a simple nod, ignoring her body's reaction to the sexy male. "Good morning," she responded, avoiding Marc's simmering gaze. "Edith will be over to take your orders shortly."

His dimpled smile never wavered. "Ahh, still too shy to talk to me, are you? It's been how many months now?"

Ava didn't respond as she turned to walk through the door to the kitchen area of the diner.

*Too shy to talk to him? Gods.* If he knew how bad she wanted him, he'd be running in terror until he reached the Atlantic Ocean.

Shaking the thought from her head, she headed toward the stock room where the other waitress, Edith, was gathering a few items.

She looked over at her. "I was *not* expecting that morning rush today," the aged woman said. "I know it's Friday, but golly."

Ava nodded in agreement. "Right? I have no idea where that crowd even came from. Is there some sort of special event going on in the city?"

Edith's gaze turned thoughtful. "If there is, I haven't heard about it. Chicago is pretty big, so there's no telling."

"Hmm. Well, your favorite customers are here. I'll finish stocking while you take their orders."

Edith blinked in surprise, her wrinkled gaze turning dreamy. "Marc and Duncan?" She let out a little happy squeal, dropping her handful of straws and condiment packets. "Oh, cripes," she muttered, crouching down to pick them up.

Ava got down to help her. "Don't worry about it. I'll get these. You go on."

Edith gave her a small frown. "Ya'know, Ava, I've been wondering for a while now... You're so nice to everyone that comes in but you always avoid those two. Why is that?"

Ava felt her cheeks heat just a bit. *Damn those old eyes of hers.*

She kept her head down, focusing on picking up the dropped items. "No reason," she mumbled. And damn herself for not being a good liar. What was the purpose of being a demon, known for their manipulation and cunning mental prowess, if she couldn't even master the art of telling a lie?

She knew that pathetic excuse wouldn't stop the other woman from prying. She was like a fluttering grandmother, always attempting to piece things together.

"Child, they're both drop-dead gorgeous," the woman continued. "They're cops, and neither of them has a ring on his finger." She paused for a second. "Wait! Could it be *because* they're cops? I know some people who tend to avoid the law at all costs. Is that the reason?" She looked around suspiciously before lowering her voice to a whisper. "Are you on the run from the authorities? Are you worried about getting deported? Don't. I won't rat on you."

Ava let out a small chuckle. In the few months since she'd been working there, she'd learned how much of a chatterbox Edith was. She voiced all her thoughts and opinions without a care in the world. Half the time Ava was sure the woman didn't even realize it. "Deported?" she asked, smiling.

Edith nodded, tapping a bony finger to her wrinkled cheeks in thought. "Yes, deported back to Mexico where you came from."

Ava shook her head. "I'm Italian, Edith, not Mexican. Two completely different countries on two completely different continents."

Edith waved that away. "Whatever. I'm not so good with all these different accents. Too many of them sound alike."

Ava only continued to smile. Despite Edith's claims, Ava's Italian accent was very faint. She'd spent a great number of years all over America, so she often picked up on their ever-changing lingo. The only time it became noticeable was if her emotions surged, which had yet to happen since working here.

"There are plenty of other police officers who come in here, and I have no trouble talking with them," Ava responded. "Honestly, I don't have an issue with either

Duncan or Marc. Let's just say I'm fairly shy around men who look that good." It was a lie, but she couldn't very well tell the woman she didn't talk to Marc because his very presence was enough to make her body tingle with desire. *Talk about embarrassing.*

"Oh well, I suppose that makes sense. Ever since you started working here, you would clam up and act all shy with only those two. Especially Marc. *That's* the one you need to shag."

Ava shook her head again. "Shag? What does that even mean?"

The woman stood up, raised a brow and put a bony hand on her hip. "You know what I mean. He's young and virile. You're young and gorgeous. You're both single. And I see the way you look at each other when no one's looking." She winked at that. "If I was just a few years younger, I'd mount that stallion in a heartbeat."

Ava bit the inside of her cheek to keep from laughing out loud. *A few years younger? Yeah, right.* They both knew full well that Edith was in her seventies — wrinkles, gray hairs and all. "Polite pass, Edith. I'm just not interested in seeing anyone right now."

That much was true, at least. Dating or even purely sexual relationships were impossible for her. *Hell, with my bad luck, it'll probably always be that way.*

"Oh well, your loss then, honey," Edith said, shrugging. She smoothed the front of her apron and straightened her thin shoulders. "How do I look?"

Ava rose as well, smiling warmly. "Fabulous."

Edith grinned and made her way back to the front, putting a little sway in her steps. Ava shook her head, still smiling. *That woman is really something else.* She was living proof that anyone is only as old as they feel. Well, to humans anyway. Time had no meaning to most demons.

She'd grown quite attached to the woman and her husband, Mr. Tommy. Though they had incredibly different personalities, they were both so sweet and generous. There'd been a few times when she'd seen them take people off the streets, offer them a hot meal and warm bed, clean them up and give them a job at the diner before helping them find something better. There weren't very many demons, if any, who would do such a thing without expecting something in return. It was the kind of pure, human love that made them want to help each other.

She placed the fallen items into the trash and washed her hands. She then pulled on a fresh pair of latex gloves, grabbed more condiments and went back to the front, where Edith's flirtatious giggling could be heard.

Ava hid a smile and began stocking the bins underneath the counter a few feet away from them. The woman was married and old enough to have great-grandchildren, yet she still flirted away with the younger men. It was fairly amusing, and the guys all went along with it.

As always, she was aware of Marc's presence. Over the smell of grease, butter and the other employees and customers, his scent stood out the most. It was a mix of his aftershave and his own personal aroma that filled her senses, making her head spin. That alone was enough to drive her mad with want.

And it was such a nuisance. She loved humans, but he stood out like a sore thumb—a very sexy, enticing sore thumb. And it was bloody frustrating because she didn't even know why. Why was it just him she felt so enamored with? Why did she feel such an intense reaction? Why did her heart jump every time her eyes met his? Yes, he was extremely attractive. Then again, so was his partner and several other men she'd come across. *So why only him?*

Speaking of his partner, she looked over at the Scot out of the corner of her eye.

Duncan looked normal enough, but he wasn't human. Oh, he very much smelled like one and did well to hide it, but she knew better. Demons could always sense another demon's presence.

Unlike Marc, Duncan's reddish-brown hair was longer and brushed back, the tips curling around his ears. His face was clean-shaven with a faint scar running from his chin up to his ear. However, it did nothing at all to take away from his handsome features. If anything, it gave him more of a gruff, sexy look, like those proud Highland warriors she'd seen on the covers of romance novels. But there was just something in the air around him that was demonic—a deadly, powerful aura that never failed to make her wary.

Oh, she wasn't afraid of him. She could hold her own against most demons. She did, after all, possess the blood of Royal vampires, some of the strongest demons to ever walk the earth.

However, Duncan was… Hell, she didn't know. His eyes were dark green with flecks of yellow around the pupil, but they held a predatory gleam that hinted at his demon side. It was like he was always searching for his next meal. That made her think he was some sort of shifter. Whether it was canine, feline or something else, she had no idea, but either way, he'd be a dangerous adversary.

Duncan was talking to Edith, making her laugh. When the woman turned away to place their orders, he looked over at Ava out of the corner of his eye, catching her watching him at bay. He winked and gave her a knowing smile. He knew she was a demon as well. It had been evident when they'd first met each other months ago, though neither of them had ever once mentioned it.

And why should they? Most demons were naturally private creatures. It wasn't like they often sat around a campfire holding hands and singing songs about peace and love. The thought made her give a soft snort.

*Still...* More than once she'd wondered what kind of demon he was and why he was parading around as a human cop. The intelligent look in his eyes told her he was far older than he appeared. He was a demon who'd lived a long life and had many stories to tell.

She gave another small shake of her head. *Oh well.* No need for dwelling on such trivial thoughts. Even if she had the answer to that question, it wouldn't change anything. As much as it would be nice to have demon friends she could feel comfortable around and let her fangs down with once in a while, so to speak, she would just have to keep dreaming. She wasn't the safest person to be around. And Marc...

He was a human. Getting involved with one was something she'd sworn to never do. She'd interact with them, even take their blood when she needed it. But with Marc, she wanted him in a way she hadn't ever felt before.

That in itself was dangerous. She would have to keep her distance from him. She feared that once she gave in to her carnal desires, it would be hard to stop.

And she would never forgive herself if something were to happen to him, all because she'd brought him into her world.

"Hey, Ava, come listen to this story," Edith suddenly called out. "It's intense."

Jarred from her thoughts, Ava bit back a sigh. *Damn you, Edith*, she thought. She was a character, but she was nosey as could be—nosey, and always trying to play matchmaker between her and Marc.

Ava picked up a clean blue towel and slowly walked over to them. The closer she got, the more Marc's scent clouded her mind. He was smirking as if he knew the effect he had on her. *Damn him too.*

Even as she silently cursed him, she was powerless to fight the way her body clenched in response to his look. *I'm worse than a harpy in heat, for crying out loud.*

"Thanks for joining us," he said playfully. Ava shrugged, annoyed that her tongue was dry. The more she looked at him, the more drawn she became. He was undoubtedly human, but he had a certain pull about him that could rival that of a full-grown incubus.

She began to dry the already-dried coffee mugs under the counter, setting them in their proper places as she listened.

Duncan was the one continuing the story. From what she'd learned from Edith, he had been born and raised in Scotland up until he'd been a teenager, then he'd moved to the US where he'd become a full citizen. He still had a thick accent when he spoke.

Although, with him being a demon who probably aged much more slowly than humans, it was no doubt just a cover. Not that he wasn't Scottish... The thick brogue and powerful aura gave him a warrior's presence that couldn't be faked. However, he could have spent several centuries in his homeland before coming here. *Who knows?*

"Anyway, one day we got a call about this drunk guy running down the street in this old neighborhood. It's broad daylight and he's just running, screaming at the top of his lungs. So we answer the call and roll up on this guy, expecting him to be high as shit. When we found him, he was rolling around in a field of grass screaming *'They're inside of me!'* This wasn't the first nut case we'd come across, so the procedure was pretty standard."

While Duncan continued with his story, a prickling sensation slid down Ava's neck, causing her to look up. She glanced around the room, but none of the patrons were out of the ordinary. The feeling became stronger and it was one she was all too familiar with. She narrowed her eyes, peering out of the large, shaded windows. She trusted her senses more than anything, and right now they were telling her something sinister was nearby.

She was never wrong.

Sure enough, across the street in the narrow alley stood a lone, cloaked figure. Even with the daylight outside, it was still dark between the two buildings. The humans on the other side of the street continued walking, completely oblivious to the danger standing within feet of them. To anyone who could see it, it would look like an ordinary person dressed for the changing weather.

To Ava, the figure stood out. It wasn't a human. It was hidden deep in the shadows, but she could make out two glowing-red eyes from under the hood it wore. Even with the distance, her enhanced eyesight allowed her to see the creature open its mouth in a wide grin.

*Found you*, it mouthed.

Her heart raced in her chest as she broke out in a cold sweat.

*Damn, damn, damn.* She'd known it might only be a matter of time before she was discovered, but she'd been too reckless. She'd hoped she had finally shaken the ghouls off her tail and had allowed herself to get too comfortable. *Curse it all.*

There was the sound of glass breaking, followed by a sharp pain in her hand, but she didn't even flinch. She glanced down at the shattered cup she'd grasped too tightly, watching as her blood flowed onto the sink and countertop.

She hissed, quickly running the water and holding her hand under the faucet.

*By the gods.* Now, with the scent of her blood in the air, it'd be even harder to make an escape. She'd just dug her own damn grave.

Edith appeared at her side, trying to help Ava with her wound, even as she was beginning to panic. Even Marc and Duncan look alarmed, and she could see Duncan's nostrils flaring, his eyes widening as he caught her scent.

*Shit and double shit.*

She had to make a quick escape.

Though most ghouls preferred night over day, there were a few who were strong enough to withstand the burning sunlight for a certain amount of time—like the one across the street, for example. And they were definitely not afraid to kill any humans who came between them and their target. If she stayed much longer, no doubt everyone in the diner would be injured…or worse. They would be collateral damage.

Wrapping her hand in the blue cloth towel, she turned to the small square window separating her from Mr. Tommy. She clutched her bleeding hand to her chest. "Sorry, Mr. Tommy, but I've got to go." She didn't even wait for a response. She took off her apron and sped out of the back, ignoring calls from her coworkers. She burst through the door and raced down the street. She knew the ghoul was following. She could feel it moving swiftly through the streets and alleys, following her scent. Her superior speed was near blinding compared to the ghoul's, but even then she didn't have much time. Once one of those creatures caught a scent, it was damn hard to get rid of them.

She only prayed her sudden departure would cause the creature to avoid harming anyone near the diner.

Home of Erotic Romance

Sign up for our newsletter and find out about all our romance book releases, eBook sales and promotions, sneak peeks and FREE romance books!

# About the Author

Sandra Carmel is an Australian-based author of engaging, thought-provoking romance novels, novellas, short stories and poetry, who writes for the pleasure of stimulating herself and others with words. An obsession with classic romance novels, particularly *Jane Eyre*, combined with marrying her own Mr Rochester, were key motivators in commencing her romance-writing journey. So far, she has taken the scenic route from contemporary to paranormal to erotic, creating provocative stories that delve beneath the surface of desire. She reads and writes a lot, frequently disrupted by her ever-attentive, cheeky cats, and sinfully amorous husband.

Sandra loves to hear from readers. You can find her contact information, website details and author profile page at https://www.totallybound.com